Readers love Under Cover by Amy Lane

"Lane masterfully weaves a narrative that balances action, romance, and suspense, making it a compelling read for fans of the genre."

—Next Page Reviews

"I have never been let down by Amy Lane and this one keeps that record going! There's not a character in this book that isn't interesting and compelling, good guys and bad guys."

—Love Bytes

"Congratulations, Ms. Lane, you truly have learned your craft!"

—Paranormal Romance Guild

By Amy Lane

An Amy Lane Christmas
Behind the Curtain
Bewitched by Bella's Brother
Bolt-hole
Bowling for Turkeys
ChrisMyths
Christmas Kitsch
Christmas with Danny Fit
Clear Water
Do-over
Food for Thought
Freckles
Gambling Men
Going Up
Hammer & Air
Hiding the Moon
With Andrew Grey: Holiday Cheer Anthology
Homebird
If I Must
Immortal
It's Not Shakespeare
Karma Kitty Christmas
Late for Christmas
Left on St. Truth-be-Well
The Locker Room
Mourning Heaven
Phonebook
Puppy, Car, and Snow
Racing for the Sun
Raising the Stakes
Regret Me Not
Shiny!
Shirt
Sidecar
Slow Pitch
String Boys
A Solid Core of Alpha
Swipe Left, Power Down, Look Up
Three Fates
Truth in the Dark
Turkey in the Snow
The 12 Kittens of Christmas
Under the Rushes
Weirdos
Wishing on a Blue Star Anthology

BENEATH THE STAIN
Beneath the Stain • Paint It Black

BONFIRES
Bonfires • Crocus
Sunset • Torch Songs

CANDY MAN
Candy Man • Bitter Taffy
Lollipop • Tart and Sweet

COVERT
Under Cover • Let the Wolf

Published by Dreamspinner Press
www.dreamspinnerpress.com

By Amy Lane (cont)

DREAMSPUN BEYOND
HEDGE WITCHES LONELY HEARTS CLUB
Shortbread and Shadows
Portals and Puppy Dogs
Pentacles and Pelting Plants
Heartbeats in a Haunted House

DREAMSPUN DESIRES
THE MANNIES
The Virgin Manny
Manny Get Your Guy
Stand by Your Manny
A Fool and His Manny
SEARCH AND RESCUE
Warm Heart
Silent Heart
Safe Heart
Hidden Heart

FAMILIAR LOVE
Familiar Angel • Familiar Demon

FISH OUT OF WATER
Fish Out of Water
Red Fish, Dead Fish
A Few Good Fish
Hiding the Moon
Fish on a Bicycle
School of Fish
Fish in a Barrel
A Perfectly Sonny Daye
Only Fish
Devil and the Deep Blue Fish
Assassin Fish

FLOPHOUSE
Shades of Henry
Constantly Cotton
Sean's Sunshine

GRANBY KNITTING
The Winter Courtship Rituals of Fur-Bearing Critters
How to Raise an Honest Rabbit
Knitter in His Natural Habitat
Blackbird Knitting in a Bunny's Lair
Weddings, Christmas, and Such

Published by Dreamspinner Press
www.dreamspinnerpress.com

By Amy Lane (cont)

JOHNNIES
Chase in Shadow • Dex in Blue
Ethan in Gold • Black John
Bobby Green • Super Sock Man

KEEPING PROMISE ROCK
Keeping Promise Rock
Making Promises
Living Promises
Forever Promised

LONG CON ADVENTURES
The Mastermind • The Muscle
The Driver • The Suit
The Tech • The Face Man
The Grifter

LUCK MECHANICS
The Rising Tide
A Salt Bitter Sea

PRINCETON ROYALS
Riding Shotgun
Running Scared

TALKER
Talker • Talker's Redemption
Talker's Graduation
The Talker Collection Anthology

WINTER BALL
Winter Ball • Summer Lessons
Fall Through Spring

Published by DSP Publications

ALL THAT HEAVEN WILL ALLOW
All the Rules of Heaven

GREEN'S HILL
The Green's Hill Novellas

LITTLE GODDESS
Vulnerable
Wounded, Vol. 1
Wounded, Vol. 2
Bound, Vol. 1 • Bound, Vol. 2
Rampant, Vol. 1 • Rampant, Vol. 2
Quickening, Vol. 1
Quickening, Vol. 2
Green's Hill Werewolves, Vol. 1
Green's Hill Werewolves, Vol. 2

Published by Harmony Ink Press

BITTER MOON SAGA
Triane's Son Rising
Triane's Son Learning
Triane's Son Fighting
Triane's Son Reigning

Published by Dreamspinner Press
www.dreamspinnerpress.com

LET THE WOLF

AMY LANE

Published by
DREAMSPINNER PRESS

8219 Woodville Hwy #1245
Woodville, FL 32362 USA
www.dreamspinnerpress.com

Trade Paperback ISBN: 9781641089104
Digital ISBN: 9781641089098
Digital eBook published May 2026
v. 1.0

Mate—like Joey, I'd be feral without you. Mary—we'll dance in Italy someday, I promise.

Author's Note

This is where I say it's "all made up," but Jesus, the news these days is a horror show. I have no idea what I'll make up to be worried about in my dark imagination, only to find that some asshole did it darker, bloodier, and worse. Let's say this one is written "in hope." As in "I hope somewhere out there are heroes who really put victims over bureaucracy, and right over easy." Don't we all.

Prologue
Look What Wandered In

GIDEON CHADWICK said goodbye to his last guest and closed the door to his midtown Manhattan apartment with a soft sigh of relief. His days of academia were as far behind him as his days in the military, and sometimes he wasn't sure which group of people made him the most uncomfortable. While it was true the doctors and lawyers and forensics specialists—who were often both—liked to talk about books and theories and the root of all political problems and had read Pynchon and Goethe, there was almost always a moment in the middle of the flowing conversation when Gideon found it absolutely, positively necessary to leave the room.

He'd excuse himself to the bathroom, check his watch, the security feeds on his phone, look to see if his alphabet division of the justice department, the Special Crimes Task Force, had caught any cases, and stare longingly out his third-floor window and down the fire escape as he remembered his covert ops days under Jason Constance when he would have thought nothing about spider-climbing out the window and ghosting into the misty September night.

Then he'd remember that he liked these people and had kept in touch with them on purpose after school, and his breathing would grow normal again, and he'd be able to return to the erudite, purposeless discussion of people who had achieved importance—but not enough. Certainly not enough importance to change the world in such a way as to lessen the uphill battle they all fought every day to fix the horrors they saw.

Tonight he'd grabbed an extra bottle of wine as he passed through the open-area kitchen and topped everybody's glass off before he settled himself around the coffee table. No dining table—unlike some of his friends, his apartment was small, with two rooms and a counter that separated the kitchen from the living room and just a big enough living room to put a couch, a love seat, and a stuffed chair.

His dinner parties always ended up with somebody, usually himself, on the floor, sitting cross-legged, trying hard not to fall asleep.

Of course that was because most of the people from his special ops unit were someplace in the desert in California, hunting serial killers. Dammit, he'd left that unit too soon.

Except he liked where he was. *Loved* the SCTF. He worked with an incredible group of people. He couldn't make them his life, though, could he?

The question was tickling his forebrain as he surveyed his apartment after the guests had left—the comfortable leather couches, the Persian rug he'd had shipped from Fallujah, the hardwood floors he'd buffed up after he'd bought the lease.

He'd always been an odd duck—too smart for his peers, too active for academics, too dry for people to get his jokes, secretly laughing at the dark, the macabre, with nobody to smirk with.

Suddenly the hackles on his neck lifted like a porcupine's spines, and he found himself breathing very softly through his nose, scenting the air.

Silently, he glided by the table, picking up a cheese knife from the charcuterie board as he passed. Useless fucking thing, he pondered grimly, flipping it from hand to hand. Good thing he'd taken special classes in useless objects and how to make them kill. He paused for a moment, to the side of his bedroom door, still tasting the currents that swept in through the now open window near the fire escape.

Worn, well-oiled leather. The hint of an organic bourbon-scented soap, the faint hint of wine from a glass Gideon himself had set on the end table near his bed when he'd excused himself from the room.

The wine had been disturbed—and consumed.

Gideon's heart rate, which had never climbed above sixty when he'd thought there was an assailant in his bedroom, suddenly skyrocketed.

"God, they were boring," Joey Carlyle said from his cross-legged perch on Gideon's bed. "I thought they'd never leave."

Gideon tucked the charcuterie knife up his sleeve. "Well, if you'd knocked on the door and started talking about ripping out deer hearts, you could have sped them up."

Joey grinned, the expression feral, like a wolf's, in his strong-boned, insanely beautiful face. His skin—a pale gold—showed traces of his Native ancestry, but Joey Carlyle's granite cheekbones and oval eyes really gave away the whole package.

Or at least the physically attractive package.

"That Elaine girl," Joey said as Gideon sat down. "You nailed her yet?"

"Dr. Aiello?" Gideon asked. "Chief Forensic Pathologist to New York State? No. I'm a peon, Joey. She only dates stallions. The fuck are you doing here?"

He thought he might know, but that could only be wishful thinking. He and Carlyle had worked together for a while. Gideon's contact with Constance had gotten him put on special assignment with Clint Harding for a year when he'd been in the service. Harding had been impressed enough to make him one of the first recruits for Harding's task force. Natalia Denison had been the actual first—she'd been Harding's partner in the FBI, then Kylie the texpert (as Carlyle called her) and wily, deadly Gail Pearson. A year and a half ago, Harding—operating on intel Chadwick couldn't fathom—had recruited big, beefy Judson Crosby, who was an astoundingly good operative for all he'd started his life as a flatfoot. Carlyle, fresh out of the service and still twitchy, had come along about the same time.

For some reason Gideon had never understood—maybe it was his stillness in the wake of Carlyle's constant motion—Joey Carlyle had gravitated to Gideon like a feral cat gravitated to a favorite yard.

He sought out Gideon's company for assignments. Asked for his opinion. Hopped in his department issue SUV without being asked or ordered.

Opened his mouth and showed the edges of his pointy teeth when Gideon told a joke, which was a thing Gideon would love about him forever.

Gideon had always thought wistfully that would be brotherly love, right up until he'd smelled Joey Carlyle and the petrichor of September rain in the city.

"You're a peon?" Carlyle asked, eyes darkening in the shadows. "You're a… what?"

Gideon blew out a breath, not wanting to dwell on the melancholy of his own insecurities tonight. "It's not important," he said. And then, because he knew Joey after all this time—*knew* he'd never tell Gideon when asked straight out—he asked a sideways question. "What'd you think about the new guy?"

Carlyle's eyes flickered, from the dim lamp to the open window and back. "Garcia?" he asked.

"Yeah."

"He's great," Carlyle said. "He's half in love with Crosby already, and Crosby's still in the hospital."

Gideon couldn't help the low moan that issued from his throat. "God. Yeah." Crosby and Garcia had followed a hunch, and Crosby had ended up getting shot in close quarters. Even with Kevlar, the force of the bullets broke his ribs and punctured his lungs. He was going to be out for a while, and Gideon couldn't help it. He'd felt protective over the kid—God, they *all* had. The rest of the squad, they'd nursed at the breast of the DOJ, all of them training for this job in one way or another through special forces, covert ops, or plain old book learning. Gideon had hit the Princeton for four years, Marines next and *then* finished the book learning with his PhD, but he'd been good at his job. Particularly the wet work. Something about his dry dispassion had made him clean, methodical, and not particularly remorseful, but that could be because he was called upon to kill very, very bad men.

Crosby had thought the world was fair until being a flatfoot in a shitty Chicago precinct had taught him different. He'd caught a serial killer single-handedly and headed off a gang war and then had stood up against the entire force when his partner had gone rogue. If Harding hadn't picked the kid up by the scruff of the neck and hauled him to New York, Crosby would be dead already. Such a sweet baby boy, and he had thrown his heart and soul into his new job.

"He wasn't supposed to last," Gideon said fretfully, perhaps to mask his concern. "I took one look and told Harding, 'Oh my God, he's going to end up in the river if we don't turf him somewhere else.'"

"I thought he'd done that himself with the fucking dogs," Carlyle said, and while a stranger might have heard the disgust, Chadwick had been there the day Crosby had turned his back on the dogfight dog in favor of the drug dealer who'd trained it. Chadwick had dispatched one drug dealer, Crosby had dispatched the other, and Carlyle had ripped up his T-shirt to use as a bandage to keep Crosby from bleeding out—after killing the dog.

"He popped back up and learned," Chadwick said, shaking his head. "But yeah. The 'Oh God, they killed Crosby!' game is old already. I would like to not see that boy in the hospital."

"Do you want him?" Carlyle asked, his eyes on Chadwick's face.

"I thought *we* were partners," Chadwick said mildly.

"But you seem in love with Crosby."

It was time for Gideon to interrupt. "No," he said gently. "I'm not in love with Crosby. He's a friend, like he is to you. We, you know, love the guy, but we don't *love* the guy."

"Garcia will," Carlyle said. Why was it that only Gideon could follow him? It always seemed to him like Joey Carlyle left a clear and distinct trail.

"You think so?" Chadwick murmured. He closed his eyes in the dark, knowing he could because Joey would watch out for him. He scented the jacket again, the soap. The dark animal smell that was Joey Carlyle, that seemed to feed Gideon's soul.

"I can see it," Joey said. "They're… they're two halves, one coconut. Like you and me."

"But Crosby and Gail are pretty tight," Gideon said curiously. "I would have thought it would be them."

"She's like his sister," Joey said. "Same pheromones, practically. They *smell* the same. Can't you smell it?"

Chadwick grimaced. The "what do you smell" game was one of the other things they had that nobody else did. "Milk and blood," he muttered, almost embarrassed.

"Yes," Joey said, following him with ease. "They're both wholesome and dangerous." His smile went wolfish again. "Garcia isn't wholesome—but he'll wash off pretty with Crosby. They'll be good once Crosby gets better."

Chadwick let out a long sigh of relief. "That's good to know," he said, smiling. He didn't doubt Joey's faint clairvoyance. It was something they'd never talked about, but when Joey said, "Our subjects are in that building, overdosing," Chadwick knew to bring his gun and put rescue workers on notice because Joey Carlyle wasn't wrong about those things.

And sometimes he was right about good things too. He'd known Kylie, their texpert, wasn't coming back from her honeymoon. He'd known Kylie had been pregnant probably before Kylie had. That was good. He'd known Gail Pearson, who looked like the Swiss Miss Hot Chocolate girl, was in truth a knife maiden with superlative skills who didn't shy away from blood work.

And now apparently he knew that Garcia and Crosby would be a thing.

Good for them.

"Is that why you came?" Chadwick asked, his throat suddenly dry. "To tell me that Garcia and Crosby are going to be a thing."

Joey shook his head, his eyes—a dark, dark ochre color—fastened upon Chadwick's face like Chadwick was a magnet. Chadwick knew for a fact he wasn't handsome. Every line or angle, from his nose to his chin to his cheekbones, was sharp and beveled like a hatchet, and he wondered uneasily what Joey Carlyle saw in him.

"Then what?" Gideon rasped, suddenly conscious of the moment. The soft patter of the rain on the deserted street below, the darkened, empty apartment, their proximity on the bed, the quiet harshness of their breaths.

The deliciousness of Joey Carlyle's skin.

"Because Crosby is taken now," Carlyle whispered. "Which means there's only me."

And Chadwick followed him there too. He swallowed—twice—because longing rushed up so thickly to block his breathing.

"Joey Carlyle," he rasped slowly, "what makes you think that Judson Crosby—or anybody else for that matter—would ever be competition for you?"

Carlyle's grin went full wolf right before he captured Chadwick's mouth, and Chadwick was fallen upon and devoured by his desire.

Wolf Song

A Year and a Half Earlier

JOEY CARLYLE sat on the bus and stared at his phone, wishing he was better with tech. He'd spent years in special ops—a Green Beret, nominally, but so much on the fringes, practically a killer for hire or a tracker to paint the target on the deer.

He'd spent part of his childhood on the res, learning how to hunt and track and move silently, all from his mother's father. He'd been able to sneak out of a lover's bed from the age of fifteen, and he'd never been caught.

But dammit, he wasn't great at keeping his father from tracking his goddamned phone.

We know you're stateside, Joseph. Stop fucking around and come home.

Except his father's home had never, ever been his home. The reservation had been his home until he'd turned eight and his father had shown up, wanting to "give the boy every opportunity." Joey *had* opportunities, he'd thought then. He had opportunities to track game, to learn the different smells of the wind, the temperature of water as it formed ice in the tracks of his prey. Opportunities to learn how to cook venison and squirrel, and how to find shelter, how to hide in knotholes so small not even badgers could find him.

So no. Stevie Carlyle's mansion, the place Joey's mother had been working when Stevie had knocked her up, was never going to be Joey's home. He'd visited his grandfather as often as possible after his grandfather—pressured, Joey was sure, by Stevie threatening to take resources away from the already struggling reservation—grudgingly allowed Joey to go.

"Learn to walk in the white man's world," old Joseph told him gravely. "You can't hunt prey when you don't understand how it walks."

And Joey had gotten it then. His father, his father's fancy wife, their employees, the kids he went to private school with—they were prey.

It was so much easier to be alone when you could think of your tormenters, the people who exiled you to corners or to your room or to the far end of the playground, as prey.

But you did not think of your prey's den as a home, and Joey had never, ever fallen into that trap.

A thing that had probably saved his soul as he'd learned more and more that his father was prey in the same way a venomous snake was prey.

You only hunted a cobra or a cottonmouth if they were out to kill your livestock or your family. Otherwise you simply allowed them to be—and stayed away from their den.

Joey and his father had been engaged in warfare from day one. He'd been shipped off to military school at fourteen and had joined the Army at eighteen for a reason. And while his father had stopped sending him texts during his time in the service, Joey had known it would take him a minute, maybe two, to learn that Joey was stateside again.

But not without a plan.

I have a job, he texted. *LEO. Stop texting me if you don't want them to track your phone.*

He'd lucked out. "The debacle," as his COs had called it, had happened near the end of his stint, and before it had occurred, he'd been thinking "Hey, I've been here for six years, and I've learned a lot, but I'm pretty much done." After the debacle occurred, he'd been recovering in the hospital and a persona non grata, which was when he'd gotten a letter—an honest to God letter—at the base in Bogota where he'd spent most of his deployment.

It had been from one Clint Harding—and it hadn't listed his rank or anything, although the man was *legend*, and Joey knew he'd retired just before being promoted to colonel. That legend said it was to *avoid* being promoted to colonel, which made Joey worship him a little more.

I run a new alphabet agency, the SCTF, and your CO tells me you'd be an outstanding new addition. We need somebody with your particular skills, but somebody who can show deference to civilian well-being. Major Corrigan told me that you managed to keep an entire village safe from your own troops. He said that the US Army may not appreciate your inability to follow a bad order, but that he did, and he felt the entire human race would benefit from you having a place where your common sense and compassion are allowed precedence. I think my agency can be that place.

And Joey, who was not prone to shows of emotion, felt his eyes burn. They'd threatened to *hang* him as a *traitor* when he'd come in from that op, but everything he knew about predator and prey and the evil of senseless slaughter of deer told him that those people had needed to be protected, not mown down. He didn't give a rat's ass that the president himself had signed the order. Everyone knew that guy was full of shit anyway.

And while Major Corrigan hadn't said anything—other than telling the three lieutenants out for his blood that they were in the wrong and Joey was welcome in his unit anytime—the fact that he'd been keeping a quiet eye out to make sure Joey landed after he'd practically been handed his papers wasn't lost on him.

He recognized kindness because his grandfather had been kind. His grandfather had passed before he'd enlisted, but that didn't mean Joey wasn't grateful.

Even predators recognized the signs of an alpha, taking care of the young in its den.

And the letter from Clint Harding indicated the same thing. They'd be the best of predators, wolves or mountain lions who didn't kill for sport but for food, and who cared for their helpless ones.

Joey had that letter in his knapsack, along with the paperwork showing he'd passed his Federal Law Enforcement Training Center courses in the last month.

Joey Carlyle had actually been stateside for a month, but he'd only in the last week been officially exited from the Army. Oh, his father must have some deep tentacles in the information superhighway, because he wouldn't have dared text his son at FLETC.

You're my son, Joseph—you belong in the family business.

You may have spawned me, but I will never be your son.

And with that he decided he didn't need technology right now. He had the address of Clint Harding's SCTF office in Manhattan, and he'd secured an apartment there using his own money, which he'd long since divorced from his father's, although he'd made steady withdrawals from his trust fund, which he'd placed in his own accounts.

His father had stolen him from his grandfather when he was eight years old—he figured that money was still collecting on an old blood debt.

He definitely had enough money for a new phone.

With a yank at the old-fashioned window clips of the aging Greyhound, he tossed the phone out onto the turnpike, where it would be hopelessly shattered on the rolling pavement below.

HE WAS standing in Clint Harding's office twelve hours later, his dusty Army duffel at his feet, the rubble of sleep in his eyes.

"You're ready to work today?" Harding said, a kind smile on his craggy face. Harding was surprisingly tall, with broad shoulders that didn't think of stooping, Nordic features, and a rather dominant nose. Still, he had that magnetic appeal that came with confidence and command. Would Joey hit that? Sure. Would it be necessary? No. "Wouldn't you like to find a place to sleep, cop a shower, get settled first?"

Joey blinked multiple times and tried to squelch a yawn. "Not necessary, sir."

"Well, as your SAC I'm going to have to disagree," Harding said briskly, something about his voice recalling the military, which was probably a canny move on his part, because Joey took that as an order. "Do you have lodging?"

"Furnished apartment," he said. He'd seen pictures. It was a spartan sanded floor, white tile sort of place. "Haven't been there yet."

Harding's eyes widened. "Well, maybe you should check it out, hit your rack, get a hot meal, and be back here tomorrow. Don't worry. Plenty of bad guys tomorrow."

Joey wasn't sure if Harding was mocking him or not, but he caught the kind crinkles at the corners of his eyes and realized that he was just making a joke.

God, he really *must* get to sleep if he was about to take issue with his SAC for cracking a joke.

"Yessir," he said, giving a crisp nod. "Oh-eight-hundred?"

"We'll have coffee and pastries," Harding told him soberly. "But I suggest you eat before then. Trust me, the takeout sitch is target rich in this city."

Joey grimaced. "Need a phone for that, sir. Mine was… damaged in transit."

Harding grunted and pinched the bridge of his nose. "How far away is your apartment?" he asked.

Joey gave him the address, and Harding's eyes did that widening thing again.

"That's forty blocks away," he said. "How were you planning to get there?"

Joey shrugged. "Walk? I understand there's buses. I've got plastic." And while his insouciance spoke of many years on his own, of tracking down prey in the jungle or wandering strange cities, he'd realized on the way in that nothing had quite prepared him for the human and concrete density of New York City. It wasn't as humanly dense as, say, Myanmar or Tokyo, but there was an unyielding quality to all those tall buildings, the acres of automobiles.

And he felt very much like a sidewalk flower, searching for the sun.

He'd learned very early on to not admit weakness and to never be lost, but for the first time in his life, it hit him that now would be a very good time to learn to ask for help.

Harding didn't make him ask.

"You know what? We've got nothing doing at the moment. The rest of the team's on desk duty until we get a call. Kylie, our computer genius, usually runs point, and she'll let us know if anything in our purview falls out. Here, let me call Chadwick. He lives in the city. He'll be able to give you some tips. Let's go."

Joey barely remembered almost tripping over Chadwick on his way to Harding's office. That would nag him later, how little he'd *seen* the man.

Sure, he was angular—face like a three-dimensional trapezoid, with a knife-blade nose and cheekbones that could cut steak. His mouth was a lean slash, slightly off center, as though he was trying not to let on that he saw the world sideways.

Joey, who had been silently laughing at fear, at his fellow students, at authority for his entire life, should really have seen the kindred spirit.

But right then all he'd seen had been Harding's derpy friend.

He didn't see much more as Harding called Chadwick over and told him they were going to run their new member to the home he hadn't seen yet.

"You got an apartment in the Upper West Side?" Chadwick asked when he heard the address. "Fancy."

"I have no idea," Joey said, suddenly aware that he may have wanted to do more research about his new residence. He'd been so grateful for the job. "I was looking for a place I could afford is all."

Chadwick didn't say anything then, didn't make fun of him, didn't mention that if Joey could afford the Upper West Side that meant he could afford a hell of a lot. He simply gave a shrug.

"There's people in Manhattan that know every back street, every restaurant, every building," Harding said. "And every day they profess to be surprised. Or cheated out of real estate. As long as you got a place to hit the rack and hang your hat, we're calling it good."

"Other new guy doesn't even have that," Chadwick muttered. "Rooming with a DJ, for sweet fuck's sake."

"A good one?" Harding asked, and Chadwick shrugged.

"Making a name for himself," he admitted. "Crosby's big concern is the substance abuse in the apartment—not by his friend, which is funny, but by the hangers-on."

"Not by the DJ?" Harding snorted. "That's unlikely."

Chadwick made an unconscious gesture then that, to his knowledge, only Joey noticed. It was a small double tap of his thumb against the base of his forefinger, and Joey wondered what it meant.

"I've met Toby Trotter," Chadwick said. "He looks like he's had some health problems—congenital most likely. I sincerely doubt he'd be abusing substances, but I can see how he wouldn't want to make a big deal about it if somebody else was. I just think we need to keep a weather eye out for Crosby is all."

Harding nodded. "He may do better than you think."

"I've read his docket," Chadwick said mildly. Then he gave Joey a sideways glance from slightly crossed hazel eyes. "I'll get to yours."

Joey knew guys in the service with eyes set like that—they were often the best shots, because they'd had to work hard to focus their entire lives. Suddenly he was a little uncomfortable. "Do I get dockets?" he asked, trying to be alert, and to his absolute horror, he let out a yawn. Oh God. Both sides of his family would be mortified.

"I emailed one to you," Harding said dryly, "but apparently your phone was damaged. Chadwick, go get your shop. I'll check him out a phone. You're certified in every weapon we have—we'll let you choose your service revolver tomorrow."

So Joey found himself trotting—yes, trotting, because Chadwick was as tall as he was angular, and Joey had always been smaller and more slightly built. To his profound relief, Chadwick didn't adjust his stride. That would have been humiliating, and it would have meant the man wouldn't trust him when shit got real. Joey liked being invisible, but he wasn't too keen about being underestimated.

"So what do you need to settle in?" Chadwick asked, with all the paternal warmth of an analyst asking how to boost internet output.

"Basic rations," Joey replied, thinking protein bars, potable water, fruit. "Blankets." He thought for a moment about clothes—because when he was stateside, he did love to dress well sometimes. "A leather jacket," he said, because his trunk of possessions was currently in storage somewhere upstate, and after his father's text, he was reluctant to go claim it. "And cleaning supplies."

Chadwick blinked slowly, and for a moment, Joey wondered if he was flummoxed by something.

"Where are your clothes?" he asked, eyeing the duffel Joey had slung over his shoulder.

"I—"

"See, it would be one thing if you just wanted a jacket," Chadwick said, as though musing to himself. "A jacket is warmth. Most of us are fans, particularly in the spring. You're wearing a hoodie, so you apparently noticed it's not warm yet. But leather is a choice. Most people who want a *leather* jacket have a style in mind. So you don't have blankets for your bed yet, but you want a leather jacket. This implies you've *had* a leather jacket and it isn't here. Where is it?"

Oh God. Joey was too tired for this. "A storage facility I can't get to," he said. "I miss it."

Chadwick nodded as they hit the elevators, presumably for an underground garage. "Anything else there you miss?"

"Stuff," Joey said noncommittally.

"Huh. Do you know it's all still there?"

"No."

"Can you check to see?"

"No." Joey wasn't sure whether to be irritated at the intrusion into his life or impressed.

"So it's Schrödinger's stuff," Chadwick said, and laughed quietly to himself. Joey stared at him, trying to process. He knew who Schrödinger was—he *thought* he knew who Schrödinger was—but while he could probably run ten miles this tired and then swim twenty laps for fun, his brain, usually adept with recall and wordplay, had shorted out.

Predators don't need to know who Schrödinger was, he told himself grumpily.

But Chadwick—whoever he was—wasn't stupid. "Sorry," he said as the elevator doors opened and he led the way to a guard kiosk to check out a vehicle and grab the keys. "Most of my jokes are really best in my own head."

Joey had no idea.

All he knew was that, while the bus ride had been impossible to sleep through with every moment spent assessing the traffic, the stops, the way his father could possibly track him from Washington, DC, to NYC via Greyhound bus, as Chadwick talked and told him to hop in the back so he could chill while Chadwick negotiated traffic, Joey's eyelids started to droop.

He didn't worry about it. He'd gone without sleep for three days before. In fact it was part of covert ops training. Forty-eight hours was no big deal; he'd sleep when he got safe.

Then Harding got into the SUV, ordering Chadwick into the passenger's seat because in his words, "My heart isn't as young as it used to be." The minute he turned the key, Joey's head hit the seat rest and he was out.

HE AWOKE twelve hours later, on the fully made plain wood bed he'd seen pictured in the pamphlet when he'd leased his apartment. He was in the T-shirt and briefs he'd put on two days ago, but his jeans and hoodie were neatly folded and hanging on the chair at the foot of the bed. His duffel sat on the chair too.

He had to pee fiercely, and he wasn't sure where the bathroom was.

He sat up and peered around, wincing at the sterility of the room. The comforter was nice—tan and green—although he couldn't remember purchasing one. Oh Jesus, he hoped there was toilet paper.

He spotted the en suite bathroom and toddled in to sit on the throne with a blessed, blessed sigh.

Toilet paper, he noticed with relief, and a freshly opened package in the corner. Towels—two new towels in navy that matched the navy-and-tan patterned rug on the floor—hung from the rack.

And there was a new bar of soap with only one or two rinses in the soap holder, and a basic men's shampoo/conditioner bottle in the shower.

Oh God, he felt ripe and rotten. When he'd finished his business, he grabbed the clean, dry, matching face cloth that was hanging with the towels and hopped into the shower, wondering who his fairy godmother was. He'd been told the place would be barren and ready for him to move in, but someone—the Realtor?—had apparently thought to welcome him here.

How did he get here again?

He was still wondering that after his shower. He put on his last clean clothes and hung up the towels before emerging into the living space in his bare feet.

He saw takeout bags in the new trash receptacle by the sink and, following his nose, opened the small refrigerator to find orange juice, Chinese food boxes (half-full), eggs, milk, cheese, jelly, and lunch meat. On the marble counter he saw bread, apples, onions, and peanut butter.

After he pulled out the takeout cartons, he found a table service for four in the cupboards, the same in silverware in the drawer near the sink, and a brand-new pan, stickers still on it, on the stove next to a new chef's knife and a spatula.

He was still pondering his good fortune when the microwave binged and he heard a snore, choked off midway, and he found himself in a crouch, looking over the kitchen counter to the front room.

Chadwick—all six-foot-something of him—lay curled up on Joey's couch, a spare pillow under his head, a tan throw—as new as the bedding in Joey's room—thrown over his lean and angular body.

He was scowling toward the kitchen. "Oh," he said groggily. "You found the food."

"You…." Joey was at a loss. "You bought me food." Lightbulb! "And bedding. And towels. And dishes. Holy crap." He no longer had exhaustion as an excuse for being an asshole. "Thank you," he said humbly, still trying to digest it all.

"Harding and I went halfsies," Chadwick mumbled, sitting up and rubbing his eyes. "What time is it?"

Joey swallowed and checked his new phone, which was plugged in and charged on the counter. "Five o'clock," he said. "Is that a.m. or p.m.?"

Chadwick laughed. "A.m." He yawned. "Harding brought me my laptop, I worked here. You were so out of it, we didn't feel right about just leaving you in a strange place. I mean, it was bad enough leaving Crosby with his roommate. Felt like leaving a puppy in a wolf den. We couldn't do that shit again."

"This Crosby must be the second coming," Joey muttered. "You haven't shut up about him."

Another dry analytical laugh. "Just not our usual," he said on another yawn. "God, five?"

"Early?" Joey asked.

"I usually get up at six thirty. I got department-issue sweats in the bag and a department issue in your parking spot. Let me get another hour in, cop a shower, and we can go in together. Any questions?"

Joey hated to ask, he really did, but… "Washer/dryer?"

"Behind the screen in the hall. I guess you had them installed when you got the place, like the fridge."

Joey grunted. "Sleep," he said. "I may take a walk, but I'll be back in time to wake you."

"'Preciate it," Chadwick said, another yawn seeming to pull him sideways on the couch, dragging the throw with him.

Joey spent a moment watching him, thinking about the kindness—for that had been what had driven Chadwick and Harding—he'd been shown. Part of him was trying to retroactively panic. He'd shown his throat! He'd let strangers see him vulnerable! He'd barely let guys from the unit see him sleep. His room in his father's house had been a landmine—soda cans on strings, squeaky toys, coffee tables placed at shin height—all of it designed to not let his father sneak up on him at any time.

The first night he'd spent in his father's house, he'd woken up with his father's knife at his throat, because his father had gotten around all the booby traps Joey had set up before going to bed.

Their relationship had only deteriorated from there.

He'd been eight.

And he'd never trusted his father.

But apparently he trusted these two men on his new team enough to not only sleep in front of them, but to continue sleeping while they put him to bed like the child he never had been and set up his apartment.

It was a welcoming. A homecoming that he hadn't seen since his weekend visits with his grandfather.

Joey finished the Chinese food in the dark and the quiet—he never had turned on the lights. He could see fine in the ambient light from the windows. He was thinking that without realizing it, he had found a pack. Harding and Chadwick, at the very least, he could trust.

Without conscious thought, Chadwick's little quip about Joey having "Schrödinger's stuff," popped into his mind, and it hit him then.

Schrödinger's cat. Joey wouldn't know if the stuff was there until he checked. Until then it was both there and not there, but since Joey had no access to it, they might as well believe it was not there.

Hence all of the "Schrödinger's stuff" in Joey's apartment.

The smile was there before he could stop it, but since nobody was awake in his new den to see it, he allowed it to be. Deer. He could be comfortable with Chadwick, with Harding, because they were deer.

Carnivorous Deer

"How'd the new guy settle in last night?" Harding asked as Gideon poured his coffee. The coffee station at the SCTF was pretty swank. No cappuccino machine, but a choice of creamers, flavors, a French press, and hand grinders—caffeine was the blood in their veins, and Harding made sure it ran sweet and true while Gideon helped by finding the super fancy stuff. Not necessarily sugar, but the choice imported beans, the richest creamers, syrups instead of plain white granules—although there were plenty of those.

And the coffee cups had become a tradition.

Only Harding and Gideon would know this. For a short time, during a dangerous joint task force deployment in covert ops, Harding had been Gideon's CO. They'd been far away, in the Afghani desert, living in a big tent with the other ten guys from their unit. Harding had provided them with a coffee station then too; nobody knew how he'd done it. Coffee and books—their unit had them when nobody else did. There were even (oh dear God!) cookies. Oreos and E.L. Fudge.

Gideon, one day when the boredom of "hurry up and wait" had been *killing him*, had asked his stepmom, Trish, if she could ship coffee mugs to the middle of the goddamned desert. He could never explain how he'd gotten the idea, but something about the depersonalization of the OD green and desert camo had worn on him worse than the heat. He listened to the men's conversations, their music, their discussion of books, their families.

They were individuals, even Harding, who kept the best stone face on that Gideon had ever seen.

But still… Gideon had caught him laughing at jokes somebody texted him every morning. He'd seen him read *every* book in the lending library, and he and Gideon had discussed some of them at length. They both enjoyed political thrillers, because—as they both said *often*—nothing in the books was as scary as what they knew about real politics.

And on a daily basis, they donned native clothing and slipped into the desert to do dangerous things, and if they got killed doing them, nobody would ever know who they were, what they'd done, or what sort of men had died protecting their country.

He felt like they needed something to say "an individual was here."

His stepmom—sweet woman from whom he'd never asked a thing until that moment—had asked for specifics and had come through.

He would never forget the day the case had arrived. Each cup had been wrapped with exquisite care, and the coffee cups were the sturdiest she could buy. There was a funny cartoon or inscription to match each man in the unit but no names.

They spent the day playing "match the coffee cup" and setting up the box they'd come in to hold them between uses. It was a wooden crate, and there was a hope the cups would sustain the periodic shelling that happened in their area.

Two weeks later, they'd gone out on a mission and had come back short one man. Garfield Molloy had died in Chadwick's arms while Harding tried to bandage together what was left of his chest, and they were both hollow eyed and empty as they walked into their tent.

Then Harding saw the coffee cup, and for the first time in their yearlong deployment, Chadwick saw fury cross his features. He strode up to the coffee station, picked up the cup and stared at it, jaw working, and for a moment, Chadwick thought he'd shatter it on the hardpacked dirt beneath their feet.

He hadn't, though. After a moment, his face had relaxed a little, and he'd allowed profound sorrow to cross his craggy features.

He held up the cup. It featured the orange cat from the comics, standing on the scale in bewilderment, accusing it of lying. While whippet lean, *their* Garfield had often contested facts like that. "Naw, it can't be this cold in the desert. The thermometer must be lying."

"To Garfield," he'd said softly.

"To Garfield," the rest of the men said. Very carefully he set the cup down in the wooden crate, and it wasn't taken out again.

They lost three more men before that mission was complete. Before the remaining eight men shipped home, they sat outside on camp chairs around a bonfire that they'd earned by making the area safe from insurgents and toasted their friends with their coffee cups—but this time filled with wine.

After the last toast, they hurled the cups at the rock they'd camped behind, one after another, the fragments and dust mingling, because they all knew that their friends were not the only parts of themselves they'd leave in the desert.

Harding and Chadwick had gone their separate ways then. Harding retired from the Marines and joined the FBI for five years, while Chadwick had finished his stint and gone on to earn the post-graduate degrees he'd contemplated before he'd signed up, and that done to join the BAU. When Harding secured the funding to start the first branch of the Special Crimes Task Force, designed to piggyback off the FBI's infrastructure but answerable to and run by Harding himself, Chadwick had been the second person he tagged after his own partner in the FBI, Natalia Denison.

Between the three of them and their previous experience, they'd brought in computer genius Kylie Grant and—fresh out of FLETC—former NCIS officer Gail Pearson. And with the acknowledgment it was only until they could recruit two or three more officers, a slight, gentle-looking man named Harman Blodgett, who had worked for the FBI as a consultant—Gideon had used his services on occasion—and whose day job of all things was as an ER doctor.

And who, Chadwick had quietly deduced, had been Harding's romantic partner for at least three closeted years.

Nobody said anything about it, although Natalia was *very* open about her wife and two children, one of whom had been born right before she'd accepted Harding's invitation to this very new experiment.

The five of them had spent some time scouring reports of various stars of the ATF, FBI, and NCIS corps, searching for an indefinable something that would make somebody want to put their career on almost permanent hold to come work for a unit that was designed to protect the victims more than it was designed to make spectacular busts.

In the meantime, Harman Blodgett and Clint Harding had been called in to help a Chicago flatfoot who thought he had a serial killer on his hands and who couldn't get a single goddamned person in his department willing to help him hunt the guy down.

After Crosby had brought the guy in single-handedly, his department had turned on him and had set him up to either be as corrupt as they were or to die, along with his bleed-blue parents.

Crosby had rejected that scenario too, but he'd needed a hand out of the windy city if he was going to survive.

And Chadwick had gotten word from a colonel who'd taken some of his criminology classes about a Green Beret who had defied orders to protect a village and like Crosby had practically earned a death sentence from his former colleagues for doing the right thing.

Harman Blodgett's last day had been the day Joey Carlyle had enrolled in FLETC. Crosby arrived from his own training the day after.

Harding said the unit still needed three to five more people, but they had enough, and enough of them were highly trained and super intuitive enough to make do until then.

But Chadwick had taken a personal interest in making sure their new recruits landed. It was like those goddamned coffee mugs in the desert; sometimes simple kindness, simple smiles, simple acknowledgments of human beings under the uniforms and the orders, could make the difference between somebody coming back from an op or never coming home.

And knowing that if you didn't come home, your brothers would remember you.

Harding hadn't commented on the assortment of mugs that Chadwick brought in. He'd just taken his "Don't make me talk about my feelings" mug and given Chadwick a nod. Natalia had spotted her "Goddess who smites" mug—complete with a lightning strike and pentagram—immediately. Kylie—who had recently become engaged at the time—smirked at the "Here comes the bride" cup with a sardonic twist of her full lips, and Gail had cackled at the cartoon cat holding the knife. *Gail's* docket contained very classified details about Gail's work in covert ops. She was disturbingly good with knives.

Harman had taken his mug with the teddy bear in scrubs with a stethoscope with a raised eyebrow at Chadwick, who had winked.

One of Chadwick's clues to Harm's and Harding's relationship was that he'd heard Harding use the word *Barchen* to refer to Harm under his breath.

It meant "bear" and had obviously been an endearment.

Gideon had wanted Harm to know that the secret was safe with him.

So now he had two recruits to buy coffee cups for. It was actually not a bad task; it forced him to connect with people, to study them, not just as a subject as he had in the BAU, but as a friend.

He and Harding had doubts that Crosby would be there that long. The kid was good. He'd tracked down a serial offender on his own using personal intuition, street smarts, and a sort of dogged integrity that had also gotten him kicked off the Chicago force and almost killed for reporting a *very* unrighteous shoot by his racist partner. But he was also… well, sweet.

Gideon hadn't wanted to say anything, but he'd seen the open admission in Crosby's face that he wouldn't have even *dreamed* about a unit like the SCTF, much less thought about applying. This kid had been born and almost died thinking Chicago flatfoot was the be-all and end-all of his existence, and frankly, Harding's little experiment needed people to dream bigger than that.

But Gideon still needed to buy him a coffee mug, because just getting here was an accomplishment for Judson Crosby, and that needed to be acknowledged.

And as for Joey Carlyle….

"Thoughts?" Harding asked him after he'd shown Carlyle where to get outfitted for weapons and tactical gear and handle other administrative tasks.

"Feral," Gideon said bluntly. "And I get he lived on pine nuts and universe juice for two months, keeping his own unit away from that village, but I think it goes deeper than that." Carlyle was two months out of the Green Berets, and Gideon had been able to see his ribs still. Part of that was that FLETC was no joke, but Gideon had seen his appreciation for the food on the counter. He wondered if Carlyle would have survived on more pine nuts and universe juice if they'd left him to his own devices.

"Same," Harding said. "You know who his father is."

Gideon grunted. "Stevie Carlyle, of your higher-end mobsters. Yeah, I know. You think he's getting away from that sitch?"

"I'd place money on it," Harding told him.

"Or our lives." Gideon didn't flinch.

Harding grimaced. "Yeah. Or our lives. But he didn't have to protect that village. Those people could have been displaced or killed and we never would have known about it. But he kept his own people off their backs while they found a way to get the whole village out of the way of Uncle Goddamned Sam. I think if he was a dyed-in-the-wool mobster's boy, that sitch wouldn't have bothered him one bit. His CO was adamant that Carlyle was absolutely on the side of using his considerable skills to protect people. And he's obviously a survivor."

Gideon wanted to protest that—the kid had slept long and hard after they'd guided him up the stairs to his apartment, and that wasn't usually a survivor's skill.

Maybe he felt safe?

"He's planning weapons training today," Gideon said, "while he gets used to the setup. What have you got for me?"

Which meant that the subject of Joey Carlyle was tabled for the moment until they could see him in the field. They'd both seen his marks and reports—he was dead-on with short work, knives, pistols, crossbows (crossbows? Holy crap!), and the like, and could apparently track a snowflake in a blizzard. But he'd never been partnered up. Clint Harding was adamant about not letting his people go into the field alone, which was a tough sell for everybody here except Clint himself and Natalia Denison. Kylie was used to working in her ivory tower as overwatch, Gail had obviously been sent on independent missions (she made a lousy honey trap, she'd told Gideon during her interview, but a really great hotel maid who could search things) but seemed to enjoy working with a team, and Harm—as Clint had noted grimly on more than one occasion—was practically an empath.

Sure, Clint's boyfriend could kick tactical ass, which was surprising given his slender form and sweet little face, but he was *really* good at reading any partner's emotional cues and then using that to advantage to track down a suspect.

If it hadn't been for his barely suppressed tendency to psychoanalyze anybody he was in close quarters with, Gideon might have harbored a crush, but as it was, he was ready to wave the man a fond farewell.

And Crosby had *always* worked with a partner—the question now was could he ever trust one again.

Gideon had ridden with him a couple of times, and he wasn't bad. For all he presented himself as a dumb flatfoot, he was intuitive and clear in his intentions *and* his communications, and as a pleasant surprise, he was pretty good at talking a suspect down from critical moments, only going for his weapon as a last resort. Natalia had reported the same things, and Clint was going to see how well he paired up with Gail.

Which meant that, depending on how things fell out, Gideon might be taking Carlyle on his first tactical or probative run. So wondering what they might have brewing was a good question. Gideon was going to want to be prepared.

"Turns out," Clint said, going to his terminal and pressing a few buttons, "I've got something you may want to check out. Let Carlyle get settled in, and if we're still quiet tomorrow, maybe start hunting down leads on this. Study it. I got a phone briefing, but I want your take." He blew out a breath. "Blodgett's going to regret missing this one."

"Where's it from?" Gideon asked, knowing the file had been sent to his computer. Yes, the iconic manila file folder still existed, but for a casual "Take a look at this, would you?" with somebody who still had clearance, a computer link worked too.

While not a leader—oh fuck no—Gideon *had* worked in Behavior Analysis, just like Harman Blodgett, and for a little while, like Clint and Natalia, and he hadn't lost his clearance rating when he transferred out. In fact that had been part of the condition of his transfer—one that Clint had asked for and Gideon hadn't.

But it had come in handy these last six months, and apparently it would now.

Three and a half hours later, Gideon's eyes felt like sandpaper, and the water flask that sat at his desk was bone dry. He kept trying to drink out of the aluminum bottle and grimacing when there was nothing in it, but so far nothing had inspired him to get up and move.

It wasn't until he reached for his water bottle for the umpteenth time and sweet, sweet nectar of life poured into his mouth, making him sputter, that he realized Joey Carlyle had been sitting at his desk, silently watching him for God knew how long.

"Holy fuck," Gideon said, wiping his mouth off with the sleeve of his white dress shirt. The dress code here was much more casual than the FBI—but it was still "Look good to impress civilians." Gideon went with a sport coat, oxford shirt, jeans, and those wonderful soft-soled lace-up things that were being worn as office-friendly now but let him tear up the street when he was running someone down.

He'd shed his sport coat the moment he'd sat and opened the damned file.

"If I'd been hunting you, you'd be dinner," Carlyle said, and Gideon glared into those disturbingly red-brown eyes. According to his file, Carlyle's mother had been born on the First Nations reservation near Carlyle's father's home in Massachusetts. The two had never married, and Joey's mother had passed away when he'd been an infant. His grandfather had raised him until he'd turned eight, and then his father had taken partial custody, sending him away to military school when he turned fourteen.

Sounded like a dick move to Gideon, who would bet the kid missed his grandfather, but he wasn't about to ask. He wasn't going to ask where Carlyle got his skills at tracking and absolute quiet either. It was enough that the kid was like a ghost.

"Not when I think I'm safe," Gideon retorted now, not liking that the kid thought of their office as a hunting ground.

Joey gave a slow processing blink. "Understood," he said. "Apologies."

Well, okay, then. "No worries," he responded. "And thank you for the water. It was considerate."

"When do I get a coffee cup?" Joey asked, surprising Gideon.

"When we know who you are," Gideon replied. It was funny—he'd always been good at languages. Spoke Spanish, Farsi, and French. He found that talking to Joey Carlyle was a little like learning a new language. One with few words and lots of intuitive leaps.

Another slow processing blink. "Will I like it?"

Gideon cocked his head. "I hope so. They're not supposed to make you feel bad. They're supposed to make you feel welcome."

A blinding thing happened with white teeth against his faintly dusky skin. His eyes narrowed, the apples of his cheeks popped out—a dimple emerged.

Oh dear God, it was a *smile*. Gideon could actually *feel* his pulse shoot up.

"That Crosby kid doesn't have one yet."

"He got here a week before you did," Gideon said, wrinkling his nose.

"You should get him a *puppy*."

Gideon shook his head. "Not until we know he'll laugh," he told Joey soberly. "It's important."

Joey sighed and nodded. "I'm done with weapons training. What else?"

Gideon *longed* to go back to his file, because the reading had been fascinating. People had been disappearing around Burlington, Camden, and Ocean counties—all of which were in proximity to New Jersey's famous Pine Barrens.

Kathy Novacek, the profiler who'd started to build the case, had been sure the people had something else in common. They'd all lost—or gained—significant money in the stock market recently. Two of them *were* stockbrokers, which would make them guilty of insider trading, but she was having trouble pinning down the firm. Kathy didn't follow the market, and while Gideon wasn't obsessive, his father *was*, so Gideon could talk financial planning like the best of them.

The finances Kathy had sent over were a tangle, and Gideon should have given up and asked to show them to his father two hours ago, but God, he hated to cry uncle.

But Carlyle was important too. He had responsibilities to this kid.

"Where's Crosby and Pearson?" he asked.

"Tracking down a drug addict who killed his dealer, but not for the reasons you'd think."

Gideon cocked his head. "Really?"

"Yeah, Pearson knew the guy, said he wouldn't hurt a fly. But the dealer was doing that free candy thing."

"Oh God—grade school?"

"Middle school. The addict made six calls to the cops, but they ignored him. He took matters into his own hands, there's a manhunt, and they're off trying to keep the police from gunning him down."

Gideon grimaced. "Well, that's gawdawful and depressing."

"But also they don't need help," Carlyle said.

"No, they do not. Too many of us looks like we're taking over turf, and that's not what we want. Okay. So how about you go get your computer setup from Kylie. She's—"

"Over there." He nodded to a closed door from which emanated Pearl Jam at top volume, which indicated Kylie was doing silent overwatch for Pearson and Crosby and a lot of research for Natalia and Harding. "In the SCIF."

Gideon nodded, impressed yet again. "Yeah—it's not, like, *presidentially* secure—we're not even supposed to *have* a Secure Communications Facility. But Kylie encrypted a lot in there for when we need it." He shrugged. "Eighty-five percent of the time, we run overwatch from a laptop and a tablet out here or from Harding's office. We're a small unit—everybody does double duty."

Carlyle nodded. "I would be *terrible* at that," he announced, surprising the hell out of Gideon. "And please don't think that means I wouldn't like to do it. Do you know how ADHD works?"

Gideon blinked. It hadn't been in the kid's file. "You can't concentrate on anything because you're concentrating on *everything*?" he hazarded.

"Yes," Carlyle said. "Or you can't concentrate on anything because you've locked on to *that one goddamned thing*. So you have enough brain cells to keep you alive while you're tracking the mastodon by tracking the saber-toothed tiger on your ass."

And Gideon got it. "But not always enough bandwidth to see the big picture when you're running hot. I get it."

Carlyle appeared relieved. "I would need training," he said frankly.

"Everybody does," Gideon told him. "We're big-picture people. When you're ready, tell us."

"Thank you." Again that puzzled blink. "So after I check out my laptop and set up my desk?"

He glanced around, and Gideon nodded to the desk across from his. "It doesn't mean we're partners—don't panic. It just means the last guy sat there."

"Was *he* your partner?" Carlyle asked.

"No, he was sort of pro tem. Until now, we've been switching off, except for Harding and Tal, because they've got that FBI dynamic that you can't lose."

"Sleeping together?" Carlyle asked clinically—not lasciviously, Gideon thought, but once again, as though scenting his territory.

"Dear God no." Gideon shook his head. "Natalia's married to a lovely woman who just had their second child."

Carlyle didn't *smile* smile, but one corner of his lean mouth curved up, which was enough for Gideon. "Understood." For a moment that almost permanent at-attention faded, and he seemed to deflate.

"What's wrong?" Gideon asked.

"This place is… not what I expected," he murmured, and before he could elaborate, Gideon's extension rang.

Hoping it was Kathy Novacek about the file, Gideon nodded at his new charge. "Go get set up, then order us some takeout—ask Kylie what she wants and how everybody else is for food. It's not a unit rule, but it's always nice to ask, and also to label leftovers for public consumption if there are any. There's a Sharpie in the drawer with the forks. Let me take this. Talk in half an hour."

Carlyle nodded, looking relieved to have some concrete directions, and made his quick and silent way toward the SCIF.

WITH POINTY TEETH

"BUT HE'S a stockbroker," Joey said for what felt like the fifth time.

Joey didn't so much *hear* Harding and Chadwick's collective breaths as feel them in his bones. Dammit. He wasn't going to be able to keep this job, this sense of safety, these nice people who would coddle him through orientation and feed him, if he kept being stupid about things.

But Chester Schumer was obviously a stockbroker. Everything on the screen Gideon had brought up indicated… well, boring white-guy vibes. Joey knew not all white guys were boring—his father being a slithering, venomous, carnivorous example—but this guy?

"He's a stockbroker with a history of legally screwing anyone who invests with him," Gideon corrected. "I know you don't have behavior analysis training, but one of the things we've learned is that 'boring white guys,' as you put it, can be chameleons. *Look* like respectable businessmen, *are actually* raving lunatic sociopaths or toxic narcissists. Or both. They mask well, and, you know, people who look like me and Harding get away with a lot."

Joey blinked… and assimilated. As somebody who'd been aware he was *passing* for a white man, because his skin color was a pale dusky clay instead of a dark ochre, he'd been peripherally aware of this. He'd just never heard a white guy *say* that. Apparently part of analyzing behavior was actually voicing what much of the world refused to acknowledge to get to the truth of things.

"A raving lunatic sociopath?" he asked, considering the idea for the first time.

"Or a toxic narcissist," Harding reminded him dryly. "Witness certain politicians we're all painfully aware of. They *look* like milquetoast with a Maalox chaser, but the way they think, their ability to coldly abuse *millions* of people for their own political gain, to dismiss the deaths and suffering they cause, that's sociopathic, narcissistic behavior. The only difference between them and literally millions of people behind bars is the bank account they were born to and the color of their skin."

"And they think bigger," Chadwick muttered bitterly. "The only difference between those people and this guy is this guy's decompensating before they do."

"Decompensating?" Joey asked, fascinated. This explained *so much* about those orders he'd defied. Who would do that? Order a village razed, order the people to evacuate or die, just because they wanted to access the lake the people had lived on for years. For that matter, it explained so much about his own heritage, how his father could seduce and abandon his mother, how the Europeans could befriend and abandon the natives of the land, marginalizing them to tiny plots of inferior land while scrubbing the resources of the other lands bare.

What could stop swarms of human locusts?

"Spinning out," Chadwick told him, pulling him back to the convo with a yank. "Making mistakes. Kathy did a pretty comprehensive background here. If we look at it, we'll see that these three people—Connie Norway, Craig Baugh, and his wife, Angie—all went missing in a span of a year. The couple made the news, although the suit they were about to file against our Chester Schumer did not. Connie was young, liked to party. She didn't even rate a bump in the newspaper, because misogyny sucks, but *she* was linked to a watering hole for the people in Schumer's company. By all reports, Schumer liked to hit on her, and she liked to tell him no. Does being rejected automatically mean he killed her? No. Does filing a suit against your stockbroker because he benefited from a trade that sucked away your retirement mean you have to worry about said stockbroker wreaking revenge? I hope not. But it's building a pattern. People who make Schumer's life inconvenient don't do well. That was three years ago. The year after that it was this guy—" He pointed to an equally bland white guy. "—who stole clients from Schumer because they followed Schumer's trades closely and didn't like what he was doing. By now Schumer's company has a low-level buzz going. Not enough to fire him—he's making *them* money—but enough for a sort of… vague warning when people asked for a recommendation."

"He starts making less money," Joey deduced, and Chadwick lit up. *He likes it when people follow his brain.*

"He does indeed. He's got a big brick of property in New Jersey and a really nice house, and suddenly his mortgage is not guaranteed." Gideon pointed to a bullet-pointed list, complete with chart. "If you see here, suddenly he's *hustling* for new investors. He's wining, dining, the whole sixty-nine yards. And he gets them. He can be charming when he tries. He gets a *whack* of them. But at this point, I don't think he knows *how* to make money unless he's fucking people over. It's like a compulsion with him."

Gideon pointed to three other faces on the board.

"Boom, boom, boom," he said.

"Three of his new investors who are now broke and pissed off disappear," Joey followed, excited now. This was a new kind of hunt, he realized. A new chase. This wasn't tracking somebody through underbrush or scouting terrain. This was putting a bunch of disparate clues together to form a path.

A pattern of behavior.

Oh wow. He got it now. Got what Chadwick and Harding and whoever this Kathy Novacek woman was that Gideon couldn't shut up about all *did*. Too bad the prey was so… ew. *Boring.*

"Exactly," Harding said. "In the space of four or so months. So he's escalating. And he's not being as careful."

"And then…." Joey frowned at the screen. "It's… they're all the waitress," he said.

"Noticed that, did you," Harding commended. "Yeah. Blond, in their twenties. Four of them, spread across all the counties touching the Pine Barrens."

Joey turned toward him, frowning. "Wait—is that what that area is?" He motioned toward the map, circling the big blank spot. "Isn't that where the Jersey Devil is supposed to live?"

Chadwick snorted. "If the Jersey Devil is this guy, then sure. But seriously"—he sobered—"all we've got is conjecture.

The odd word dropped by the odd witness. An escalating pattern. First he killed the woman who rejected him. Then he killed the couple that dared to call him out at work, and then he just kept doing both. But those last four disappearances were only since December. That's what we mean by decompensating."

"He can't keep up this pace," Joey said, nodding. "A murder like the ones he's doing—luring his prey, executing the murder, hiding the body, covering his tracks—that's a lot of work. It's exhausting. You do too much of that, you make mistakes."

"I'm sure if we interviewed his contemporaries at work, we'd see a pattern of odd behavior," Clint said. Then he eyed Joey and Chadwick. "Gid, it's your call. You and the kid take his office, or leave that to me and Tal while you and the kid take Chester Schumer himself for a preliminary interview."

"They need to happen simultaneously," Chadwick said, completely focused on the board. "He can't know he's a suspect. Let's do it on an off day. Tomorrow's Saturday, the market's closed. You and Tal start interviewing the people from his office, and we can say we're part of a team. Joey and I can even hit some other office people afterward. But he can't think he's singled out, or we'll lose him."

"Your call," Harding said. "Meet here tomorrow. Crosby's here to take an online class, so he can do overwatch while we're out."

Chadwick gave a sweet little smile, and Joey's heart twisted. Why should he care? Why should he care if this thin, dry man sounded all warm and gooey when he was talking to the BAU lady, Kathy whatever? Why should he care if Chadwick seemed to have a hard-on for the other rookie? This wasn't what that was about, was it.

"His second weekend doing online classes here," he said. "Kid seems to be throwing himself into it."

Harding grunted. "He told Gail he wasn't sure when we'd realize our mistake, and he wants to learn as much as he can while he's here."

Chadwick groaned. "Oh God. Fuck me. We're keeping him."

"So far she says he's pretty field-ready," Harding admitted. "And the best part is he admits what he doesn't know." He nodded at Joey. "Witness."

Joey realized then that while they hadn't necessarily meant this meeting as a test, he'd still passed by being willing to learn stuff. On the one hand, he felt a warmth in his stomach, one that he'd gotten while learning to hunt and track with his grandfather. It was a pride of sorts for being the best he could be, for pleasing an authority figure who neither demanded nor ridiculed.

He hadn't been aware that feeling could be replicated.

But on the other hand, he realized that he'd walked in here with a sort of arrogance. He knew he was hot shit—he was the best tracker his unit had ever seen, and he'd heard that again and again and again. He'd been able to stay out of his father's clutches while he lived with the bastard; he'd always thought that should qualify him for some sort of award. He was silent, he was able with any kind of weapon, and hand-to-hand? Forget about it. He could take out guys three times his size, which was a good thing because height and mass were not his friends. If the stupid major in the stupid Green Berets had just listened to reason, he wouldn't have had to leave deployment, or the military, and he wouldn't be stuck pencil pushing *here* in this building where the fluorescent lights made him half blind.

Except that wasn't the case at all, was it. He'd defied a direct order. He could have been arrested for *treason*. Instead the other major, the one who wasn't even his CO, had bailed him out for no other reason than it *had* been unfair, and now he was here where he *didn't know anything*.

He'd *thought* he knew things—his FLETC training had gone fine, but that thing they'd just done—where they reasoned through a mass of facts and found a suspect, then decided how best to investigate him—that was *new* to him. He'd asked questions because it was interesting, not because he'd realized he was a weak spot on the team.

And he'd met Crosby. Big dumb Irish flatfoot who was probably right, his being there had been a big mistake. Except that big dumb Irish flatfoot apparently knew more than Joey fucking

Carlyle, because he was already coming in here on his own time, making up for what he realized he didn't know.

And Carlyle, who thought he was *hot* shit, had just realized that he didn't *know* shit instead.

Oh fuck. He needed to up his game.

And that started with not being jealous or mean about the big dumb Irish flatfoot.

"What kinds of online classes?" he asked, and he must have been abrupt about it, because both Chadwick and Harding got the sort of expressions on their faces when a kid did something oh so precocious.

"I'll get you a catalogue," Chadwick said mildly. "There's time. Any other questions?"

"What should I wear tomorrow?" he asked.

"Black tracksuit is fine," Harding said, glancing at the new outfit Joey had worn that morning. "In fact, it almost looks more professional than a sport suit and tie."

"Fuck you very much," Chadwick said with a grimace. "If they had a Grim Reaper outfit, I'm sure that would suit me better."

Harding chuckled, and Carlyle realized that these two men had known each other for a while. Unlike with Crosby—or that Kathy person who still pissed him off because he'd heard Chadwick's voice warm—Carlyle didn't feel any jealousy or one-upmanship with Harding over Chadwick. Maybe it was because the two of them together had done that sweet thing with the food and the making sure he didn't wake up in a strange place alone. Or maybe it was because Harding was so overwhelmingly his CO. But either way, Harding had orders or lessons or suggestions.

Chadwick seemed to have more than that.

Carlyle didn't understand the hold, but he did understand he needed to trust his instincts. Whatever fascination he had with this very smart deer, he needed to observe the deer and maybe learn from his behaviors if he wanted to keep this job.

ALL THAT self-searching and he *almost* let some *other* hunter kill his fucking deer!

"Nice digs," Joey said as he and Chadwick disembarked from the department-issued SUV. The place backed up against the national forest that housed the Pine Barrens and, thanks to the thick growth of oak and pine that made up the place's name, was out of sight from its nearest neighbors. It stood two stories, both levels having big bay windows that looked to the road and an overhanging awning that would keep the porches shady in the summer and rain and snow free during the other times of year. There was an attached garage and no outside stairs, so they approached the front door with its nice little stoop and a solidly built mat with bristles at the bottom designed to really *clean* the sole of a boot.

"God forbid we track the forest in," Chadwick muttered.

Joey cocked his head, listening for those mutters. They'd spoken a little on the two-hour drive from Manhattan. Chadwick had asked him about his interests—movies, TV, music—and Joey had been… embarrassed.

"I don't… listen, a lot," he said, thinking about the noise of these things. "I… if you can't hear the silence around you, you could be in danger."

Gideon frowned. "But if you don't hear the music around you, you could miss out on a lot of joy," he said, concerned. "C'mon, Carlyle—it's not neuroscience. What makes you *happy*?"

Gah! Joey racked his brains. During deployment, he'd wandered environs, watching the small victories and tragedies of flora and fauna around his seemingly oblivious unit.

"Snakes and birds?" he said. "Monkeys." He paused. "Did you know the Spider Monkey is endangered because of habitat loss?" He sighed. "And it doesn't get laid enough. But it has a prehensile tail. Not a lot of the New World Monkeys do."

Chadwick appeared bemused. "I did not know that," he said, as though assimilating that very fact. "That is sad—but very cool. Tell you what." He fiddled with the radio for a minute. "I'm going to play some Imagine Dragons, because they're old school, but you might have heard them, and you tell me about New World Monkeys, because I am seriously fascinated."

At first Joey thought that would be too much noise, but Chadwick seemed to have a knack for picking just the right amount of noise for the occasion. The music was loud enough so, when Joey ran out of things to say about monkeys, a song called "Radioactive" that Joey remembered from grade school was playing, and he could hear enough for it to be familiar.

"Oh," he said in surprise.

"What?" Chadwick asked.

"I know this song." He hummed a few bars. "I like it."

And then, for the first time, he saw a *truly* joyous smile break out on Chadwick's face. "*Awesome*," he said. "Next stop, Broadway!"

Joey frowned. "Broadway? Like… I don't know. Plays?"

"Broadway like *musical theater*!" Gideon almost crowed. "I've got tickets to see *Wicked* tonight. I'm stoked. I know it's not your thing, but give it some time in the car, you and me, and it *will* be."

Joey had snorted, but now, as they neared the suddenly foreboding and very expensive house, he heard Chadwick humming something under his breath.

I wonder if that's from his musical?

Joey got it then. *He* thought about creatures to calm himself down. Stalking mountain lions, protective wolves, swift and muscular deer. The poor doomed Spider Monkey with its rare-for-South America prehensile tail.

Chadwick heard music.

He was interested in mine. He wants me to be interested in his.

Oh. Was this part of the new job? Being interested in the people around him?

Joey got being interested in protecting people, or serving people, or avoiding people, or sometimes killing people, all in the name of making the ecosystem work. He understood ecosystems. His grandfather had taught him well about the predators not overhunting, about the prey needing to be culled.

But while he'd been glad to let pregnant does or young, untried stags pass unhunted in the name of keeping the ecosystem sound, he hadn't wanted to share musical tastes with them.

The same went for bedmates—his personal ecosystem enjoyed the physical contact, but he was content to make the kill, as it were, and then fade from their existence, a one-off in the night.

Joey realized that if he was partnered with this man, he needed to not fade from his existence. They needed to be *real* to each other.

Joey was starting to see he had a lot of weaknesses, and it didn't please him at all.

Chadwick was talking to himself, which brought Joey back to the here and now.

"So what do we have here, Mr. Boring White Guy," Chadwick murmured as they neared the house. "Could be a stockbroker, could be a monster. Until we open the door, it's both. Schrödinger's monster." He chuckled to himself then as they neared the door, and Joey found his lips twitching.

Out of nowhere, he *longed* for Chadwick to turn to him, that self-deprecating smirk on his lips, and invite Joey in on the joke. Joey actually *got* the Schrödinger's cat jokes. He *got* the dry, subtle digs at his own age. Joey had never really *gotten* another human being before, and except for the thing with American musical theater, Joey was starting to think he could *get* Chadwick. He couldn't *fuck* Chadwick—for one thing, Chadwick apparently had game that nobody had suspected. Joey knew for sure that Kathy Novocek woman who had sent him the files on Chester Schumer had been angling for an invitation to Gideon Chadwick's bed for the last two days. Joey could practically *smell* her pheromones through the phone, not that Chadwick responded to any of that noise.

But Joey had to leave the man alone that way. This thing they were doing—tracking prey together—they couldn't contaminate that with any other smells.

Still, they were what? At the den of a fluffy bunny today? Joey had seen the boards, had even bought into the reasoning, but he couldn't get over that mild, deer-in-the-headlights expression of the puffy-faced man with the white-blond hair and big wet blue eyes.

"Remember," Chadwick said as they neared the door, "you have to go to the bathroom."

Joey grunted, clearly recalling the distraction method they'd talked about on the ride over—in between discussions of *Wicked* and whether or not jaguars should be classified as endangered because their population was dropping.

Chadwick would establish rapport, and then Joey would ask politely to use the bathroom. Doing so while Chadwick engaged would give Joey a chance to scope out the place. Joey figured that finding traces of things that shouldn't be there was something he could absolutely do.

The door opened, not forebodingly at all.

"Chester Schumer?" Chadwick said, smiling pleasantly. The expression made the back of Joey's neck tighten. "Hello, we're from the SCTF. My colleagues and I are doing a canvass of people from your firm for some extra information on some of your clients. Do you mind if I come in?"

"We can't do this out here?" Schumer asked, and while he kept a pleasant smile on his own face, it was the same smile Chadwick was showing.

Joey knew his assignment. Tightening his glutes and affecting an impatient bob and weave, he gave his best look of apology. "I'm sorry, man. I've really gotta hit the head. We're so far away from a gas station, my only other option's behind a tree, you know what I mean?"

"Besides," Chadwick told him, giving a nod to Joey, "I'll be recording your answers so my colleagues and I can compile a timeline with what they get from their interviews, and the breeze out here"—it was something, actually; there was a storm brewing this early April day—"will play havoc with the sound."

Schumer scowled. "You're interviewing everybody?" he said, as Joey gave an impatient little bob.

"Yessir," Chadwick said. "It's standard procedure. Your coworkers will report the same thing." And oh, hadn't Chadwick been smart about that. Joey had thought it was a stupid precaution, doing all the interviews at the same time, but immediately their boy's shoulders relaxed, and Schumer seemed to relent.

"I did not know that," he said with dignity. He had a good voice, Joey thought. Joey had expected it to be high and squeaky, but it was low and cultured and mellifluous. Schumer probably got lots of people to trust him as a stockbroker on his voice alone, but Joey's entire alert system was suddenly on high. The back of his neck, his thighs—his sphincter was so tight he'd be squirting diamonds for a week.

Chadwick didn't wait for the rest of the invitation. He took a step forward and Schumer gave way. Joey followed him into a cavernous foyer with a staircase to the right and what seemed to be a sitting room to the left.

"I hate to impose," Joey began, and Schumer gave him a disgusted look and gestured curtly up the staircase.

"Top of the landing, third door to the right."

"Cannot thank you enough," Joey said and practically hurtled up the stairs.

For one thing, he really did have to pee, but he made short work of that and took his time flushing and running water afterward. While the water ran, he put on gloves and gave the three closed doors in the hallway a try.

The locked one got his immediate attention.

For one thing, it was back-to-back with the bathroom in a way that indicated it also had plumbing. For another, while the other two doors hid a master suite and a guest bedroom and opened easily, showing off rooms done in cream, beige, and ecru, with wood accents, this one was, well, *locked*.

And while part of Joey wanted to toss Schumer's bedroom and look to see if there was anything in the drawers, Joey had never been one to let a locked door keep him out.

He kept his lockpicks with him always. He'd mentioned to Gail Pearson, who had helped him check out his weapons and tactical gear, that he had a set, and she told him to consider them like a drop piece or an extra knife, so he didn't mention the 3-inch Schrade blade tucked against his back or the .38 Berretta in his ankle holster either.

Now the picks fit against his fingertips like they'd been missing all along, and he did that carefully orchestrated fiddling dance, thinking, "How long can I wash my—"

Plink. And he was in.

He swung the door open, expecting to do a quick assessment of a dark room or a closet, and then he gasped.

The SCTF had an up-to-date situation room, in which everybody had iPads hooked up to a projection screen, and a "murder board" or bullet-point list of the team's reasoning could be called up on a moment's notice. There were even, in the background, whiteboards, and Joey was sure that they'd gotten hard use before electronics had come along to render them obsolete.

This place had whiteboards, with the victims' pictures mounted on them, almost like a legitimate murder board, because these were pictures of bodies.

And Joey's blood ran cold as he scanned each picture, because he knew that his entire doubt about this case had stemmed from the fact that the police hadn't seen a single drop of blood.

And according to the 8x10 glossies affixed to the whiteboards with magnets, there had been considerable blood—all of it from a small wound at the base of the jugular.

A narrow knife? A *stiletto*? Oh my God. Oh my *God.* The pale balding man with the big wet eyes and the baritone voice was exactly what Harding and Chadwick had pegged him as and….

And Joey had left his partner *downstairs with a serial killer*.

Oh God. Chadwick, with his love of musical theater, who had slept on his couch and made sure he'd landed in his apartment and had set aside *this case* to make sure Joey had been welcomed to the unit as a whole and….

Joey left the water running in the bathroom and the door open to the murder room and bolted down the stairs.

To his horror, he could hear his own footsteps above the beating of his heart.

TEETHING

GIDEON'S BACK had been up before Schumer had even opened the door. He knew for a fact nobody else was being recorded. Harding and Denison would be taking notes on their phones. Gail and Crosby—who had both given up their other plans that weekend to canvass employees when they learned what was up, as had Kylie, who was on overwatch instead of Crosby—were doing the same thing.

Gideon wanted a direct line to overwatch while they were in that house.

There was something in the air. Gideon wasn't sure if Carlyle could feel it, but for Gideon it was almost like a smell, rancid like meat that had *just* gone bad in an ice chest, and Gideon wanted to stick his nose in the air and peel his lips from his teeth and scent the wind.

Instead, he watched as Carlyle disappeared up the stairs, and while Gideon wondered what he'd find up there, he kept his eyes very firmly fixed on Schumer.

"Can I interest you in a drink?" the man was saying as they entered the sitting room. A wet bar stood in the corner, white marble, ebony cupboards, gray tile. It was almost as unsettling as the gray rug on the gray tile on the floor—absolutely monochromatic.

Gideon wondered if the guy had, like, a *thing* about color, any color whatsoever. Even the stairs had been a black wrought-iron railing against a white marble staircase. No runner.

Ye gods.

"No, thank you," Gideon replied to the drink offer. For one thing, it was only 11:00 a.m., but for another? Even if he'd been dying of thirst, nothing in this place made Gideon want to accept any offers of hospitality.

"Do you mind if I get one for myself?" Schumer asked. "Tonic water and lime. I like the bitterness."

"Knock yourself out," Gideon replied, not able to suppress a shudder. Soda, yes. Selzer water, fine. But quinine in the morning? Blech.

And while part of him wanted to take this opportunity while Schumer was busy to glance around the house, part of him—the animal part—didn't want to think of turning his back.

Schumer busied himself behind the bar, and Gideon, still standing, started small talk. It wasn't his favorite; the conversation he'd had with Joey about Spider Monkeys and *Wicked* had been much more satisfying, because in spite of Carlyle's short responses, the kid (must think of him as a kid, because otherwise, damn, those cheekbones!) had been thoughtful. Not always funny and not always kind. But thoughtful.

Gideon rather hoped the team was growing on him. He'd certainly been impressed that Crosby, Pearson, and Kylie had volunteered to work this canvass on their off day, the better to keep Schumer from thinking they were on to him.

"So," Schumer said, pulling Gideon's attention sharply back to the present. "you guys don't have anything better to do on a Saturday?"

Gideon snorted. "Oh, we do. Theater tickets, sports events. One of us even knows New York's hottest DJ. We're a rockin' bunch."

"But you made this a priority." His voice was flat—not questioning—and Gideon's hackles actually *ruffled*.

"A friend of mine called," Gideon said, shrugging. "She'd been putting pieces together on her own. My unit thought she'd earned some help."

"And how *is* dear Kathy doing?" Schumer asked.

Gideon was alert to the danger now, keeping his eyes on Schumer's hands. Not Schumer's face, because that bland, all-purpose smile hadn't shifted once since they'd started talking, and neither had that ripe baritone. A true sociopath wouldn't give anything away in his voice or his face; he didn't feel enough to let it show. It was his *hands* that would be busying themselves, and while Gideon could see that Schumer was cutting a lime up and putting it in a glass bowl, he could also see the occasional little twitch or quiver that said he wanted to go for something but was too conscious of Gideon's regard.

"You know Kathy?" Gideon asked, and *there*. Schumer had palmed something as he'd bent to put the limes in the refrigerator.

"She's been around the office," Schumer said offhandedly, coming out from behind the bar. He'd left the drink, fully made, on the counter of the bar, and Gideon almost missed what happened next from checking.

"Oh yeah? What fo—*oh fuck*!"

Schumer rushed him, rounded shoulders down, a stiletto held in his left hand, the same hand he'd used to cut the limes. Gideon might have been gutted by that thing—long, thin, sharp—if he'd been caught unawares.

As it was, he squared to meet his opponent, waited until Schumer was almost upon him, then stepped smoothly aside and seized Schumer's wrist, pinching hard at the ulnar nerve, between the thumb and the forefinger.

Schumer moaned and sagged, releasing the stiletto, but just as Gideon caught it, the guy rallied, pushing up and surging against Gideon's chest.

Gideon fell backward over the coffee table, and it shattered under this weight, but he didn't let go of the stiletto. Instead he held it front and center, and Schumer fell on it, throat first.

Gideon scrambled out from under the gush of blood and the fleshy body, not minding the glass, although he could feel the cuts in his hands, his elbows, fuck, his *ass*, and knowing he needed to answer Kylie's urgent summons from the phone in his pocket before she sent in the Marines.

"Chadwick!" Joey called, surprising Gideon into glancing up from Schumer's still-thrashing body. He *should* try to staunch the bleeding, but, oh, hey, open wounds! That would be a *bad* idea.

"Chadwick!" Joey repeated, rounding the staircase and hitting the foyer before rushing into the sitting room. "He's got a *kill* room! I thought this guy was a *stockbroker*."

"So did I," Gideon said, straightening his tie with a bloodied hand and then reaching for his phone. "And then he went to get himself a drink at the bar and tried to rush me with a stiletto."

Joey gaped at him, and Gideon felt a little bit of disgruntled pride kicking in.

"Did you get pictures of the kill board? Harding's going to want those so we can justify this fucking corpse on the floor."

Joey had scowled at the man, whose hands had flailed in his own blood as it had pooled underneath him. "Nice job," he grunted.

"Thank you," Gideon said, feeling better about the whole thing. "My special forces commander taught an entire class on how to use an attacker's weapons against him. I was sort of hoping for a cheese knife, because I always thought that would be *cool*!"

Joey's cackle surprised them both. "That was good," he said in surprise. "Next time you have thoughts on Schrödinger's cat, you should let me in on the joke."

Gideon grinned at him and reached into his pocket to put Kylie out of her misery. "You want to come with me to see *Wicked* tonight?" he asked. "It was gonna be Kathy Novacek, but she's going to be up to her eyeballs in paperwork."

"Yeah, sure." Carlyle checked out the body again, shaking his head. "A stiletto. Yeah. Well, wait until you see the wounds on the other guys. It's his favorite toy."

Gideon stared at the now-cooling body of what had once been Chester Schumer, and resisted the urge to kick the rat bastard in the gut. "Not anymore," he said grimly. Then, "Kylie, my dear, you need to get a bus out here—coroner's, not for me—and tell Clint to save the interviews for the Feebies, but we need dogs out here, and searchers and—"

Carlyle was flagging him down.

"What?" he asked.

"A *murder room*," Carlyle told him, like he was expecting Gideon to remember what he'd been saying as Gideon had been brushing glass out of his hands. "He *documented* where he buried all his bodies."

"Gid?" Kylie said over the phone.

"Well, we'll need all those same people, sweetheart, but their job is going to be a lot easier than you thought."

"Chadwick, you're bleeding," Carlyle said, his voice hitching. "Holy shit. I'm partnered one day and you almost die on me. Do you realize what would happen?"

Gideon gave him a dry glance and grimaced because his cuts were starting to drip and he was contaminating the scene. "I'd miss *Wicked*?"

"I'd get *fired*, you asshole! Why didn't you call for help?"

"Because my special forces commander would take a flight from the fucking desert in California and kill me twice if I had to call for help over this piece of shit and his pigsticker. Jesus, Carlyle, chill out and go take pictures of the murder room. But don't touch anything. I'm *fine*."

HE WAS not, Harding told him grimly one hour later, *fine*. "Get on the bus, get stitched up, then go home, grab your date, and see your musical—"

"Carlyle's coming with me. Kathy's stuck here."

"You bet I am!" she shouted across the room, where she and her unit had set up an op center using the intel that Schumer himself had left them. "Thanks for the help, Gid—you couldn't have interviewed this guy on Monday? I was looking forward to tonight."

"Sorry, Kathy," Gideon muttered. She was pretty—compact, blond, a fresh girl-next-door face. He might have gotten laid, he thought irritably. Now that they no longer worked in the same department, Kathy had seemed more than amenable to his textbook three moves: self-deprecation, casual kindness, and—his best—"Hey, staying friends is my strongpoint." Gideon had a lot of casually kind friends, but few long-term lovers.

His passion just seemed to revolve around other things. Kathy's did too, which had made the idea seem perfect, but Gideon found he was actually more excited about taking Carlyle and popping his theater cherry. Carlyle didn't smile much—Gideon wanted to see if he'd be as excited about flying monkeys on stage as he was about Spider Monkeys in the jungle.

Harding glanced up at Carlyle, who had been watching the crime scene processing with avid, interested eyes, but who hadn't left Gideon's side since he'd taken the pictures of the murder room to show Gideon. For his part, Gideon had allowed himself to be sat on one of the barstools, over the marble-tiled foyer, so he could bleed as sterilely as possible.

"Good," Harding said shortly. "I'm glad Carlyle can take you home and make sure you have an early night. Why wasn't he with you when the guy came at you with a stiletto again?"

"He was upstairs finding the murder room," Gideon said. "I swear to God, Harding, we were textbook—"

"Except for the lockpicks," Harding said dryly.

"The suspect was acting suspiciously," Carlyle said, virtue writ large across his puckish features.

Harding eyed the corpse, which was getting zipped into a black plastic bag. "I think you lucked out in that way," he said. "Given how this fell out, nobody's going to question the access to the murder room. But next time, keep the lockpicks to yourself unless it's an emergency, okay?"

Carlyle tilted his head. "Define emergency?"

Harding grimaced. "You'll know it when you see it," he said. "But this wasn't it. Don't worry. Schumer took care of a lot of our problems by ending up dead."

"I took care of a lot of your problems by *not* ending up dead," Gideon told him, and at that moment the EMTs finally arrived to take him to get stitched, so he could only watch Harding roll his eyes.

CARLYLE FOLLOWED in the department issue, and sat by his bedside during the stitching, bitching at him like an inconvenienced spouse the entire time.

"I don't understand how you saw it," he said finally. "How did you see that this guy was off, and you hadn't even met him."

"Did you see that he was off when you met him?" Gideon asked, and this was a real question because your partner's instincts were part of your own arsenal.

"Definitely. I almost threw up when he smiled."

"Same. Let's just say that with practice and study, you can see those same things—those same things that made him 'off,' in his pattern of behavior, in his color choices—"

"No color," Carlyle said. "The upstairs was everything from pale beige to anemic ecru, and downstairs…."

They both shuddered.

"Exactly," Gideon told him. "It doesn't work this way for everybody, but colors tend to evoke emotions. If somebody is *that* obsessive about monochrome, it *can* be that they have a problem responding emotionally to their environment, and, hey, hello, socio- or psychopath."

Carlyle nodded. "But not always." His eyes went sideways then, and Gideon would place bets that he hadn't added anything to the sterility of his apartment since Gideon and Harding had walked Carlyle into his own bedroom to fall asleep.

"Not always," Gideon said. "This guy had obviously spent a lot of time and money on his house making it that sterile. There's a difference between a concerted effort and spending all your time at work."

Carlyle's lips twitched. "I have some *very* colorful dress shirts," he said.

"I am reassured. Maybe we should swing by your place to grab one before we go to my place to find something less…." He gazed woefully at the plastic bag containing his tweed sport coat with the hand-sewn patches at the elbows. It had been a gift from his father and sort of a favorite.

"Shredded and bloodstained?" Carlyle asked, but not without sympathy.

"It would be best," Gideon told him. "But reading a file gets to be a skill—one I practiced for a couple of years before Harding called me up to the SCTF." He shrugged. "That's how we landed the case. Kathy wanted a second opinion, and, well…."

"Your opinion was we should check out this guy before he killed somebody else," Carlyle said, nodding. "I get it. I mean, I *get* it. But if you've got any beginning profiling training programs or books, I'd love to bone up. I can't promise I'll ever get, like, Gideon Chadwick certified, but…."

Gideon gave him a slightly goofy smile. He'd been given some oral painkillers, because the number of scratches in his arms and the sides of his hands and his shoulders were truly too big a job for lidocaine. When that table had disintegrated, it had gone with a vengeance.

"It matters," he said, "that you study, that you try. You said something today about not wanting to get fired because the guy rushed me. What mattered today was you saw he was a threat and came to back your partner. Don't worry, Carlyle. So far, your job is safe."

"What's it take to get fired?" Joey asked.

"Gross incompetence," Gideon fired back. And then, remembering one guy they'd considered for about a week who had wanted to shoot a suspect *through* a hostage, because he'd seen that in a movie once. "Or gross human indifference," he added soberly. "Harding wanted to form an agency based on not traumatizing a victim or an informant or even an unsub—provided they can be talked down—any more than possible. It's weird how wanting to found law enforcement based on human kindness can inspire a lot of interagency bloodshed and hatred."

Carlyle's face went carefully blank, and Gideon wondered if he was thinking about how he and three hundred villagers had hidden in the jungle, literally climbing trees and crossing swamps, to keep from coming up against Carlyle's own unit.

"There's got to be a better word than weird," he said flatly.

"I'd settle for 'awful,'" Gideon told him. It would be good if the kid learned that partnership went both ways.

WATCHING CARLYLE absolutely entranced by the theater was one of Gideon's best things *all year*. He was tired, his painkiller wore off by the beginning of the second act, and neither of them had remembered to eat, but Gideon felt like he was made whole by listening to Carlyle's quick, delighted catches of breath during the show.

They talked about it fast and furiously as they walked the twenty blocks to Gideon's apartment, and Gideon was relieved to see the fresh fruit on the counter where he'd left it the night before, because he was now officially starving.

They made do with apples and grapes while Gideon fixed them both bagel sandwiches, talking about the political and emotional implications of doing what was expected of you for appearance's sake or resisting conformity to live an honorable life the entire time.

Finally, Carlyle literally took Gideon's shoulders and walked him to bed, much as they'd walked Carlyle to bed when he'd arrived in the city midweek.

"I'll crash on your couch if you don't mind," he said, and Gideon yawned and told him there were extra blankets and pillows in the cupboard.

When he woke up the next morning, the blankets were folded neatly and the pillows stacked on top. There was no note, but there was a steaming cup of mocha-flavored coffee on the counter.

Gideon sipped it, pleased that it was still a little hot, and thought that maybe, in spite of the intention he and Harding had stated that they'd try different people out as partners, Gideon had found *his* partner without that.

He and Carlyle seemed a really good match.

Carlyle laughed at his jokes and seemed to appreciate musical theater.

Gideon was willing to learn about monkeys.

There were so many worse ways to enter into a work marriage. Gideon was much encouraged.

Puppies and Teeth

"Hey, Crosby, how's it hangin'?"

"Low and inside, Chadwick, like a good curveball, right?"

Chadwick's laugh at the tired joke set Joey's teeth on edge. Six months in, he was starting to appreciate a few things. The job and how it varied day to day. The unit and how everybody wanted to learn, to get better, to make their world better. The weather—it got cold in New York, even in the fall, and having gotten there in April and surviving the salt-mugginess of the summer, Joey was thrilled to experience the honest to God cold of October. After six years of hot in South America, the cold he remembered from a childhood in Massachusetts was to be appreciated.

And Joey had started to appreciate Chadwick. A lot. Because he was wicked smart, wicked funny, and a wicked stone-cold killer.

Chester Schumer wasn't the only psychopath they'd come up against, and Gideon Chadwick—who looked like a college professor and analyzed with the clear-eyed precision of a human computer assessing other humans—could draw his gun and fire without batting an eyelash.

And his marksmanship was outstanding. Joey had been the hotshot of his unit, but he and Chadwick competed weekly, and after six months were in a dead heat for small weapons.

They were both aware that the rest of the team had stopped betting on these occasions. You could only have a draw so many times.

And while Chester Schumer was one of three fatalities over that time (and the only one killed in hand-to-hand combat), after twice watching Chadwick *literally* shoot the hat off a suspect's head and then watching the suspect drop to the ground in fear and surrender, Joey was starting to feel safe with the guy.

Sure, he'd drag Joey off to a rock concert or a stage musical whenever he could score tickets, and he'd literally *forced* Joey to read a book by Richard Feynman (that Joey reluctantly enjoyed), but that just meant that, like the combat skills and the brilliant analytical mind, Chadwick had *depth*.

Joey, who had always thought his ability to survive was the one thing that made him unique, was starting to appreciate *depth*. In fact he was starting to appreciate how being partnered with Gideon Chadwick seemed to give him *more* depth.

But what he didn't particularly appreciate was how happy Chadwick was to *spread* the depth.

The Kathy thing hadn't lasted long. Yeah, they'd done the thing. She'd come up to Manhattan or he'd go down to DC for a weekend, but after two months, Joey had seen him getting bored, and with that sort of commute, it was easier to let it fade. Joey didn't ask, but he was sure it was done "amicably," because that's how you did things when you enjoyed something, but it was too much hassle to continue for long.

Joey hadn't been happy about the Kathy situation, but Kathy hadn't taken much of Chadwick's focus when he'd been at work, or even *off* work, so he'd dealt.

But the Crosby situation… that was *irritating*.

Joey couldn't even say *why* it was irritating. Crosby himself wasn't as bad as Joey had first thought. He *looked* like he should be a meatloaf. He held himself with the sort of humility that recognized he would *always* be a meatloaf. But while Chadwick and Joey held the small-arms title in their unit, Crosby held the long-range weapon title, from bolt-action to semiauto, from hunting rifle to extreme long-range sniper rifles. Crosby had the fortitude, patience, physics awareness, and instincts to fire a projectile across several football fields and have it go exactly where he'd planned.

It wasn't a stupid man's specialty.

Neither was Crosby's people sense, which was unfailingly on point. Joey and Chadwick would arrive on scene, and Chadwick would start scouting a profile, and Joey would start scouting evidence and opportunity, and Crosby, without fail, would be talking to the actual victim or sometimes the perpetrator. Nine times out of ten, Joey had watched him de-escalate a situation by treating somebody scared and freaked out and terrified into remembering they were a human fucking being.

It was that one time out of ten, when they were dealing with a psychopath, that Crosby needed the entire unit to back him up.

And usually he had Pearson. Joey would have said *she* was a psychopath, except she wasn't. She was *terrifyingly* good with knives and carried an illegal five-inch fixed blade in a holster in the small of her back and another three-inch at her ankle. Of the three fatalities, one had been Denison—the perpetrator had been too high to even know she was cutting off the air in his windpipe with her garotte as he held a gun to Harding's head. One had been Chadwick's sure shooting—the bad guy had been rushing Joey with his knife out while Joey was handcuffing the man's brother, and nobody was close enough to take him down any other way. And the other had been Pearson.

She'd been grappling with a man twice her size, and when she'd broken away and pulled her defense weapon, he'd laughed and jumped right on top of her.

And had been dead before she'd sidestepped him as he hit the ground.

Joey had seen the aftermath. You'd *think* there'd be a lot of blood with a heart wound, but she'd hit it so cleanly, it had stopped beating before much blood had spurted.

Nobody on the team was afraid of battle—not even Crosby, who had fired a couple of shots to wound and had done it accurately without hesitation.

So Joey couldn't pinpoint his irritation with the guy. He was friendly, paid his bar tabs when everybody went out after work, contributed to the conversation, and was often even funny. And he spent his Saturdays either taking seminars, working on classes, or helping with open cases with the rest of the unit.

He was like the guy at school who was the class president, the school valedictorian, the guy who tutored kids on the side for his church, and who, in person, was funny and decent.

Joey couldn't *stand* that guy.

But here, now, listening to Chadwick greet him with genuine warmth and Crosby reply with a shy smile, he *really* couldn't stand him, and that's when it got him.

Oh fuck. Joey was *jealous*.

Not romantically (really?). Joey didn't advertise, but he wasn't particularly discriminating when it came to the gender of a sex partner. Mostly he thought of them as fallow deer who were to be set upon, devoured, and then left behind.

He didn't… couldn't think of Chadwick like that. It was much more visceral than that. Chadwick was *Joey's*. Sure he could have other sex partners, as long as his main focus was *Joey*. And while Chadwick didn't seem particularly romantically interested in Crosby, he *could* be, and that would be a threat to *Joey*.

As Crosby made small talk about how badly New England sucked in the playoffs, and Chadwick asked him how close he'd gotten to playing pro ball, Joey realized how small that made him.

"Yeah, I was only a few games away from the end of the season," Crosby said with a philosophical shrug. "We were set to win division and compete in the Citrus Bowl when that illegal tackle came out of nowhere. It would've been nice, but then I wouldn't have ended up here."

Oh Christ. He was so fucking earnest. Joey had *read* the guy's file, trying to use Gideon Chadwick skills to see what Gideon Chadwick saw in him. What he saw was that this guy had gone against his entire department to find a serial murderer who'd been trying to start a gang war, and his house had been so grateful for Crosby bringing the guy down single-handedly, they'd tried to kill him when he'd gone against another flatfoot who'd shot a Black teenager in the back.

Crosby had done more than just have the bad luck to blow his knee out like every other jock on the planet. He was there through character, hard work, and intelligence.

Joey *hated* that guy.

But he couldn't be cruel or dismissive of him either.

Fuck.

"Well, we're all glad you're here," Harding said. "But we've got to get you a better coffee cup."

Harding glanced pointedly at Chadwick, who grimaced. Joey wondered about that. Pearson's coffee cup was a cat holding a bloody dripping knife. Chadwick's cup was a fox in a cap and gown. Everybody had personalized coffee cups except him and Crosby.

Except last week Joey had run down a suspect by following his trail through a park, noting the way his footsteps had disturbed leaves and left impressions in the soft ground. The chase had ended when Joey had executed a flying tackle and handcuffed the guy when they landed.

That Monday, Joey had gotten to work, and in the place where his usual cup—plain white porcelain with Joey's name in Sharpie—usually sat was a cup with a cartoon wolf on it, wearing a slick suit.

And Joey had seen the cup and gotten it. He'd tracked that guy down like a wolf, and he liked a slick outfit after work.

Nobody said anything (except Pearson, who'd saluted him slightly), and Joey realized that the cup needed to be earned.

And Crosby didn't have one yet.

Oh. Bummer.

Abruptly Joey hated him a little less.

And with that lessening of distracting emotion, he could pay attention to the situation Harding was rolling out.

"Meet Kent and Colin Gleeson," Harding said, firing up the screen at the end of the conference room. "The Dogfight Brothers."

"Brothers?" Denison was the one to say it. Kent Gleeson was six two, Black, with two thick braids coming from his temples down his back, and heavily tattooed with handsome tribal markings. Colin was White, five six, with brown hair buzz-cut into a ragged mullet and pale blue red-rimmed eyes. They were as different as two humans could appear, right down to Colin's yellow meth teeth and Kent's gold inlaid grill.

"Oddly enough, no," Harding said. "Same last name, same taste for candy, same idea to run dogfights out of Red Hook. Kent is muscle, Colin is greed. I don't know which one is brains, because so far we haven't seen a damned thing about them that's smart."

"What are they wanted for?" Crosby asked. "Besides being garbage humans. Because dogfighting is the fucking worst."

A little more of Joey's frozen black wolf's heart melted at that. Of *course* Crosby would champion dogs.

"They are wanted for the disappearance of this man," Clint said, tapping on his tablet. The screen flashed, and the image of the Gleeson brothers was replaced with a picture of a rather sweet-faced middle-aged man wearing a tweed suit and carrying a small white Chihuahua. "This is Tad Spencer. His dog, Carl, was, well, sort of the terror of their Haworth, New Jersey, neighborhood. According to police sources, Carl was under quarantine for biting a woman at the dog park when he disappeared. The enclosure in the back was *totally* secure. The only way the dog could have escaped is if he had help."

"Wait," Joey said, not sure if Harding was having him on or not. "The, uh, Gleeson brothers kidnapped a Chihuahua for dog fights?"

Harding grunted. "Apparently the little-dog fights are some of the most brutal. I guess the story spread—the woman who was bitten was a social-media influencer, and Carl gained some notoriety. Mr. Spencer went looking for him, and after asking around, told his husband he was going to Red Hook to get his dog back. When he didn't return that night, the husband called the FBI."

"And they turned it over to us because…?" Pearson asked. "I mean, who has jurisdiction with this sort of thing?"

"These days? Who knows," Harding grunted. "Which is why the ASAC kicked it over to us." He let out a long breath. "Seemed to think it was amusing. Deavers, the ASAC, called the gambling commission, and Jay Arnold apparently brought her attention to the whole thing, so he was willing to send us backup, which is both human of him but also a copout. It's like he doesn't want to be seen handling this mess. But these guys are dangerous. Anybody who will torture a dog to make him vicious will have no problem assaulting a human being. Spencer and Carl disappeared yesterday, and the fights start in a few hours. We have a limited amount of time here to save the dog, and nobody laugh but—"

"I mean, poor little guy," Crosby said, sounding distressed.

Fuck. Joey was *really* going to have to let go of his grudge, wasn't he?

"Yeah," Harding said with a sigh. "I don't know the odds of him being alive, but, you know, it would be nice."

"Well, if he's being used as a star attraction for the preliminary rounds," Chadwick said, the only one in the room not losing their minds over the tiny dog, "we should be able to get to him. And I would imagine Tad Spencer is simply going to be held until the fight is over and then released after his dog is dead."

"Released? Not killed?" Harding asked.

"Possible," Chadwick admitted, nodding. "Because dog fighting *is* big business. If they attract a big enough crowd with a celebrity hound, and the owner gets disappeared, we could have a real problem."

"These men are frequently spotted carrying weapons," Harding said, flashing more pictures of the two men going about their day with the butts of large pistols showing in the backs of their jeans. "The weapons are registered, but they're obviously used for intimidation."

"I take it we don't have enough for a warrant," Natalia said thoughtfully. "Otherwise the gambling commission *would* take this over."

"Pure speculation," Clint confirmed. "Obviously the brothers are under surveillance, but nobody has spotted Spencer or his dog."

"Do we have a list of their properties?" Kylie asked, her own laptop in front of her.

Harding paused to forward those to her and then straightened. "And while she's doing that, we should take a look at their, uhm, employees."

"Henchmen?" Chadwick supplied coyly.

"Flunkies," Pearson suggested.

"Minions?" Crosby asked, and Joey rubbed the back of his neck.

Goddammit. He was funny too.

"Known associates," Harding told them, trying to be stern. "And here we go. It's a rogue's gallery, as you have all guessed."

Harding gave them the run-through of who might be expected to pop up with a gun, and about the time he wrapped up, Kylie chimed brightly, "And here we go! Here's the winner of the 'Where's the dog fight going to be tonight?' contest!"

"The Gleesons own—or squat in—a couple of properties out in the warehouse district of Red Hook," Kylie continued. "But this is their biggest." She put up an overview of a property lot, one with a big building that, if hollowed out and filled with bleachers, would be a good stage for a fight. And three outbuildings that would be *great* places to house animals starved and beaten to the point of madness.

"Why's this the winner?" Crosby asked.

"There's two others," Kylie said. "One of them just had all its buildings knocked down—" She flashed a slide of a bunch of demolished construction materials. "—and the other was the site of a bust three months ago." And there was a nice press shot of the two brothers being led away in handcuffs.

"Wait," Joey said. "What are they doing out if they just got busted?"

"Bail," Harding said grimly. "Dogfighting isn't legal, but it's not necessarily a high arrest priority either."

"But if they kidnapped a guy…," Chadwick murmured, and he and Harding locked gazes and nodded.

"What?" Joey demanded. "What? What are you thinking about that we don't know?"

"Why we got the case," Natalia said with disgust. "Politics."

"I don't understand." Oh hell. Even Crosby looked like *he* got it, and now Joey hated him all over again.

"It's not a high-profile crime," Gail explained patiently. "But Harding's superiors hate it as much as we do. So they gave it to us when *they'd* been told to sweep it under the table. So if shit goes bad, we get the blame, but if we make a positive bust and save the poor dumb dog owner and maybe even the poor dumb dog…."

"The FBI and the gambling commission get the credit," Joey said slowly. "Oh. Oh hell. Jesus, this is stupid. Can't we just shoot those assholes?"

"Sure," Chadwick told him soothingly. "But only if they're aiming a gun at us."

"What do we do?" Carlyle asked. "Serve them a warrant?"

"We don't have one to serve," Harding said. "But we *do* have a warrant for surveillance and covert search."

Denison whistled. "Who did you have to blow to get a covert-search warrant?"

Joey expected the world to stop and a record player somewhere to scratch to a halt, but Harding merely snorted. "The list is long and distinguished and classified. But we got it, so we're gonna use it. And since we've got ourselves a couple of stealth operative specialists, I'm gonna use them. Carlyle? Pearson? You guys game?"

"Wire us up, Chief," Pearson said, grinning. "What's the uniform? Camo?"

Harding shook his head. "Urban variety. You two get scruffy, dirty up your faces a little. Pearson, find a stocking cap and tuck that shiny gold hair up, darlin'. I'll be up top for on-site overwatch. Kylie," he grunted. "Normally, I'd like Crosby up there with a long-range weapon, but see that?"

"Oh shit," Chadwick said. "Is that really a rec center?"

"Yup—not three hundred yards from the back fence. Sorry, Crosby."

"No worries, Chief," Crosby said. "You don't fire a gun unless you know what's going to be behind your target. Too many friendlies there for something that can go fifteen hundred yards."

"Yup," Harding said. "So I'm doing overwatch, you and Chadwick do backup, Carlyle goes east, Pearson goes west. Tal, where do you see a hole?"

"Rec center side," she said promptly. "If there's dogs loose, guys, that's a danger. I'll filter along back there. When we going, Clint?"

"Weapons check in five," he said. "Everybody, suit up."

The SCTF tactical gear requirements were very tailored to the operative—with the exception of vests, which Joey and Gail put under their baggy T-shirts. Pearson preferred knives and one small gun which she wore in a side holster, and Joey was pretty much on board with that. They could move silently, both of them wearing oversized street clothes, frayed and yellowed with too much washing and too much hard use. Gail took Harding's advice and tucked her hair under a hat, and Carlyle used another—frayed and unraveling—to hide his raven's-wing black hair, which shone when clean, and then went for some pale, loose cosmetic powder to make his complexion lighter and added little patches of eyeliner rubbed into his skin to dirty it up.

He was in the middle of doing that, using the mirror in his locker to check his work, when Chadwick blew out a sigh and pushed him aside by virtue of a bony hip.

"Turn around," he grumbled. "Here." He grabbed the makeup from Joey's hand and, using a sponge he'd produced out of nowhere, started blotting the eyeliner. "It looks like a high school play. Subtlety here, Carlyle. Subtlety."

Joey was trying to think of something—anything—to retort with, but he found his breath had seized. Wide-eyed, he stared at Chadwick's once-ordinary hazel eyes and tried to remember how to push oxygen in and out of his lungs. Maybe even through his vocal cords; he understood that was cool.

Chadwick's features—always lean and hatchet thin—were suddenly… warm. Close. Touchable.

Attractive.

From fucking *nowhere*. Six months of working together, and suddenly Joey noticed that he was working with an attractive, beddable, *fuckable* man.

The realization was both humbling and exciting, and Joey couldn't decide which dominated.

Gideon… fuck, *Chadwick*, was searching his work for a flaw, and suddenly he caught the direction of Joey's gaze.

Chadwick's eyes—not hazel, repeat *not* hazel but more of a muted falcon's gold—widened fractionally, and for the span of a few heartbeats, they were… arrested, stilled, lost in a bubble in which only the two of them existed.

"Hey, guys," Gail's chirpy voice called from the doorway of their locker room. "Let me look!"

Chadwick stirred first, turning to take her in. "You're perfect," he said proudly.

"Thank you, Papa," she replied, giving a cheeky grin. "You taught me well. Pay attention to him, Carlyle—he's good at this part."

Joey's heart started thudding slowly in his chest again, and his breath resumed its usual function.

"Thanks," he said gruffly to Gid—*Chadwick*. "I—"

But Gideon was inhaling lightly through his nose like a mountain cat, and he tilted his head. "Blood," he said thoughtfully. "Not old… just… blood and pine trees." He shook himself. "That's weird," he said. "Sorry. I get that way. Crosby smelled like puppies. Clint like rock face. Tal, of all things, like snickerdoodles. It's not always the same smell… but it's only something that happens with people I'm close to."

He gave a fleeting smile and took a step back. "You look good. Meet you at the shop in five."

And then he was gone.

And Carlyle was left to close up his locker and remember how to walk. For a moment, he'd thought he wasn't special, like that moment hadn't been real, and Gideon Chadwick had *always* been that intense and he'd simply missed it.

But then it sunk in: Gideon had said he smelled like blood and pine trees, and Joey felt those things in his marrow.

And Gideon hadn't been appalled. Just… just accepting. Like he knew Joey by his smell alone.

The moment had been real. Gideon smelled him—*saw* him.

And Joey was never going to forget that wave of attraction, that wave of raw desire that had stopped up his breath and blood.

HE WOULDN'T forget it—but in the meantime, he had a job to do.

"I hear them," Crosby said over comms, and Joey grimaced. He and Gail had been creeping around their assigned paths for half an hour, sweltering in their layers of clothes in spite of the crisp October breeze. The property was all concrete base and aluminum buildings—it was probably twenty degrees hotter there than the ambient temp. Crosby and Gideon were supposed to be *their* backup, while Natalia and Harding took care of the holes in the surveillance.

That Crosby had stumbled on the place where the dogs themselves were being kept was just fucking aces. Gideon would probably raise an erection, erm, erect a monument, to his golden boy's prowess now that he'd managed to crack the op.

Stop it. Crosby is a good operative… and your friend.

Goddammit, it was no good if—

The thought died in an explosion of barking and Crosby's deep voice calling out, "SCTF, freeze!"

"Who? That isn't a real thing!" The voice was a cackle—uneducated, slurred. It had to be one of their subjects. Given the pitch, Joey would put odds on Colin, their White meth buddy.

"We have a warrant to search if we hear anything suspicious," Crosby said, "and all the barking coming out of that building you're leaving, that's suspicious."

Joey heard a door slam, and with it a silence that made him realize there was a racket he hadn't marked.

Well shit. Crosby *had* found the dogs. And now *he* was the one who needed backup.

Silently, Joey rounded the corner behind Crosby and saw the scene as if through a wide-angle lens.

Front and center, he could see Crosby, small weapon (a Glock, which wasn't *that* small) drawn, sighting down the smaller Gleeson brother, who had just closed the door on a long, low building that could be used to house dogs. They had initially dismissed it; there was a layer of trash that made it appear partially collapsed. But Joey thought with a flash of insight that Crosby would have used it as cover. He'd gotten close enough to hear the dogs past the insulating trash.

Well *shit*.

But that was in the center. On the peripherals, Joey could see two things. One was the other Gleeson brother, rounding the corner, gun drawn.

The other was on the complete other end, but not for long. Charging headlong for Crosby, teeth bared in a salivating grimace, was one of the biggest fucking dogs Joey had ever seen.

Later he'd take in the details: the mixed Rottweiler breed, the scars on its back and around its face, the barbed collar, the near emaciation. All the things that would make a dog savage—pain, hunger, mistreatment—had been leveled against this poor creature.

At that moment all he knew was that the dog was, for once, a more dangerous predator than the two men with guns.

Per all protocol, Crosby was focused on the armed, drug-impaired criminal, but God, that dog was coming in fast.

Right as Joey swung to focus on the dog, the other Gleeson twin raised his gun toward Crosby too.

"Drop it!" Joey shouted, swinging around to aim at him.

Dog dog dog dog dog....

"Both of you are covered," Crosby barked. "Lower your weapons and nobody gets hurt."

Kent Gleeson looked gaunt in real life, so he and Colin probably did their meth together. He grinned, the light bouncing off his grill.

"Nobody?" he asked.

And Colin gave a piercing whistle and a short, harsh command. *"Attack!"*

As they both dropped their guns.

Crosby lowered his weapon—his training was spot on.

Joey kept his up, and he refocused on the dog as it charged Crosby, jaws open, and bit the soft inside of his thigh.

Crosby howled, both Gleeson twins went for their guns, and three shots rang out.

One from Crosby, hitting Colin Gleeson solidly in the body.

One from Gideon, hitting Kent Gleeson neatly in the forehead.

One from Joey, nailing the dog in the side of the head.

The targets dropped, and so did Crosby, gushing blood from an artery and trying not to cry out.

Gideon secured the dead criminals, and Joey holstered his weapon before rushing to prize the dead dog's jaws off his friend's leg.

"*Fuck*," Crosby gasped, and Joey was too busy to curse. With a growl, he ran toward the trash pile and grabbed an iron bar he'd spotted, sticking out and ready to trip the unwary. As Gideon spoke into the comm link at his collar, Gail hurtled around the low-slung building.

"Goddammit, Crosby!" she cried. "What in the actual fuck!"

"I'm fine, Elsa," he rasped, using a pet name for her that Joey didn't understand. "Just…. Jesus, fucking dog."

"Yeah, fucking dog," Gail muttered. "Only you, Olaf." With an oath, she tore off her loose sweatshirt and wrapped it around her hand, grabbing the dog's lower jaw around Crosby's oozing flesh while Joey slid the prybar into the hinge. Joey used his iron lever, and Gail gave an assisting yank, both of them grunting in exertion.

With a terrible *crack* the bones gave way, and Crosby started gushing blood for real.

Joey tore off his own oversized sweatshirt and used it as a pad to put direct pressure on the wound, and Gideon—still giving situation details to Harding, Natalia, and Kylie—pulled off his own belt and secured it around the pad, the two of them working as a team like they did field dressing every day of their entire lives.

Far off in the distance, they heard an ambulance wail, and Gail knelt on the filthy, oily ground and pulled Crosby's head onto her lap, while Joey worked to elevate his leg.

For a moment, the only sound was their labored breathing and Crosby's surprised murmurs. "Seriously. The dog. I saw him, but… usually it's the people…."

Joey held on to the acid retort about how only a moron wouldn't know a predator when he saw one.

Crosby had done everything right. In fact, he'd played it smart, he hadn't panicked, and he'd had Joey's back. If Joey wasn't mistaken, he'd shot and hit a live, moving target as the dog had been sinking its teeth into Crosby's inner thigh, and goddammit, if that wasn't good enough for Joey Carlyle's standards, he was aiming too goddamned high.

Suddenly it didn't matter if Gideon liked Crosby best. *Joey* liked Crosby. Not best, but it didn't matter. Crosby wasn't just a coworker; Crosby was a *teammate*. And, Joey thought miserably as he watched the man's face turn powder gray from shock and blood loss, he was a good friend. A good guy.

Joey had never had friends, really. Hell, he'd barely had teammates. He'd always been their lone wolf, their scout, the squad's quiet cutting edge. He'd seen men die, and while he'd felt a dispassionate sense of loss, he'd never felt anything like grief.

As Crosby labored for breath and Gail berated him with legitimate anger and a voice broken with tears, Joey realized he would grieve his teammate if Crosby didn't recover. He would grieve his friend. His team would be struck with an irrecoverable, unassailable sense of loss.

And Joey was part of that team.

The fear of that emotion was *crushing*, and Joey stared helplessly at Gideon, knowing that Gideon was probably more lost than he was.

But Gideon was suddenly at his side, their arms touching in a simple animal way that Joey appreciated.

"He's going to be fine," he said, his voice tight with strain. "The ambulance is one minute out." Gideon froze and swore, obviously responding to something on comms. "I need to go help Tal. Watch for animal control. She got in the back way and found our dog owner and his caged Chihuahua but would like some assistance." He glanced from Joey to Gail unhappily, and then Crosby. "I'm the only one who's not covered in blood," he said apologetically, and then knelt by Crosby's side. "Hang in there, kid."

He tousled Crosby's hair like a little brother's and then strode over Colin Gleeson's body and into the building, the shrill echoes of frenzied dog barks starting and stopping with the closing of the door.

THREE HOURS later, Joey and Gail were seated shoulder to shoulder in the same bed, next to Crosby's. Both of them had been cleaned, checked for bites, and debriefed by the head of the gambling commission (like that asshole had the balls to understand what had gone down), and they were waiting for Crosby to come out of the anesthetic from the emergency surgery to close off his artery so he could answer the same stupid questions.

And, Joey understood now, they were there to see how their friend was doing.

"A dog," Gail said for what was probably the tenth time. "I mean, who would have fucking thunk it."

"How could he not see?" Joey asked for the first time.

Gail glanced at him. "See what?"

"That the dog was… was a predator. Not even a reasonable one. It was… it was *created* to kill. You can't take your eye off a predator. You just can't!" His voice rose an octave, and he was remembering the sound his phone had made when he'd thrown it on the pavement from the bus those months ago. He'd been waiting for his father to text him since, and he kept wondering what he was risking by not watching his back twenty-four seven. He couldn't, though. He had to watch his team's back.

That threatened loss as Crosby had been bleeding out on the dirty pavement resurfaced, and he realized with a faint shock he would have been just as frightened if it had been Gail or Harding or Natalia or Kylie.

For a moment his thoughts strayed to Gideon, bleeding out like Crosby had been, and first came that moment in the bathroom, realizing Gideon's ordinary hazel eyes were really muted gold, and then came a terrible moment of vertigo, followed by queasiness so bad he'd almost popped his head over the side of the bed to toss his cookies.

Pain. Pain like you haven't felt since Grandfather... oh God. Can't think. Pain.

And for the first time, Joey realized that there were big holes in his life where his heart had been as a child, and these people here were offering to fill them.

For a moment, on the bed next to Gail, he wanted to walk away. He thought about quitting. Going underground. He could spend his entire life living off the grid, doing odd jobs, drifting from place to place. His father would never find him, and he would never find anybody he cared about like the people who'd had his back for the last six months.

Crosby moaned from the bed like he was coming out of it, and Joey realized he had one foot on the ground in what even he had to admit was flight.

"The fuck are *you* going?" Gideon asked irritably, striding into the room. "You get one grilling from the gambling commission and you're out of here?"

Carlyle stared at him. "Soda," he said weakly, not sure how transparent he'd been.

Gideon snorted. "The hell," he said.

Crosby moaned again, and both their attention turned toward him on the bed.

Gail hopped off and now stood at the side of the bed, murmuring, "Heya, Olaf—how you doing?"

"Ow," he said, eyes still closed.

"Yeah, so we heard. You up to a debrief?"

"From who?" He could barely talk.

"Some asshole from the gambling commission who wants to know if there was any way we could have avoided shooting the dog," she said, her voice laced with disgust.

"Send him in," Crosby breathed. "I'll bleed on him."

And then he passed out.

"Really?" Gideon asked, his eyebrows raised. "*Really*?"

"Shh!" Gail shushed him, and Gideon gestured them outside the room.

"Really what?" Joey asked as they settled in front of the door. Then, "Are we sure he's okay?"

"His vitals were fine," Gideon reassured him, but not absently. "I checked in with the nurses. He's not supposed to come to for an hour. Which is how long we waited on-site while animal control came and bailed out all the fucking dogs, taking most of them to shelters." His voice grew thick. "Most of them will have to be destroyed, and it's a goddamned shame."

"Our civilian?" Gail asked, and Joey could have kicked himself. He'd almost forgotten.

"Is fine. So's his little dog, who was in the cage next to the giant dog crate where they were keeping the civilian." Gideon's face fell. "They were practically hugging each other as the paramedics escorted them out."

And again that curious sense of vertigo. In the military, Joey would have regarded the civilian and his dog with a grim duty. The man, anyway, was whom Joey was assigned to protect. But no affection, and certainly no pity.

But here, after the horrific death and desecration of the dog that almost killed his friend, the thought of that perfectly nice man with the unruly Chihuahua walking away from that entire nightmare situation made Joey feel…

Better.

Not awesome. Certainly not like good triumphed over evil, because if that were true, somebody would have struck those motherfuckers dead before they'd had a chance to weaponize Fido. But better.

They'd been there for a reason. There were innocent people involved. The innocent people (yes, he was counting the dog) walked away.

Didn't always happen.

And suddenly Joey could see what his team was pushing for.

He hadn't seen it during that first bust, the serial killer. He'd seen he almost let his partner die—that had been bad. He'd seen there were things to learn about human behavior that he'd never even fathomed. That had been fascinating.

But he hadn't seen that what his team had been pushing for that day, all of them coming in on what was supposed to be a day off to chase down Gideon's hunch, had been this.

There had been people on Chester Schumer's hit list who would never know their lives had been in danger.

Thanks to Gideon and Joey, their lives *weren't* in danger anymore.

And a New Jersey suburbanite got to walk away from a nightmare with his Chihuahua.

"Carlyle?" Gideon said sharply, and like that, Joey was back in the hospital hallway, his dual realities merging, where suddenly he *was* that guy who would be glad there was a happy ending for somebody, and who would share worry with a teammate and friend about another teammate and friend.

"Yeah, Gid," Joey replied blandly. "We're glad they're okay. Anything else?"

Gideon's eyes hardened. "Yeah, how long did the gambling commissioner talk to you guys? You're giving me the jeebies."

"An hour," Gail said flatly. "He debriefed us both for an hour, and then tried to push into the room to yell at Crosby while he slept, I guess. The nurse kicked him out, but that's one of the reasons we stayed."

Oh yeah. Joey was mad all over again. Now that his own emotions had labels and boxes, he was suddenly *pissed* at the guy who'd tried to bully Crosby *in his sleep*.

Gideon's thin face grew a curling Disney-villain smile. "Where is he now?"

"Right there…." Gail was spared from pointing at the guy by Gideon giving them both an angry head nod back into Crosby's room.

"If he tries to get in there again," Gideon said, no ounce of play in him, "take him out. Cuff him. You both still have weapons. Be prepared to use them. Go."

And then they were on the other side of the door, with their ears pressed firmly against it.

"I need to get in there."

Joey and Gail exchanged scowls. Jay Arnold, the gambling commissioner of NYC, was young—early thirties—with slicked-back hair and a sharp brown suit that he probably thought looked good but simply made him look small and pasty because the lapels were too wide. He spoke with a natural pomposity that made any reasonable person want to smack him with a sap.

"I am SA Chadwick from the SCTF," Gideon said, his voice flat. "That's my man in there. He was injured in the course of doing your dirty work, because whether you want to admit it or not, this was your case we were executing. You don't deserve to speak to him, and if I have my way, he won't ever know you exist."

Joey sucked in air through his teeth in surprise. He'd heard Gideon speak to his coworkers, to Harding, to perpetrators, and while he could be dry and funny, or no-nonsense and analytical, hard-assed and frightening, Joey had never, ever heard him be so… *disdainful* of another human being.

"I need to know how he managed to shoot a dog in the course of a routine investigation—"

"Shoot the dog?" Gideon asked, and something about his tone—baffled and outraged—made the air freeze in Joey's lungs. That moment in the locker room… Gideon's face so close….

"People are going to be outraged—"

"My man almost *died*," Gideon snarled, and Gail and Joey both gasped. They'd heard the thump of Jay Arnold's body as he'd backed up against the wall next to the door.

Or had been shoved there.

"Due to his own—"

"Bullshit," Gideon snapped. "Who do you think we are? Your basic flatfoot with a six-month sponsorship from our left cousin's buttcrack? Those two agents you just grilled? They are U.S. Special Forces—a Green Beret and a covert operative. The guy on his back? Tracked down a serial killer single-handedly, brought him in, and made the case stick. I've got more letters behind my name than you can probably use to spell, and our SAC? Has more medals on his chest in the military and out of it than you could carry. Do you understand? Our specially trained, carefully nurtured operative was attacked by a dog trained to kill *on your turf*. *You* are responsible for him almost bleeding out on a filthy concrete floor. *You* are responsible for us having to shoot a dog who had been tortured into savagery. You knew this was happening. You were too afraid to tackle it. Too afraid a couple of methed-out fight promotors were going to make your boys look like chumps. So you called our guys in on it. Good move, because if your boys were as incompetent and lazy as you are, you probably would have shot the hostage *and* his Chihuahua, and then *fed* them to the monster that almost killed Crosby!"

Gideon's voice grew louder, more filled with righteous fury, with each word, and Joey, ear pressed hungrily to the door so he could catch every syllable, had to swallow against a sudden ache in an unexpected place.

His groin.

Dear God.

He had an aching, unassuageable erection from hearing Gideon take this motherfucker down.

"Oh my God," Gail whispered. "Who knew Chadwick could be that sexy?"

"I'm sayin'," Joey muttered back, glad she'd put it in that zone before he had.

"Agent Chadwick?"

Joey and Gail were going to hyperventilate. That deceptively mild voice had been Harding's, and in six months, Joey had never heard that tone.

"Sir?" Chadwick replied respectfully.

"Your work here is appreciated, but it's my turn. Go check on Crosby, would you?"

"Yes, sir," Chadwick said, and Gail and Joey had to skitter back as he opened the door.

"And Gid?"

"Sir?"

"Don't let anybody but our unit and medical professionals into his room." Clint Harding's voice developed a blinding edge. "You're authorized to use deadly force if they try."

"Sir." And Gideon stepped into the room and shut the door in time for Joey and Gail to lean on it again.

They had to. They'd held their breath so long on big gasps of air, they were both, Joey surmised, a little dizzy.

"You heard?" Gideon asked the two of them dryly.

They rolled their eyes at him.

"Just remember that," Gideon said. "We have each other's backs."

They both nodded solemnly before Gail scooted back and motioned Gideon to the spot between them so they could *all* listen through the door.

Gideon took it, and for a full ten minutes, through a truly epic ass-chewing by Clint Harding, one that would go down in agency lore forever, Joey was face-to-face, sharing breath with Gideon Chadwick of the hooded falcon eyes.

His aching, insistent erection didn't ease until Harding stepped back from the wall Jay Arnold had sweated against, and they had to let him into the room, along with a couple of patient, wise nurses.

When they finally left the room so Crosby could sleep, Joey noticed two things.

One was that Gideon's presence, his heat, his *smell*, seemed to have imprinted itself on Joey Carlyle's consciousness like a mountain lion's scent mark on its mate.

The other was an unfortunate body-sized wet mark on the hospital wall, where the NYC Gambling Commissioner had sweated through his ugly, overpriced suit.

STAKEOUT

"GOD, WE need more people," Gideon complained, leaning his head back against the rest. Carlyle sat next to him, quiet and still, which he'd been doing a lot since Crosby had been hospitalized.

But maybe he was, like Gideon, exhausted.

They were stretched thin, and Pearson and Kylie had been partnered with Kylie running point from a laptop in the passenger seat while Pearson hauled ass through NYC and much of the East Coast, terrifying the unwary, because the two of *them* were still allowed their weapons, while Gideon and Carlyle were on administrative or surveillance duty after the shooting.

Kylie had confided that while Crosby and Gideon were the *fastest* drivers of the unit, Gail Pearson was the one most likely to die as a grease spot on the highway, for impossible turn reasons.

But Gideon's and Harding's encounter with Jay Arnold hadn't been without repercussions, and one of them had been a come-to-Jesus meeting with the FBI *about* the NYC Gambling Commissioner, and how long it had taken him to take down the Gleeson Brothers.

It turned out their supposition about politics had been right on. Arnold had called in favors with Connie Deaver, the Manhattan based ASAC—the big cheese, the one that Harding *sort* of reported to—to get an agency that he had no jurisdiction over and no connection with, to close down the dogfighting ring.

He'd been getting an *amazing* amount of heat about it, and they knew that because Deaver had authorized a wiretap and a culling of all Arnold's professional and private records regarding the operation.

And they'd discovered that a local businessman known for his absolute lack of ethics, his shoddy workmanship, piss-poor deals, and the string of suicides he left in his wake when his business partners found themselves bankrupt and without legal or financial recourse had listed Jay Arnold on his payroll for the past six months.

In fact after Kylie had run their financials, she'd commented acidly that Jay Arnold was the *only* person Halsey Garber had ever paid on time.

And in return, Arnold had stayed carefully away from certain business enterprises—like the Gleeson brothers and their junk business, which was the official title on the deed for the property.

So now they knew why Arnold had pulled the one favor Connie Deaver owed him from college to get a smaller, lesser-known agency involved with the Gleeson brothers, and at first they thought that the civilian abduction—and that of his Chihuahua—had been a windfall.

But then Natalia had commented in the middle of the group debrief—Crosby joining by Zoom from his hospital bed—that Arnold must have been biting his nails hoping for something to happen so he could authorize the operation to get shut down without tipping Garber off that he'd had anything to do with it.

And the entire room had gone silent.

"Guys?" came Crosby's voice from Kylie's computer screen. "Guys, do you really think…?"

"Somebody pulled their strings," Harding said. "And it was probably Arnold. That's why he was so freaked out about us killing the dog. If he got nailed for it, he'd be included in the cruelty to animals charge."

"I don't know if the charges would be any worse," Gideon mused. "Maybe it's just his own guilty conscience."

"Arnold's or Garber's?" Pearson asked.

"Arnold's," Gideon said decidedly. "Garber hasn't shown an ounce of guilt or even an iota of responsibility his entire career. Arnold actually worked his way up through the ranks in Atlantic City before he was elected gambling commissioner here."

"What was the charge? Blackmail or corruption?" Carlyle asked, his voice clinical and removed.

"Which guy?" Harding asked.

"Garber first," Carlyle told him. "Arnold was weird and erratic—and an asshole—but he seemed… I don't know. Human. The rest of this is off the rails inhumane."

"Corruption," Gideon said, glancing at him. He wondered for the umpteenth time how Joey Carlyle had managed to escape his father's clutches with only that coldness as a scar. Carlyle had used that tone of voice a lot when he'd first started, but over the past six months—particularly in the past week since they'd broken up the dogfighting ring—Gideon hadn't heard that tone so much.

Given that he knew who Joey's father was, Gideon had begun to assemble a private and very personal, unofficial, undocumented profile of his new partner.

And he was somewhat impressed.

Joey Carlyle had grown up with a conscience, but not because his father had ever given him one. In fact, much of the coldness, the predatory aloofness, that Carlyle had exhibited when he'd first arrived at SCTF appeared to be in defense of living in close proximity to a known sociopath.

But since that first day, when Carlyle had realized his lack of instincts regarding Chester Schumer had almost cost Gideon his life (no matter how many times Gideon reassured him that Schumer had a lot of people fooled), Carlyle had been working on improvement.

Gideon hadn't missed his steady thawing toward Crosby, and it didn't surprise him. Crosby was warm-blooded, an instinctively good protector, sensitive and attuned to other people's pain.

Carlyle had probably spent much of his childhood insulating himself from somebody he was afraid of. He'd had no room in his psyche for that sort of empathy, but he did have a clear set of rules that he played by.

Protect the innocent. Well, that was the code of the Green Berets and most advanced military units. But also there was the language he used—predators, prey, hunters, meat. Carlyle was a firm believer in not destroying the helpless unless there was a reason.

And in human terms, he'd realized there was never a reason.

These rules were hard and fast, and the more he interacted with his unit on a human level, the more that bare-bones conscience grew.

Finding Carlyle and Pearson sitting in the bed next to Crosby's to defend him from Jay Arnold had been a surprise.

Gideon had expected to find Pearson, but he'd expected Carlyle to be doing something useful but not nurturing.

Instead he'd been shoulder to shoulder with his comrade in arms, and he'd been defending their friend.

And, well, obviously panicking about it, but Gideon couldn't blame him really, even if he'd had one foot out the door.

It was encouraging, Gideon had thought, pleased. It meant that his and Harding's faith in the little shit wasn't misplaced. But it was also reassuring to hear that ice-cold intelligence coming into play. While Carlyle had been upset his human instincts hadn't picked up on Schumer, it was that cold analytical side of him that had come rushing to Gideon's aid and helped them recover the bodies of Schumer's victims.

Carlyle had come to them lacking certain skills but proficient in others. If he could pick up what he was missing, he'd be a superlative agent.

He was already a decent partner.

Reluctantly, Gideon shook off that moment when the three of them had been listening to Harding's takedown of Arnold. He and Joey had been face-to-face, breath mingling, and the heat in those obsidian eyes….

Gideon had felt it in his gut, hard, warming… *warning*.

He'd taken enough chemistry classes to know some combinations were explosive. He had to be careful—very careful—of not allowing the two of them to mix in the wrong way.

He wasn't sure there was a device made that could pick up the fragments if they exploded.

But for now Carlyle was reserving his cold, predatory side for analysis and strategy and allowing some warmth, some human connection, to seep in regarding his colleagues. Gideon would take it. It was a win.

Especially because Gideon hadn't ever had a partner he'd enjoyed as much as Joey Carlyle.

Ruthless and predatory? Absolutely. But he was also funny, curious, and as excited about learning as a child. That first odd venture to Broadway hadn't been their last. Once a month—sometimes once a week—they saw a show. Or live music. Or listened to buskers in the park. Stakeouts and travel times were filled with battling playlists and discussions as to what the lyrics said, how the songs were put together, how the music *mattered.*

And Gideon now knew more about monkeys than a *Wild Kingdom* special.

Gideon had to admit he'd been having a lot of fun, but it was good to know he wasn't having fun with a complete sociopath. Watching Carlyle slowly learn to care about his teammates had been a huge relief.

"What about Arnold?" Carlyle prodded during the staff meeting, his reserve of judgment proof of everything Gideon had come to believe about him.

"For Arnold I suspect blackmail," Gideon had responded slowly. "What do you think, Clint?"

"Why do you say that?" Harding returned—one of his most irritating qualities, actually.

"Because he's only now on the payroll," Kylie said promptly. "Like, he's resisted being on the payroll for years, and what he's getting now? It's not very much."

"And he was sweating through his suit," Gideon added, remembering that encounter in the hospital. "He… he was fixated on shooting the dog, because he *likes* dogs. It was like the legal implications had gone to the wind. He was going to bully a man under anesthetic because we shot the dog."

"Well, then," Harding murmured, "if we think it's blackmail, we need to find out what Garber has on him. Which means…."

"Aw fuck," Carlyle muttered, seeing the implications for surveillance. "Goddammit."

"Half of us are out for active duty anyway," Clint said with a shrug, which was true since Gideon *and* Carlyle were out for another week, until their shooting cleared Deavers's desk, and Crosby was still laid up. Technically, the whole squad should have been doing paperwork, but they were pissed. They felt used, and one of their own was down, and they'd killed two men and one whacked-out Rott-something because a businessman had a gambling jones.

They wanted some payback.

And, as Carlyle had intuited, the only way to get it was….

"I fucking hate stakeouts," Carlyle muttered now in the car that had been their home in the last week, ever since that meeting. During normal work hours they rode their desk and did paperwork. After they'd ostensibly clocked out, while the others chased down leads relating to Halsey Garber and his tentacle-like hold on the gambling industry in the state, Gideon and Carlyle sat here, keeping an eye on Jay Arnold, hoping to see Garber in person. The man was oily and rancid, but all accounts said he stuck his oily and rancid fingers into all his personal pies.

"You only hate stakeouts because it's my turn with the playlist," Gideon said with satisfaction.

And here they were, stretched thin but reluctant to call it a night. Jay Arnold had been closeted in the three floors of his Upper East Side apartment for the last week after working hours. It was not the biggest or fanciest of the buildings in the area, although the size of the space was quite impressive. Apparently Arnold had tried for five years to buy property in the neighborhood, and the sale had come through about a year after his appointment to his current job.

Next to Gideon, Carlyle spoke, and as he often did, he sounded as though he'd been reading Gideon's mind. "Do you really think he felt bad about the dog?"

Gideon grunted. "Yeah. Why?"

"Because it's… it seems so out of character for a man who has all this money and shit." He paused, and Gideon let him search for words. "In my experience, men with that sort of bling have removed conscience from the equation."

Gideon should have let the matter drop, but he couldn't. Not after watching Carlyle grow these past six months.

"Was that your father?" he asked quietly.

All the oxygen left the vehicle.

When Carlyle did breathe again, it was slowly, in and out, as though he were fighting the impulse to do something he'd regret.

Like run.

"Yeah," he said after that moment. Just that one word. "Not yours?"

"My dad's rich. He was an engineer, super bright, has lots of patents, who went into finance. Not really…." Gideon searched for words as well. "Effusive," he said after a moment, remembering how after his mother's funeral, his father came in, sat next to him on his bed, and simply… sat. Before he'd gotten up, he'd said, "I'm sorry, son. I'll try to find a nanny to watch you after school. I know it won't be your mother. I-I wish I was better at this."

And then he'd gone to prepare for dinner.

"Cold?" Joey asked, but not dripping with pity.

"Not really," Gideon replied, surprising himself. "In fact, he's quite kind. I mean, he *did* fall in love with his assistant when I was twelve, and he's really adorable around her. He just grew up when men didn't communicate their feelings. He's been practicing since he and Trish got together. The other day he sent me a link to an article on finances and told me that he hoped I had a portfolio, but if I didn't, he and Trish had plenty of inheritance to give me. And I know that doesn't *sound* exciting, but think about what he was offering—"

"Shelter," Carlyle said, boiling it down to its most animal essence in one heartbeat.

"Yes," Gideon said, nodding. "And every Christmas, every vacation, I head over to Dad's house in the suburbs or Trish's house in Pennsylvania, and they decorate or plan outings. And nobody has asked me once if I have a girlfriend or demanded I produce offspring. They just… you know. Talk. Dad's still quiet, but he's always glad to see me. So not cold, but not… touchy."

Carlyle's mouth canted up. "What do you suppose that's like?" he asked, almost wistfully. "To live with someone you're so comfortable with, you touch?"

"I vaguely remember it," Gideon said. "From when my mother was alive. But not as an adult."

"Your relationships?" Carlyle asked, and his eyes… darted.

The vehicle—a plain unmarked, nice enough to not get reported on this street—suddenly heated up in the October chill.

And Gideon knew exactly what he was asking.

"The women are all sleek and sophisticated and professional," Gideon admitted with a quiet laugh. And then, carefully, "The men are usually in law enforcement—not a touchy-feely bunch. You?"

Again that sudden shifting of oxygen in the vehicle. "No cuddling," he said after a moment. "With either one. Just sex. Touch and release, I guess."

The coldness didn't surprise Gideon, but the wistfulness—that cut him deep.

"Maybe we'll know," he said. "We'll know when we've found someone real, when there's lots of touching."

He couldn't help it. The fantasy flowed through him of rolling over one morning to find Carlyle in his arms. That wiry power, that subtle strength, the ruthlessness, the curiosity, the surprising gentleness that was emerging bit by bit….

Gideon hungered for it so acutely his stomach ached.

Carlyle turned to him slowly, while Bruce Springsteen—a mutual favorite—played "Secret Garden" softly on the stereo, and for a moment, Gideon thought, "Yes. I will let this happen. We will explode."

And then in the corner of his eye, he saw movement.

In a heartbeat they were both on alert as a kid—he looked young, barely college aged if that—slunk into view.

His eyes were fixed on the lit window of Jay Arnold's apartment building, and he was sobbing as he spoke.

Whisper soft, Carlyle killed the radio while Gideon lowered the window.

"But it's been almost a month, Jay. Nobody will know. Please, I've got to see you. You… you told me you loved me. Was that bullshit?"

Gideon and Carlyle locked eyes for a surprising moment.

Blackmail.

Jay Arnold was a bachelor—that's what his bio said. Famous for dating lots of high-powered women, but none of them for more than a week.

But he was also currently working under a conservative administration, with a direct line to what was left of the gutted Department of Labor and Statistics, and Gideon had a sudden insight as to why this boy was so very dangerous to Jay Arnold.

Blackmail indeed.

"But, but Jay…. Fuck."

With a dispirited sigh the young man shoved his phone in his pocket and leaned back against one of the great trees lining the walk. He paused for a minute and wiped his face on the inside of his shirtsleeve and was going for something—probably cigarettes—in his pocket.

Before he could get them, Carlyle was at his side, and Gideon had to check the seat next to him to realize that his partner had made a decision without him.

Careful not to startle, Chadwick slid out of the car and shut the door with a muffled thud. He watched as Carlyle held out a lighter for the kid's smoke and then tucked it back in his pocket like he did stuff that smooth every day. Gideon had literally seen the kid walk away from Kylie on her knees in front of a mound of paperwork that had slid out of her arms because it didn't occur to him to help her.

"Thanks," the kid muttered as he exhaled. "I've been trying to quit. *Jay* wants me to quit, but…." He sputtered what was supposed to be a defiant laugh into the moist, foggy air. "Fuck him."

"I wouldn't write him off yet," Carlyle said, catching Gideon's eyes as he drew near. "I would put actual money down on him blowing you off to protect you."

The kid—well, maybe mid-twenties like Joey himself, but he *seemed* younger, dressed like a student or a barista or something *not* a vital part of Manhattan's cutthroat political scene—frowned.

"What do you mean?"

"Well, kid, if my partner and I are right, your rich, powerful boyfriend just double-crossed the devil to do his job and *not* out you to the entire nest of pit vipers he's swimming with. He's probably eating his heart out, thinking he's trying to do right by you. Want to ask him?"

The kid's hand fell to his side in the middle of raising the cigarette to his lips, and the smoke dropped to the ground to be killed by the wet leaves.

Gideon smiled to himself. Well, it wasn't like Carlyle was wrong, but it was good to see he hadn't changed completely. Gideon rather liked him the way he was.

"Maybe give him a few more details first," Gideon said softly. "Kid? You got a name?"

"Kael," the kid said, studying the two of them with a little bit of fear. "Like the vegetable but spelled weird. Kael Rogers."

"Like Captain America, but with vegetables, right?" Carlyle asked, and Kael nodded, a surprised smile popping out.

"Sure. Who are you?"

"Well, the last time your boyfriend saw us, he"—Carlyle indicated Gideon—"was yelling at him so hard your boy left sweat prints on the wall he was backed up against."

"That was Harding," Gideon corrected with a faint whine. He was not that scary.

"Anyway, I would bet his boycott of America's favorite veggie started that night. Would you like to hear the story?"

"Does it have to do with the mobster that started hanging around about six months ago?" Kael asked grimly, and Gideon and Chadwick locked eyes again.

"Very probably," Gideon said, surprised that Kael had been around that long. "You want to tell us about him?"

Kael shuddered. "We… I mean, I knew I had to be his dirty little secret. I knew it from the minute I served his coffee."

Gideon wanted a medal for pegging *that* right, but he let the kid continue.

"But Jay's… well, kind. At least he was when we met. We'd been together for a few months, and we had a system. I knew when it was clear to come over, and he'd set up the back entrance for me—har-har, right? Back entrance? But he'd set it up for, well, *me*. I had a key, and he'd leave little gifts when he wasn't there. It's sort of an entrance to the old maid's quarters, but he fixed it up nice, with a desk to study at, and books and a TV. It was like… like the rest of the house was his job, his public life, but those rooms were *ours*. And then one day, there we were, watching TV, and this slick guy walks into *our space*, and Jay takes one look at him and then one look at me, and he turns *white*. And he tells me to go to the kitchen and fix us something to eat. I do—scared the bejeezus out of the *actual* housekeeper, who's really nice, by the way. When she tries to shoo me back into our quarters, I tell her somebody's there, scaring the shit out of Jay."

Wow. This was—well, *frightening* was what it was. Not that Gideon approved of keeping your lovers hidden from the world, but it seemed like Jay Arnold had been doing the best he could with what he had.

"Do you know who barged in?" Carlyle asked—probably too soon, but the kid was on a roll, so it didn't seem to put him off.

"Halsey Garber," Kael muttered. "And yeah, I know who he is and why Jay shouldn't be having any conversations at all with him. But at first it didn't seem to matter. Jay said he had it handled, the housekeeper showed me three different secret passages out of the apartment floors, and the next time Halsey Garber arrived unannounced, Jay was there, feet up, watching *Celebrity Bachelor*, and I was in the housekeeper's closet, which she'd set up with a comfy chair, a pillow, and a little monitor of our room so I could, you know, make sure the mob wasn't killing my boyfriend."

Gideon found an unexpected bark of laughter stopped up in his throat. The kid was funny—but he was also very *real.* No wonder he'd been heartbroken. Gideon had assumed he'd been a sidepiece, used and ignored and cast aside when things got rough.

But that's not what this setup sounded like. Not a picnic, no—and not the way Gideon would lead his life—but this didn't sound like a sidepiece. This sounded like *love*.

"So things were tense," Carlyle prompted. "But not urgent."

Kael nodded, started patting his pockets for cigarettes again, and then let his hands fall.

"Yeah," he said softly. "Not urgent. I… I probably could have lived like that for a while, until politics changed, you know? Until he could bring me to parties, make me his special friend. Come out without worrying about his party turning on him like a pack of pit vipers. But I knew Garber was putting pressure on him for something—only Jay wouldn't share that with me. He kept saying he wanted me out of it. He'd managed to keep my name from the guy, keep my picture. Halsey knew I existed, but he doesn't know who I am. And then a couple of weeks ago—" He glanced pointedly at Gideon. "—that changed. What changed?"

"What changed was that Garber was asking your boyfriend to ignore a dogfighting ring," Gideon told him bluntly. "And apparently Jay Arnold is the last honest man in New York, because that didn't sit well with him. And when he found out Halsey had authorized a dognapping—and a kidnapping when the owner came to find the dog—he used our people as pawns to make it stop without telling us what we were walking into."

Kael closed his eyes. "Shit."

"Not his greatest moment," Gideon admitted. "But not strictly illegal either. But if your boyfriend was a pawn too, maybe we could help each other out."

"Halsey Garber's a piece of garbage," Kael said with loathing. "Every real estate broker in New York knows he doesn't pay his workers, and his projects all go bust. It's like he makes his living out of declaring bankruptcy and leaves this… this trail of broken lives behind him."

"You sound like you know," Carlyle said perceptively.

"I *had* a college fund," Kael told him, the bitterness palpable. "And then my father's company invested with that asshole. Now my parents don't even have a house, and my dad's a greeter in Walmart when he should be retired. So I know Halsey's bad news. And whatever he wanted to involve Jay in, it had to be shady." His voice dropped miserably. "And I guess the only reason Jay would be involved with something shady was me."

"You can't blame yourself," Carlyle said, and he sounded kind—and sincere. "You wanted somebody to love. That's not supposed to be a bad thing. But yeah, Jay got put in a spot, and he did something stupid, and now we need his help to get the bad guy off the street."

"I'd do a lot to fuck up Halsey Garber," Kael said.

They didn't need to meet eyes again, but they did anyway. That shit was starting to send a thunder through Gideon's veins.

"Can you introduce us to your boyfriend?" Carlyle asked. "We haven't spoken for a while, and it's about time we did."

GIDEON TEXTED Clint a quick debrief as Kael led them down the side path to the stairs that took them up to Jay Arnold's level. This wasn't strictly surveillance, but all they were doing was visiting a contact, right? No need for weapons—this *was* administration.

Except in person.

Right?

Once they were upstairs, Kael pulled out a key and let them into a tiled hallway that led to a large airy kitchen—or would have. Kael turned instead into a doorway right off the entrance, one that Gideon would have thought led to a laundry room, and they found themselves in a cozy little apartment, carpeted, with a couch and a minifridge and two recliners. There were bookshelves and a television, and even a small desk in the corner, and a doorway in the back that led, Gideon assumed, to sleeping quarters.

The furnishings were masculine—leather and dark wood—and the carpet was a tasteful Berber. There was an art rail, though, with some rather glorious cityscapes, and the couch was navy blue and looked comfortable. There were some throw pillows there with dents in them, and a warm throw in a muted purple along the back, a napping couch that had seen a recent nap.

Kael let out a sad little sound and walked over to plump the pillows and refold the throw.

"He's been sleeping in here," he murmured. "He… he has this big bedroom upstairs, but he says he can't sleep in there, and he can't sleep in our bed without me, so he'll…." His voice broke a little. "He missed me."

Gideon could admit it—he'd carried a grudge. Jay Arnold had put his team in danger to cover his ass, had bullied Pearson and Carlyle when they'd been sheltering their injured colleague, and had threatened to bully Crosby—*Crosby*—who had been injured while caught up in Arnold's subterfuge.

He'd been pissed.

But this little domestic scene softened him. *Kael* softened him. He'd been right. The kid wasn't a sidepiece. This was protection right here.

This was love.

But that didn't mean Arnold didn't need a little come-to-Jesus.

"Call him," he told Kael, but Kael grimaced.

"Do we have to?"

"We do," Carlyle said earnestly. "Because a predator has already been in this den. Halsey Garber was *here*. He's seen your face. Eventually it's going to come down to threatening *you*, and I don't think your boyfriend wants that. Which means he needs our help."

Kael swallowed and nodded, pulling out his phone.

"Jay?" he said softly. "Yeah, I'm—"

At that moment, they all heard the door to the hallway burst in, and a voice Gideon didn't recognize screamed, "Arnold! Arnold, get down here or your twinkie is toast!"

Gideon and Joey didn't even *need* to meet eyes. Joey, who was nearest to Kael, grabbed him and shoved him toward the sleeping quarters. “Bathtub?” he whispered, and when Kael nodded, Joey said, “Get in it, get down, cover your head.”

Kael disappeared while Gideon pinged at the comm on his collar.

“SCTF, overwatch,” he enunciated as Joey got behind the couch and he got behind the door, arm braced so it wouldn’t rebound off his face. “Hostile intruder at the house of Jay Arnold. We are inside, without weapons, protecting a civilian asset. Request immediate backup, going silent, out.”

And after dropping that bomb, he crossed both his arms in front of his face and sucked in his gut. This would hurt.

Hurt it did, but it worked like clockwork.

The door cracked open and bounced off his crossed wrists like a blow, and Gideon took advantage of the bounce and thrust forward, shoving an unsuspecting Halsey Garber back into the doorframe. As he stumbled back, whacking his head hard enough to leave hair and blood, Joey shoved the couch sideways against him, hitting his knees and hips. He went over, hard, landing on his stomach, and Joey catapulted over the sofa and landed on his back. Joey pulled his drop piece—the wicked little dagger—and held it at kidney level, hard enough to pierce the man’s gray wool coat and the sweater underneath.

“Help!” Halsey wheezed, and Gideon wiggled from behind the door and knelt on his wrists, to keep him from going for a weapon.

“SCTF,” Gideon said, knowing his comms were picking up the exchange. “Halsey Garber, you’re under arrest for breaking and entering and threatening the occupants of a private residence, with other charges pending. You have the right to remain silent….”

He finished reading the man his rights and watched as Jay Arnold rounded the corner, his personal weapon held out in front of him in a credible three-point stance.

“Mr. Arnold,” Gideon said in his calmest voice. “We were let into your residence by somebody with a key. This man, Halsey Garber, damaged your door, and he’s been subdued. He was threatening bodily harm to somebody you know. Would you like to press charges?"

Jay Arnold wasn't slick and in control—not tonight. His hair was wet, like he'd been in the shower, and his eyes were red-rimmed and hollow, like he'd been crying there. He was wearing old sweats—too small, perhaps Kael's—with holes in the knees, and a cheap, threadbare hoodie. Yes, he was in his early thirties, but he suddenly seemed young and sad and overwhelmed, and when his gaze fell on an infuriated, and now *handcuffed*, Halsey Garber, terrified.

"Oh God," he whispered, glancing from Halsey to Carlyle to Gideon. "He *broke in here*?"

"And threatened someone you know," Gideon said softly, with meaning.

Jay's expression of pure panic was enough for Gideon to forgive him.

"Somebody who's safe for the moment," Gideon said meaningfully. "But who won't be if we have to let this man go."

And he could see it, the whole of it, crossing Jay Arnold's face. Confess to being blackmailed, to using his job to leverage law enforcement, to turning his back on a dogfighting ring in the heart of the city and not doing anything until a civilian was threatened. None of what he'd done would get him prison time—Gideon had no doubt—but all of it was potentially career ending, including the poor barista currently hiding in the bathtub with his arms over his head.

Gideon kept his face calm and impassive as he watched the war of the wolves on Jay Arnold's face. One wolf wanted his career, power, the things he'd worked for his entire life.

The other wolf wanted the kid hiding in the bathroom, and a small three-bedroom home, and love.

Gideon thought he'd be hard-pressed to know which wolf would win in his own heart, but then, he'd never been in love.

Abruptly the war was over. Kael Rogers must have fed Jay Arnold's soul well, because with a deep breath, Arnold's shoulders relaxed, and he turned a look of resignation toward the thrashing, furious man on the floor.

"Yes," he rasped, and then tried again. "Yes," he said, his voice even. "I *would* like to press charges. And I do believe I should call the New York DA and my own counsel."

"Understood." Gideon allowed his eyes to dart toward where Kael had disappeared. "You may want to use the landline in the bedroom," he said, with the emphasis on the landline, although which phone Arnold used wouldn't matter.

Arnold's eyes widened, and he nodded. "Thank you," he said, with dignity before stepping over Garber's furious form and walking toward the darkened room—and presumably the bathroom—with admirable restraint.

"Close the door," Gideon called, and Arnold did just that. Garber would never know that Kael had been right there and was a potential witness. Arnold would take all the heat, and that was exactly as it should be.

At that moment Pearson and Kylie called through the door, emerging with their weapons drawn, and Gideon and Carlyle could turn Garber over to people who *weren't* on administrative leave.

He was a bulky middle-aged man with a soft stomach and the wide shoulders of a linebacker.

"I'm going to fucking kill you all," he frothed as Pearson grabbed his bicep. "I know politicians in this town. I know people. I will *eat* your families with my fuckin' *eggs* in the morning."

Gideon laughed dryly. "My family goes best with cornflakes. Carlyle?"

"Arsenic," Carlyle said. "You're welcome to them."

"Cheese danish," Pearson said cheerfully, holstering her piece as Garber became more and more under control. "You?"

"Fruit and yogurt," Kylie said, just as cheerfully. "Nope—no eggs here."

"By the way," Gail said, hauling Garber through the door, "do you know that our friend Agent Chadwick has his recorder on? We have every threat you made in the last ten minutes *on tape*. And given what we know about your criminal activities, I think that shit's going to court with you. I don't think eggs are gonna taste so good in prison. You may want to go with Carlyle's arsenic, right?"

Gideon laughed weakly as they went around the corner, and Carlyle did the same, leaning against Gideon with an easy familiarity.

That quickly the moment from the car was back, the intimacy, the yearning to explode.

But Gideon remembered the two wolves. Had Joey Carlyle fed his wolf enough human kindness for that wolf to win if they met each other skin to skin?

Harding and Talia arrived next, and they straightened up and "professionalized," as Gideon thought of it, but as they ran through the procedure and the upshot and the paperwork they'd need to file, Gideon watched Joey prowling around that little love nest like a puzzled wild animal, sniffing at the corners and listening intently for the sounds of solace and reconciliation in the next room.

Not yet, Gideon thought. *Not yet. But God, someday he's going to offer his throat. What're you gonna do then, Gid?*

And the thought of the two of them in bed, feral, demanding, skin to skin, inside each other, flashed behind his eyes with passion and violence.

Take it. In a heartbeat. Even if he eats my liver for breakfast.

Oh.

Well, now he knew which wolf would win.

A Well-Fed Wolf

JOEY RESISTED being overwatch as long as he could, and then Pearson broke her leg and he absolutely couldn't avoid it.

The year had gone by fast after the dog-bite case (as they called it, to Crosby's eternal discomfort). After four weeks, Crosby was back on the job, but this time with a coffee cup that *Joey* had picked out, one of adorable puppies tumbling across the ceramic surface.

Crosby had given Joey a horrified grimace. "Really? I thought you liked me, sort of."

"I love you, man," Joey said, and he *meant* it, and now he *knew* that he meant it, which for him was a big deal. "Just remember that sometimes a puppy is a cute fluffy animal, and sometimes…."

"It'll kill ya," Crosby said, laughing a little in spite of himself. He gave a mock-salute with the mug. "Thanks, man. I'll try not to shove it down the garbage disposal or something."

Everybody laughed then, and Gideon—oh God, after those delicious, fraught moments, it *had* to be Gideon, at least in Joey's head—winked at him before they started their morning debrief.

And after that first hurdle of learning to love his teammates like the family he'd always wanted but had never had, he seemed to take *all* of it—the psychology classes, the electronics classes for surveillance, the communications classes—to heart.

He'd joined the military because it got him away from his father. He'd stayed there because he seemed to have skills compatible with survival there.

But that one dumb fuckup—as he'd thought of it then—that one refusal to bow to the power because the truth was power was corrupt, had brought him here. And here—here he didn't merely survive.

He *thrived.*

He was a respected member of an amazing team. A member who'd managed to avoid the ultimate responsibility of overwatch until two things happened.

The first was that Kylie, funny, voluptuous, va-va-va-voom Kylie, had gotten married and gone on a month-long honeymoon. It wasn't that she didn't *deserve* a honeymoon or didn't have the leave coming, but goddammit, Harding still hadn't been able to find anybody to replace her, and he'd been searching! Gideon and some guy named Blodgett, whom Harding consulted a lot, as well as Natalia, spent a lot of their time leafing through folders, trying to find the right fit. They'd actually *found* more than one candidate, but unfortunately, by the time *they* got to the person, they'd either resigned in disgust with the entire law enforcement system, gotten promoted to a place where they could invoke change, or—and this had apparently happened more than once—they'd been killed, often by their own squad, for being insubordinate or "just not fitting in."

And right when Harding got a line on somebody—undercover, yes, but Harding seemed *really* excited about this agent's potential—Gail Pearson had to go do the other thing that landed Joey on overwatch and break her goddamned leg.

The worst part was, he'd been there when it happened—it could have happened to *him*.

The thing to remember about Gail was that she may have *looked* like the Swiss Miss Hot Chocolate girl—or, as Crosby called her, Elsa from *Frozen*, which Joey understood now, but she was, in fact, fierce as a snow lynx, quick, ruthless, and unafraid to shed blood.

So partnering her and Joey was probably a bad idea.

But Kylie was out, Gideon was overwatch, and Harding and Natalia were needed to interview the zillionaire who had given his thug the kill order for a sweet older couple who owned a mom-and-pop business. Apparently the zillionaire didn't like being told "no" when he asked them if he could purchase their bodega at half its value—go figure. While the zillionaire told Harding and Natalia that "I didn't think Gregor would take me seriously," Joey and Gail were chasing Gregor through a back alley while Crosby hauled ass around the block to cut the behemoth off from the other side.

What they hadn't counted on was the stacks of pipes in the alley, apparently all ready to get laid to replace leaky plumbing, and how easy it would be for their perp to shove a pallet of them over so they clattered and clanged on the concrete and each other and the brick wall across the alley.

Joey, skills honed by running through the forest in the winter, dodging trees, animal lairs, holes under the snow, managed to dance his way through the minefield, but he had just cleared the mess—and Crosby had just rounded the corner to take out their fleeing perpetrator with the bulk and fearlessness of the football player he'd been in college—when Joey heard it.

A horrible, sickening *snap*, and as he turned in slow motion, Gail's leg bent *backward*, in a way no leg should ever bend, and as Joey watched, horrified, she went down, whiter than a ghost, and the rest of the pipes battered her slight body.

"*Fuck*!" Carlyle screamed, and then, before he could control himself, his mind replayed that "*snap*" and he bent over and threw up, barely missing his own shoes.

He recovered quickly—he had to—because Gail was whimpering and Crosby was…

Well, brushing past him, saying, "Get our suspect—he's down and cuffed but feisty."

"I'll call it in," Joey said, wiping his mouth and trying to recover from the ignominy of blowing chunks at a takedown.

Crosby spared him a glance, and because it was Crosby, it was a compassionate one. "Been there, brother," he said before getting to Gail's side.

Gail didn't want Joey anyway, he thought as he started speaking immediately into his comms unit while pulling their suspect to his feet. Gideon, who was running overwatch from his department issue, parked haphazardly at long-term in Kennedy airport, where he'd spotted their rich douchebag—had already called for an ambulance at their location.

"I heard the snap," he said sickly.

"Did you hear me blowing chunks?" Joey asked, disgusted with himself.

"Yeah, well, good thing Crosby was there, because I almost hurled out the door. God, that fucking *sound*." They both shuddered and then got to the business of handing their suspect over to the flatfoots who had arrived on the scene, broken and panting after being ditched at the start of the chase.

Once that was done, Joey had no choice but to human.

Crosby had shoved his leather coat under Gail's head to shield her from the concrete as he lifted the pipes off her body. Joey helped with that and then took off his own coat to cover her shoulders while they waited in the fall chill.

Nobody, he noticed, could look at her leg.

"God, it's bad," she sobbed. "If neither of you bozos will give me grief about it, it's gotta be bad."

Crosby sank to one side of her, and Joey sank to the other. Crosby smoothed flyaway strands of her blond hair back from her brow, and Joey thought that she looked unbelievably young.

"Elsa, I can't lie," Crosby rumbled. "You're gonna be on your ass for this one. But don't worry. We'll treat you with the same care and consideration you showed me when I was out."

"Aw fuck," she groaned. "I'm never gonna hear the end of it. Gail Pearson, taken down for trying to lay pipe."

Joey was surprised into sputtering laughter—and even more surprised to see he was sputtering a few tears. Oh God. This was what being human *did* to him, wasn't it? It made him feel for his fellow humans, and right now, the perky, fey little assassin who could keep up with him in a chase was making him wish *he* was injured instead.

It was scary. Terrifying. But it didn't keep him from holding her hand, like Crosby, until the EMTs arrived to stabilize her leg and take her away.

When they were gone, Carlyle found he was leaning against Crosby, vision black, because the pop and squelch of flesh as they stabilized the wound almost destroyed him.

"Easy there, Carlyle," Crosby soothed, and Carlyle straightened almost angrily. He had *killed* people. He had thrust his knife between an enemy combatant's ribs and shoved it until it thudded in his attacker's heart.

But you've never held a friend's hand while she cried out in pain.

Somehow he made it through the rest of the day. The wait in the hospital, Harding sending them the paperwork that they all signed with their phones as they paced. Finally—*finally*—Gail was out of surgery, and everybody got to go home, even Crosby, whose roommate sitch with his old college friend was still insane and showed in his shadowed eyes every day.

And without quite knowing how it happened, Joey was in Gideon's department issue, being ushered up the stairs to Gideon's brownstone apartment, being settled on the couch with a rum and coke—something he'd discovered he enjoyed this last year as he and Gideon had hit music venues with things like two-drink minimums.

Gideon didn't hoard a full bar, but the liquor he did have, wine, beer, a few spirits, tended to be top shelf.

The first swallow of rum was absolutely bracing, and Joey let out what felt like his first full breath.

"I didn't use to be like this," he said, not sure it was going to come out of his mouth.

"I know it," Gideon said on the other side of the couch, nursing his own R&C. "I am well aware."

"I hate this feeling. *Hate* it. Hated it with Crosby. Hated it with Gail. Why can't I make it stop?"

Gideon let out a sigh. "Because you care about your unit, Joey. It's not a bad thing."

Joey took a breath and then another. "But… but I've *killed* people!" he explained, taking another swallow. The rum was good—so good—and it didn't burn down. It slid, satisfying and almost fattening, the way a really good cock sometimes filled his throat.

That image made him widen his eyes—and almost made him choke on that oh-so-smooth drink.

Oh, it had been a long time since he'd gotten laid. Either sex. Yeah, sure, he'd spent his first six months wandering around the city, hooking up when he felt like it. Condoms and PrEP and he could fuck an army and be nothing but a little sore in the morning.

But in the last year, as he and Gideon had found more and more concerts to attend, spent more and more nights in Gideon's apartment, listening to albums—vinyl, CDs, streaming—and had started a heated rivalry playing *Law & Order* Bingo when attending theater productions, the need for that kind of quick-and-dirty sexual encounter had waned.

Joey hadn't wanted to articulate it, but he knew what was happening.

Sex—feral, animal—had been the only real human connection he'd allowed himself to make. But this last year, it hadn't just been Gideon—although his connection had been strongest, the *most* feral, the *most* animal—it had been all of them.

From that terrible moment when Crosby had fallen and Joey had needed to kill the gods-benighted dog to now, the steel sinews of his once purely autonomous heart had bound so tightly to the other people in his unit that he felt his chest tighten with the need to breathe.

"Shh…." Gideon had moved closer, had his hand on Joey's knee, and dammit, Joey *needed* that connection.

"This is stupid," he said harshly and went to set his drink down on the coffee table so he could storm out, but he ended up knocking it back instead.

To his surprise, Gideon refilled it with the bottle and can on the table, and he took another swallow, his hands shaking.

"It's not stupid," Gideon said, and this time he wrapped his arm around Joey's shoulders. Joey found himself sagging against Gideon Chadwick, the man he'd once thought was weak, a rabbit or a deer, and trusting all his weight on the thin, wiry frame. "It's human."

Joey let out a bark of what was supposed to be laughter, but that's not what it sounded like, even to himself. "I'm not human," he muttered. "I'm a wolf."

"Sure you are," Gideon murmured. "You're a badass little wolf. We all know that. You take down prey, you protect your pack—but even a badass wolf doesn't like it when his pack is injured."

"I hate this," Joey said, his voice cracking. He heard the crack and tried to hold back his horror. That sounded like… that was almost like….

He wasn't aware that Gideon had taken the now-empty glass away from him. He wasn't aware that he was slumped against the one human on the planet he trusted with his throat.

All he was aware of was that Gideon's arms, sinewy and strong, were wrapped around his shoulders as he buried his face in Gideon's throat and howled.

IT WAS not the first time he woke up on Gideon's couch, his mouth tasting like rum or beer or wine. It *was* the first time he woke up with a roaring headache and a hangover, though. Gideon was crouching eye level with him on the couch with a big glass of water and two ibuprofen.

"Don't worry about work," he said. "For one thing it's Saturday, and we don't have anything active and pressing. For another, Harding texted everybody with strict instructions to stay home. Apparently he's got a meeting with Deavers so he can clear Gail's injury before Monday."

Gail's injury. "*Fuuuuuuuck…*," he managed before tossing down the meds and taking a swig of sweet, sweet water.

"Yeah. Crosby's been in the hospital room all morning with her. You and I get to pull a shift in the afternoon. Clint and Tal get tomorrow. She's coming home on Monday, and Crosby's going to need our help outfitting her place so she can do things like use the bathroom and take a shower. She's got a roommate, but I guess she's a big cheese in the 43rd Precinct and isn't going to have a lot of time to babysit. We're on."

Joey nodded, and then realizing Gideon's pewter-gold eyes were level on his face, measuring his every microexpression, he grimaced.

"I'm fine," he said gruffly.

"No," Gideon said, smoothing his hair back from his face. "Don't give me 'fine' bullshit. I know, Joey. I know who your father is. I've *studied* what it must be like to grow up in a home like that. I get it. Your whole last year has been learning what a real family is about, and it's only possible because most of us are predators, like you."

"'Cept Crosby," Joey said, trying for disgust and ending up with admiration. Crosby the fuzzy bunny. Crosby the puppy. Crosby the solid-ass citizen who could give Joey a look of kindness after Joey hurled his cookies.

"Well, yeah." Gideon laughed, shaking his head. "Crosby's an anomaly. But we're a bloodthirsty lot. I mean, Pearson was an *assassin*, for sweet fuck's sake. And Clint's a scary motherfucker in battle—I've been shoulder to shoulder with him."

Joey felt an unwelcome shaft of jealousy and tamped it down because any idiot, even Joey, could see it would never be like that between Gid and Clint.

"But…," Joey started to say it, but the words stuck. God, how long had Gideon known about his father?

"But we're your pack now," Gideon said softly. "We might be the only people who *could* be your pack. You know what happens to lone wolves in the wild, Carlyle?"

Call me Joey.

But he was already nodding. "They don't make it," he said, because as romantic as the idea was, the truth was sad and desperate for an animal that had no den and no place to turn.

"You're going to make it," Gideon promised, raising his hand to Joey's face again, presumably to push back his hair in that same sweet gesture Crosby had used. But Gideon's hand didn't complete the movement.

It froze. *He* froze. His palm cupping Joey's cheek.

Joey swallowed and met his eyes again, and he was horrified when Gideon took a deep fortifying breath, swallowed, and moved his hand.

"You're tired," he said, his voice gruff. "And you spent the night drunk and crying on my couch. This—this can't happen when you're feeling weak, Carlyle. You'll never forgive me."

But I want!

It was a mewl, not a howl, and goddamn Gideon for being right anyway.

"You're probably still sleeping with Dr. Death," Joey muttered, pulling back and turning his head so as not to assault Gideon with the dead animal he felt crawling out of his mouth.

"I have never slept with Elaine," Gideon told him primly. "She's part of my outside-of-work friend circle, that's all."

Elaine Aiello was the Medical Examiner for Manhattan's Lower East Side, and Joey could admit she was hot, blond, and smart. And while Gideon didn't really care about the blond—or the female, by his own admission—hot and smart seemed to be his candy.

Although Elaine had been the only lollipop Gideon had been eyeing as of late, which was probably why Joey felt that irrational hatred start up again. It had once been aimed at Crosby, but he was much more comfortable now that he could aim it at somebody *not* in the unit.

Elaine was a handy target to hate, and he couldn't even lie to himself anymore about why he hated her.

Which was why the smile snuck up on him so quickly. "You're not?" he asked, nakedly curious.

"Sleeping with Elaine?" Gideon clarified. "No." His face grew sober. "And if you have to ask why, maybe I should."

Joey felt the growl in his stomach, and Gideon's arched eyebrow indicated he heard it.

"I don't have to ask," Joey snarled, and then he swung his legs around and stood. "I'm going to shower."

He'd started keeping an extra set of clothes in Gideon's drawer after the first few times he'd fallen asleep on the couch. He knew where his clothes were, where his toothbrush was, even knew where Gideon's electric razor was and that he was invited to share.

As he stalked to the bathroom, he realized he was scanning the rest of the apartment for other marks that he was there, that he'd already begun to make this place his den.

When he didn't see any, he found himself asking why. He started *planning* to leave things, to bring them from his own still-sterile apartment. *If you have to ask why, maybe I should.* The thing in his chest that had lain dormant in the last year, only poking its nose out occasionally, the thing that wanted to bite Gideon on the neck, the shoulder, the hip, the thigh, leave sign, leave scent that Joey owned him—*that* thing—was awake now, screaming for release.

Joey's animal knew the difference now, between packmates and *mate*, and it was ready to make its needs known.

BUT STILL he held off. He wasn't sure why. Part of it was that the next six weeks were a flurry of being stretched thin in an already understaffed unit. Gail was back in two weeks, casted leg elevated, laptop computer seemingly welded to her fingertips, and the understanding was, she'd be their permanent overwatch until she healed, but then Joey and Crosby needed to be up to speed.

They'd been looking forward to Kylie returning, but the day Harding walked into the briefing both pleased and grim, they all knew. Kylie had decided *not* to return.

And even though she'd never been a predator, or a warrior, really, or even a solid cop, like Crosby, Joey could admit to himself that he'd miss her. She'd been dry and funny and so super competent it was almost pornographic.

Joey was almost afraid to fill her shoes, but Harding didn't miss much.

"Since we don't have any pressing cases at the moment," Harding intoned, "I'm going to have Chadwick give us all a refresher on overwatch protocol and ways to organize your screen to keep track of your targets. Gideon, spend the day prepping. Everyone else, physical and weapons training today, take your pick. I'm doing paperwork—somebody shoot a paper file for me, right in the face."

"Can do, sir," Joey told him. An hour later, he and Crosby were in the basement shooting range, pulling back their targets for small arms practice and comparing shots.

Joey was mortified to realize that Crosby had bested him.

"Damn," Crosby said, voice loud over their protective gear. "You must be having an off day."

"Or you're getting better!" Joey shouted, but he felt his brows draw close.

Or he was distracted.

"What's wrong?" Crosby asked, removing his earwear and stepping away from the shooting corridor to the table in the back, where he pulled out his cleaning kit and proceeded to break down and empty his weapon to clean. Joey did the same, the space eerily silent since they were the only two down there for this session.

"I...." Joey was horrified to find himself tempted to blurt out all the... the *things* going on in his chest about Chadwick, but Jesus, poor Crosby. Who wanted to be subjected to *that*? Joey had the feeling Crosby had his own problems. He'd been sleeping on Gail's couch a lot in the last few weeks so he could help her with basic stuff: dressing, bathing, getting to work. If he'd ever thought the two of them were sleeping together—and he hadn't, because Gideon said the smells weren't meshing—that idea would have been killed quickly watching Crosby's patient *brotherly* concern over his friend and partner since she'd been down for the count.

But he *did* have something he could share. "Overwatch," he said after a moment. "You feeling up to it?"

Crosby grimaced. "I ran it a little when I was recovering from that dog-bite thing. Not my favorite, no, but mostly 'cause... you know. You worry. It's like, 'Hey, I just sent my friends there. I hope they don't get dead 'cause I made a fucking decision,' you know?"

Joey grinned at him. "Yeah, I fucking *know*. It's like, 'I'll face that shit myself, thank you, but don't let me throw someone else at it because, *damn*.'"

Crosby nodded glumly, his handsome All-American football hero face assuming an anxious expression that made Carlyle appreciate him more. "Well," he said, after a few moments of replacing his gun and cleaning kit in the case, using precision and care also at odds with his appearance. "Maybe Harding's new hire will be King Shit Overwatch, and you and me can relax."

"New hire?" Where had Joey been for this?

"Yeah, heard him on the phone with Blodgett. Said the guy was the best he'd seen since you, so, you know, you don't have to be King Shit New Guy anymore."

Joey snorted. "I wasn't the King Shit New Guy, Crosby. That was you."

It was Crosby's turn to snort. "Fuckin' Jesus, a year and a half and I finally barely beat you at small arms? What're you drinking?"

Rum and coke. The thought came out of nowhere and made Joey smile.

"Whatever it is, it means I'm too stoned to do overwatch—so there."

Crosby's deep chuckle was reassuring. It meant that even if one of them ended up alone with a computer screen while the other was following his orders into hell, neither one of them were really alone.

A WEEK later, Calix Garcia swaggered into the staff room. Joey saw it happen. He took two steps in, his eyes sought out Judson Crosby, who was sitting next to Gail, assembling info on their perp, and he froze. Joey wasn't sure if anybody else could read his face, his reactions, the way his breath caught and his brown eyes widened, the tautness of his compact, muscular body, but Joey could.

He'd remember it forever because he'd never seen anybody actually find his mate at first sight before. Except that wasn't even the real words for it. It wasn't *find his mate*. It was—

No. No no no no no no....

Because admitting something like that was real was like admitting he still believed in Sky Woman or Maple Sapling or Flint—the old stories his grandfather told when he was still a child and allowed to hunt by his grandfather's side.

It was impossible. It was….

Harding called them all to order, and all thoughts of that gnawing in his chest, the need that had only grown since that night on Gideon's couch, fled.

They had an active perpetrator on a killing spree, and it was all hands on deck.

CHADWICK AND Carlyle got to the deserted nightclub just as the two ambulances were leaving, and Joey heard Gideon's voice pitching as he spoke to Gail over comms.

"He *what*?"

"He was wearing a vest," Gail said, her voice gritty, "and the perpetrator shot Crosby point blank before Crosby brought him down. Cracked ribs. Punctured lung. He's on the way to the hospital for surgery. Garcia and Harding have custody of a witness who's going to need some cozening—maybe a night in one of our emotional trauma centers, someplace safe. Crosby picked up on the fact that this kid was abused a lot at home, and even though he's not a minor, his family isn't going to be too excited about him being involved at anything at a gay nightclub."

"Shit," Gideon muttered. "Does Garcia know the particulars?"

"I don't know," Gail muttered. "Yes. Probably. Fuck."

It was the first time Joey had ever heard her rattled as overwatch. Fucking Crosby.

"We'll take care of them," Gideon promised, and while Joey heard the stress in his voice, he was pretty sure he sounded reassuring to Gail. "Don't worry. You keep us apprised on Crosby, and we'll make sure our wits land and the new guy isn't terrified. Square?"

"Four by four," she replied, and Joey breathed out a sigh of relief.

Gideon disconnected and spent a moment hunting for a parking spot that wouldn't snarl traffic for miles in either direction. He found one and paused for a moment, eyes closed, face toward the sun.

"Gid?" Joey asked hesitantly. "We okay?"

"You know, you and me were both only children. I think Gail and Tal have siblings. As far as I know, Clint sprang up from the earth like a mushroom. But this—this must be what it's like to worry about one kid—one kid who's always getting hurt. One kid who's always about to go tits up. I just… you wouldn't think it was Crosby, would you?"

And Joey felt it, not for the first time. Gideon's attachment to the unit. The way he regarded all of them as his people. Like they were the only group he could ever be comfortable with.

And how Joey felt the same way.

"He's going to be fine," Joey told him inanely. Nobody knew that for certain.

Gideon turned his head and gave him a tired grin. "Let's go see how Calix is. I mean, one day and his partner's shot? Might make him rethink the whole works."

Calix Garcia was not rethinking anything. In fact he was already ahead of them all. They had another witness in protective custody with his family, and Calix had already made arrangements with Clint to keep the detail until the boys could be debriefed, as much to keep an eye on them as to keep them safe from the guy Crosby had already taken out. He'd already made mental notes of things Crosby knew that he wanted to learn, protocols for making sure witnesses and victims landed, knowing resources to call on so that people who were in a shitty situation didn't completely lose their footing—or their housing or their family—because a criminal had cut a destructive swath through their lives.

Harding, who had to deal with authorities in Queens and the brand-new gambling commissioner replacing Jay Arnold because their perp was making book on local high school ball clubs and probably sixty-dozen people Joey *didn't* know about, was happy to turn Garcia over to them while he did his damned job.

One of the first things they did, while escorting Garcia's witness to the safehouse with the other wit, was stop for food for both of them. Garcia was pale and woozy at that point, and his witness probably wouldn't turn down a cheeseburger.

Through mouthfuls of burger, Garcia admitted that Crosby had been going to brief everybody on his blood sugar and how it could be a touchy thing. Not diabetes—not yet—but he ate right and tried to keep food on his person at all times.

"No worries," Joey said through his own mouthfuls of burger. "Harding forgets to fuckin' eat. We *always* have food on us. Protein bars, apples—we'll treat you right."

And Garcia, who looked like a tough little bird, much like Joey himself, had grinned at them, all peacock, and Joey felt that particular wrenching again. *Sky Woman smiled on the two lovers in the glen, and everywhere they lay, flowers bloomed.*

His grandfather's voice, telling Joey a story that had never been in a book, never told at a campfire, just, well, told because his grandfather liked telling stories.

He could see it so clearly—Calix Garcia, mid-sized, tightly built, cocky as fuck, and their solid, earnest Crosby. Why he'd never really thought Crosby would be bisexual before, he couldn't say, but Joey suddenly knew, without a doubt, that he and Garcia would fit in all the ways.

"We about done?" Gideon asked, wiping his mouth. "I gotta say, things always look better after food."

"Soundtrack is mine," Joey claimed without thought, and Gideon's private, just-for-them grin locked something in his stomach.

Tonight, he thought. And a logical part of him knew that Gideon would have company that night. He'd been planning sort of a wine-and-cheese thing for the friends he made outside the unit. Part of it was that Gideon was sort of brilliant, and he didn't get to discuss academics a lot when he was chasing down suspects and dodging bullets, but partly—and Gideon had admitted this—it was so he could remember that there was a way of thinking that didn't always involve life and death. In his own words, it helped him "human better" when he interacted with humans who didn't always boil behavior and circumstances down to bare survival.

He doesn't have to human with me, Joey thought. *Tonight it will be animal to animal.*

THAT NIGHT, he stood on the street, staring up to the window through which he could see the shadows of Gideon's bedroom. There was a flickering of lights, the suggestion of chatter, but the October mist oiled his face, his jacket, as he stared up, and he could not feel the heat of the room.

He might not want you.

But Joey remembered that look from four weeks ago when he'd awakened on Gideon's couch. How it had burned.

You'll never forgive me if this happens when you're feeling weak.

But Joey *wasn't* feeling weak. He was feeling *ravenous*. He couldn't logic his way through him and Gideon Chadwick anymore. What he wanted was beyond words.

With a leap and a grunt, he grabbed the ladder of the fire escape and started to climb.

DEVOURED

OH GOD, he tasted like prey, like blood, like power and song.

Gideon moaned and pressed forward, expecting fight, resistance. He knew Joey Carlyle inside and out, and his boy didn't give over easily, and certainly not skin to skin.

But Joey surprised him, going limp, yielding in his arms, falling back against the bed and accepting him greedily as Gideon kept tasting him, their mouths meshing, retreating, their kisses urgent and hard.

Gideon's hands shook as he shoved them under Joey's shirt, the fabric still smelling of the leather jacket currently draped on a chair by the bed. The scent triggered something in Gideon. He wanted to smell *all* of Joey Carlyle—his sweat, his sex—smell and taste and *bite*.

He licked instead, nibbled along defined abs, sensitive ribs, to cover a dark brown nipple with his mouth and suck.

The sound that came from Joey's throat was feral, needy, and his hands tunneled through Gideon's hair, fingers clenching as he arched his back.

Gideon moved to the other nipple, thrusting his hips into the mattress, half-hard and aching already. He lifted up enough to pull the hoodie up over Joey's head, and together they fell back on the mattress as Gideon moved up to his throat.

To his eternal shock, Joey tilted his head back to give him access, and Gideon felt it hard in his stomach what this meant. Joey Carlyle might not understand it—not yet—but this was submission. Total. An admission of need. An invitation not just to fuck, but to mate.

Gideon was *there*. He was *mated*. He'd been longing for this for *months*. Joey's smell was in his pores, in his dreams, and he wanted this man's mark on his skin.

But Gideon wanted to mark him first.

Joey's breathless cries, his needy grunts, drove him on. Gideon pulled hard on his neck and then moved before he left a mark the world could see. He made his way back down Joey's chest, getting to his hip bone and sucking hard, adding teeth until Joey cried out again, almost desperate.

Mine, Gideon thought, but they were beyond words.

With shaking hands, Gideon stripped off the tight black jeans, knowing the boots and socks would have been removed already. The black briefs underneath were too small to hide many secrets—beyond the fact that Joey waxed—and Gideon would have ripped them, broken them, destroyed them, if that wouldn't have taken precious time.

It didn't matter. In a heartbeat, Joey Carlyle was stretched, naked and vulnerable beneath him, and Gideon *wanted* him as he'd *never* wanted another human being in his life. He'd wanted water in the desert, food after days of foraging, heat when he'd nearly died of exposure—those things he'd *wanted* with this intensity. *Those* things had taught him what need felt like.

He sucked Joey's proud erect cock into his mouth, into his throat, with that level of need.

Joey didn't cry out this time, and Gideon looked up to see his eyes closed, his entire body immersed in pleasure, and his teeth softly sinking into his lower lip.

He'd been caught by surprise, Gideon thought, heart aching. Joey Carlyle wouldn't make noise in bed, probably had never been vulnerable in bed. And he wouldn't respect Gideon ever again if Gideon didn't make good on his promises.

Gideon took him down to the back of his throat again, working those muscles while cupping those slim hips with his fingers. Joey tried to thrash, tried to arch, but Gideon didn't let him, holding him still while he used all his empirical evidence for how to please a male body on the one he wanted most of all.

A slow retreat, a quick advance, and Joey's breath grew quick, quicker—he'd been clenching the sheets after Gideon had undressed him, but one hand was back in Gideon's hair now, making his eyes tear with the smarting pain. Gideon refused to relent, and Joey's other hand beat the mattress at his side until Gideon took it in his own, weaving their fingers together.

That brought a noise from Joey's throat, and Gideon released the other hand on Joey's hip to grip his shaft, to squeeze and stroke, while he worked his tongue and teeth.

"Gid," Joey pleaded, and they both knew it for a plea. "I'm gonna come."

Gideon pulled back enough to lick Joey's head with a flattened tongue. "How many times?" he asked, and Joey's laugh was semihysterical.

"Usually just the once, but—"

Gideon heard it even if Joey hadn't meant to say it. He came once, he always topped, he was probably gone before the condom hit the trash.

Not this time.

Very deliberately, he said, "I didn't wait a year and a half for you to come once and run."

Then he shoved Joey's thighs up, up, parted his cheeks, and licked long and hard between the crease. Joey didn't cry out, still biting his lip, but from his chest came a *ngungh* sound that gave Gideon the shivers.

That much repressed passion had to come out somewhere.

Joey's thighs suddenly shuddered and clamped around Gideon's ears. Gideon lunged up past them to take Joey's cock in his mouth, while thrusting a slickened finger into his asshole, and then, oh God, Joey made that sound again, that low, tortured *ngungh* sound, and he came, thrusting into the back of Gideon's throat and pouring ejaculate, thick and basic, down.

Gideon swallowed and kept stretching with that finger.

"Oh God," Joey whispered, shuddering. "God—"

"Gid," Gideon corrected. "Here, you beg *me*."

Joey shuddered hard, suppressed a whimper, and broke.

"Gideon," he rasped. "Please."

"Stay there."

Gideon was still clothed, but not for long. His slacks and shirt crumpled to the floor, and his boxers slid down his thighs. Joey reached out from the bed as he undressed, trailing nimble fingers down his flank, his backside.

"I want to touch you," he said, but his voice was garbled, hazy with pleasure, and Gideon knew this wasn't the time.

"Later," he promised. "There will be later."

Joey made a negative sound, but Gideon wasn't going to have that discussion now. He paused to grab a tube of slick from his drawer and then turned back toward the bed. Moved by a sense of exhibitionism that had rarely, if ever, gripped him, he whispered, "Watch."

Joey turned, mouth slightly parted, and watched as Gideon oiled his own erect cock, hard and slow, letting his head tilt back and enjoying the sensation.

It had been a while, and then the relationship—a woman that time—had been tepid and halfhearted. This was Joey fucking Carlyle. Every sinew of Gideon's body was committed to this.

Joey made that sound again, the one that told Gideon he was aroused beyond endurance, and his hand came out to feather along Gideon's cock.

Gideon stepped away, not to be cruel but because Joey wasn't the only one at the cliff's edge.

He moved up from the bottom of the bed again, pulling Joey's thighs over his shoulders and meeting his eyes as he positioned himself.

"You ready?" he asked, and he saw Joey swallow before nodding.

Oh God. He couldn't do this without…. He lowered himself, let Joey's legs slide down, and kissed him, not hard but tenderly, intimately, the way he'd wanted to touch him from the first.

"It'll be okay," he promised when the kiss ended, and with a little shimmy, he felt himself thrusting forward, breaching Joey's stretched body.

Joey nodded again, but no words, nothing but that bitten lower lip and the arching of his hips as he sought to impale himself on Gideon's girth and length.

Gideon shuddered. "Come on," he urged. "We can do this. Relax."

And that did it. Joey's knees fell open, his body went pliant again, and Gideon surged forward slowly, with care, but inevitably, like the rising sun or the smell of mist on concrete.

He was there, unmistakable and real.

Joey's eyes closed, his mouth parted slightly, and he let out a sigh of completion as Gideon seated himself entirely in Joey's body.

Gideon stayed there, letting Joey relax around him, and waited until he felt that first visceral shudder.

"Go—Gid," Joey begged. "Please."

"Oh yeah," Gideon told him, pulling back and thrusting. And again. And harder. Joey's knees came up, clenching around Gideon's hips, and still he kept thrusting, kept fucking, his body hungry, *starving*, devouring Joey's surrender like it was the thing he needed to sustain his very life.

And finally, finally, Joey opened his mouth, cried out, said, "Gideon!" so desperately, Gideon wouldn't have been able to deny him *anything*.

"Come," he growled, thrusting hard, hitting that spot, the one that made most men quiver, and Joey was no exception.

First he made that sound, *ngungghhhh*, and then he used it to power a tortured, "*Yes*!" that sent shudders of electricity all along Gideon's skin.

"Yes!" Joey cried again, his asshole clenching on Gideon's erection, and that quickly—oh God, Gideon saw stars and hurtled off the precipice to orgasm, falling so hard, so fast, he barely felt the hot spurt of come scalding the inside of Joey Carlyle's body.

Joey's next sound was lost as his own spend coated their stomachs, and Gideon, still spasming, lowered his head and took his mouth again, easing him down and down until the chaos of orgasm passed.

Joey fell back against the pillows, eyes closed, his body falling absolutely still, and Gideon pressed a kiss to his forehead, recognizing the haziness of subspace, of *forcing* your body to relax so what should be a pleasurable experience didn't become a painful one.

"Hang in there," he murmured and got up, unsteady himself, to turn off the lights, double-check the apartment's locks, fetch a washcloth, and arrange the blankets. He got back, shivering a little from running around naked, and after wiping them both down, he nudged Joey a little until he was on his side and then spooned him from behind.

It wasn't until he'd wrapped his arm around Joey Carlyle's chest that he allowed himself to think about the enormity of what they'd just done.

He shuddered hard and drew Joey closer, and Joey whimpered in his sleep.

Now he would make the noises he wouldn't let Gideon hear when they were making love.

"Oh, kid," he whispered into Joey's hair. "You and me—it's going to be such a tricky dance." And it would be. Gideon was cautious, but Joey was *damaged*. Still it was too late for either of them. Gideon had known it the moment he'd smelled Joey Carlyle in his darkened bedroom.

The moment Joey had shown Gideon his throat, their destiny was locked in stone.

Gideon was never letting him go.

But it wouldn't be easy. Gideon knew that. Which was why he wasn't surprised when, after an hour of sleep, he woke to feel Joey trying to slip away.

THE CAUTIOUS HUNTER

JOEY HAD been able to sneak out of a lover's bed from the age of fifteen, and he'd never been caught.

Until Gideon Chadwick.

"Don't go," Gideon murmured, rolling over in bed and wrapping his long ropy arm around Joey's chest.

Joey went completely still. "You're supposed to be asleep," he said stupidly, because they were. *All* his lovers were. Just because he'd obeyed the stupid compulsion to… to… *stalk* Gideon, to *fell* him, to *devour* him, that didn't mean there would be conversation afterward.

You didn't talk to your dinner, particularly not after it had been enjoyed.

But Joey should have known better.

When he'd been still mostly a child, learning those long-ago lessons of stealth and deadly intent, he'd once gone missing in the woods for three days. He'd been staying with his grandfather for a week; the one concession his father had made to how Joey had grown up had been letting Joey go to the reservation on school holidays.

They'd gone on an outing, and Joey had simply vanished from his grandfather's side, because that was how it had always been with them. His grandfather, knowing Joey, had simply continued to track Joey as Joey tracked a mountain lion through the woods. Joey had wanted to see it kill, watch it prey, study the techniques.

His grandfather, comfortable in Joey's woodcraft, knew that he could survive for far longer. He had a canteen, water purifying tablets, a small tent, a formfitting shearling cocoon to sleep in. But old Joe would still track him, to make sure.

In the end, Joey had watched without passion as the mountain lion took down an elderly deer, quickly, cleanly, and without malice. He'd seen the thing feed, and then drag the deer by the haunches back to his den.

He'd hiked back to his grandfather's house then, and when his father—who had been alarmed when he couldn't make contact with his son—had greeted him with drama and fury, Joey had simply shrugged.

"I wanted to see how a real predator kills," he said. "Not one who kills for money or show."

His father, who had been in mid rant, hand raised as it often was in anticipation of violence, took a step back and swallowed, reassessing his quiet, wayward illegitimate son with newer, harder eyes.

"What did you learn?" he asked, chest still heaving.

"Even if you enjoy the kill, you don't celebrate it over the cooling corpse," Joey replied, eyes even.

His father swallowed again and dropped his hand. "When do you celebrate it?" he asked, and he was cocking his head as though trying desperately to hear something funny in their exchange.

"When your belly is full and your family is safe," Joey had replied.

His father had taken another step back and then had simply taken Joey home to the daunting mobster's mansion on the other side of the res. Shortly after that, Joey had been enrolled in military school, and while he and his grandfather had written, his trips to the vast wilderness of the reservation were over until Joey had joined the military and had been selected for Special Forces training after only two years.

By then he had killed. By then he'd become good at it. And he'd learned that rule—lived by it, in fact, both in his personal life and his professional one.

He'd been scenting Gideon Chadwick for a year and a half now, since he'd been recruited for the SCTF. At first he'd seen the tall, angular man with the hatchet-thin face and the nose like a knife blade and thought, "Deer. He's obviously a deer." He'd expected Gideon to haunt the home base and radio in ops info.

He remembered how stunned he'd been on their first case, when he'd found Gideon standing, dripping blood over the corpse of a killer who'd been impaled on his own stiletto.

He felt that same sort of surprise now as Gideon pulled his body close.

"Do you think I'm stupid?" Gideon asked softly, rubbing his nose along Joey's ear.

Joey closed his eyes; the sensation was soft and sweet, and he wanted more.

"N-no." Uncertainty? No. This was absolutely not who he was. With every lover he'd ever had, he came, he took what he wanted, and he retreated to his lair and indulged in his conquest.

He conquered you.

Well, fine. So Chadwick had topped.

Joey didn't want to tell him how that had never happened before. It seemed so… so *inconsequential* to their coming together. But how would he know how he felt about it until he had a chance to roll the whole thing around in his head, retrace Gideon's path on his body with his own hands? He… he needed to *think* about it, and he couldn't do it with… with….

He moaned softly.

"You still want to go?" Gideon asked, and now his hand was moving languidly on Joey's chest. "I won't stop you."

"But… ah…." Joey's cock was starting to wake up, and he realized that he must have slept, because he was *clean*. God, how had he allowed this man access to his body while he'd dozed?

"You want to go?" Gideon's fingertips slid along Joey's hardening length. "Go." One of them toyed with the end, with the pre that was already dripping the tiniest bit. "Just roll out of bed and go."

Joey gasped and moved his own hand down to wrap around Gideon's, both of them stroking his cock while Joey spread his legs and pressed his feet against the mattress, arching up against their hands.

Chadwick nibbled on his neck again, lowered his mouth to Joey's nipple and licked, and Joey wasn't thinking about leaving anymore, about indulging in his full belly after his feast.

Oh, fuck it all, he was *starving* again, and when Chadwick rolled between his spread thighs and made himself at home, Joey had no option, none, but to welcome his cock—an amazing piece of equipment, that, thick and long like all of Gideon's substance was there in that one part of his body—as it thrust inside.

Joey, who preferred his sex silent, intense, his own quiet banquet, cried out and then silenced his sounds with his mouth to Gideon's chest.

He tried not to bite, failed, and Gideon simply fucked him harder.

And harder.

They cried out together as the crest took them, and Joey wanted to sob as he felt the slick heat of come inside his body once again.

He wanted to trap it there, keep it, stay filled with it, because even as he felt himself drop off to another unguarded sleep, he knew that hunger, that need to be filled, would be waiting for him when he awakened.

Oh God, how had he not known *he* was the deer?

GIDEON'S BODY had never been so sated. He lay in the predawn chill coming through the window and wondered if he should let Joey leave this time.

Sure. Why not? They would be meeting for work again. Crosby was down for the count. It was their job to show Garcia the ropes.

Nothing had changed there, although everything, *everything* had changed here, in Gideon's bed.

He'd let Joey go, meet him in the office, let his eyes roam where his hands had taken liberties, and keep all his sly jokes, his dirty innuendo, to himself until….

Oh God.

Until it was them alone again. Together.

He allowed Joey to slide off the bed this time, to disappear into the bathroom, to dress. And then he waited.

Come on, Joey—what's it going to be? The door? The window? The door? The window? One says you acknowledge this was a thing that happened once, says you're hoping to keep it hidden, even from yourself.

So when Gideon heard that indecision, that moment of hesitation as Joey emerged from the bathroom, he knew what the kid was thinking. And when he—predictably but sadly—reached for the window, Gideon let out a sigh, thinking he'd hoped for better, for easier.

But he could keep his own counsel, right? He'd been looking at Carlyle from under hooded eyes, thinking, *That kid is out of my league, but my God is he beautiful*, for a long time.

A year and a half.

They could dance some more, right?

He thought he'd resolved to do that, so his own voice, coming low and imperious as he feigned sleep, surprised him as much as Joey.

"Grab my keys so you can bring coffee when you return."

"What?"

He smiled but kept his eyes determinedly closed. "You're not coming to my bed like that and not bringing me coffee in the morning, Joey. I like caramel."

"Chocolate," Joey snapped, and Gideon opened his eyes and saw that he was irritated.

"Good," he said softly. "If you know what kind of coffee I like, next time you can just get it and come back to bed."

He saw that lean mouth part, probably to argue, to pretend, to push back.

"Fine," Joey said, the bafflement in his voice gratifying. "Where are your keys?"

"The bowl by the door," Gideon murmured. "I'll take a breakfast sandwich too. I'll be showered when you get back. We can go in and do paperwork today so we're ready to train Garcia on Monday."

Gideon heard him stomp his way through the apartment and then let himself out through the front door. He left the window open, in case Carlyle was tempted not to return, though—what had happened the night before was really too important not to show his throat.

Let the Wolf Choose

THAT FIRST time was easy, like an accident. Gideon wandered into his room one night and there Joey Carlyle was, in his bed, waiting for him to be done with whatever people were there.

Gideon frequently got the idea that other people were not quite real to Joey Carlyle. The team was—but Gideon had seen that happen step by step as Joey began to feel affinity, then affection, then protectiveness and a fierce loyalty for everybody on the team. Gideon was real because he was on the team, but Gideon had a feeling, a nagging gut instinct, that Gideon wasn't real to Joey as a *lover* after one roll in the hay, no matter how insistent Gideon had been on the morning after.

So the first time was easy, but the second would take more finesse. Gideon had to seduce a man without touching him, without making eye contact, without flirting. Not that Gideon was good at those things anyway, but he'd capitalized on a certain slow sideways glance or a deliberate quirk of his lean mouth to get a lover's attention. But Joey was a wolf—Joey was *the* wolf—and as with most wolves, the wrong touch, reaching too quickly, even just brushing the guard hairs at the ruff wrong, all of that could lead to the loss of fingers, or even a whole hand.

Or even a whole heart.

So the first time was easy, but the second time Gideon had to pretend like the first time never happened. He tried once or twice to nudge Carlyle into decision, but no dice.

"Don't forget you've got stuff at my place."

"Fuck off."

Oh. Okay, then.

"Do you like orange juice in the mornings?"

"How do you know I'll ever be at your place in the morning again?"

Oh. Well, then. Gideon had to find another way.

He waited patiently, knowing that Joey might be out sniffing other asses like a dedicated wolf might, but also knowing that Gideon already had an advantage. He was real to Joey Carlyle like most people weren't.

He held on to that, even knowing in the time that followed their first encounter (ha! First mauling, both physically and emotionally) that Joey might go sniffing in other lairs to make sure he hadn't made a mistake.

There were days—many of them—in the two weeks after their night together—when Gideon would scent the air, shiver, and rush to the window to see if he was there.

Most of the time, he wasn't, or Gideon only caught the sound of his footsteps on the wet or icy pavement below.

One night, though, Joey waited a breath too long before disappearing, and for a moment, they locked eyes, staring at each other in the distance between the third floor and the pavement, and Gideon could see it. Yearning. Gideon was *wanted.* Carlyle was *dying* for him.

But Joey, Gideon was sure, was very much afraid that one night had been a mistake.

Gideon would do anything to prove that they weren't a mistake.

So he kept his sideways glances and casual touches to himself, but he kept his ears alert for things that would make Carlyle particularly alert to Gideon.

When the thing came, Gideon almost missed it.

"Everybody, we caught one."

They'd just come off one, an emotionally grueling case of a political zealot, a man who had once been a beloved father, husband, baseball coach, killing a small-time politician and his family in their beds. The team had tried hard to take him alive—finding out where the crazy came from, making it public, was *so* important—but he'd had a semiautomatic weapon in a public place, and just the sight of Natalia and Garcia had made him fire randomly. Crosby, back from the hospital early but still on restricted duty, had been overwatch, and he'd been so fucking smart he'd stunned them all. On his direction, Joey had made the kill with one of his wicked knives, silently, and Gideon had seen then the way his boy could pull on pieces of his armor like tiny panels around his heart. He'd made the kill two days before, and that night he'd been caught outside Gideon's apartment.

If Gideon had half Joey's skill at tracking, he would have followed his bleeding wolf home.

But yesterday had been paperwork, and today had been physical training or cryptography classes—at least that's what had been on the roster.

Then Clint had shown up at briefing typing furiously on his tablet, his craggy face folded into a scowl of concentration. "No," he muttered. "That's our case. It is. Yes, it is. See? Yes, asshole, that's our case. Good. Now back off."

He said that last with a flourish of his fingers pounding out a message on the tablet and then glanced up at the expectant faces around him.

"So," he said, as though they hadn't all seen him fighting for turf. "We've had two kids disappear from a local LGBTQ shelter—fifteen and sixteen, both assigned male at birth, but trans. Their supervisor said that both kids were in full dress, very female in appearance, because they were going to a school dance. He's…." Clint looked up and swallowed. "He's afraid they might have been bullied, and the local law enforcement thinks that, and I'm quoting here, 'Any tranny in a dress is probably out tricking.'"

The unit sucked in an angry breath, and Clint nodded grimly. Special Crimes Task Force was there for all sorts of reasons—serial killers, fugitives on a spree, organized crime—but also, clearly stated in their mission statement, they were in charge of "crimes against marginalized persons or vulnerable communities." This meant that Gail—leg freshly healed—and Garcia had spent a week tracking down a poor Amish drug addict who'd just wanted to go home. And it meant that these two trans youths, who had probably been kicked out of the house and had landed in one of the most organized shelters in Brooklyn, were suddenly the two most important teenagers in the world.

"So this is definitely our case," he said in the silence. "Pearson, Crosby, you got five minutes to bring us up to speed."

Gideon used that time to get their two IT rats coffee, but found Calix Garcia was there first, black eyes snapping in a little circle of a face.

"I got Crosby," he said, as though he hadn't just joined the task force four weeks ago, in time for Crosby to get hurt.

Gideon let him, getting Gail's coffee without comment, making sure to use the special cat-with-a-knife coffee cup that was Gail's signature. He and Joey had called it that moment in bed that Garcia and Crosby were a thing. *They* might not know it yet, but Garcia's possessiveness was unmistakable.

Gideon yearned to be that possessive, but he knew he'd need both hands and all ten fingers to negotiate what was to come. Joey was smart, agile, and could plan ahead to take an objective, but true to most warriors, he didn't think of what came after: How does one occupy territory?

Gideon had to make his wolf occupy Joey's.

There were worse occupations to have.

His musings were interrupted by Joey at his elbow, taking the coffee carafe so he could brew another. "You got your eye on that?" he asked nonchalantly, as though the idea of hitting on Gail Pearson wasn't abhorrent, like sleeping with a sibling.

"No," he said shortly, adding cream and sugar. And then for spite, because he was stung, he added, "Work entanglements never work out."

He left Carlyle glaring at his back and sat down next to Crosby for the briefing. He'd missed Crosby's no-bullshit flatfoot perspective since he'd been out, and while Judson Crosby's wide cheekbones and blue eyes weren't really to his taste, hey, Crosby and Garcia weren't sleeping together *yet*, so he might as well piss *everybody* off today, right?

But then Crosby and Pearson launched into their spiel, and Gideon forgot about office lonely-hearts games and really focused on the two missing girls.

They'd been captured without makeup in one shot, both of them growing their hair long, plucking their brows, using moisturizer and toner to minimize their pores. And after a bare breath of adjustment, Gideon could see them—*see* them—for who they wanted to be. Two dark haired girls with squirrel-bright brown eyes and wide laughing mouths. The taller one looked a little sadder—there was something in her eyes that said this laughing moment wasn't easily found—and the smaller one held her hand over teeth that might have been crooked while biting her lip. Self-conscious, Gideon thought with an aching heart. Both of them self-conscious, a little afraid—like every other girl in high school, except these two girls had generations of hatred and ignorance to overcome every time they put on their makeup and fluffed their hair.

But God, they were pretty and happy and young.

Even happier in the next picture, which, Pearson pointed out, had been taken last night—hours before they'd disappeared. They were dressed in sequined party dresses with sleeves and appropriate wraps (so not like whooores, Garcia said bluntly, giving the extra-slutty *oos* to the word), and while Chadwick couldn't see them, he assumed they were wearing heels.

"I'm going to give you their deadnames in your briefing," Crosby said, "because we may have to deal with the parents who kicked them out, and you need to have that information. But to us, they're Tasha, to the left, and Arietty, on the right."

"I read those books when I was a kid," Gail said softly, and when they all looked at her, she said, "*The Borrowers*. It's about little people who steal things from the human world to live. Arietty was…." Her full mouth quirked. "She was feisty and smart, and the only person like herself that she knew."

"Oh," Natalia Denison said next to her, and they didn't need any elaboration after that. Poor Arietty.

Gail cleared her throat and went on, explaining how both girls had left for school that night, taking a bus to a dance at a nearby high school. While they attended school at the shelter, the high school aged students were often involved in activities at a larger public school, and the shelter administrator, Eli Engel, had assured the police that the girls had been welcome to the dance—and that they hadn't been a "surprise," as the officer taking his statement had intimated.

"It says here that the high school is very LGBTQ friendly," Gail read. "And it has a very strong antibullying policy—apparently Mr. Engel is something of a bulldog, trying to make sure his students have access to the high school amenities that the shelter doesn't have, but also that his kids stay safe."

"What did the principal of the other school say?" Garcia asked, sounding dubious.

"He said the same thing," Crosby told them. "But he said the girls didn't show. He was expecting them—they were coming early to help decorate—but when they didn't get off the bus, he called Engel to make sure they were on their way."

A diagram of the bus route popped up on their big screen, with a route penciled in. The high school was only ten blocks away. Most New Yorkers could walk that easy, Gideon thought in detachment, but the girls had been wearing heels and their best dresses. They hadn't wanted to arrive sweaty and messy when this had been a big deal to them.

"Two stops," Pearson said, using the tablet to put two dots on the map between where they'd gotten on and where they should have gotten off. "We've got two places to search, although both schools have had service groups canvassing the stops all morning. This place—" She tapped what on the map looked like a small series of alleys. "—is a nest of drug dealers and gang activity. It's actually a drug *mart*, one the police crash at least every two weeks, but I guess they do too much business to move it someplace else. We've advised Rainbow House to steer clear of that area—too many kids, too much danger. This other place"—she tapped the other stop—"has small shops lining both blocks—two small bodegas, one on either side of the street, a check cashing place, a cobbler, a diamond seller, and a watch repairman. Those are the street-level businesses. Most of them have two or three businesses in the upper levels before they become walkups."

"So lots of places for these two girls to get lost," Harding said.

"Yup," Pearson told him. "But the good news is there were a lot of long-term passes being used on the buses last night, so we've got a record of who boarded when. One of us," she said, looking at Crosby reprovingly, "can start calling people up to see if they spotted anything."

"And call up the security footage from the buses themselves first," Harding told him. "I'll send you the federal passcodes."

"Ooh," Crosby muttered. "Fancy."

"You're with the Feds now," Harding said dryly. "We pull out all the stops. Speaking of which, Pearson, you and Garcia go to the 12th and Whitcomb stop, and Denison and I will hit druggie central. Chadwick, Carlyle, you go to Rainbow House and see if there were any other kids going to the dance who might have seen anything. I know the cops might have asked them, but they might not have. It sounds like the locals are being assholes, and the shelter director is pretty protective of his kids. Crosby's running point from here, since he can't really run. And he needs to alert the hospitals and morgues so they know what to look for."

Gideon actually felt the air pressure in the room change.

"That's not the outcome any of us wants," Harding said softly. "But we've got to prepare for it. Everybody, good hunting."

And with that, everybody gulped what was left of their coffee, snagged a last pastry or bagel, and headed toward their weapon lockers before they went downstairs to the garage to claim their vehicles.

SCTF Lonely Hearts Hour was over, and they were at work now.

Crosby, who had been *very* nervous about taking overwatch duties, was actually *stellar* at his job, because they hadn't gotten more than two blocks when they got a call from Elaine.

"Hey, Gideon, long time no see!"

"Hey, Elaine," Gideon said in genuine pleasure over the SUV's intercom. "Good to hear from you." He hadn't seen her since the night of his get-together—the night Joey Carlyle had come to his bed and had obliterated the thought of any other potential partner from Gideon's mind.

"You have some time to talk?" Elaine asked, and Gideon risked a glance at Joey, who gave him an absolutely flat, expressionless face back.

"We're on our way to a call," Gideon apologized. "You caught us in transit. Elaine, Joey Carlyle. Joey, Elaine Aiello, Chief Medical Examiner of New York."

"We've met," Joey said, his voice as flat as his eyes. "What can Gideon do for you, Ms. Aiello?"

Gideon's eyebrows went up. Elaine might not recognize his very purposeful distancing, but *Gideon* did.

"That case you're checking out," she said. "The two trans girls in Brooklyn?"

"Missing for fourteen hours," Gideon recited, a chill in his stomach. "We're heading to interview the LGBTQ shelter right now."

"I'd suggest you detour here," Elaine said, no nonsense. "I don't have your girls, for which I'm grateful, but I do have a body that came in last week and hasn't been claimed, and you might want to take a look."

Next to him, he felt Joey's active hostility begin to ebb away.

"We'll be there in ten," he said, and Joey—who wasn't Catholic in the least—crossed himself.

"Oh God," he muttered. "Here it comes. And I thought Crosby was bad."

"Crosby *is* bad," Gideon muttered, slamming on his brakes, taking a hole on his left, and racing to cut in front of a car four cars ahead of where they'd just been. "I'm *good*. And I'm faster than Crosby!"

They made it in seven, and the smoldering hostility from Carlyle had completely disappeared.

IF THIS bitch put her hand on Chadwick's sleeve one more time, Joey was going to stuff her in her own goddamned hurt locker.

Elaine Aiello was lovely, blond, fortyish, which put her a few years older than Chadwick, but most people wouldn't notice the difference. She had a charming smile, kind manners, and was *very* concerned over SCTF's missing girls.

And she had reason to be, Joey grudgingly admitted after he saw the body.

The girl's makeup had been smeared off her face when she'd been brought in, and her wig had been ripped off, as had her corset, leaving bleeding crescents on the thin, breastless chest where the underwires had dug in. She'd been anally violated, and her genitals had been taped to her thighs with duct tape, which had been torn off brutally, ripping hair and skin.

Aiello's compassion for her dead victim was absolutely heartbreaking to witness, which was the only reason Carlyle *hadn't* killed her yet.

"She showed up a week and a half ago," Aiello said, covering the body and asking her dieners to return it to its spot in the refrigerator racks. The drawers were for active cases. The racks were awaiting identification or disposal. It wasn't pretty—or dignified—but it was a small bit of land with a lot of dead bodies, and space was at a premium. "COD, asphyxia."

"Manner of death?" Chadwick asked, seeming to ignore the way her hand rested on the bend of his elbow as he tapped notes into his phone.

"It appears as though her face was held in sand," Aiello said. "Which is a horrible, horrible way to die. But I brought you in because it looks as though she'd been held and abused for a good two days—or a gawdawful two days—and that could give you a small window to find your missing girls. Also because the sand is specific, and I'll send my lab results to your point man when they come back in an hour."

"You really put a fire under the lab," Gideon said in pleased surprise.

"The minute I saw your case run across my feed," she verified, and her swallow of anguish was very real. "My youngest sibling was trans," she said softly. "He… he walked into a bar for a drink, and somebody spotted his binder and…." She shook her head. "He died two days later of a brain hemorrhage, and my parents buried him under his deadname. This hits close. Nobody's looking for her," she said, her eyes overfilling, and Carlyle hated her even more because he didn't hate her at all.

He disappeared for a moment, running out of the cold room to the vending machines, and he came back with a water as she and Gideon were entering the corridor.

"Here," he said, producing a bit of toilet paper he'd grabbed while he'd been at it. "Sorry. Couldn't find any tissues."

"There's some in my office," she said, her voice clogged as she took the tissues. "But thank you. That's kind." She wiped her eyes carefully and blew her nose, then accepted the water. "Both of you—I know you've got to run, but let me know if I can do anything else."

"Where was the body found?" Gideon asked.

"Under the carousel at Adventure Park," she responded. "It was shipped to Manhattan because they don't have any special-victims facilities or personnel."

"We've gotten that impression," Carlyle growled. "Our victims disappeared from Bed-Stuy, and the officer who took their guardian's statement was—"

"A piece of work," Aiello confirmed. "Yeah, my friend who works in Bed-Stuy wanted better for our girl in there." She gave a weak smile. "And lucky me, I got you guys." Her smile dimmed. "Bring them home, okay?"

"We'll do our best," Gideon said and kissed Aiello on a messy cheek.

Then he turned, and Joey stuck to his heels as he strode toward their vehicle, already on the phone with Crosby to alert the rest of the team.

Crosby really *was* efficient running point. Fifteen minutes after they were on their way to Bed-Stuy, he was back with coordinates. Garcia and Pearson had picked up their victims' scent at a diamond store, because somebody had seen a customer she'd remembered with two teenaged girls, both of them seeming "a little freaked out." The woman had looked up the customer's name and address—five blocks down the street from the diamond store and within walking distance of Adventure Park.

There was a construction site with a sand pit next door.

He lived in the basement of a walkup, and by the time Chadwick squealed his SUV to a halt and Joey found his stomach and his eyebrows, the other two units were in place.

Denison took point, Harding at her heels, while Pearson and Garcia took the back.

It was Chadwick, with his wandering eyes and amusement park brain that glanced up.

"Oh shit," he said softly. "Oh shit."

The girls, both of them, naked except for white cotton granny briefs with little flowers on them, were on the third-story ledge of the apartment building, backs against the wall, both of them terrified.

"Tell them to stay there," Joey muttered.

"You tell them," Chadwick snapped before giving his badge number and location to the local fire department.

So smart, Joey thought, before spotting his hand- and footholds, taking a running jump, and climbing the side of the crumbling building like a rock wall he just hadn't had the chance to practice on yet.

GIDEON TRIED to remember his words as he communicated with the fire department. Joey Carlyle in action was something special. His hard, fit body scaled that wall like a lizard's might, sinuous as a gecko, fluid muscle attaching itself to the nooks and crannies of the crumbling mortar and broken siding like he had claws instead of fingers.

A sound from the ground floor broke his trance, and he heard Denison call, "Watch him, he's going out the side!"

Gideon sprinted into position as a wriggling body slithered through the window from the underground apartment, small and slender and naked in the late fall chill.

This isn't the perp, he thought. *This is another victim.*

Still, he needed to stabilize the situation. He called out, "Law enforcement! Freeze!" as the figure ran through the narrow alley between buildings, helpless sobs issuing from a throat that sounded shredded with screaming.

"It's not the perp!" Gideon shouted. "Talia, it's a vic!"

"Got her!" Gail called, sprinting up alongside that shivering adolescent figure and—instead of tackling, placing her body between the shaking victim and Garcia, who was coming up behind.

"Fire department and EMTs are on the way," Gideon called, and then, inexorably, his vision was called up. "Denison, Harding, our girls are on the ledge.... *Fuck*!"

That last was because as he'd looked up, he'd seen Joey scrabbling onto the ledge with the girls on it to find his footing just as another figure, fiftyish or so, male, in a cardigan and corduroy pants, of all things, fell halfway out of the once-sealed window that the girls had crawled out of.

Gideon couldn't hear much from the three-story distance, but he could almost make out shouting, ranting, spittle flicking from the attacker's lips as the girls huddled on their ledge, unable to move farther away because of a crenelation they couldn't step around, and so close to the attacker they could probably smell his breath.

Joey was edging on the ledge from the other side as the fire department, sirens down like Gideon had demanded, pulled onto the street.

They couldn't use the ladder, Gideon thought, because their attacker was up there, a knife in his hand, lashing out toward the girls.

Joey shouted something, and the man glanced at him but kept his focus on the two victims, seemingly too crazed to recognize a threat. And then, while Gideon watched, horrified, Joey ceased to *be* a threat. The ledge under his feet broke off, and he lunged for the window as he fell, seizing on it with one hard hand and dangling like a heroine in a Stallone movie.

Now he had their perpetrator's attention.

Gideon had his weapon out before the man could bring the knife down on Joey's head, and the shot rang out before he knew he'd aimed.

Overbalanced, the body toppled over and out the window, landing on the pavement with a sick sort of thud/crackle/plop as firefighters setting up the emergency airbag dodged out of the way.

Gideon was the one who broke the stunned silence by shouting, "They're still up there! Fuck the body and get that thing out!"

It took minutes to position but only seconds to inflate, and Gideon looked up and shouted, "Tasha! Arietty! Hold on! Carlyle, hold on!"

But the ledge wasn't that strong to begin with, and the smaller of the two girls, the one closest to Joey, lost her footing as the mortar crumbled. She would have fallen on top of the laboring firemen, but Carlyle caught her with his free hand, and for a perilous moment they dangled, while Gideon's heart threatened to freeze in his chest.

There was a *whoomp*! Almost as loud as an explosion, and the airbag was in place. As Gideon stared up at the third floor, spots swimming in front of his eyes, he felt rather than saw the others drawing near. Pearson had handed off her victim to the EMTs to be checked over and given aid for shock and, God, everything else, and together, he and his team stood, eyes glued to the spectacle in fear.

But the airbag was the climax. With some coaching, Joey flung the girl holding on to his hand out and then let her go. She fell onto her back, like she was supposed to, after windmilling her limbs. Arietty was pulled off the bag, and then Tasha went, a simple jump, her descent more controlled and less panicked.

Carlyle struggled for another handhold, found it, and then *pushed* off the wall, executing a neat back flip before landing solidly on his backside, limbs extended.

Next to him, Gideon heard Clint muttering, "Fucking show-off," and Natalia say, "I'll fucking kill him."

Garcia said, "Righteous!" and Gail said, "Not one of you tell Crosby about that. Not one."

And Gideon almost passed out, because Carlyle was getting helped off the bag, and suddenly he could breathe again, and the oxygen made him dizzy.

DEBRIEFING THE victims at the hospital was painful.

Gideon could see them reliving that moment on the bus, when they went from "happy and excited" for something as simple as a school dance—one where they'd be welcomed and feel as though they belonged—to the absolute simplicity of terror.

Crosby had sent them footage of one Morten Donald Johns thrusting a knife against Tasha's ribs and whispering in Arietty's ear.

"What did he say to you there?" Natalia asked softly. "We just need to know what the threat was."

"He said," Arietty whispered, "that he'd gut her. He'd stick the knife through her ribs to her heart."

"That's really scary," Natalia told her, and Gideon could see the mom in her coming out for this. "You were really brave."

"Is Greta all right?" Arietty asked, her voice breaking. "She was there before us… she was in a bad way. He'd… he'd killed her friend, and she was… we had to keep her from… from…."

"Hurting herself?" Gail asked. Both the women had seen their roles and moved in quickly, surrounding the girls with nonthreatening energy and genuine kindness.

"Yeah." Tasha started to cry then, and she and Arietty clung together for a moment while the nurses and a trained psychologist moved in.

Their unit met outside the glass and briefly discussed what Crosby had turned up, as well as what they knew about the new victim.

Morten D. Johns had been, until two months earlier, a mild-mannered accountant who lived with his mother. The old woman, by all accounts, was a piece of work—bitter, vitriolic, prone to homo- and trans-phobic outbursts on the regular. Morten was heard to echo her while at the same time accessing porn on the internet that was… well, contrary to her beliefs was one way to put it.

"Hot tranny on tranny action" was how the internet site put it, and while Gideon wasn't one to kink-shame, he knew an unhealthy fixation on something forbidden when he saw it.

And then Morten's mother had died. He had been left alone, which was apparently a bad thing. All that repressed self-loathing, all that screaming id, none of the social skills that some decent parenting might have given him, and Morten was abducting his favorite candy from buses and—now that the nearly vacant walkup was all his—he was doing with them what he wanted.

Greta was the nearly naked victim who had escaped from an impossibly small window, gone screaming into the alley, and—fortunately for her—straight into Gail Pearson's arms. She'd needed sedation and clothes and to be treated for everything from dehydration to the consequences of being violently assaulted for several weeks without aftercare.

She was currently on twenty-four-hour watch, with a seasoned rape counselor crocheting in her room and another one prepared to take her shift.

Maybe in a couple of weeks, the SCTF would interview her to finish their paperwork, but that was going to wait until she was well enough to talk.

When she was, they'd tell her what they'd told Tasha and Arietty when they'd asked about the fate of one Morten D. Johns.

Gideon's shot to Johns's forehead had killed him immediately, but even if it hadn't, he wouldn't have survived the three-story headfirst fall. And even if he had, when the airbag had been deployed on top of the body, it had broken every bone he possessed in the series of mini explosions that activated the giant airbag in seconds.

So Morten D. Johns had been a grotesque raping monster, but he was dead now. Very, very dead. And they would do their best to make sure his surviving victims would grow up to live their best lives. Johns would not be mourned.

Tasha, Arietty, and Greta would be *celebrated.*

It wasn't great comfort at the moment, but hopefully someday it would help.

And then it was time to return to HQ and fill out their action reports. Gideon would be on desk duty for a week or two while his use of force was investigated, but Harding had sort of a magic touch for pushing that paperwork through.

It helped that he tended to recruit assassin (or assassin-adjacent) personalities for his task force, though. The odds of one more kill pinging Gideon's conscience were slim to none. Gideon wasn't losing any sleep over Johns's death—he knew that for a fact.

That moment Johns raised the knife over Carlyle's head, however?

Oh yeah. That would be waking him up in a cold sweat for a long, long time.

After a few hours of paperwork, Gideon asked to check out a vehicle and said he'd drive himself and Carlyle home. No big deal—he'd done this before.

But Carlyle knew something was up.

"What's up?" he asked, sounding uncertain, a rarity for him.

"Nothing," Gideon said shortly.

"Are you really going to take me to my apartment?" he asked cagily.

"Not a fucking chance," Gideon replied calmly. He hadn't even had to think about that one.

"I'll walk home," Joey said, like he was trying to be nonchalant.

"Funny you would think so." Gideon's voice sounded strange to his own ears. Disassociated. Detached. "I don't see that happening."

"Gid?"

Gideon heard it then—a tremble. An uncertainty. Knowing what he did about Joey's father, Gideon had to take a deep breath and pull up the words to reassure them both.

"We're almost there," he said. His place had paid parking, and they'd left early enough for Gideon to have a spot. "I've got food in the fridge." He did—lunch meat, some tomatoes and onions, pickles and condiments. Bread, even.

But neither of them was dependent on food.

Gideon was aware of the nervous glances Joey cast in his direction as they tromped up the stairs, and a part of him was thinking, *This isn't smart. This is so not smart. You were going to dance. You were going to let him seduce you. Let him choose.*

He can choose. But he needs to know what he's choosing.

They got through the door, and Joey said, "Gid?" and Gideon whirled him around, his back to the door, and held him there, their breath mingling, his hands shaking on Joey Carlyle's shirt.

"You terrified me," he hissed, and for a moment, he thought Joey was going to try it, that sly grin, that "The danger is the joke!" smile.

But Joey swallowed instead. "You had my back," he said softly.

"I will *always* have your back," Gideon ground out. "Do you understand? If we're sleeping together, if we're not, as long as I'm alive, I will have your back. That's not what this is."

"What is it?" Joey asked, no smile at all. Deadly serious.

"You will choose me, or you will walk away," Gideon told him. "But you will not taunt me. My heart froze. My breath, my blood—the only thing that worked was my gun hand. If I am going to be that terrified, I need to know who you are to me. Either way it's fear, but I need to know what kind."

Joey tilted his head back as though he was savoring the contact, the bare hint of violence, Gideon's fury.

"I will never walk away," Joey said, like it was a dare, and that was the end of Gideon's restraint.

His mouth on Joey's was hard, furious, without mercy. His hands, ripping away the clothes, leaving Joey Carlyle's fine golden body naked down to his boots, were hard and without hesitation.

"With my boots on?" Joey tried to tease, but Gideon, who was kicking off his own shoes—a sort of oxford/walking boot crossbreed—couldn't return the jibe.

"On or off," he panted, dropping his sport coat on the ground and fumbling with his belt. "As long as I'm inside you."

He heard a small welcoming whimper from Joey's throat, and somehow the boots disappeared.

"Where are you going?" Joey complained as Gideon stalked toward the bedroom.

"There's lube in here," Gideon called back, and when Joey snarled, "*Fuck lube*!" Gideon turned to scowl at him.

"No, Joey. We will use lube. And care. And tenderness. If you are choosing me, I'm not going to abuse that choice. Do you understand? Not even if I want to fuck you so bad I can't breathe."

Joey beat him to the bed, scrabbling for the lubricant as Gideon finished dropping his clothes.

He turned to find Joey Carlyle ass up, his fingers deep in his own asshole as he spread the lubricant, groaning with pleasure.

Gideon was just hard and angry enough to take him that way, thrusting inside brutally, leaning forward to pull him up by the throat and pressing his front along Joey's back while embedded deeply in his flesh.

"You chose me," he growled.

"Yes," Joey gasped.

"Then don't scare me. Don't tease me." He punctuated the orders with thrusts.

"No," Joey panted. "I won't."

"When you want me, come in."

"I will!" Gideon thrust extra hard. "Gid, I swear, I'll come… come in… oh God, I'm gonna come…."

Gideon released his throat and pushed down with a hand on his back and fucked him brutally, still angry and scared and needy. Beneath him, Joey groaned, spasming around Gideon's cock while he came, and it was almost enough, not quite enough, Gideon was going to… going to….

The sound Joey made then was not quite human, a deep groan of surrender, of giving, and inside his body, his flesh softened, relaxed, *bloomed* around Gideon's cock, and suddenly Gideon was there.

His vision washed white, and his fingers tightened on Joey's hips, and a cry that felt like it was ripped out of his chest with barbed wire sounded in the still apartment around them.

"Dammit!"

He had no idea what it meant, but his orgasm took over, shaking him hard, pouring his entire heart into Joey Carlyle whether he'd planned to hold back or not.

It didn't matter what he'd planned. He fell forward, clutching his lover to his chest in the cool autumn chill of the apartment, their naked bodies clammy with sweat.

Their breath sounded strange in that stillness, and for a moment Gideon wanted to cry with shame. It was clear now that Joey had thought he was safe, and Gideon—God, had he just betrayed what he wanted most?

"I knew it," Joey said, speaking into the void.

"What?" Gideon was still holding him close, praying he wouldn't try to wiggle away, because after what they'd just done, Gideon would have to let him.

"I knew it." With a grunt, Joey backed up against him, snuggling in, accepting Gideon as the big spoon. Gideon reached below him, grabbed the throw from the foot of his bed, and pulled it up to keep them warm for a few more moments while they were still joined.

"Knew what?" Gideon asked, running his lips over Joey's shoulder because he couldn't help himself.

"Knew you were the wolf," Joey said dreamily. "Knew you were the wolf. I've never been the prey before. But I knew you were the wolf."

And there they were. In the strange language of hunter and hunted, one that Gideon understood.

He licked the sweat from the back of Joey's neck and then bit him softly, enjoying Joey's faint, "Ah!" of pain and pleasure.

"I don't know who you're kidding," Gideon whispered in his ear. "But we're both the wolf."

In his arms, Joey Carlyle shook hard. Orgasmic aftermath—or anticipation. As Gideon hardened inside him, he realized it could be both.

Joey grunted and bore down, squeezing him harder. "Fuck me, wolf," he dared.

Gideon closed his eyes for an instant, now seeing how trapped he was—how trapped they both were.

And his hips started moving, and he started mating once more.

FINALLY, *FINALLY*, their passion eased. They may have slept, but Gideon, true to those years in the military, was immediately awake and in the present when he felt Carlyle try to slip out of bed.

His arm tightened around Joey's stomach, and Joey grunted. "I swear to Christ, Gid, I just have to pee."

Gideon sighed away some of his panic. "Okay," he conceded. "I'll go when you're done."

When he got back, Joey had a bag of pita chips and some hummus on a towel on the bed. Gideon raised an eyebrow, and Joey glared at him.

"Yes, I'm a barbarian. No, I don't always eat in bed, but…." He glanced away. "I wasn't sure if you'd let us eat on the couch."

Gideon shivered. "Grab some sweats," he murmured. "We haven't eaten all day."

A short time later, they were both sitting cross-legged on the floor, the coffee table laden with snacks, including a bowl of microwaved popcorn, something Gideon had only begun keeping when Joey had started coming over to his place and asking for it.

After eating in silence for a few, Joey started talking as though they'd never stopped.

"I… the one time I had a girlfriend," he said, his voice low, "my father paid one of his men to seduce her—or assault her, I never knew which—and get her pregnant. Her parents were too scared to press charges. But you… you learn really quick not to get attached. Every encounter—you stalk, you fall, you eat, you walk away." He shrugged. "My grandfather taught me how to hunt. He made it… honorable, I guess. I tried to be honorable." His voice had a note of pleading in it, and Gideon got it.

"No strings, no promises, everybody knows what they're getting," he said, and Joey nodded, relieved. "That's a hard way to live."

He'd meant it to comfort, but the expression on Joey's face was suddenly stripped bare.

"I didn't mean to taunt you, Gid," he said, staring at Gideon's face with naked begging now. *Please understand me. Please.* "I just didn't know how to ask for more than that."

Gideon nodded and leaned into Joey's space, relieved when Joey leaned back.

"We can't do this if we don't trust each other in the bedroom the same way we trust each other in the car," he said gently. Joey shifted a little, but that was only to lean closer. "Do you trust me?"

"In the car, yeah," Joey said, and Gideon nodded, thinking he'd take it. It was a place to start.

"What are you afraid I'll do here, flesh to flesh?"

Joey made a sound then, a grunt of terrible fear. "You don't know what he could do," he whispered.

Gideon nodded. "I've been studying up, Joseph Carlyle. Believe me, I know exactly what I'm getting into."

Joey pulled back and stared at him skeptically. "You've said that," he said. "I don't think you can get what you need from—"

But Gideon wouldn't apologize, not for this. "You were very candid in your interview with Clint. The DOJ doesn't want to touch your father with a barge pole because he's got his finger in too many illustrious asses, but we know who he is." Gideon regarded him compassionately, but levelly too. Joey was too smart to jerk around. "Stevie Carlyle is a functioning sociopath, and he's wanted for a fair number of killings, some of which we think he's done himself. We *know*. And I know who *you* are. You may not be great at relationships, Joey, but you *are* an honorable man."

Joey's cheekbones and the slight cant to his sepia-colored eyes often made him seem inscrutable, but after a year and a half, Gideon could read the tilt to his chin, the sheen to his eyes, the slight—oh-so-slight—quiver to his lean lower lip.

"You believe that of me?" he asked, and the formality of the language was like a giant arrow pointing at Joey's heart, blinking "This is important!" in neon.

"After working with you for so long?" Gideon asked, continuing to lean, continuing to treasure the heat of Joey's body as he leaned back. "Of course."

"I'm not always nice," Joey whispered, still staring at the remains of their late-night feast on the coffee table.

"I know. Neither am I."

Joey gave him a quick glance. "I won't make this easy on either of us."

"Just remember what I said when we cleared the door," Gideon told him, and suddenly his heart was pounding in his ears.

"I won't taunt you," Joey said softly, and his lean body softened, became pliant. "I won't betray you."

Gideon let out a laugh that was almost a grumble. "I had honestly never thought about you doing that," he said. "Just remember, Joey—I know what you grew up with. I've profiled men like your father before. As much as you might think you're damaged beyond repair, *I* know, you're more human than most people parented by monsters. I know who's been in my car, I know who's in my bed. We're both the wolf, Joey. If you will trust me not to turn on you, I will trust you with my life and my bed. It works both ways."

Gideon felt the tremble where their arms touched, and he couldn't help himself. He wrapped his arm around Joey's shoulders and drew him close, nuzzling his cheek, where he found telltale dampness, and nuzzling his neck, where Joey's pulse throbbed.

"I'm so tired," Joey whispered. "I couldn't sleep all month."

Oh, baby. "Let's clean up and go to bed," he said. "Tomorrow we'll get up and go to work like we always do. And we'll be us, like we always are. This is my den, Joey. You are always welcome."

Joey let out a strained chuckle. "Maybe make me a key. I hate that you've been leaving your window open."

Gideon grunted. "I hate that you wouldn't come in," he muttered.

"I'll come in from now on," Joey said. "I promise."

Gideon nodded, and tiredly they got up and began to clean. Their bodies were replete now, and their hearts were eased.

Sleep came swiftly, and if either of them dreamed, they were wolfish dreams that needed no words.

WHEN SNOW COATS THE GROUND

JOEY UNDERSTOOD that in many families, people keep time by the events in the family. September was when everybody had a birthday, or April was when somebody was expecting, and the entire year hinged around those moments.

September was when Garcia arrived and Crosby got shot, and Joey had to accept another person into their family—and worry about the brother he already had.

September was when he'd first slunk his way into Gideon Chadwick's bed, and Gideon had mastered him there, not just *fucked* him—and damned well—but *mated* with him.

Possessed him. Kept him. Had given Joey haven, safety, home.

Joey hadn't had a home—a real home—since he was eight years old.

He wasn't sure what to do with it. He wasn't expected to spend every night there, was he? Their partnership was well established, but this other thing was in its infancy. Surely Gideon would need some nights to himself.

Every second or third night, Joey would say he needed space and spend the night in his apartment. He never slept those nights, simply lay awake in the bed that had come with the apartment, under the bedding that Gideon and Harding had bought him, and waited for something, anything, to break through his door.

For a year and a half, as he'd learned more about electronics, he'd set up his own surveillance in that apartment, had cameras, had alarms, and nothing had disturbed his sleep *then*.

Two nights with Gideon and it no longer felt like his den.

And right when he was starting to get a handle on why he was so jumpy, the thing happened that shattered all his peace.

They'd just hit a big case. Joey had made the kill this time, with a crossbow in a cemetery while Crosby had distracted the killer, a man about to annihilate his entire family with a 9mm in his daughters' brains after he'd already done the same for their mother. Joey had spent the night in his apartment—he'd been closer to the scene when Crosby caught it, and Gideon had taken overwatch from the office since he'd only just arrived.

Joey had wanted him there so bad. Something about the silence of the crossbow bolt, the awfulness of what had almost happened, and even the cemetery plot—labeled the Island of Hope, a place for unidentified murdered children, of all things—had depressed Joey in ways he didn't think he *could* be depressed. Not after his childhood. Not after his adulthood, for fuck's sake. Not after all his internal bullshit about predators and prey.

It was beginning to dawn on Joey Carlyle that sometimes you were neither the wolf nor the deer. Sometimes you were just a human fucking being depressed by what other human fucking beings could do to each other.

So he was in the back of the SUV as they returned to the office—via the nearest food venue, since Garcia professed to be hungry and Joey knew Gideon often went without food in the morning—when his phone buzzed.

He glanced at it numbly, for once looking forward to the time off after a weapons discharge or a kill, and thinking it might be Gideon with his order.

Come to the compound for Christmas.

Joey gaped. No return number, but there didn't need to be one.

Fuck off and lose this number.

Shit. He was going to have to requisition another fucking phone.

You think you're invisible? Your little unit is making waves. It's time to come home.

He sucked air in through his teeth. They hadn't made any explicit plans, but Gideon had said something about forgoing his trip to Pennsylvania this year to his stepmother's place so they could spend Christmas day… whatwuzit? Joey touched the face of his phone and remembered Gideon's nonchalant invitation.

We can eat good food, watch stupid Christmas movies. You know—give each other dumb presents. Pretend like we're normal. You think?

I dunno, Gid. What's a dumb present? I need specifics.

You ever play with Legos?

Joey remembered now, how he'd snorted and rolled his eyes, and Gideon had nodded like giving a grown man a Lego set was totally reasonable.

And for some reason, Joey had looked forward to that.

They'd had Thanksgiving at Natalia's house, and Joey and Crosby had spent the day playing with her two children to give Tal and her wife a break. They'd pretended to be choo-choo trains and bears while everybody else sat at the table and drank wine and adulted.

Joey had loved that. Loved the safety of the cubs rolling around on the carpet, loved the kindness of the adults, even loved the smell of wine on Gideon's breath when they'd gotten back to Gideon's apartment and fallen into bed.

But the idea of a holiday where *he* got to be the child, watching cartoons, opening "stupid presents," that had filled him with this sense of contentment he hadn't known he was capable of.

You don't know where my home is, he sent to his father now.

There was no response, and for a whole forty-five minutes, Joey believed he was safe.

Then, as he was exiting the elevator into the office, the rest of the unit in front of him, all of them bearing takeout bags, his phone buzzed again.

He managed to pass the bag absentmindedly to Gideon before he wandered to his desk, sank down, and checked his phone.

And swallowed.

There was a picture of his apartment building on his phone.

Granted, the picture was from a block away, and it was grainy, so it had been taken from probably farther away than that, but he knew what the picture intimated.

It said, "I do too know where your home is, and you're no longer safe there," in a way that left no mistaking the threat. And no proving it either.

Joey wiped a suddenly shaking hand across his face, and instead of seeing his father, he saw the crossbow bolt as it entered into their perpetrator's back that morning.

I'm a killer too.

He might have sat there forever, but a nonrecyclable food carton hit his desk with a thud, and Gideon stood there, staring at him with concern.

"What gives?" he asked quietly.

Joey swallowed and privately bid adieu to that promise of sleeping in with Gideon, watching movies, eating Gideon's food—which was always top notch—and opening a box of something stupid and wonderful and remembering what surprises were like. The good kind.

"I think," he said, smelling the food and feeling sick, "I need to visit my father over Christmas."

Gideon's eyes popped open. "Do you *want* to visit your father over Christmas?" he asked carefully.

Joey shook his head and showed him the picture on his phone. "Not particularly," he said.

Joey realized he'd never seen this expression on Gideon's face before. But after an entire day of Gideon waging a subtle campaign of "Let's ask Clint what he thinks," and "Maybe the unit would prefer you stay at my place for Christmas," he thought he might understand what it was.

This was Gideon Chadwick when he was afraid.

But the good news was that Gideon Chadwick, afraid, was just as smart as Gideon Chadwick, cool, calm, and analytical.

Joey had tried to detach himself at first. "I'll stay at my place from now on," he'd murmured that night as they'd headed for the garage. "You can drop me—"

"No," Gideon replied. "No."

Okay, then. "Gid, it's only a matter of time before he figures out where I'm spending my nights—"

"You change your habits now, he'll come looking for me," Gideon said shortly. "And I'm not letting you go there alone, not tonight."

Joey sighed. "I can't move into your apartment—not now."

Gideon had turned to him in the elevator, the fury on his face unmistakable. "Tonight, Joey. That's all I'm asking for. Tonight." He took a breath, and some of the fury relaxed. "I said I knew what I was getting into, Joey."

"But now you want out," Joey said with resignation, sagging against the back of the car.

Gideon's mouth on his, brutally, was not the answer he anticipated. But he responded, the hurt, the fear, the anger roiling in his gut unable to leave any room for hiding.

Everything—*everything*—was in that kiss, and Joey, heart, soul, *being* invaded with Gideon's surprising heat, clung to him in panic as he'd been afraid to cling to him with emotional need.

The kiss was over as quickly as it had begun, leaving Joey to pull his brains back inside his head as the elevator doors opened and they made their way through the lobby to hail a cab to the apartment.

Except Gideon didn't hail a cab. Apparently still pissed, he took off along the crowded sidewalk, Joey striding beside him.

Joey wanted to protest, say something like "All forty blocks?" but he didn't. They were both fit—Gideon was a runner, as unlikely as he looked, loping along in a ground-eating pace with those long slender legs. Forty blocks was not a hardship.

Joey kept pace, and after the first twenty blocks, Gideon's stride slowed a notch, became less fierce, less angry, and more accepting. His chest opened up enough that—had either of them been demonstrative at all—Joey could have seized his hand.

For the first time in his life since he was a child going shopping with his grandfather in the city, Joey wanted to hold somebody's hand.

The thought startled him, and he almost stumbled, but it burrowed in, making him yearn for something he'd never known he missed, almost consuming him as he followed Gideon up the stairs to the apartment, the corridor echoing with the voices of the other building residents as people prepared dinner or hurried out to eat.

By the time Gideon opened the door, his movements were calm, measured, thoughtful, and Joey realized that he'd needed the activity to work things out in his own head. The thought soothed Joey—he used physical activity to think too, and he often forgot how similar he and Gideon were about some things.

It meant Gideon wasn't angry at him.

Until that moment it hadn't occurred to him how much he relied on Gideon Chadwick's good opinion. That the foundation of his attraction—his *need*—for Gideon's touch was built in his rock-solid respect for Gideon's goodness and his intelligence and the thoughtful way he approached his fellow humans.

The thought drew him up short, and as he closed the door behind them, he leaned against it and tried to think about what he could do to not make this moment any more difficult than it was.

"I don't *want* to stop seeing you," he said into the sudden silence.

The face Gideon turned to him was—oh God—*hurt*, and he realized why people like his father hated empathy so damned much. Because when somebody you empathized with *hurt*, so did *you*, and that *sucked*.

But Joey didn't care—he'd feel this again and again if it meant he could keep walking through Gideon Chadwick's door.

"Then stop using that as an option," Gideon said, closing the distance between them.

Joey nodded and reached out a hand. He couldn't seem to stop himself, but that touching thing he and Gid had talked about was real—they *touched* behind Gideon's door, and it *meant* something to him.

Gideon didn't leave him hanging. He reached out and twined their fingers, and they drew close. Gideon leaned his forehead against Joey's, and Joey supported some of his weight as they sagged against the door.

"I don't want him to hurt you," Joey confessed, his chest raw.

"Same, Joey. Do you think I'm not afraid for you?"

Joey nodded. He'd known that. He may not have articulated it in his head, but he'd known that's why Gideon had been so angry.

"I can take care of myself there," he whispered. "I-I don't know how to take care of other people there. The only way to protect you, Gid, is to keep you secret." He flashed, then, to the long-ago case with Jay Arnold, protecting his poor barista. Gideon had been so much kinder than Joey would have been—but that's because Gideon had seen, even then, how sometimes what you wanted for your lover and what you had to offer were not the same thing.

Gideon nodded now and let out a sigh. "I don't want to be your secret," he murmured. "But we've been partners for a year and a half—nobody's going to question that we're close. We've both had other relation—" He paused, and Joey gave a green smile. "Sex partners," Gideon finished dryly. "The squad has no reason to think we've changed."

Joey put his hands on Gideon's hips and drew him even closer, until they were no longer leaning against the door but on each other, Joey with his head on Gideon's shoulder.

"Just stay safe, Gid," Joey begged.

"You too," Gideon said. "Or…. God, Joey. Do you really have to go?"

"Yeah. But only for a few days." Joey raised his face for a kiss, a thing he never thought he needed but had come to crave.

Gideon didn't leave him hanging, lowering his head and taking Joey's mouth with an aching tenderness Joey couldn't ever remember being touched with.

"And not now," Joey whispered, pulling back for a moment to smooth his hands through Gideon's perpetually tousled hair.

"Not now," Gideon echoed and bent his head to take Joey's mouth again.

"YOU HAVE to go?" Gideon asked for the umpteenth time as they strode through the slush toward the subway that would take them to the train station. They each had their packed duffels over their shoulders, and Gideon wondered if anybody else could spot the military in the two of them, the way they carried their duffels, the way they marched. The synchronicity that had dogged them since Joey Carlyle had come pounding down the steps trying to shoot a stockbroker about to stab Gideon in the eye with a stiletto.

"If this goes south fast, I'll be at your place when you get back," Joey said, sidestepping Gideon's question about their Christmas destinations easily.

Gideon's place. Of course he'd be at Gideon's place.

Joey and Gideon had made a couple of trips to Joey's apartment since Joey had been texted, ostensibly to get something Joey needed for work, in the middle of the day, or after work on the way out to a venue, including the office Christmas party. Twice with Harding—and twice Harding had gone without them—to install new security attached to *all* their phones and sporadically timed lights to make it look as though Joey's hours were so demanding that was the reason he was seldom there.

Of course Gideon had clued Harding in about Joey's visit to his father. For one thing, since Stephen Carlyle was well known for illegal and dangerous activities, it was important Joey be aboveboard about his interactions so he didn't get suspicion thrown on *him*, but for another? Gideon wanted help with this one, and since his former CO was across the country hunting monsters, Harding was his best bet. And a good, good friend.

A friend who didn't ask too many questions when asked to pick up spare sets of clothes for Joey so he could stay at Gideon's one more night than planned.

Not that Carlyle didn't have plenty of clothes at Gideon's already. In the months since Garcia had arrived at the SCTF and Joey had ended up in Gideon's bed, Joey's clothes had been… well, everywhere in Gideon's apartment. In drawers where Gideon kept tablecloths, hanging behind the valances in the living room. Three days before, Gideon had gone to pull down his duffel so it would be packed as soon as their leave came due, and he'd found three pairs of boxer briefs, black, microfiber, sized M.

Gideon wore size large tighty-whities himself.

Like so many things about what they'd been doing since the fall, Gideon had said nothing about it. He'd simply taken the underwear, put it in a drawer he'd emptied, and gone about his business.

The next morning he'd found one of Joey's T-shirts doubling as a plant doily.

"It will get dirty here," he told Joey, and draped it on the back of the chair, in place of the runner that normally went there.

He'd… oh God. He'd been so looking forward to spending the holidays with Joey Carlyle. Two Christmases they'd been partnered, and once they'd worked, giving Natalia the night off, and once Joey had spent the time getting laid and Gideon had spent it at his father's. Not once had Gideon had somebody special (and wasn't *that* a tepid word?) he wanted to spend a holiday with, somebody he wanted to see light up with simple things like kids' movies or a dumb present, and God, wasn't Joey Carlyle all the things he'd want in a Christmas lover?

But then Joey had gotten that fucking text, and all those visions had dissipated like the bubbles in flat champagne. Gideon had accepted his father and stepmother's invitation to their second home outside of Philly and told Joey that if he managed to get away early, he could join Gideon there.

"Or you could come back to Manhattan," Joey said stonily, although Gideon recognized by now that he was trying to mask the hurt of having to give up the same dream Gideon had cherished.

"I *like* my family," Gideon told him, hoping for gentleness. "My stepmother hates red meat, and she's making a *roast*, medium rare, on Christmas Eve. That's a big deal to her, Joey—I can't shit on that."

Joey frowned, his funk palpable.

"You could just not go," Gideon said now, for the three-thousandth time.

"My father's dangerous," Joey repeated bluntly. "And he has 'business' to talk to me about, as you very well know. I told you I don't want you anywhere near it. It would be like inviting you into a viper pit."

Gideon wondered for the thousandth time how much of a thing they were. Joey Carlyle's *stuff* was *all over* his apartment. If any of their friends walked in on any given day, they'd *know* somebody was sleeping there, and since they all knew Joey wore trendy, tailored, and pricey, they'd know *who* was sleeping there, and the jig would be up.

Gideon didn't care. Joey was *so* out of his league. Every moment that feral forest creature decided not to shift his den from his apartment back to his bare stone woodland abode was a moment of PFM, as the Navy called it.

Pure Fucking Magic.

"I've been in viper pits," Gideon said, hoping for a last-minute reprieve, a chance to accompany Joey, a chance to protect him. "True story. Took a trip to India when I was in college." He shuddered. "Took all sorts of antivenin before I went in, and had a hook and a slipknot handle thing when I walked in. Steel-toed boots, leather chaps—"

"Are you trying to turn me on?" Carlyle asked, sounding bored, but he was giving Gideon a sideways glance, as if to assess whether or not Gideon would *really* wear chaps.

"Not the assless kind, and no tassels anywhere," Gideon said dryly. "Get your mind out of the gutter. I'm making an analogy here."

"That if you've taken your anti-snake juice, you'll live," Joey retorted. "Yes, I get it. No, I don't want you to jump in the pit with me."

"I'd have your back, Joey," Gideon said, his hurt surfacing when he'd been trying to bury it for weeks.

Carlyle glared at him. "Of course you would. That's not even a question. Just go eat your red meat and don't dream of snakes. For me. My treat."

Gideon scowled. Of all the stupid things. God help him, Joey Carlyle was ten years his junior and he was *protecting* Gideon.

"I'm not helpless," Gideon muttered, not wanting to let his wounds show.

"If my father was going to attack you with a stiletto or a cheese knife, no, you are not," Joey said, and while he still sounded hard, there was a definite sheen to his eyes. "But he'd attack you with his words, or he'd sabotage that portfolio you don't admit you have, or he'd go after your parents in their nice little New Jersey suburban house and then take on your stepmom's holiday place and *her* family. And yes, you could probably defend yourself if you had to, but since you don't have to, go have a merry fucking Christmas. I've taken my antivenin too, Gideon. Please, for all that's holy, protect yourself."

Gideon chewed on that for a little bit, and part of him was chanting, *Three months. We've only been doing the thing for three months. You are under no obligation to put yourself or your father in danger for a three-month relationship.*

But the other part of him was saying, *He's my partner.*

And he wasn't sure how that applied. It was equally true for a work partner or a domestic partner, but he didn't think they were to the place where he could point that out, no matter how many times he opened his kitchen towel drawer and came up with Joey's soft white tank-tees.

He sighed. "I'll protect you until the day I die," he said, surprising even himself with his passion. He was not necessarily a passionate man, the increasingly intense interludes with Joey notwithstanding. Those were the exception, not the rule.

"And this is me," Joey said, his lean, hard mouth softening. "Doing the same." Then he let out a breath. "You're going to miss your train, Gid. If we weren't out in public I'd kiss you goodbye, but we are so never mind. I should be home on the twenty-sixth. It's only three days. Enjoy your roast."

And with that he was gone, blending in with the train-station crowd so easily not even Gideon could find him.

But maybe Gideon's eyes were blurring for stupid reasons. The kid could blend in seamlessly whether in the city or the woods.

He could track a deer for miles—or an armed perpetrator. He was closer to being a serial killer than a victim, but still….

Still….

There was something vulnerable about him.

Gideon shook himself. He'd done his best. He couldn't make somebody take help. He couldn't *make* Joey care about him.

He'd rechecked his duffel that morning to make sure he'd included his father's and stepmother's gifts and had found one of Carlyle's favorite sleep shirts in his duffel. There was no reason for it to be there, except to replace the fancy underwear. If Gideon put it on, he'd look ridiculous. It probably didn't clear his navel, and it would make even Gideon's narrow shoulders seem broad.

Gideon had rolled it super tight, so that it barely took any room, and wedged it in the corner of his bag. The thought of it now calmed him down a little.

Maybe you didn't have to make somebody care about you when they packed their favorite sleep shirt with your underwear on purpose so nobody could mistake that you were taken. Maybe that meant they already cared. Gideon thought that might be a good rule. He'd remember it.

Let the Wolf Come Home

Joey saw the car waiting for him when he got off the train—and neatly avoided it.

He wasn't going to accept his father's help, for one thing, and he didn't want to be trapped in his father's house, for another. The storage facility he'd told Gideon about on his first day in the city was less than a mile from the train station, and it didn't only house a steadily depreciating investment in pricey menswear.

Joey's winter boots were prime, well-oiled leather, a rubber sole that made running easier and gave him traction through the snow on the side of the road. He stayed behind the tree line, on the shadowed side of the interstate, knowing his dark clothes and OD green duffel would be harder to spot. When he got to the facility, he didn't go through the front; he vaulted over the wall in the hole in the cameras.

And when he drove his fully charged electric motorcycle out, he was so stealthy the security guard didn't even see him.

He really loved this thing. It was like riding a dragonfly. Quick, quiet, went for hundreds of miles on one charge, and wearing dark leathers and a slate-gray helmet, he could be absolutely invisible.

It also went off-road.

Joey knew the backroads of this area of wilderness—much of them were on the reservation, where he and his grandfather had tramped and camped for weeks at a time. He knew the naked area that abutted his father's property, and the tiny line shack that still stood close to the hole in his father's security.

Or what *would* be the hole in his father's security, thanks to the class the whole unit had just attended on how to jam security cameras and break into compounds without being seen.

After stowing the bike behind the shack and covering it up with the camo tarp that had been in his storage facility, he also tucked away a change of winter clothes, a lined denim jacket, and a bedding roll strapped to the back. There was cash in there too, hidden in a pocket in the bedroll. He didn't *plan* to get trapped in his father's place, but he had a five-mile hike in and out. He could do it in his underwear if he had to, but he wanted warm clothes at the end.

The hike through the woods up to the long driveway of the house as the sun sank beneath the tree line was almost cathartic. Part of it was the rather childish exercise of picking up small rocks and taking out the security cameras that he saw every hundred yards or so, once when the camera was especially high, by using his new scarf as a sling. But mostly it was the physical exertion. His body was fit for it, but it had been a long time since he'd exercised in raw wilderness, and everything from the wind in the trees to the sound of game—wild turkeys, peafowl, wild rabbits, deer, and the occasional forbidden wolf smuggled in by his father's gamekeeper to balance the ecosystem—made him remember his original den.

And there, pungent and powerful, the smell of the ultimate predator on the property, the one even the wolves feared.

Joey had no idea if his father knew it was there, but he rather suspected he didn't. The gamekeeper, a silent old Mohawk man whom Joey surmised was being threatened with blackmail to tend to his father's acreage in such a way as to keep it wild and stocked full of game for his father's hunting friends, had enough bitter lines around his mouth and eyes that Joey wondered sometimes if he hoped the mountain lion would take Joey's father out one day.

Joey liked that plan. It had a certain poetry to it, but he didn't count on it happening.

Still, he was glad the creature—the family of creatures—survived in the back quarter, in a rocky den that most humans didn't approach. As Joey passed the lair, scanning his surroundings carefully to make sure he didn't cross any boundaries or miss any scat, didn't disturb the creature any more than necessary, the pewter gray sky opened up, and snow began to fall.

Joey pulled a stocking cap from the pocket of his leather jacket, as well as some warm, stretchy gloves he'd worn under his leather motorcycle gloves and pocketed for later. Around his neck he had a black-and-gray cashmere scarf that Gideon had given him, something handwoven and tailored that he'd practically thrown at Joey the night before, presented in a box with a stretchy, festive silver ribbon.

"It's my Christmas gift," he'd said stonily when Joey had been surprised. "Just because we're not spending the day together doesn't mean I didn't get you a present."

Joey had clutched the thing to his chest, absurdly touched. "I was expecting Legos," he said, feeling lost as a child. *He* hadn't gotten Gideon a gift yet. Every fiber of his being had been taken up with countermeasures for facing his father without putting Gideon—or hell, anybody in his unit—in the old man's crosshairs.

Gideon had sighed and pulled him close—that thing they both claimed they didn't know how to do, be close, touch easily, seeming to come more and more often as Christmas loomed—and feathered a kiss along his temple.

"Only request is that I get to see you wear it," he murmured. "Which means you have to come home."

Joey had nodded and had threatened to strip down to nothing, wearing *only* the scarf, and Gideon had pretended to be horrified, claiming that was a terrible thing to do to cashmere.

What had followed had been naked and intense, because they didn't do sex any other way, Joey was starting to learn. After so many years of simply brushing up against bodies in the night, he'd expected sex to pall after a few months with this one person.

Apparently that's not what mating *was*. Mating was *never* boring, and it was *never* repetitive. Yes, sex itself was basically the same motion, repeated until orgasm, but *mating*…. Mating was the smell of Gideon's skin suffusing his senses. It was the warmth of his bony fingers stroking Joey's flesh. Mating was the swell of emotion as urgency built between them, and the *explosion* of pleasure, of safety, when climax tumbled over them both.

Sex was rudimentary.

What happened when Gideon Chadwick touched him was something else entirely.

Joey found he was clutching the scarf tightly around his neck as he hiked, not because he was cold but because it was as though he was holding fast to that memory of the two of them together the night before.

The memory lingered, and he could still hear Gideon's harsh breath, his cry of completion as he poured his orgasm, once again, into Joey's body. Joey had stopped protesting to himself that he "didn't bottom." With Gideon, he did. With Gideon, he *needed* Gideon's flesh inside his. He *begged* for it. It grounded him, pulled him into the world of Gideon's arms, made the two of them whole.

And it was that wholeness that he wore like his leather jacket as he rounded the last bend of the long driveway to his father's mansion. It was that wholeness, supple as calfskin, warm as cashmere, as impervious as steel, that he used to defend himself against his father's acid tongue.

Joey didn't knock on the great oak door—he punched the code and entered.

He'd expected his father's bodyguard on the other side, but found his father there instead.

When Joey had been small, learning how to navigate a world in which the predator was his guardian, he'd kept expecting his father's face to change. Stephen Carlyle was a handsome man, with a high forehead, a bold nose, and a square jaw. His gray/blond hair was receding, but even that was occurring handsomely, in a fashionable widow's peak.

Joey always expected the bones under the skin to morph, the flesh to sag, to melt, the entire visage to contort into grotesquerie to show the world his father for the monster he was.

But now, after eighteen months with the SCTF, after encountering monsters like Chester Schumer and Halsey Garber, he'd come to appreciate that his father's face *was* the face of evil—people just didn't always recognize evil when they saw it.

"You could have let us know you had a way home," Stephen said almost before the door was open.

"I told you when I'd be here," Joey said. He'd added an hour and a half to the train's arrival time. "You were trying to ambush me. Are you going to move, or would you like me to turn around and leave?"

Silent intimidation was one of Stevie's favorite gambits. Grudgingly he stepped back half a step, and Joey didn't move. He kept up eye contact until Stephen took another half-step. And then another.

He tried to draw a line in the sand, to refuse to go any farther, but Joey shook his head.

"Far enough back that I can't smell your fetid breath, Stevie. This is going to be a short visit."

With a growl, he took a full step backward and gestured grandly to the interior of the entryway.

"Come to the study," his father said. "Leave your things in the hallway. Someone will move them to your room."

Joey kept his duffel on his shoulder. "Nobody touches my shit but me," he said. "And I'm going to the kitchen for something to eat. Whatever you want to say to me, you can say to me there."

He removed his hat and gloves and tucked them in his coat pocket as he went. So far he'd gotten the physical intimidation and the subtle threat to steal his stuff to leave him stranded—a thing his father had tried before. If the past told him anything it was that his father was going to demand he return to the family business, threaten all his friends, threaten his family's property on the reservation, and threaten his life if he refused.

Joey had locked up his grandfather's property using his trust money and used it to house and fund a school—it was untouchable. He could kill the old man with a twitch of a knife, but chose not to so he could continue to live *his* life the way he wanted to. And until now, until his eighteen months with the SCTF, he had avoided having any friends who could be harmed by the human cancer huffing behind him as he headed down the hall, ignoring the baroque gold-and-black decorations, the heavy blood-red carpeting and gold-tinted blue furniture, the oak trim that matched nothing, because his father, like Chester Schumer, had no sense of humanity in his décor.

He thought longingly of Gideon's little apartment, of eating dinner on the floor by the coffee table, of the way Gideon had picked out each piece—often mismatched—lovingly, because he liked it, and was comfortable that his taste might not be anybody else's.

He burst into the kitchen, badly startling this year's cook. A new kitchen staff tended to rotate in, because Stephen Carlyle was an ass who thought everybody was trying to poison him and didn't know the difference between homemade gravy and sauce from a jar.

"Uhm, Mr. Carlyle…?"

"I'm sorry," Joey said bluntly. "I just arrived. Is there any way I can get a sandwich? I'll make it myself so I don't wreck your timetable."

Gideon had taught him how to cook just a bit, and in watching him try to plan a meal in his tiny kitchen, Joey had learned the importance of not getting in a cook's way.

"Not a problem," the cook replied. He was a young man who might not have looked as frightened before he took this job, but who had definitely developed some prey responses since. "I… we have sourdough rolls, the usual condiments, meat, cheese—"

"Anything I can't touch?" Joey asked kindly.

"The prosciutto and the hard cheeses?" the cook said on a gust of relief. "I had plans for dinner."

"Of course," Joey told him. "Any juice?"

"Orange and cranberry."

"I'll try not to leave you high and dry."

With that, Joey turned to an unused counter space and spent five minutes assembling a sandwich with some chips he found in a cupboard, and a glass of OJ. His father, unmindful of the cook and a couple of assistants moving around trying to prep vegetables, stood in the center of the kitchen, arms crossed, until Joey took his lunch and moved out of the kitchen to the breakfast nook, just to get himself, his father, and his father's fucking bodyguard out of the poor chef's hair.

He sat down to his sandwich with a sigh of contentment. He needed food for fuel, and while his father might not know the difference between quality meats and Oscar Meyer, *Joey* did now after eighteen months as Gideon's partner, and he was super excited not to be eating reconstituted ramen or processed bologna.

"Joseph, are we going to talk?"

Joey swallowed a bite of a first-rate dagwood. "Thanks for the sandwich, Stevie. Merry Christmas. I'm not coming back to join the criming. I'm a Federal Agent now, and they won't let me."

Joey had his sandwich in his hands so he could finish it when his father ripped the plate out from under it and pitched it at the wall behind Joey's head.

Joey ducked and took another bite of sandwich—after inspecting it for pottery shards, of course. He leaned his head back and shook out his hair, listening to a faint sandy tinkle, and he felt a trickle of blood down the back of his ear. But the sandwich was fine.

He swallowed. "That doesn't make the job more attractive," he said.

"I'm your father, Joseph. The job doesn't have to be attractive. You took my money, you *owe* me your skill set for my business—"

"You took my real family away," Joey said, and this bite had no joy in it as he thought longingly of his grandfather. "You isolated me in this hellhole and then sent me to military school. I lost years with somebody who actually cared for me because you thought I was a pretty trinket. I didn't give a *shit* about your money, but given that I inherited it legally, you better believe I used it. I also make my own." He shrugged. "And my skill set? You've taught me *nothing*. But would you like to know what I've learned in my new job?" He sucked bread off his teeth so he could give a pointy smile. "I've learned all the ways you broke the law to *make* that money. Think about that for a sec."

He took a swig of OJ and watched his father do the math.

"You wouldn't *dare*—" Oh yes. Now Stevie got it.

Joey looked his father in the eye. "Where in the hell do you think I've been for almost ten years, Steve? You sent me to military school, and then I went into Special Forces. What do you think I dared to do there?"

"You were kicked out," his father said, almost triumphantly.

"But not for refusing to dare," Joey told him. "And you got me here by threatening the people I work with. Do you have *any* idea who they are?"

His father's face went blank, which was a tell.

"That information is heavily classified," his father said primly.

"Well, you won't learn from me," Joey replied, equally prim. "But imagine an entire unit of assholes just like me, but better. Smarter. Quicker on their feet. And they *know* about you. They've *profiled* you. They have *files* on you." Oh yeah. Gideon had been right—telling Clint Harding and giving him permission to tell Tal and the mysterious Blodgett person had been right on the money. The others might not know about his father, but if they had to, his team would have his back.

And telling his father that they had Joey's back had made his father's pale brow grow even paler.

"Give us a reason to *dare*," Joey said, finishing off his sandwich. "Or maybe? Just leave us alone. If you don't cross our path, we've got no beef with you. But man, give us a reason. And before you ask? Abducting me, forcing me to stay here against my will? That would be a reason."

His words were aimed at his father's bodyguard, who had been stealthily reaching for his weapon as Joey spoke.

They locked eyes for a moment, and the bodyguard made a show of relaxing his hand, which didn't fool Joey at all. He was making his own show of doing the same. When the guard struck to draw his weapon, quick as a snake, Joey was ready with one of the three blades he'd tucked behind his belt.

His aim was true, and the guard gave a strangled cry as the blade pinned his jacket to his hand, where presumably he'd been reaching for his weapon.

Joey stood up and threw the cloth napkin he'd used to wipe his mouth at the bodyguard, who caught it with a grunt and used it to pull the blade out.

"Set it on the table," Joey said with all the inflection he'd use to say "Pass the milk."

The guard dropped it, and it clattered, not even spattering blood since the jacket had cleaned it on its way out.

Joey picked it up but didn't return it to his specialized little holster.

"Thanks for the sandwich, Dad," he said. "I'll be going now."

"You think you can hide out on my own property?" his father sputtered, and Joey smiled thinly, thinking of the broken cameras he'd left in his wake and of the motorcycle hidden far from his father's clutches.

It was growing dark now—he might not make it back to the bike and the bedroll before he was forced to take shelter and hide—but his father hired city thugs, and Joey had been raised on this land.

"It'll be a fun game of hide and seek," he said pleasantly, twirling the fixed blade between his fingers. "Just remember what's hiding in the bushes. The wilderness isn't always a great place to be lost in the dark."

And with that he strode past the bodyguard, past his father, and toward the living room.

There had been a throw on the back of one of the couches—it had looked like genuine mink, which was tacky and stupid and wasteful.

But it would be *very* warm as the temperature dropped below freezing, and it would be black as night as his father's men searched.

He grabbed it on his way toward the foyer, glad he'd never taken off his jacket, had never relinquished his hat, his gloves, his scarf.

"I'd say you'll be seeing me," he told his outraged father, "but not if I see you first."

He used the knife to fix the mink around his shoulders like a cloak before he slid to the side of the driveway and started his sprint.

GIDEON CAME from money—not, say, Joey Carlyle's father's kind of money, with the extensive grounds and the small army of security and the files of blackmail bait that Gideon had begun to suspect Carlyle knew about, but comfortable enough. Mountain Lakes wasn't Essex Fells—but it was close.

Gideon had gone to Princeton after high school and had been slated to get his doctorate there immediately, but he'd served with the Marines and done Officer Candidate School instead. He'd gone back to Princeton *after* his ten-year stint, and graduated in four years, with honors, with a masters in criminology and his PhD in psychology. Which had made him a perfect candidate for the FBI Behavioral Analysis department—until his old CO's friend, Clint Harding, had approached him about creating a new kind of alphabet unit, one as intent on addressing the needs of the victims as it was on stopping the perpetrators.

Gideon had been in on the SCTF from the ground floor, and he knew things—uncomfortable things—about every one of his coworkers, because he'd been one of the three people in on who the unit hired since the very beginning.

He wished he could say he'd seen this thing between him and Carlyle coming, but he hadn't, and the solace of his stepmother's big-assed two-story second home off Lake Erie in Pennsylvania was a particular balm after he and Joey had parted at the train station.

On the one hand, he was hurt and furious, but on the other hand, he was *worried*. And while he had indulged in the hurt and the furious during the train ride from Manhattan, by the time his father picked him up at the train station, it was the last part that had settled in to ache.

While not as stiff-necked as a New Englander—or as close-mouthed as Joey Carlyle—rich people had their own reserve. People in Gideon Chadwick's family did not *talk* about their feelings. The only reason Gideon knew his father cared for his stepmom was because he got this baffled, melty expression whenever she asked him to do something for her. Gideon had often thought that it was a good thing Trish was a good person, and the things she asked for were trips to the store or for a new trash can or sometimes even a new kitten, because if she ever asked Gideon's dad to knock over a bank, Gerald Chadwick might be in the middle of a heist before he realized exactly how that had happened.

So imagine Gideon's surprise when, in the car halfway from the train station in Philly, his father said, "Anything going on that I should know about, son?"

While for some parents, that might have been a regular occurrence, for Gideon, the last time he could remember his father asking him such a thing had been after his mother died, when he was seven, not-so-promptly followed by Gideon's mostly private decision to enlist in the military after his first stint in college.

The end.

Gideon glanced at his father, taking in the same narrow frame and hatchet nose that Gideon had sported his entire life. But Gerald wore his with a certain dignity, a certain peace. None of the subversiveness or restlessness that Gideon had always possessed. Gideon had seen things wrong in the world, and he'd been supremely aware of his privilege. It was his job to *fix* those things. For the first time in his life, he saw the slight stooping, the enhanced sharpness to the cheekbones, the crow's feet at the corners of his father's eyes. His father was over sixty, and while not *old*, he was certainly *older*. And the sideways glance he cast Gideon was almost wistful.

His father had been a prominent, successful businessman who, while not unkind, had always worked prominent, successful businessman hours. Lots of trips, lots of late nights, one night out as a family for dinner, and the occasional vacation to someplace warm with lots of sun.

Not distant, not cold—but not overly involved. When Gideon's mother passed away, his father had hired a series of nannies and kept the same schedule, until Trisha had arrived. Gideon may not have been the warmest child, but Trisha—who had started out as his father's admin when Gideon was in junior high—had often told him that his rare smiles had been like a fully fleshed out performance review. "Excellent" rating.

Trisha was the reason Gideon had returned either to the house in Mountain Lakes or Lake Erie for holidays (they switched off—Trisha was reluctant to part with the Lake Erie estate, and Gideon had fond memories of the lake as a teenager), but seeing his father having reasoned, adult conversations with him had been his reward for opening up to another human being after that long, windswept silence of his childhood.

His father had retired in this last year, and Gideon wondered if he'd started to regret—or at least rethink—some of the emotional habits that he'd inherited from *his* father.

He must have, because he didn't let Gideon's stunned silence stop him.

"See, Trisha, she's starting to worry about you being alone so much. Now I know you've probably got friends in the city, but see, nobody you've cared for enough to tell us about. But…." He trailed off, glanced at Gideon again since they were at a light, and sighed. "You just look… worried."

Gideon blinked and decided to throw his old man a bone. "I am, sort of. My—" Partner? Friend? Lover? "—colleague? He, uhm, is not looking forward to visiting his family for the holiday."

His father snorted. "Colleague?" he echoed, and Gideon winced. Not involved—but not stupid.

"Friend?"

And his father rolled his eyes in that supremely superior, sarcastic way that Gideon was aware he'd inherited straight from the old man. "Weak shit, son."

Gideon managed a chuckle. "Weak shit? Did you hear that from Trisha?"

His father's expression—almost eternally closed—softened. "She listens to podcasts," he said mildly. "*Very* liberal podcasts." He sobered. "It doesn't bother us, you know, if your 'colleague' is, you know, male."

That touched Gideon. "Thanks, Dad. Of all the things I'm worried about, that wasn't one, but thank you. It's nice to know."

"So why are you worried? About him. Your 'colleague'?"

It was Gideon's turn to snort. "Because he's so emotionally closed off he makes us look like open fire hydrants. And because I offered to go with him, and he pretty much said he didn't want his father to put a hit out on me. *Or* you. *Or* our unit. So, uhm, yeah." And then, because his father had given a harsh bark of laughter—but had *not* told him he was being crazy or overreactive or, well, any of the things he might have said when Gideon was younger—he added, "I asked him to come with *me* instead, but he seemed to feel that would get him the same result." Gideon sighed. "I… you know. Wish he felt safe."

Gerald nodded slowly, as if digesting all of that. "Do you really feel safe, visiting home?" he asked, and Gideon could hear the hope in his voice. *Bless you, Dad. You really do try.*

"Yeah, Dad. You and Trisha make a nice home." He smiled. "*Homes*. I hope you shower that woman with presents and praise, because she really is more than the two of us deserve."

His father's smile was… boyish, and fond, and Gideon realized that, in spite of the *very* pricey and rare pocket watch he'd packed as his father's gift, his *real* gift had been that statement right there, heaping praise on the person who had saved Gerald Chadwick from a lonely life as King of the Hill.

"She is," Gerald said. "What did you get her for Christmas?"

Gideon grinned. "Tickets to the Tonys this year. I got her two, so you'd better be nice or I'm going with her."

"Oh, that's lovely!" His father's face lit up. "How did you spring that?"

"Well, a *different* colleague of mine is buddies with Toby Trotter, who's—"

"Manhattan's hottest DJ?" his father supplied and then laughed. "Don't look so surprised, son. You know Trish reads the entertainment blogs."

"Yeah, well, I had Crosby ask his friend for the hookup. He was pretty happy to do it. He's a good guy."

"But not *the* good guy."

Gideon's cheeks heated. "Well, not *my* good guy."

"Why not?"

They were nearing the house now, and Gideon realized he only had a small pocket of this seemingly magical honest time to give a real answer.

"Crosby's a nice guy," he said after a moment. "And I am… not always. Carlyle isn't always a nice guy either. I don't have to worry about hurting him with my lack of niceness."

His father made a distressed sound. "You seem nice to me and your stepmother," he said.

Gideon gave a weary sigh, the kind that reminded him why he'd come home after his last deployment and slept for a month before going off to school.

"You and Trisha haven't done horrible things to other people," he said softly. "If I'm grateful for nothing else, Dad, I'm grateful that you're both unequivocally on the side of the angels."

His father *hmm*ed slightly as he made the left turn up the long driveway to the solid, sweeping brick house. "I don't know about angels, son, but you look tired. How about you nap in your room before dinner."

Gideon nodded. "But first I hug Trish."

"Who says you're not a good boy?"

GIDEON'S "OLD room," which Trish had set up for him during high school and college when they'd visited the house in the summer, had been converted into a guest room about six months after he'd deployed. It sported a queen-sized bed with warm flannel sheets and a snuggly comforter with a linen duvet in the summer and a flannel covering in the winter. It had been done in warm, masculine colors with a soft carpet and pad under his feet, and he almost wished he'd let Trisha do his room as a kid, because the comfort here could not be denied.

He *did* settle himself down for a warm winter's nap before dinner, thank you, and he'd awakened trying hard to figure out if the darkness meant he'd awakened in the crotch of dawn or in the dark of the long winter afternoon, when his phone buzzed in its charger on the end table.

He picked it up and squinted at the text.

Made it. Fought. Left. Sleeping here instead.

The picture showed an almost idyllic snowscape, with a shallow divot carving its way into the side of a hill.

A cave.

I'm napping in flannel sheets with a floor heater under the bed, he typed back. *Join me instead.*

Sadist, Joey replied. But he didn't say he wouldn't, which meant he really *had* spent his day fighting with his father.

I'm just trying to present you with viable options, Gideon texted. *Don't shoot the messenger.*

Your life might not be so peaceful if I showed up at two in the morning.

Gideon's chest seized. He didn't even want to know how Joey would get from the wilds of Boston to Lake Erie, but he wanted him there badly.

My folks wouldn't care, and I'd consider it my Christmas present.

Your Christmas present was my T-shirt so you didn't forget who you belonged to.

I'm not forgetting. Come here and belong to me back.

His phone buzzed, and he hit the Call button.

"He wants me to quit and join the family business," Joey said softly.

"You knew that might happen," Gideon said, but inside he'd gone cold. He and Clint had kept their research of Joey's father superficial because they needed some serious encryption to not trip every alarm the man had, but they *had* done research and had both given Joey input on how to shut his father down.

Still, they'd known it would be dangerous. Gideon wouldn't be okay until Joey was home.

"Yeah, I was neither disappointed nor surprised," Joey said dryly. "But it's dark, and I won't be able to get out until dawn."

"You're *trapped* there?" Gideon asked, trying not to panic. He scrambled to a sitting position, mind racing with exfil scenarios. He should call Clint, he should alert the team, he should—

"It's fine. We've done this before," Joey said calmly. And then his voice dropped, and Gideon could swear he heard the snow falling around him. "It's just this time I've got a real reason to leave."

"I'd come get you," Gideon said, and he heard the hardness in his voice and knew that, of all people, it would give Joey comfort. "I know I'm not an army, but you and me—"

"We'd do all right," Joey said, and he *sounded* comforted. "Thanks, Gid." Some of the anger slipped from his voice. "I'll be okay."

"My father would love to meet you," Gideon said simply.

"That's a nice promise. Merry Christmas, Chadwick."

"Merry Christmas, Carlyle."

"I'll see you on the twenty-sixth."

"Stay warm. And safe."

"Stay single."

Gideon wanted to laugh then. As. If. He opened his mouth to say something else, but Joey ended the call, and Gideon had worked enough missions to know you didn't call the guy out in the cold.

There was another picture, though, and Gideon stared in fascination at a mountain lion stalking out of the cave. The picture was taken from an elevated perspective, and Gideon realized Joey had cut off the convo so he could climb a tree.

He wanted to laugh, but his chest still ached, a stupid, purposeless thing. Downstairs, he could hear Trisha and his father talking—simple, easy conversation about pot roast and salad, and the smell of dinner was wafting up the stairs. Trisha had domestic help, and there was a lively conversation coming from the kitchen as the table was set, and Gideon suddenly wanted Joey here with everything in his heart.

Another picture. This one bloody, because the mountain lion had brought down a hare, and somebody wouldn't go hungry tonight.

Sleep well, Carlyle. Get warm. Find some food. He texted the words, not wanting to get more sentimental but wanting Joey to have better.

As long as I don't kill anyone, it will be a good night.

Gideon heard himself telling his father that he and Joey were not nice people.

Predators want full bellies and safe homes too, he thought.

He stood and dressed for dinner, remembering to wet-comb his wild flyaway hair. As he made his way downstairs in his loafers, he found himself missing his wolf, their cozy den in the city, and the feeling of being on the hunt together.

He found himself angry at the mountain lion threatening his wolf. Together, he thought grimly, *together,* they could make a feast of the lion and cozy up in their own safe cave.

SUCH A strange twin plane of existence. On one plane, Gideon spent the next two days with his chest constricted, in a constant state of panic while he worried about Joey, living for the vibration of his phone against his thigh. Texts like *Out of the compound* or *Staying at a hotel* kept him grounded, gave him peace, allowed him to return to his other plane of existence, where his father and stepmother were trying hard to have a peaceful holiday.

The third time Trish watched him jerk upright at the dinner table and then surreptitiously check his phone, she laughed.

"Gideon," she said warmly, "you can just put it next to your plate. I get it. You're worried about somebody. It's got to be hard being here when you want to be there."

Gideon did what she asked and then turned a truly apologetic face toward the kind woman who had tried to mother him for nearly thirty years. "I am so grateful to be here," he said, meaning it. "I appreciate you and my dad, and the decorations and the good food—I didn't want to be rude."

Trish had never been beautiful—not by the standards of Gideon's father's friends. She had an unruly mop of curly hair that had once been red, a round face, and a round bosom and plush hips and, as far as Gideon could see, didn't regret a single morsel to cross her lips, nor should she have. Her smile was glorious, and her eyes—a little droopier than they had been thirty years ago because she had no time for cosmetic surgery and no shyness about aging—lit up with a joy for life that made the years fall away.

Now she gave Gideon a soft look that made him wish, not for the first time, that he'd been less reserved as a child. He *so* should have let himself be mothered by this woman.

"It's okay to be worried about someone," she said. "I don't know if this is job related or not, Gideon, but it doesn't matter. I used to worry about your father when he had a long commute. I worried about you when you were deployed. Your father and I spent an entire year jumping at every text, because you had gone dark and we were waiting for *any* word." Her eyes grew bright. "I remember your Christmas text that year. We memorized it. '*I'm fine. Merry Christmas. Have a drink for me.*'" She gave half a laugh. "We had an entire bottle of pino grigio for you, Gideon. I don't know if we ever told you that."

Gideon gave her a helpless smile. "No," he said. "I didn't know that. I hope it was a good one."

She shrugged. "It paired well with chocolate. My point is, I get it. You're worried. Keep the phone on the table and tell us about this… colleague that you're so worried about. Don't worry—nothing classified, and we're quite fine with violence. Watch it all the time on TV."

Gideon felt a laugh bubbling up. "God, Trish, I really love you. In case I don't say it enough."

She laughed, and he set his phone on the table as requested.

And then spent dinner telling them about Joey Carlyle.

He skipped the worst parts—he held enough dinner parties to know what made a good story. The gory details about the dog? Out. Joey's choice of the dog cup for Crosby? Definitely in. Joey, doing a backflip off a building onto a giant inflatable fireman's airbag? Oh yes, that story got told. Gideon dragging him back to the apartment to fuck him senseless? No, that would stay private. But his father wasn't a stupid man—and Dad knew what it was like to love somebody and to worry.

"That must have been a little hard on your heart, though, right, son?"

Gideon took a sip of wine before he answered. "We had a talk," he underplayed. "I asked him not to scare me like that again."

They both nodded. "And so he's texting you when he can tonight," Trish said perceptively. "Good. Let us know what you hear. I really can't wait to meet him."

"I warn you, though," Gideon said, figuring this woman could take it, "he's sort of… care resistant."

Trish snorted wine all over herself, making Gideon and his father jump in surprise, and she was still chuckling as she wiped her face and her blouse with a napkin. "Really, Gideon? You'd choose somebody care resistant as a mate? Because *you* were a *pussycat*."

Gideon, remembering his reserve, his careful attempts not to get attached, not to hug too tightly, not to show this woman too much affection, not to welcome her into his little bubble of existence, right up until he left for deployment and realized she was weeping on his shoulder and holding him too tightly to not hold her back, gave her a sheepish grimace.

"He's younger than I am," he said with dignity. "We're all stupid when we're young."

That made her laugh harder, and Gideon glanced at his father to see that baffled, melty expression on Gerald Chadwick's face, and his eyes grew suddenly bright.

Trish would have Joey Carlyle eating out of her hand.

Bidding them goodbye the morning of the twenty-sixth was both really difficult and a profound relief. He'd come to cherish—truly—the peace of their home, the haven of kindness, of grace that they'd created.

But his last text from Joey had come at 5:00 a.m. It had said, simply, *Almost there*. And Gideon *needed* to be where that text came from.

It was dark by the time he got to his apartment, his bones aching from the long train ride so hard on the heels of the one on the twenty-third. Still he moved carefully, opening the door to his apartment quietly but not silently. Making sure his keys clattered as he dropped them in the bowl by the door. Turning on the light in the kitchen as he passed by so nobody who slept with his knife under his pillow would be startled when he woke up.

But the light from the kitchen allowed him to see that Joey was still sleeping, curled on the couch under what looked like a battered, sap-stained fur coat. His boots stood sentinel at the foot of the couch, and his head was pillowed on his duffel, while the throw pillows littered the floor.

With a surprised grunt, Gideon dropped his duffel by the couch and knelt down beside him, murmuring his name softly. He'd *love* to do the Sleeping Beauty thing and kiss him, but that was a good way to find a knife in his jugular before Joey Carlyle was quite awake.

"Joey, baby, how long you been here?"

Joey grunted. "Are we using endearments now?" he asked. "Did this clear committee?"

"Fuck off, Carlyle," Gideon told him, but he was relieved. That sort of talk-back couldn't happen if he was irreparably damaged, either emotionally *or* physically.

Joey's eyes opened, and he yawned and sat up, arching his back like a cat. "Endearments are a go," he said, reaching out to feather a touch along Gideon's cheek. "God, is it dark already? How late *is* it?"

"Six o'clock," Gideon said, taking Joey's invitation to squeeze in next to him. "How long have you been sleeping?"

Joey grunted, and then shocked the hell out of Gideon by resting his head on Gideon's shoulder. "Since around noon. I had to find someplace to house the bike—"

"Bike?"

"Motorcycle," Joey said through a yawn, "and then go visit my own apartment so I'd show up on video. I showered and repacked, changed my jacket and put on a different hat." He let out a sigh, and his hand went to the rumpled cashmere scarf at his throat. "Couldn't bear to part with this, though. You may have to peel it off my neck in April. So warm."

Gideon let out a rusty chuckle. "I'll get you another one." He wrapped his arm around Joey's shoulders and held him close. "That's some nap."

"First sleep I got since we left town," Joey confessed.

"I thought you found a hotel!" Gideon asked, dismayed.

"Yeah, caught a couple hours there, but…." Joey's shoulders twitched. "Too close to Dad and not close enough to here. Can't explain it. Had to leave."

Gideon nodded. "I trust those instincts," he said softly. "I'm glad you're home."

"Mm…." Joey snuggled in closer, and the battered mink coat? Blanket? Fell from his shoulders as he thrust one hand under Gideon's coat, his warm hand welcome as it spanned Gideon's stomach. "Still flat," he said, patting it. "Not enough red meat."

Gideon smiled even as he shuddered at the touch. "Plenty. Trish is a good cook. *I* spent my Christmas eating and sleeping. Maybe next year you can come with me."

Joey grunted and moved to pull his hand back, but Gideon trapped it there. "Nobody said to stop," he grumbled. "And Trish wants to meet you. It's going to be weird but pleasant, I warn you. She'll try to mother you. I suggest you let her."

Joey let out another little grunt, and started to feel Gideon up in earnest. “A thing we can discuss later,” he said, and Gideon wanted to protest. He’d just sat down. He felt travel-worn and a little ragged, but there was something… necessary in Joey’s touch.

He kissed Joey hard, like he meant it, tasting sleep on Joey’s breath but not much else, and bore him back against the cushions. Joey went pliant, needy, almost immediately, and his breath when Gideon pulled back shook hard.

“Please…,” he whispered, then swallowed, looking dismayed and a little wild.

“In the bed,” Gideon whispered back. “Come on, baby.”

“I prefer ‘fuck off,’” he grumbled, but he stood and followed Gideon through the doorway.

“Tomorrow,” Gideon promised. “Tonight you’ll get ‘baby’ and like it.” God, those kisses had been so desperate. For a moment as they moved through the dimly lit apartment, Gideon felt… unworthy. Inadequate. Joey was a wild creature, and tonight he was nearly feral, and the things he needed from Gideon demanded passion and fire. Until this moment, until this *relationship*, passion and fire had not been his forte.

Joey hesitated, though, as they entered the darkened bedroom, and Gideon, turning to see his face silhouetted against the faint glow of the living room, saw a primal need for warmth, for comfort, for possession.

Gideon turned on the lamp by the bed on instinct and turned toward his lover with intent, taking Joey’s chin between his two fingers and tilting his face up so Gideon could take his mouth, hard, no hesitation, no overthinking.

Joey sighed and shuddered, melting into Gideon’s arms. His hand shook as he cupped Gideon’s cheek, and Gideon pulled him tight, so tight, their bodies aligning perfectly. He continued the kiss, some of his travel exhaustion falling away as desire swept him. This. *This.* There he’d been, in his parents’ fortress of kindness, of warmth, and he’d been cold, alone, missing his mate.

His mate was *here*, and he *needed*, and Gideon had no choice and no desire to turn him away.

He made quick work of Joey's clothes—*Gideon's* clothes, hanging from Joey's smaller frame. And Gideon saw it now, the claiming, the nesting behavior, knew it for what it was. That shirt in the bottom of his duffel was no more an accident than the one being used as a runner on the back of his stuffed chair, or the remains of the white tank currently hanging on his stove so they could dry their hands on it.

This was Joey's home. *Gideon* was Joey's home, whether there were signed papers or declarations of love or rings or never would be.

Joey scrambled under the covers, naked, while Gideon toed off his shoes and shucked his overcoat, pulling his sweater and henley over his head in one motion before letting them all fall where they landed.

Joey made a forlorn sound, huddling under the comforter, and Gideon finished undressing and crawled in, surrounding Joey with his heat, his bare skin, his animal presence, a thing Joey seemed to crave as much as Gideon needed to give.

"Shh…," Gideon murmured, taking his mouth again, running his hands along Joey's shoulders, his biceps, down to the ends of his fingers. Joey grabbed one hand and clasped it, a shudder racking his body, and Gideon soothed him again.

"Please…," Joey whispered, and Gideon went to work, lowering his head to Joey's nipple to pull.

"Harder!" he cried, but Gideon released him and kissed down to his naked groin.

"I will not hurt you," he said with certainty, knowing that, of all things, that needed to be the lesson here.

"Gid!" he pleaded, but Gideon had reached his cock, and he swallowed it down with one motion. "*Gideon*!" he gasped, and that was better, but not enough.

Gideon kept his hand stroking and repositioned himself between Joey's thighs, knowing he felt vulnerable but unable to do this any other way.

He shoved Joey's legs up, spreading them, and spat on his hole. Crude, yes, but Joey's harsh breath told Gideon he'd needed that, the animal, the visceral. As he rose up and swallowed Joey's cock down, he thrust a spit-slick finger up Joey's tunnel, and Joey's next cry was shattered, close to climax, every barrier between need and oblivion blown apart by Gideon's aggressiveness.

"More…," he moaned.

Gideon fumbled for the lube they kept under the pillow now, breathing a sigh of relief when he found it. He clicked it open and dumped slick on his fingers, his stomach shuddering at Joey's breathless prayer of protest.

"No… no, don't… don't stop…. Gid… I need—*ah*!"

Covered in slick, this time Gideon thrust three fingers in, and Joey cried out again, holding his thighs out, spreading himself for Gideon's invasion while Gideon bottomed Joey's cock out in his throat.

"*Yes, please*!" Joey cried, and Gideon added more lube and one more finger, curling the front two up, finding the sweet spot while Joey clutched at his hair and screamed.

And came, and came and came and came.

And when his balls were dry, he still shuddered, clenching around Gideon's fingers. He cried out when Gideon withdrew them, and Gideon whispered, "Coming, baby. I'm coming," as he repositioned himself, thrusting up and inside Joey's still tremoring body.

The little mewl that issued from his lips destroyed Gideon's heart as it drove his body on. Joey wrapped his legs around Gideon's hips, and Gideon thrust again and again and again, wiping his fingers off on the sheets so he could pin Joey's shoulders against the bed and plunder his mouth while he plundered his body.

Joey's movements, his noises, were no longer pleading, no longer desperate—they were fierce. He thrust his hips up to meet Gideon's and battled for supremacy in the cage of their kiss.

Gideon welcomed it, loved Joey Carlyle's fierceness, loved his fight, wanted his lover whole and powerful as they took each other, met equally on the battlefield of passion.

His own climax threatened, and he growled, trying to drive it back, knowing Joey needed him there, thrusting, *fucking*, for as long as possible, but Joey raked his nails across Gideon's lower back.

"Don't you dare," he commanded, the first sane thing he'd said since they'd gotten to the bedroom. "Come on, dammit, come in me—*come inside me*!"

And just knowing his will had returned was enough. He threw his head back, exposing his throat, driving so deeply into Joey Carlyle's body he thought his *soul* was thrusting inside. Joey moaned from a deep place in his gut, a place Gideon could feel down in his cock, and a last bit of come spattered from Joey's cock across Gideon's abs.

And Gideon lost all cohesion, his orgasm destroying him, disintegrating his identity, his boundaries, his inhibitions, and he howled, a guttural, visceral sound he didn't recognize as his own as he pulsed come into the haven of Joey Carlyle's ass.

He came to himself still lodged inside Joey, face buried in the hollow of Joey's neck and shoulders, his own body still twitching.

There was an angry pounding coming from the room next door, and Gideon squeezed his eyes shut and tried to place it.

"What the…," he mumbled.

Joey let out a broken little laugh. "You were loud," he said.

"*I* was loud?" Although yes—that final cry, that had been… well, a lot.

"*We* were loud," Joey sighed, his body so limp and pliant Gideon wondered if they'd fall into each other, become one flesh forever.

"Mm." Before Gideon could draw in enough breath to shout a weak "Sorry," the pounding faded, and he let out a low grunt and slid to the side. His cock slid out of Joey's body, and the gush that followed was enough to make him sigh.

"I'll change the sheets," Joey murmured. "You get something to eat."

"Sure," he said, pleased that Joey was sounding more… more *Carlyle* like, but still not quite of this earth yet.

"Never mind," Joey said, laughing a little. He slithered out from Gideon's arm and bent to kiss his cheek, lingering, rubbing his lips along Gideon's cheekbone and nuzzling his ear. "You stay there," he said. "I'll start dinner and come in with the sheets. I… I really want to eat dinner with you after this. I want to come back to our clean den and sleep."

Gideon nodded, wishing he had words yet, but he was already half asleep.

Then Joey's smell, his heat, slid away, and he was *all* asleep, and that was fun too.

HE AWOKE half an hour later to the smell of breaded chicken cutlets frying and Joey's gentle shaking. "Get dressed, clean up, and go finish dinner while I do this." The hand not squeezing his arm waved clean linens around.

He was still out of it enough to realize he hadn't said anything even as he got up to follow orders.

He was a little more awake when Joey came back out of the bedroom, and together they plated up the chicken, the microwaved potatoes, and the salad Gideon had whipped up, and brought their plates and a glass of wine to the coffee table, where they both sat on the floor and ate, their conversation minimal.

Finally they pushed their plates away and moved up to sit on the couch, Gideon leaning back so Joey could rest his head on Gideon's chest.

"Do we have to talk about it?" Joey asked reluctantly.

Gideon sighed. "Only a little," he said.

"What's a little?"

"Joey?"

"Yeah?"

"You are mine. And I am yours. However you want to define it. You belong here, in my home. I know you can't move back in now, but there will be a time when you have to let go of your apartment so we can be here together."

“We can’t come out to the squad,” Joey said, and for a moment Gideon felt a shaft of pain that took his breath away. Then Joey added, “Not because I’m afraid for me—or even *us*—but for them. What they don’t know, they can’t tell my father. If my father finds out about us, I’ll be worried for *you*, but if it’s the whole squad, we are *all* in danger. You understand?”

“They’d stand up for us,” Gideon said without a doubt.

“I know,” Joey said gravely. “I’ve learned that much. And we’ll stand for them too. Even Manny, who’s new—I like him.”

“Same,” Gideon said, acknowledging the new hire Crosby—who else—had discovered during the op that got him shot. Manny was partnered with Gail now that everybody was healthy, and Gideon liked the pairing. Manny Swan was easygoing, smart, measured, and thought on his feet. Gail was quick and fierce and sometimes was quicker on her feet than on her thoughts. They made a good team.

“But right now, I trust you to stay alive. Until we have a reason—or a way—to take my father down, let’s not give him a bigger target, okay?”

And Gideon understood. It wasn’t a picket fence, but it was enough. It was faith that someday, they’d be *them* in front of the family they had that mattered.

“As long as *you* know,” Gideon murmured into his hair. “Unless you say anything—and I mean real words, Joey—you are my person. You said once you thought *I* was the deer. We’re both wolves. *You’re* my wolf. Do you understand?”

Joey shuddered against him, but it wasn’t desperate or pleading. It was the shudder a body makes when it’s been cold too long and suddenly it begins to warm.

“You’re *my* wolf,” he whispered. “Is there a word for that?”

“Yeah. I won’t make you say it.”

“Someday,” Joey promised, but the wine and the food—and the aftermath—were settling into his bones much like they were into Gideon’s.

Still, when Joey’s breathing had evened out against his chest, when his eyes had closed, leaving absurdly long lashes the only testament to the boy Joey Carlyle must have been at one time, Gideon was awake enough to say the word against his crown.

"I love you, Joey Carlyle. Love is the word. It's the only word that matters."

He dropped off to sleep to dream of hearing the words back.

BORROWED TIME

JOEY STARED at the text again and sighed before getting up from his desk to tap Gideon on the shoulder.

"I'll tell him," he said, and Gideon nodded, starting to get up.

"It's fine," Joey said. "You keep working on what you're working on. Harding doesn't bite."

Gideon gave him a warm smile, and Joey twitched his lips in return. He may talk big, but he was very aware this was a shitty time to tell Harding that his father had tracked his new phone.

Crosby was in trouble again (goddammit, Crosby!) and this time, all they could do about it was cover for him and pray he didn't get outed in the undercover assignment he never should have been given.

The good news was that, if Joey had ever doubted that the team would stand up behind him and Gideon when they came out, those doubts were dispelled when Crosby had moved in with Garcia in March, claiming to be using his spare room.

Spare room the unit's collective *ass*. Anybody who saw them move together, heard them talk, heard them argue over what color sheets were going on the bed in the *spare room*, knew what was happening—what *had* happened—between the two of them, and the fact was, everybody was so relieved Crosby wasn't alone in the world like a lost puppy they didn't even bat an eyelash that the partners were just like Joey and Gid. *Partners* in every sense of the word.

But that wasn't the only secret that had been revealed when they'd moved in together. Crosby's past, much like Joey's, had come to bite him in the ass. He'd needed to leave Chicago not just because he refused to go along with the shooting of an unarmed Black teenager by his partner, but because his entire *department* had been rotten to the core, saturated in the stink of a white supremacy organization known as the Sons of the Blood.

And Crosby's old partner had shown up in a federal capacity to force Crosby to do his bidding.

So Crosby was working in a Brooklyn precinct under another name, pretending to recruit for the Sons of the Blood, while his unit spent every spare moment they had trying to figure out the power structure of the organization so they could bring it down and get their Crosby back.

The whole unit was being tracked by Sons' members. They'd already lived through a *very* bloody night, saving Crosby's former roommate, and a month spent looking over their shoulders and trying to keep Garcia off the ceiling from worry was wearing on everybody's fucking nerves.

Harding did *not* need the added aggravation, but given that he'd already sat through Gideon's rather dry revelation of their relationship and the upshot of Joey's visit to his father with only raised eyebrows and, "The two of you? Really? Go figure," Joey hoped their boss's legendary stoicism wouldn't let him down today.

"Boss?" Joey said, sticking his head into Harding's office. Gideon had pithily described it as a plain space with *very* comfortable furniture, including a couch that *everybody* had slept on at one point or another when a case got hairy.

Harding glanced up and then sighed and *stood* up, stretching his arms over his head.

"What time is it?" he asked fuzzily, and Joey grimaced, because that usually meant that Harding had been so busy at his desk doing one thing after another that he'd forgotten to eat, drink, stretch, or sometimes pee.

"Time to hit the head and get something at the vending machines," Joey said. "I'll tell you while we walk."

Harding blinked at him and then gave a sheepish smile. "Caught," he said. "I've been doing all the paperwork while Tal does super extra detective work on Crosby. We've got some people in the upper levels of the DOJ who might get subpoenaed if we can run this whole thing to ground, but first…."

First Crosby had to get somebody, *anybody*, who could implicate the guy he'd once testified against and who now held a knife to his balls.

"I would *love* to not have to take a different route home every night," Joey said, referring to the fact that, on any given day, one or all of them could pick up a tail. Joey and Gideon had both started hanging back, allowing themselves to be followed, and then taking radical turns into dark alleys or known body-dumping sites, their bodies wired for action. It wasn't ethical—or even moral—but God, they were both itching for a kill.

The bad night—the *bloody* night—Crosby's fragile former roommate, Toby, had been falsely arrested and imprisoned in a hostile precinct. Garcia and Gideon had gotten the poor guy out—although he was still having surgeries and physical therapy to repair the damage done to his body that night—while the rest of the squad… prowled.

Joey couldn't lie, not even to not horrify Gideon. He'd *loved* the prowl. Those fuckers. Those bloody *fuckers*. Taking an innocent guy like Toby and trying to beat him to death? Shoving Crosby in a proverbial meat grinder and forcing him to do their dirty work? He'd taken three out with his crossbow that night, because silence and stealth had been mandatory, and he'd seen the looks on the others' faces. Tal, Gail, Manny, Harding—they'd been snarling and fierce, a wolfpack still raring for the hunt, even with blood on their fangs.

But Gideon, who had kept him and Garcia alive, as well as rescuing Toby and a couple of guys who were working out well as new recruits for having the balls to stand up to their precinct that night by sheer stinking strategy—hadn't been horrified.

Joey knew this because in the locker room that morning, after the others had showered and gone out to wait so they could exit together, he'd lingered, cupping Joey's cheek and giving a feral smile.

"Did you have fun?" he asked, showing all his teeth.

And Joey knew he was *seen*. "Not enough," he'd growled.

"Don't worry, Little Brother," Gideon said, quoting an old movie that Joey had never seen. "There's more."

Joey had gone in for a quick, fierce kiss, and then they'd separated and gone out to meet the others.

After taking an hour and two different buses to get to Gideon's apartment that morning, they'd barely made it through the door before they fell upon each other and fed and fed and fed.

But that kind of high alert took its toll on a body, on a *mind*, and they were a unit under siege now. Walking through their own level of the federal law enforcement building—a rather forgotten nook on the fifth floor—they held their heads high, unafraid. It was easy because Gideon and Joey had installed their *own* private cameras, starting at the elevator that fed directly into *everybody's* computer units, so all visitors were screened and identified before they even got to the first turn of a very long corridor.

For the moment, in this specific place, they were safe.

But Gideon and Joey had gotten *very* good at installing surveillance equipment. They'd done it to Natalia's house, to her father's (he was a high-powered judge), to Pearson's apartment, and to Swan's. They'd even done it for Henderson and Doba, who had started out the only two honest flatfoots in their precinct but had graduated to protected members of the unit, complete with a new apartment that they shared (with the fresh-faced Henderson's cat and more seasoned Doba's apparently endless supply of houseplants) and were both doing a good job of assimilating into the unit. Doba had even applied for FLETC training, and Henderson was working on getting clearances as a researcher. Like Crosby, they'd taken a bad situation and made the best of it, and the unit had taken them in.

And protected them, although they appeared to have been forgotten by the Sons of the Blood. While the core members of the unit? They saw action once a week, dodging the people tailing them and sometimes, putting them in a world of hurt.

But this floor, their offices? Those were *theirs*. Harding wasn't the only one working late these days.

First the vending machines, each of them getting a candy bar, then the conference room, where the coffee was. Gideon, who had originally supplied the fancy coffees and the coffee bar, something Joey would always adore him for, had bought a new "destresso" machine, as Joey called it, because for the first week Crosby had been under cover, shopping for that fucking espresso contraption had been the only thing keeping Gideon from losing his shit.

A giant vanilla latte sure could take the edge off a guy's day.

Harding also visited the staff minifridge and was surprised to see a reusable plastic container with his name on it.

"Gideon?" he asked, pulling out his *and* Joey's—and Gideon's. There was one for each of them; Joey had helped.

"Both of us," he said, taking the two containers from Harding. "Natalia did it one day last week. Garcia keeps bringing us fruit. Swan and Pearson order takeout. We're dealing, Chief."

Harding nodded and then, spotting Gideon at his desk through the window, waved the sandwich container at him and nodded.

Gideon—who was on the phone—saluted back, and Joey gestured him over. Gideon nodded, and Joey knew he'd come in and they could eat together when he was done with his task, and then it was time for Joey to quit stalling.

Harding sank into one of the comfortable chairs around the conference table and sighed, breaking out his sandwich. "Roast beef and pickles," he said. "Gideon doesn't miss a trick."

Joey's was almost the same thing, but with bacon added on top. Still, he'd wait for Gideon to be done.

Harding was halfway through his sandwich when he realized Joey was eating chips and drinking coffee to keep him company, but he hadn't spoken yet.

"Go on," he urged through a full mouth.

Joey sighed and held out his phone.

If you touch the Sons, I can't protect you.

Harding grunted. "Darling Papa?" he asked sardonically.

"I'm afraid so. I'm going to need—"

"Another encrypted phone," Harding said on a sigh. "I hear you. More concerning, though, is the message. Did you have any idea your sperm donor was involved with the Sons?"

Joey shook his head and shrugged. "No, but it doesn't surprise me. That fucker tends to control people with blackmail, and the Sons of the Blood are *very* blackmailable, if you know what I mean."

"It follows," Harding said mildly. What he meant—and what they'd all ranted about over the last month—was that someone with the sort of pathology that had them willing to set their house on fire before letting a woman, minority, or member of the LGBTQ community lend them a hose was often weak enough to be involved in any number of sins: From drugs to prostitution to gambling, to name the big three. At the very least, fraud made a frequent appearance. Sometimes, Carlyle believed, because racists were too fucking stupid to understand that they couldn't just take shit that didn't belong to them without consequences.

"So odds are, some of the guys paying Dad for protection or whatever are on our hit list. Just… you know. Be aware."

Harding nodded and chewed steadily, setting the sandwich down after he swallowed. "I should have gotten a soda," he mused.

"I'll get it, sir," Joey said, standing up. "That way I don't have to stare at my own sandwich while I wait for Gid."

At that moment Gideon stuck his head in. "I'll get the sodas. I could really use some cold and sweet myself."

He disappeared, and Harding's unexpectedly expressive eyes caught Joey's.

"How are you guys?" he said softly. "This is a lot of pressure for two people."

Joey blinked, surprised at the question—and also absurdly touched. "He wants to be out to the team," he said. "But he gets why I think we shouldn't. I mean, Jesus, let's wait until Crosby's safe at the very fucking least, okay?"

Harding shrugged. "It's sound logic," he agreed. "But I think the team could handle it—they might boggle, cause *look* at you, but they can handle you two as a couple."

Joey shook his head and thought of how Crosby had worn an almost permanent blush the day they'd moved him into Garcia's spare room.

"Let's give Crosby and Garcia some attention," he said after a minute. "I want them home and safe and this Sons of the Blood nightmare behind us. I mean, this thing with my dad? It'll come soon enough. It's like… like when that dog attacked. Crosby shot the drug dealer reaching for his gun because that was the shot he had. I shot the fucking dog because that was the shot *I* had, and that was what I could do. We know the dog's out there, Boss. We know he's gonna bite us in the ass. But right now we've got the Sons of the Blood, and they're all fucking armed, so we gotta take care of them first. And when the dog sinks his teeth into my ass, I hope the rest of you all have my back."

"No question," Harding said soberly. "Believe it, Joey. Just like with Crosby. We didn't desert him, we won't desert you."

Gideon's squeeze of his shoulder told Joey that he'd heard and agreed.

He proceeded to set down the soda cans, one of which he pulled out of his pocket. Joey, who was almost done with his latte, gave him a smile even *he* knew was besotted.

"Carlyle?" Harding said, lips twitching as he picked up his sandwich and prepared to do more damage.

"Yeah, Boss," Joey said, jerking his attention back with an effort.

"If you don't want to be out to the team, you gotta not look at him like that."

Joey realized he had the *stupidest* expression on his face, sort of a goofy combination of worship and desire and gratitude, and he bit his lip and stared down at his own sandwich.

"Well, it's not my fault if they figure it out," he mumbled, unwrapping his sandwich with a sigh. "I mean, we work with detectives, right?"

Gideon's chuckle warmed him—almost as much as Gideon's knee, pressed gently next to his own.

"Also," Harding said, pulling a napkin from the center of the table and wiping his mouth with it, "Natalia knows."

Joey puffed out a breath, not surprised. Harding and Natalia were partners and, as far as he could see, one of the best couples he knew. Unlike him and Gid, or Crosby and Garcia, they were platonic, but super extra tight that way.

"I do," Natalia said, coming into the conference room and surprising Joey—and Gideon from his expression—but not Harding. "And since we all know, I'm going to come eat my sandwich. I've been *waiting* for this." She rummaged through the minifridge and came back with *her* paper-wrapped bundle, as well as a bottle of hand-brewed kombucha. "So," she said, elbowing Harding to let her in, "have we discussed Joey's family yet, because I am *dying* to dissect his father's brain. With a butter knife."

Joey snickered into his sandwich, and the rest of lunch was spent in a pleasant game of "revenge," and the grim fantasy did a *lot* to alleviate some of the brain-crunching stress he'd felt when his phone had buzzed that morning.

THE GAME wasn't so funny when Crosby got brought in beat to shit and mostly dead from a drug overdose slipped into his water.

He was brought to Garcia's place, hooked up to an IV, mostly unconscious for nearly three days, and the entire unit decided they'd had enough.

Joey and Gideon had been interviewing a civil engineer who kept finding bodies in the Hudson over the course of his work day when Gideon had gotten the text that Crosby had been brought in and was in bad shape. Joey saw from his eyes that something was wrong, read his silent "Crosby," and felt his blood run cold. So he'd been about to blow the poor engineer off, but that felt dishonest. The NYPD was supposed to interview him, but *they* kept shuttling his problem down to SCTF. Where the fuck were all the bodies coming from?

Clint thought that was a very good question, but their dossier was incredibly spotty because nobody in the NYPD was taking him seriously, and the FBI had to be asked in on a case and hadn't been. The SCTF was their fallback, but by the time somebody from Clint's squad got there, the staties had already taken the body to be autopsied and locked the feds out of it.

So it wasn't the engineer's fault. He was just trying to do his job, and he'd been grilled by the SCTF three times, all about stuff they *should have had* in the fucking dossier. Joey was going to tell him—a solid guy, mostly bald, with a degree in civil engineering and a New Jersey accent—that this was not his day, again, when the guy said something that made them both perk up.

"Yeah, I know I keep finding bodies, and you suits keep saying 'So what,' but you know, I got a theory about why they keep ending up here."

Gideon cocked his head, and Joey kept his peace. Gideon liked things like this—the physics, the how, the where, the why.

"Hit us with it, Mr. Rau," he said.

"Well, see, my job is to clear out the floor of the Hudson to either build the ferry docks or make sure the ferries can get through, right?"

They both nodded.

"So we get sand and silt buildup from the same places on account of the currents. I figure the bodies gotta come the same way. You look at where the currents of the river are coming from, you'll see where the bodies are coming from, right? I mean, *I* got maps and computer readouts and shit—but that's so I know which parts of the river are building up so I know where to direct my guys. But you can use that same shit to figure out where an object's gonna come from, and aren't you guys the ones who get the forensics reports? I mean, there's engineers at the transportation commission who could help you do the math, right?"

Gideon and Joey stared at him.

"Absolutely right, sir," Gideon said, thinking about it. "You are absolutely right. I mean, I'm sorry. I feel like we should have thought of this before, but I'm thrilled *you* got there, right?"

“You gonna do something about this?” the man asked. “’Cause I seen the same tattoo on some of these guys—and some of ’em are suits, but some of ’em are working guys. They all got their insides carved out and stuffed full of rocks so they stick to the bottom of the river, ’cause people don’t count on my outfit to scoop ’em out, you know?”

“What’s the tattoo say?” Joey asked. “Like, Special Forces or something?”

Their guy snorted. “Like *wannabe*, right? S-o-B. Big *S*, little *o*, big *B*.”

Joey and Gideon locked gazes.

“Shit,” Joey said.

“Motherfucker.”

No wonder the NYPD was mucking up the case and muddling up the federal involvement.

“You know who that is?” their guy asked.

“Sir,” Joey said, pulling out his card, “you have been the victim of a massive bureaucratic fuckup. We’re sorry this keeps happening to you, and you only get us when we’re run ragged from something else, but that is going to fucking change. Here’s my card. Next time you find a fucking body, you contact *us*. Not the NYPD. Not the FBI. You’ve done part of our job for us, but that’s not fair. You’re busy trying to build shit, and that’s a good thing. Keep doing that. In the meantime, send *everything* you got to this email.” He pulled out his pen and circled Gideon’s email on their business card. “That’s my partner here. He’s hella fuckin’ smart—he’s gonna take everything you just said and make the goddamned bodies stop.”

They could only hope.

Their guy went from beleaguered and frustrated to much, much happier. “That’s great,” he said. “I mean, I get it if you gotta see a couple more—there don’t seem to be much of a shortage, you know what I mean?”

“Sadly, yes,” Gideon said, nodding. “Just remember—you call *us*. Leave the NYPD out of it for now.”

“Will do,” Mr. Rau told them. “Thanks, guys.”

"Jesus," Joey said as they walked away. "That guy should be on our team."

"Shoulders like a linebacker," Gideon said. "And speaking of…." His voice dropped, and he told Joey about Crosby then.

Joey's vision went a little swimmy. Gideon's hand on his elbow helped him get to the SUV, and he refused to shake it off, even though between the Crosby sitch and Joey's father, the odds were pretty damned good they had a tail.

Fuck 'em, he thought, fighting off shivers in the SUV. Fuck 'em if they thought he and Gideon leaning on each other for strength meant they were weak. He'd show 'em weak. *They'd rip their fucking throats out!*

He was very aware of Gideon rubbing his back with his own shaking hand.

"He'll be okay?" Joey asked.

"He's at Garcia's right now. After shift, we're on for setting up a security system."

Joey nodded, thinking of Garcia's sweet little house in Queens. So domestic. Natalia did the gracious holiday dinners at her gracious family house. Clint had a house—and a husband, apparently—he kept secret and safe in Long Island. Gideon's apartment was too small for the unit, especially now that its population had grown. But Garcia's house in Queens—they'd gathered there the last nine months. It had been the den-mother house they hadn't known they'd needed. You could eat pizza while sitting in front of the coffee table at Garcia's house in Queens.

They *had* to make it safe.

"You okay?" Gideon asked.

"No," Joey said, thinking about the many eyes that could be on them right now, hating those fuckers who were just waiting for them to show their throats. He turned toward Gideon and fisted his front collar before dragging him, unresisting, until their lips touched.

Gideon must have felt like he did, because their kiss wasn't soft or comforting—it was *monster*, destructive, and angry.

And Joey pulled strength from it, the kind of strength that could lay waste to armies.

Bad guys didn't know that a kiss could do this, because bad guys didn't know shit.

They separated only to breathe, leaning their foreheads against each other as they panted into air that would soon be stifling.

"Gideon?"

"Yeah?"

"I'm tired of this shit."

"Same."

"Those guys watching us? My dad's? The Sons of the Blood?"

"Yeah?"

"Let's kill 'em."

Gideon's smile was as thin as his features, feral, a wolf showing his teeth. "Knives or guns?"

"I don't care." Joey laughed, and it was not a nice sound.

As Gideon started the car and pulled away from the curb, Joey caught sight of a guy in flannels and jeans, with a lean face and yellowing skin, glaring at them as they passed.

He had lank hair and a badger's mean eyes, and he hawked spit at them, probably hitting the back quarter panel as they went.

Joey flipped him the bird behind his back, but he filed the face away. He had a feeling he'd see it again.

THEY DIDN'T have long to wait. The team worked feverishly—even Crosby, whose eyes were practically swollen shut from the beating he'd gotten. Three days after Crosby was carted home, unconscious, Joey and Gideon were late. The plan was that after logging out, the team would leave their work phones in their offices and take their burner phones with them as they all took different routes to Crosby's house in Queens, but Gideon was going to stop by Shake Shack first, the better to grab food for everybody.

"Shake Shack?" Joey asked. "Couldn't we just order pizza at Garcia's place?"

Gideon gave him that thin wolf's smile. "We could," he said innocently. "In fact, we may want to do that anyway. But you know. There's something I want to check out at Shake Shack."

"What?" Joey asked, but he was belting up anyway.

"You know how the warehouses are about two blocks behind that strip with the Shake Shack and the frozen-yogurt place, right?"

"Yeah?"

"I… I want to check some shit out at those warehouses is all. Just…." Gideon's shoulders twitched. "You know, our nice civil engineer?"

"Yeah?"

"I've been tracking water currents with the department of fish and game and the weather people and the water department—and I've got… let's say I've got a theory."

Joey liked where this was going.

They left the department issue at the fro-yo place (after checking to see if they had pre-packed half gallons first), and then they cruised the warehouse front, noting one that was clean and bustling when much of the activity down that area had been limp and uninterested.

"Who is this?" Gideon asked as they took turns with field glasses from the roof of a building two blocks away. "I mean, which company? Nobody's this busy in this economy. Who—"

"Doesn't matter," Joey said, feeling that feral growl in his throat.

"Why not?"

"I spotted one of my tails. He's reporting to that woman with the blond ponytail—the one with the Glock tucked in the back of her jeans."

"Ooh… promising." Gideon took the field glasses from him and stared for a minute, frowning. "Okay, then," he said. "I gotta talk to Harding."

"Over the phones?" Joey asked, surprised. The guy who was putting the screws to Crosby was working *for NYPD Internal Affairs*, and their assumption had been that they could easily be tracked or recorded on their phones pretty much from day one of this whole mishigas.

"No, Joey, in person. *You're* going to stay here and track their movements and try to figure out who in the fuck is onloading what here—Crosby said there were drugs filling the streets. You know where drugs often come in from? Two hints, and the answer's *not* the Rio Grande."

"Ports, Gideon. I'm not stupid. I see where you're going." He might have sulked then, but he realized Gideon was trusting him. "So while I'm here, you're going back to the office to talk to Harding."

"And to get a covert vehicle, not the I'm-a-government-official SUV," Gideon confirmed. "Watch for me."

"What do you think Harding's going to say?" Joey asked.

Again, that feral wolf's smile, the one Joey Carlyle had thought he owned but knew now he hadn't sharpened nearly enough. Gideon's smile was as sharp as his chin, his nose, his fierce lethal brain.

Joey felt a lust rising, for blood, for sex, for *Gideon*, that he'd never known existed.

But first….

"See you in an hour," he said. "And Gideon?"

"Yeah?"

"Bring my crossbow."

That smile only widened.

AN HOUR later, Joey emerged from the shadows of the alleyway to hop in the front seat of the nondescript sedan, heart thundering in his ears.

"Half a block," he managed. "Turn left behind that outbuilding."

"What's back there?" Gideon asked.

“A great make-out spot,” he cackled.

Gideon scowled. “Now?”

“Did you bring my crossbow?”

“Yeah, yeah, I did.”

“Did Harding agree?”

“As long as we’re defending our lives,” Gideon said virtuously.

“So, let’s go make out,” Joey said. “*Right now.*”

“Oh,” Gideon said, getting it. “Now.”

Killing bad guys was remarkably easy when they were mean and dumb.

“Do you see them?” Gideon asked softly as they emerged from the car, Joey with the crossbow tucked under his jacket in the front and the knives tucked under his belt in the back. Gideon had his own knife in a sheath at his side, and of course a gun, but they didn’t want to fire their weapons today.

Their weapons and ammo were highly regulated, and that’s not what this was about.

“So,” Joey said, pulling into the shade of the brick outbuilding, making sure it was at his back. He was angled slightly—Gideon had the view behind him, toward the open water, and he had the view behind Gideon, toward the alleyway, both access points that made the two of them vulnerable. “You feeling naughty yet?”

“Feeling *horny*,” Gideon said, and that blunt word from his usually refined mouth actually *did* make Joey harden under his stretchy black slacks.

Joey’s laughter went throaty and evil, and he caught Gideon by the hips and pulled him forward. Gideon wrapped on arm around Joey’s shoulders—strategically, so their views remained unobstructed—and murmured against his mouth, “Do you see them yet?”

“Yup,” Joey said, running his tongue along the seam of Gideon’s lips. “You got one on your seven, one on your eight.”

“Yours are at your nine and eleven,” Gideon murmured. “A knife and a baseball bat.”

"You got a knife and brass knuckles."

Gideon growled, and Joey felt him reach under his own jacket for his sheath, while Joey pulled his crossbow out with one hand and a fixed blade from his back sheath with the other.

"Hello, faggots," one of their assailants laughed.

Together Joey and Gideon turned outward, back to back, weapons in hand, and Joey couldn't see Gideon's face, but he could hear the growl in his voice.

"Hello, boys. Did you think we were stupid?" he asked.

The men in front of Joey gave nasty little laughs, and the four assailants closed in.

Joey's one regret was that he couldn't watch Gideon in action. As he squared off with his opponents, he heard Gideon talking to himself. "To the right, motherfucker, to the left, one hop this time, everybody slit your throat!" And then a series of feints and gasps that to Joey's fevered imagination sounded very much like the battle was choreographed to the song.

But Joey's own attackers were getting closer, and Joey recognized the guy with the stringy, curly hair who had seen him and Gideon kissing in the SUV. He was carrying the baseball bat.

He was also the one who'd called them faggots, and Joey bared all his teeth as he wielded his knife. "How ya doin'?" he asked. "You ready to party with a *real* man?"

"Suck my fat one," the guy said, and Joey laughed unpleasantly.

"For that?" he said. "I'll cut it off."

The man closed in, with the bat coming heavily off his shoulder, and Joey waited until he got close enough to swing, the thing lifting off with a sense of lots of power but no velocity. Then he aimed the crossbow at his hip and fired, hitting the fuckwad squarely in the upper abdomen.

Not immediately mortal, no—but bad. The guy pinwheeled backward, the bat flinging from his hand and barely missing his friend as his hands felt for the metal fletching protruding from his sternum.

"But… but…," the guy muttered.

"Did you think we were going to play fair?" Joey asked, ducking as the other guy—this one smaller, quicker, and younger—came in with the knife. He toyed with the boy for a few, dodging back, trash talking.

"This what you got?" Joey asked. "You sure you want to die like this? I'm not in the mood to let you walk away."

"You talk big," the boy panted, "for a faggot."

"Do you even know what that word *means*?" Joey asked, springing from a board to a brick, to off the side of the outbuilding, each move taking him higher and higher until, after running up the side of the building, he executed a little flip over the boy's head, landing at his back squarely to grab his knife hand and squeeze the ulnar nerve hard enough for the boy to drop his weapon.

Joey jerked the kid's arm behind him and yanked with enough force to dislocate the shoulder, and unlike with Gail, who was a friend, the *pop* of cartilage and bone didn't bother him, and neither did the boy's scream of pain.

"You're young," Joey whispered into the kid's ear. God, freshly showered when the other three guys back there had been unwashed. "So I'm gonna give you the benefit of the doubt. You can keep this up and I'll kill you—witness your buddy there." Lank, curly-headed guy was down, and Joey had been wrong about the wound not being mortal. The guy was spitting up blood, his face ashen, wet, wheezing sobs of desperation coming from his sucking chest wound.

"Or what?" the boy mewled. "You let me go, they'll kill me."

"This ain't the only part of the city, boy," Joey told him. "You take what's in your pocket, you get the fuck out of here. Grab a bus to Jersey, work as a dishwasher, sleep in a shelter, but get the fuck out. 'Cause the only other way out is in the Hudson River. You ready to die yet? Are you?"

He yanked on the kid's shoulder, sending pain zinging up his body, Joey knew. He'd done this once. Wasn't a picnic.

"No," the boy whispered.

Joey threw him against the wall. "Then get the fuck out of here," he said. "If I have to fight you again, I'll slit your throat."

The kid stumbled on his way out, bent to check his buddy, who wasn't spitting up blood anymore because you had to breathe to do that. He glanced behind himself, cradling his arm, and saw that Gideon had dispatched his two assailants, one with a quick flick of his knife to a jugular, and one with a square thrust under the ribs to the guy's heart.

As the kid watched, Gideon was yanking his knife out of the second guy's chest, and the kid must have known that guy, because he issued a little moan and ran faster.

"Was that wise?" Gideon asked. He pointed at the body he'd pulled the knife from. "Get his feet."

Joey did as asked, and together they moved to the edge of the dock, where they could throw the guy off. Thanks to the two outbuildings—and the emptiness of this part of the pier—they were unobserved, although Joey suspected there might be electronic surveillance.

Good. It wasn't the government kind. He wanted their enemy to see them, know the SCTF wasn't helpless and it wasn't weak, and it wasn't going to let its people get beaten, stabbed, and drugged without retribution.

He and Gideon gave a little extra *oomph* to their body—and the two that followed it.

Joey remembered to yank the crossbow bolt out of the first casualty. Not many people used one of those, and if Harding said no paperwork, he didn't want to have to account for it.

"Poor Alex," Gideon said as they left the bodies to the vagaries of the river.

"Alex?" Joey asked.

"Our civil engineer. His first name is Alex. I suspect he's going to get a whole whack of bodies in the next few days."

"As long as none of them are ours," Joey said with satisfaction. He looked them both over. "I got bloodier than you. You're going to have to go into the fro-yo place and pick up our order."

"You ordered fro-yo?" Gideon asked, sounding touched.

"For the unit. You know. Since we didn't get Shake Shack for Garcia, I figured we could bring fro-yo for the team. For dessert."

Gideon chuckled. "God, Joey. I wish we were here to make out for real."

Joey blew out a breath in disgust. "Not me—ew. I wish we were at your apartment making out. Jesus. What a thing to say."

But Gideon kept chuckling, throwing an arm over Joey's shoulder and squeezing before letting go so they could get into the car.

They should have been more careful, Joey thought in hindsight. The Sons of the Blood—and he was pretty sure those had been the men who'd attacked them—weren't the only ones on his tail. He knew that.

AND WORSE, the run-in had made Joey and Gideon cocky. After the meeting at Garcia's house—and God, it was hard to see Crosby that weak; it pissed Joey off all over again—they told Harding they were going back to the same place.

Something about the way the men had moved, the way the kid had wept as he'd taken off in a completely different direction than the one he'd come, told them this was their *stomping* grounds. Some of the intel they'd covered at the meeting had niggled at Gideon, he said. It hinted at a warehouse, and a bunch of the guys Crosby had gotten tight with worked at a warehouse. And that warehouse had proximity to where all the bodies were being dumped into the river.

Harding had given them permission, told them to check in with him. This time Joey drove.

"You think they'll be waiting for us?" Joey said.

"They might be."

"Should we park farther away, maybe surveil from the roof?"

"Yeah," Gideon said. He shuddered. "Joey, you heard from your old man?"

"No," Joey muttered. "Yeah, gives me the creeps too."

"How do you think he's mixed up in this?"

"I think he's blackmailing the top brass involved is what I think," Joey said. "But that doesn't mean he doesn't have his fingers in the pie. The old man's a control freak. I should've taken pictures of his house. You and your pointy brain would have had a *field* day profiling him."

Gideon snorted. "You've learned a lot since you got here. What do *you* think?"

Joey was quiet for a moment. "I think the first night I slept there, he had all these toys—Legos, Lincoln Logs, shit he grew up with as a kid—and a tablet. Back then, it meant we were rich, that he'd bought his kid a tablet. Anyway, I went up to my room after dinner, and I remembered my grandfather teaching me how to camp in the wild, particularly if there were bears or mountain lions around. Lights were scary. Big noises were scary. So I was eight years old. I missed the shit out of my grandfather, and I didn't like this white motherfucker who took me away. I made traps—rigged a jump rope to trip somebody walking into the room, and if he stepped over that, he stepped on rubber balls. And I moved the bookshelves and put jacks and Legos on them so if you tripped and put your hands down, you made a racket, and I rigged the bookshelves to fall down and clatter, and on top of all of that, I rigged the tablet so that any bit of jiggling would make it screech speed-metal music at the drop of a hat."

"Oh my God," Gideon said, sounding stunned "What happened?"

"I didn't count on the fucker having put video cameras in all the stuffed animals—the one toy I wouldn't touch. I woke up, and he had a knife to my throat, but I'd slept with my own knife, so I held it to his balls."

"Jesus," Gideon muttered. "What'd he say?"

"He smiled, backed out of the room, and said, 'I'm locking the door. I hope you don't have to take a piss in the night.'"

Gideon blew out a breath. "Did you?"

"Yeah. I found a teddy bear with the camera on it and pissed on that. It was like a signal, you know? Let the games begin."

"Oh Jesus." Gideon leaned back in his seat and shuddered. "Baby. I'm sorry you had to grow up like that."

"Me too," Joey said. "Especially because, you know, all that training, growing up with a sociopath, it's told me the same thing you already know."

"What's that?" Gideon asked, but he didn't sound like it would be a shock to him.

"You and me tonight? We're walking into a trap."

Gideon was good—so good he didn't check his rearview mirror, although he must have seen their tail for the last six blocks. Joey had shaken the first one, and the second, and the third, but it became obvious they weren't getting out of here without some sort of confrontation.

"What do you want to do about it?" Gideon asked, just as an SUV with a reinforced grill and no lights T-boned them from out of fucking nowhere.

Apparently, the trap was already sprung.

THERE WAS confusion then, rough hands on his person, the pain of being dragged and restrained.

Joey fought. He heard swearing and knew Gideon was fighting too. Loopily, he pushed to his feet, started swinging, disoriented but pissed. They'd both worn seatbelts, but his neck, his shoulders—they'd be in a *world* of hurt the next morning. Hands on his shoulder, hauling *his* hands behind his back, and the rip of duct tape.

He lashed out with a kick that landed solidly in somebody's groin, and behind him he heard a pop and a howl and thought, *Hey, Gid dislocated a knee. How cool is that?*

But there were a lot of "them," and only two of him and Gideon, and eventually they were in the center of a panting, sweating, *angry* bunch of men and one unpleasant, bitter-looking woman, all of them dressed in battered jeans, denim jackets, and hoodies—the unofficial uniform of dock workers without coveralls.

"What do we do with them?" came the question. "I'd just as soon shoot 'em and shove 'em off the dock."

"They're feds, you moron," said the woman. "Their bodies show up and people start asking questions. Let me check with my guys. For now, take them upstairs and dose 'em—these two fuckers'll break free if you let 'em."

Dose. Oh shit. *Dose.* Joey had never known it was a fear. Of all the ways he'd had to come to harm at his father's hands, an *overdose* hadn't been an option. But he'd seen Crosby's face, heard the story of how Crosby had been doing okay. He'd been stabbed and stitched, had gotten into one hell of a fight, but he'd been doing okay—and then he'd downed meth-flavored water by accident and almost died.

And deep in Joey's gut started the worry, the *terror*, that all the work he'd done to be smarter, to be a more compassionate human, to love his family in the SCTF like they seemed to love him, would disappear when the drugs hit his bloodstream.

He'd seen junkies. He'd *tracked* junkies, and sometimes they were sad, and sometimes they were mean, but never, ever were they the version of themselves they'd planned to be as children.

He'd rather lose his life than lose the person that Gideon took to his bed.

The thought was shocking beyond belief, but he couldn't dwell on it because they were being dragged into a warehouse and up a set of wooden stairs to an office. He didn't need to study the place to spot the pallets of plastic-wrapped white powder that were stacked in plain sight right behind the bay doors.

Oh, these *must* be the Sons of the Blood, a group so deep in the police force they'd bought themselves a higher-up in the DOJ to force Crosby to recruit them into the nearest precinct.

But bad guys came in tangles—the dogfighting ring had taught him that—and Joey was not surprised when the biggest and oldest guy of the group that had borne them up here, kicking and fighting with every breath, stopped a younger, angrier guy from going to work on Gideon.

"But Garve!" the younger guy complained, his body primed to let a punch explode, as Gideon sat furious, zip-tied to an office chair, and glowered.

"Go ahead," Gideon snarled before hawking blood from his already broken nose and spitting on the guy's shoes. "You think a little pain is gonna save you now?"

"I'll show you a little pain—*Garve*!"

Garve clocked the guy in the jaw and stood, body between Joey and Gideon, a force to be reckoned with. Joey thought unhappily that this guy was wasted as a hood, or whatever capacity he served under Sons of the Blood, because that was some solid-balls leadership right there.

"We're dosing them," he said. "If they die from heroin, it'll be easier to deny we had anything to do with it. If they live, they'll be killed and dumped way far away from here. I don't know how they found us, but they're *feds*, Rog. Feds do check-ins. *Somebody* is gonna come lookin' for 'em, and they're harder to move when dead. You gotta trust me on this. I know. So shut up and get the doses from Big Bitch's drawer. She's always got four or five ready to go in case the boys get antsy. Too many of our boys are methed out—the horse chills them until they can come down."

Crosby had told them about the meth, but the heroin—that was something new.

Joey marveled that he was storing all these facts in his aching noggin when odds were good he was going to die with his first needleful of heroin.

Garve had wrapped the constrictor around Joey's arm first, and as he flicked the crux of Joey's arm to get the vein to pop out, he leaned close.

"You let my kid go," he whispered, so quietly Joey almost couldn't hear him over the ringing in his ears. "For that you only get half a dose."

Joey grunted. "If the other guy dies, I will burn this place to the ground."

The man flicked surprised eyes to Joey's, and Joey wasn't sure what glared back at him, but he got one solid nod in return.

"'Sides," Joey mumbled as the needle slid into the vein. "'Mm Stevie Carlyle's kid. You kill me, he'll burn your neighborhoods, your families, your whole family line. Only person who fucks with Stevie Carlyle's kid is Stevie Carlyle."

He heard the gasps—more than one—and Rog spoke up.

"Holy fuckin' Jesus, Garve, you hear that? Stevie Carlyle will fuck us up!"

"Another reason to only give 'em half a dose," Garve said, but Joey caught the reluctance there and wondered if that was because they were no longer square.

"Me and Gideon live," Joey slurred as the drug made its way into his vein, "he'll be too fuckin' busy to ever hear your name."

His eyelids flickered, but he kept them on the syringe and the needle. How much was left? Five mil? Three? Was it enough?

All the pain faded, so, so sweet, and then his vision darkened, soft and gentle, and he began to sing.

"I WAS not singing," he protested later, in the hospital bed next to Gideon's.

"Swear to fuckin' God," Harding told him, his voice harsh with worry—and with battle. Did their team come after them? Oh yeah, and they brought the fury of hell with them.

All Joey knew was one minute he was in the comforting arms of oblivion, and the next Harman Blodgett, Clint Harding's significant other, apparently, a slender man with a charming smile, a receding hairline, and balls of adamantium, had his shoulder under Joey's arm and was helping him down the back stairway of the warehouse while Iwo Fuckin' Jima was going on in the front.

"Gid?" Joey had slurred.

"Right behind us—" Blodgett began, and then Gideon started screaming "The Wreck of the Edmund Fitzgerald" at the top of his bloody lungs.

"Oh," Joey said. "We're doing that now."

And then he joined him. But that was *conscious*, he told himself virtuously. Gideon was singing "The Wreck of the Edmund Fitzgerald" and Joey was his *partner*—they *had* to sing together.

"I mean, the Gordon Lightfoot thing," Joey said, holding Harding's eyes and nodding. "Had to do that. Right, Gid? Couldn't leave you hanging."

"My baby boy never leaves me hanging," Gideon said, and he sounded sober as a judge too. Then he launched into "Right Hand Man" from *Hamilton*, and Harding took a deep breath and called for the nurse.

Joey and Gideon were *grooving* to *Hamilton* when the nurse showed up, and Harding asked if there was any fucking chance the two of them would be sober enough to go on an op in a couple of hours when he got the warrant. It was a nice thing he was trying to do, let them in on serving a warrant to the top bad guys responsible for their shitty night. Joey worked hard at keeping his voice on key so Harding would know how much they loved him.

The nurse had eyed them skeptically. "*How* much Narcan did you give them?" he asked Blodgett, who was staring at them in bemusement.

"Just the first dose," Harm told him. "Maybe give them an hour of fluids, Clint, and let's stitch their wounds and set Gideon's nose at the very least. It'll be a few hours before your judge wakes up enough to send you on your way. Might as well let them finish the concert."

"D'you hear that?" Gideon asked. "*Encore*!"

"Oh God," Crosby said, because God-for-fucking-bid Crosby be on an op without bleeding all over the fuckin' place. He was gonna be okay, he'd assured them, but he wasn't sure he knew enough of *Hamilton* to sing along.

"Your loss," Joey said.

Now, as Crosby and Harding conferred, Blodgett went out to talk to the nurse, and Harding said—loud enough for them to hear—"Jesus, don't you guys know some Led Zeppelin or something?"

So they got to change to "Immigrant Song," and that was good too. Air guitar with that one!

But back to what Harding had insisted at the beginning of that conversation in the hospital. Joey Carlyle had *not* been singing when he'd been completely unconscious and stoned.

He had way too much dignity for that.

BY THE end of the day, he'd consigned dignity to the four winds. Had they gotten the fuckers who'd fucked them? Oh yes, they had—in an explosion of bullets and blood in a conference room of police plaza, they'd killed all but two of the bad guys.

One of those bad guys would have a *very* bad time in jail, and the other one, the one Crosby had wounded but not killed, on purpose because apparently their puppy had a mean streak, was probably going to die there.

Crosby liked that idea, and Joey thought better of him for the little bit of sadism that now laced his sweetness. It was that kind of move that could keep a puppy alive.

But finally, it was over. The upper-level Sons of the Blood were being subpoenaed by the other part of their team, and the part who had gone to One Police Plaza had surrendered their weapons and were slated for depositions in the next week.

And then there was lunch. Which on the one hand felt weird after the fuckin' last week they'd all had, but on the other, sitting in a greasy spoon and eating steak and eggs with his colleagues—his family—felt like the thing that had been missing from his life.

Which must have been why he chose that moment to spill about his father.

It was either that or the heroin, but Joey hoped it wasn't the heroin, because he and Gideon had *sworn* they'd come down off their high before accepting their weapons.

But there they were—him, Harding, Gideon, Crosby, and Garcia—*plowing* through some first-rate chow, battered, bloody, exhausted, and *ravenous*, when Gideon elbowed him.

"What's up?"

Joey realized he'd been sitting in the same position, a juicy bite of steak dripping with egg poised halfway to his mouth, for a good ten seconds.

He glanced over at Crosby, who had spent some painful moments revealing his past to the entire squad so they would understand what they'd been up against in this last clusterfuck, and then at Harding, who had known about Joey's past from the very beginning and still recruited him, had faith in him.

Welcomed him into his family.

And then he looked at Gideon, who had pretty much learned to read his mind in the last two years.

Gideon's nose was swollen and taped, and he'd needed stitches on his temple and his cheek, would need dentistry—hell, would need to have his wrist set in the next two days because he had a hairline fracture that had been too swollen to do more than splint.

Gideon nodded soberly. "Tell them, kid," he said. "That way they'll be on the lookout."

"I… I don't think he'll do anything right away," Joey mumbled, and then glanced up to meet the eyes of everybody at the table. "But they… the reason Gideon and I didn't die from an overdose—well, there were a couple. One of them was that they were aware that too many bodies had gone over at the pier, and as you know, it's easier to move a live body than it is a dead one. The other two are more complicated. Yesterday, I sort of…." He felt his face heat.

"When the Sons of the Blood attacked, he spared our youngest attacker," Gideon said softly. "Let him go. I would have too. Kid was maybe seventeen, and God—so scared."

Joey nodded. "I couldn't." He finally took that bite and spoke through a heavenly burst of protein and grease. "I mean, I *could* have, but, you know. I thought it was unnecessary."

Under the table, he felt Gideon's splint bump gently against his knee. Gideon knew the truth; that was all he needed.

"Anyway, that kid's father was the one in charge of the needles. And he was going to let me live for it, but, you know, I had to have Gid's back."

"What'd you tell him?" Harding asked like he understood.

"Well, first I said if he killed my partner I'd burn his shit to the ground, and then, when he just stared at me, I…." He sighed and took another bite. After he swallowed he said, "I invoked my father. You all know who my father is?"

He glanced up and saw everyone exchange glances, and Crosby nodded, looking embarrassed, before Calix Garcia said irritably, "No. No I do *not* know who your father is. Why does everybody else?"

"Because you fell for Crosby so hard when you walked in the door, the rest of us assholes ceased to exist," Gideon said dryly, and Garcia's cheeks went dark pink under his bronze skin.

"Fair," he mumbled, before taking his own bite of steak and eggs. "So who *is* your father, for those of us not in the know?"

Joey opened his mouth to answer, but Harding did instead.

"Stevie Carlyle," he said, crossing his utensils over his cleaned plate. "One of the biggest mobsters-slash businessmen-slash blackmailers on the East Coast."

"Oh shit!" Garcia was staring at him with round eyes. "No kidding?"

"No kidding," Joey said, his mouth twitching. He'd thought this moment would be hard. "Anyway, he's been trying to recruit me pretty much since I left the FLETC. I told Harding. It's why I keep switching out phones and SIM cards—sorry everybody. I visited his place over Christmas, sort of, uhm, made an impression that I was never fucking coming back, and he needed to leave us alone before we investigated *him*."

"Could we?" Crosby asked Harding astutely. He'd eaten about half the food on his plate, but that, apparently, was what happened when you graduated from two months undercover with a shit-ton of damage and a peptic ulcer.

Harding grimaced. "Yes and no. Yes, *this* crew—you guys and the folks who went to Washington to make their own busts today—*my* squad? We could take 'em down. Won't say easy, but Harm and Gideon know you don't find this much talent just anywhere."

"But no," Crosby said, "because you don't just go after somebody like that without a reason. It's… mobsters know. Whatever their racket, they know how to stay under the radar. They're *always* under investigation, so they keep their activity levels at a place where that shit doesn't go up. If it does, they escalate violence, and everybody loses. It's an ecosystem. If you have enough wolves, the ecosystem thrives. You have too many wolves, and they're fighting for food, or they feel threatened, there's a lot of fuckin' carnage. Not enough? All the deer overgraze, and the ecosystem gets fucked. We need to be the wolves, they need to be the deer. We can't wipe out all the fuckin' deer or there's a bloodbath and a lot of dead civilians. Right, Chief?"

Harding smiled at him. "Those classes on organized crime paid off," he said mildly. "Yeah, kid—you learned some stuff."

"And I watched some of Carlyle's fuckin' nature documentaries when I was stuck in my flat under cover," Crosby said. "It's weird the shit you miss from pizza nights."

Carlyle grinned at him. "Yeah, well, I missed your fuckin' stupid shoot-em-ups."

"Don't listen to him," Gideon muttered. "We watched *plenty* of fuckin' stupid shoot-em-ups when you were gone."

There was some general laughter, and then Harding made a subtle sound, and Joey knew it was time to finish the story.

"Anyway, I said that if they killed me, my father would burn their families to the fucking ground. I know he would because he's a sadistic bastard like that, and I also know he's been tailing me. Harding knows they've got my apartment under surveillance." He shuddered. "I would *love* to fucking move, but when we go there now, we know their camera angles, and we know how to get in and out without them seeing. And I've spotted my tails a few times in the last few months." He grimaced. "Between my father and *your* problems, Crosby, I would *love* to take a fuckin' dump in peace, if you know what I mean."

Crosby sucked air through his teeth. "Yeah, I feel that." He shuddered the deep tremor of a man who'd been living in a crappy studio that had been watched over by his mortal enemy for nearly two months. "Fuckin' deeply. So why tell us now?"

Carlyle sighed and took his last bite before placing his own utensils over his plate and pushing back to sigh. "'Cause of what you said about the deer thing. You were right. Predators, prey, they form their own ecosystem. And now that we took out a bunch of wolves, my father's the mountain lion that's gonna move in. One of the things he texted me was not to go after the Sons of the Blood."

"Fuck that!" Garcia snorted, and Joey nodded.

"Harding said the same thing. But we… you know." He turned pleading eyes to all of them. "Guys, it was like one big fucking asshole at a time, you know?"

They nodded.

"So what now?" Crosby asked.

"Well, I figure we give ol' pops a chance to deal with the fallout, and in the meantime? You know those eyes we grew in the back of our heads these last two months?"

"We don't shut them anytime soon," Gideon finished for him, and he gave Gideon a grateful look.

"Yeah. And we tell the others. Like, unless we have something pressing, we should have a meeting about it special while we're wrapping this last shit up. How long you think that'll take, anyway?"

Harding grimaced. "Two weeks for Crosby to be back in the field, and then he's going back to the 43rd Precinct to help them clean up the mess those assholes made in their ranks. Between that and debriefs and testifying for everybody, I'd say six weeks to two months before we're fully operational again."

Joey nodded. "Don't count on Stevie Carlyle to wait that long," he said on a sigh. "But I'm pretty sure he'll only be after me."

"And Gideon," Harding said softly.

Joey sent him a stricken look before meeting Gideon's eyes. "Why Gid?" But he knew.

"'Cause you told that guy Gideon meant something to you, Joey. It's why you haven't let yourself get attached until now, with us."

"Why us?" Crosby asked. "Not that I'm not grateful, Carlyle. Just sucks how being special never did me no favors."

"'Cause with one fuckin' exception, Crosby, you fuckers can defend yourselves," Gideon told him dryly, and Crosby grinned at him while Calix elbowed him—gently—in the bruised ribs, avoiding the gunshot graze from that morning.

"Exactly," Harding told them, shaking his head at his wayward children. "But it's still hard to have things—people—you value when you're growing up with a sociopath." There was a gasp at the table, because this group of people knew what that word meant in their *bones*. "Sociopaths will destroy what you lo—value, to control you. Joey, your father knows what you value, and it's your partner. So both of you, keep those eyes in the back of your head wide open, okay?"

Joey nodded soberly and was relieved when Gideon did the same.

Harding gave them both kind smiles. "And in the meantime, who's got room for a milkshake?"

Surprisingly enough, everybody. Every-fucking-body at the table had wreaked violence and mayhem in the last twenty-four hours.

They could fuck *up* a milkshake.

HARDING DROPPED them off at Gideon's place, bringing them in through the alley and the back entrance to the stairs. He walked them up, double-checked the apartment for security, and then paused as Gideon and Joey wandered in, lost and exhausted and strung out, behind him. Joey stared at him, at a loss.

"Whatcha thinkin', Boss?" Gideon asked after a quiet moment.

Harding met his eyes with the levelness of an old friend.

"Remember when we moved Crosby into Garcia's, and you guys were like, 'The guest room, who in the hell do they think they're fooling?'"

Joey's eyes widened, and he glanced around the apartment again. His shirts, folded neatly on the back of each tweed couch cushion and the recliner, used as doilies. The banners they'd bought—from *Wicked* to the Stone Pony—strung together and used as curtains in the bedroom. The weapons safe next to the couch, with books about the natural world stacked on them, books Gideon had bought for Joey, since his obsession with the natural order of the animal world was still going strong.

He must have made a noise then, because Gideon gave him a reassuring smile.

"Your shit's all over the apartment, Joey," Harding said gently. "I know we've had other things on our mind, but if we're going to keep you two safe, you've got to be honest about how much Gideon means to you. You can think about what happened in two ways. You saved Gideon's life last night—I'm not going to argue. You two, all your adrenaline kept you alive to some extent, but there was a lot left over in those syringes in the waste bin. I checked. So you can either think that threat you made saved his life, and that if you two stick together as a team, as a couple, you made him too valuable to kill, or you can think you put a target on his back."

Joey swallowed. He'd been thinking exactly that.

"I… I don't want a target on his back," he said, the only thing he could think.

Harding nodded. "Then don't leave him hanging," he said gently. "We should keep up the old apartment. I wish I could let you move in here completely. But don't pull away from him to keep him safe. You see it happening all the time in law enforcement, although not"—he smiled slightly—"always with such a dramatic reason. I'm just saying, you two know how to have each other's backs. Don't stop now."

Joey nodded dumbly, and Harding gave them each a quick, hard, *careful* hug, before he strode out of the apartment and back down the steps.

Joey found himself staring at the closed door, even as Gideon came to hang a reassuring arm around his shoulders.

"I wasn't gonna," Joey said, sounding sulky even to his own ears.

"Sure you were," Gideon murmured, kissing his cheek. "Now you're not."

"I didn't know bosses could do that," Joey muttered, leaning into him.

"Fix your life?" Gideon's chest rose and fell in a soundless chuckle. "Only the good ones. C'mon—shower first or pass out?"

For a moment, Joey wobbled on his feet, but then he caught a faint whiff of… of the docks, of that awful office where they'd been tied up, of the ozone from the car wreck, and oh dear God, his own BO.

And every muscle in his body suddenly seized up, as though reminding him that he and Gid had been beat up a *lot* in the last two days.

"Shower," he mumbled. His stomach gurgled. "And an antacid."

"Same," Gideon told him. "You hop in. I'm gonna find a plastic bag for my splint." He sighed. "Joey?"

"Yeah?"

"I'm really glad you're here. That we made it. That you're in my place. I want to say more, but I know you're skittish—"

Joey turned in his arms and kissed him gingerly on the mouth. Wasn't a great kiss. They'd had a rough night, and both of them needed a toothbrush and some toothpaste and at least a moment to rinse out the blood and the eggs.

Still, it soothed Joey's soul.

"I love you too, Gid. It's terrifying. I'm not leaving, except to shower. God, I just can't."

Gideon kissed him on the forehead, the gesture more comforting than Joey had ever thought possible. "Yeah. Same. I always thought falling in love would come with more sex and less exhaustion. I'm a little disappointed."

Joey chuckled. "Think the team knows about us?"

Gideon grunted. "We may have given it away when we sang Act I of *Hamilton* in the hospital. We'll have to see." He stepped back. "Shower. Antacids. Sleep." He swallowed. "I want you in my arms, kid. It's the only thing keeping me upright."

Joey closed his eyes and steadied himself. "Same."

They made it so.

But even after the shower, as the pale sky of a spring evening gave way to a deep purple, blending with the shadows of the buildings soaring above their head, Joey couldn't sleep.

He lay there, body aching, brain buzzing, Gideon's steady breathing into the nape of his neck the only thing keeping him tethered to the planet.

"Spit it out, Joey," Gideon grumbled. "I can hear you thinking."

"Gid… what if he gets you?"

"He won't."

"But what if he does?"

Stiffly, Joey rolled to his other side so he could see Gideon's face in the descending dark.

"What if he does?" Gideon blinked. "Then you'll grieve. You'll… I don't know, mourn your mate. You'll let your pack comfort you. You'll get up, eventually, to hunt again." His lean mouth flickered briefly. "As much as I flatter myself that I'm a catch, Joey, I'm pretty sure you can find other old warriors who swing your way and will have your back."

Unexpected tears burned Joey's eyes, then spilled hotly onto his cheeks. "You're not a fucking catch, Gideon. You're fucking smarter than everybody, and you're so damned hard to follow sometimes. You think everything's a joke, and you're laughing at me now and—"

"Shh…." And Gideon's arm was around his shoulder. "No," he murmured. "I'm not laughing at you. I'm…. Don't you get it? I don't want to leave you. But look at the lives we lead. Look at *life*, period. Those fuckers in ICE are shooting random civilians on a daily basis—there are innocent people trying not to lose their lives from the same government that props us up. But you, me, the team—we have sworn to put *our lives* on the line to protect people, from our own government, from mobsters with more connections than God. I mean, today proved that, if nothing else. So yeah, you might lose me. And I-I don't even want to think of losing you. But if we're strong enough to risk ourselves, we've got to be strong enough to pick up and go on if the worst happens."

Joey stared at him, suddenly yearning for that sweet heroin oblivion. *I get it now. I never got drugs before, but I get it now.*

"Come back to me, kid," Gideon whispered. "I don't know where you went."

Joey closed his eyes tight and remembered that moment of doing a backflip off a building, and how angry Gideon had been. *Don't taunt me!* He'd promised not to do that ever again, but that was because it made Gideon angry, and Gideon was so *rarely* angry, he knew it must be important.

But now—*now*—he understood *why* it had made Gideon angry, and he swallowed in an effort to put that sudden emotional epiphany into words.

"I'm not a good person," he said dryly. "I… I was practically feral when I got here. It's taken me two years to learn how to fucking human, and *you're* the one who taught me. If you… if you die first, Gid, I got no promises I won't, you know. Go back. Get *worse*. I really *would* burn down the world if something happened to you. I… I am *afraid*, you understand? Of who I could be, of what I would *do*, if you weren't in my life. How do I… I don't know how…." And that was it. He'd said the magic word, *afraid*, and that was as far as he could get.

But Gideon was whispering soft kisses along his bruised face, feathering touches along the outside of his arm. They were both wearing underwear—Joey in boxer briefs, Gideon in tighty-whiteys, because some things never changed—and their bodies were so battered even the whisper of skin on skin threatened to hurt.

But Joey wanted it anyway. His breathing slowed, and his eyes closed, and he thought, *That's it. I got worked up is all. Gid knows. He'll get me to sleep and this will all go away.*

But Gideon wasn't that guy.

"You are such a better person than you know, Joey Carlyle," he said. "You think I'm the only one you care about here? You'd take a bullet for Harding. We both would. You'd throw yourself on top of Harman Blodgett in a firefight. The sound of Pearson's leg breaking didn't make you puke because it was a *leg*. it made you puke because it was *Pearson's* leg. And you care about her. God help us if anybody touches Natalia. We will fucking *end* them. Garcia, Swan, hell, even fucking Doba and Henderson—they're *ours*. You're the one who came into my bed talking about wolves and deer. Don't you watch your own fucking documentaries, Joey? We're wolves. We're *all* wolves. And wolves are a pack. They're a *family*. So you lose your mate. That'd suck." His lips twitched. "I'd really rather that not happen, to be honest."

"Dick," Joey muttered, but the dry self-deprecation soothed him.

"Yeah, I am. You were right. I'm not a catch." He sobered and ran his lips over Joey's eyelids, which could have been the only nontender skin on his body right then. "But you'd miss me. And it would be awful. But your pack isn't going anywhere." He blew out a breath. "You know how much you worry about Crosby? You think he's not worried about us the same? That's the thing growing up with a sociopath for a father doesn't tell you, kid. Caring for people is scary—it leaves you vulnerable. Your dad's not wrong about that."

"Then why we gotta do it?" Joey asked, those tears spilling again at the awful pit of fear in his stomach for everybody he… oh God. Loved. He loved them all. He loved Gideon most, but his team….

"'Cause it makes us better," Gideon told him and then pulled him close, mindful of the splint on his wrist. Closer, closer, close enough for Joey to sob quietly into the hollow of his neck. Close enough to kiss the tears off his cheeks.

So close that Joey could hear the beat of Gideon's heart.

Of his lover's heart.

Oh God. Gideon was right. It made him better. Loving Gideon, it made him better. Caring for his team, it made him better.

It made him stronger.

Maybe even strong enough to face the fear of what his father could do when he realized that he held the keys to his son's life in the beating of Gideon Chadwick's heart.

DANCING, DANCING, DANCE THE NIGHT AWAY

THE SATURDAY night before Crosby was supposed to come back to the SCTF in person after fixing up the precinct brutalized by the Sons of the Blood, the team took a night off together.

Harding called it "team building," and first there was an *excellent* steak dinner, and then in a club in Queens, owned by a drag queen named Chartreuse who sort of adored Crosby and Garcia, there was dancing.

Gideon wasn't usually a dancer. He was quite aware his angular, ropy body wasn't graceful on the dance floor no matter *how* much he adored music, so he'd planned to be the group's drink-bearer, schmooze at the bar, and flirt with Chartreuse, who was arch and funny (a requirement for drag queens), and who had decided to embrace all of Crosby's unit, since they'd gone out of their way to help a few of her kids—employees and young people she took under her wing in a harsh world—land someplace safe.

Joey wasn't about to let him do that.

They hadn't come out formally to the team, and they certainly weren't going to start holding hands or kissing in public *now*. God no, not even Natalia and her wife did that, because the public conservatism of law enforcement went bone deep. But something, some spine of worry, had relaxed between him and Joey since that terrible night with the Sons of the Blood.

It was as though just admitting he cared for somebody had melted that last sturdy barrier that would *keep* Joey Carlyle from caring. Admitting he was afraid for his person allowed him to be glad his person was there in the first place.

Gideon hadn't wanted to tell him, but he'd been very afraid, from their first meeting, that Joey Carlyle would have a hard time making the sort of attachment that the two of them had formed.

Every other morning or so he got to wake up with Joey in his bed, in his arms, or touching him casually as they passed each other in the kitchen, wrapping his arms around Gideon's waist as he cooked or folded laundry, or rubbing their feet together as they read at night on opposite sides of the couch. Every moment of them together was a miracle.

And they still worked like clockwork in the field.

The day before, they'd been interviewing a woman they thought was a witness until Gideon had caught her in a fairly significant lie.

He knew his eyebrows had raised fractionally—an unguarded microexpression—but he wasn't aware he'd tipped her off until she'd gone for the knife in the waistband of her jeans.

And Joey had tackled her before she'd gotten it clear of her belt.

"Good tip-off, Gid," he'd said, after wrestling her into cuffs and yanking her to a standing position.

"Anything for you, Carlyle," he'd said dryly, but inside he'd been thinking that it was a damned good thing that kid could read his mind, and that he'd been born to track prey.

Either way, two years of partnership outside the bedroom was really paying off.

And eight months of partnership *inside* the bedroom felt as necessary as breathing.

So when, as Gideon was doing a drink roundup with the fresh-faced Henderson and older, battle-hardened Doba, and he heard Joey's whistle above the music—a remix of an acoustic rock song about stolen dances—he turned just in time to watch Carlyle pop above everybody's head in a graceful leap and signal him over with a jerk of his chin.

He had to swallow, hard, because in that moment Joey Carlyle was fierce and happy and carefree, and he turned in dismay to the tray of drinks he'd been going to ferry over to the team's table.

"I'll get them," Chartreuse said, waving him off. "You people… I don't mind po-po in my place as long as you *dance*."

And Gideon found himself in the center of the dance floor with the rest of the unit, having tiny Gail Pearson whirled into his arms in a sleek river of blond hair that went all the way to the waist of her Little Black Dress.

He laughed and gallantly pulled her in so they were both facing the same direction and then whirled her out again, into Manny Swan's waiting arms.

Henderson and Doba—both as straight as rulers, Gideon knew, although they apparently were working nicely as roommates since the night they'd saved Toby, their DJ for the night, from getting beaten to death by cops—were both executing swing moves side by side, and Chadwick blessed them. Not a word from either of them about how Harding had needed to come out about being married to Harman Blodgett in the course of the *many* trials and press conferences he'd attended in the last two months, and they'd been as happy as the rest of the team to hear that Crosby was being returned to SCTF after his long-term loan to the 43rd Precinct to clean up the corruption mess.

For a moment, Gideon found himself doing a quick two-step with Natalia's lovely wife, Emily, and after five years with the unit and a lot of holidays with Emily and Tal, he treasured her happy laughter and her exquisite dancing on amazingly tall heels.

And then the beat changed, grew slower, sultrier.

Henderson and Doba laughingly went to claim their drinks, take them to the unit's table, and mark it since the place was filling up.

Emily moved into Natalia's arms, the happy slope of her neck as she rested her cheek on Tal's shoulder somehow one of the sweetest things Gideon had ever seen. Manny teased Pearson into doing a slow dance, his posture and stance that of a professional dancer, although his hand in the small of her back spoke of tenderness. Partners or, well, *partners*, Gideon had to admit, they'd *all* grown closer in the last few months, and since Crosby and Garcia had paired off, and *everybody* knew Clint was married to Harman now, maybe the SCTF would simply be a DOJ anomaly. Partners who were partners allowed.

And as he turned to Joey to meet his eyes and share the joke—and to head back to the table because God knew he was lucky not to have caught any of the women, at least, in the ear with his wild flailing elbows—he felt a small, callused hand in his and Joey's cable-strong arm wrapping around his waist.

"Oh," he said softly, assuming the dance position. "Hello."

"Here," Carlyle murmured, resting his head against Gideon's chest. "Call me sentimental, but I think an LGBTQ dance club in Queens is the perfect place to come out."

Gideon chuckled and pulled him closer, dropping their formal "dance arms" so he could hold Joey against him while Joey wrapped his arms around Gideon's neck. For all the music they'd listened to, they'd never danced like this—not even in the privacy of Gideon's apartment—and the intimacy of their bodies, the synchronicity of their feet, their movements, their heartbeats, was suddenly all he could think about.

He had no urge to glance around to see if the rest of the unit saw and approved—or disapproved—or was even surprised. Right now, with Joey in his arms, leaning against his chest, *trusting* him, all he wanted was Joey.

"Kid," Gideon said, because he couldn't break the habit, "you know I love you, right?"

"Yeah, Gid. I love you too." It hadn't rolled smoothly off the tongue for either of them at first. But then once a day, in private, one of them would stare at the other in surprise.

Joey, what?

I love you.

Yeah, that's weird. Love you back.

Or,

You thought about it again.

You complaining?

Naw, Gid. I love you too.

Or that evening as they'd been getting dressed,

What? I like this suit. (Joey always liked his suits, no matter how doomed for the rag pile they'd be in the next two weeks.)

Yeah, I like it on you.

So, is that, uhm, lust in your eyes?

No, moron, it's love. I can't lust after you in a suit that shows me how long it's been since you waxed. It feels unclean.

So "I love you" was getting easier, was starting to fit a lot more comfortably (at least more comfortably than Joey's suit, which was about to burst at the seams, and it wasn't like Joey had an ounce of fat to spare.)

And right now, the music washing over them, this thing they both loved, Gideon had no qualifiers. No embarrassment. They loved each other. This—them moving in sync, their breath mingling as Gideon lowered his mouth for a kiss—this was as happy as he was ever going to get, and it was a *stunning* amount of happiness for a man who'd never dreamed of romance or partnership or love.

It was probably a stunning amount of happiness for a man who *had* dreamed of those things, but Gideon felt so much less prepared for it than one of those other men.

And maybe a smidge more grateful. To say being in love with somebody who was exasperating, fierce, and damned near as amoral as Gideon was such an amazing surprise. Who knew life could give such a gift?

Gideon had never suspected.

The kiss deepened, and the dance went on, and like Ed Sheeran was saying, everything was "Perfect."

The dance ended, and the floor grew more crowded. Joey let Gideon retreat to the drink table while he be-bopped with Swan and Crosby. He was surprised to see the rest of the unit there, quenching their thirst and chatting happily—and more surprised to get a cheer as he sat down.

"I have no idea what you're going on about," he said, and Garcia elbowed him in the ribs.

"Crosby *so* called you guys. Kept going on and on about you two singing *Hamilton*. I thought he was crazy."

Gideon snorted. "Well, it's not like we're all lovesick and missing each other." He held his hands to his chest and batted his eyes. "Crosby, oh Crosby, why won't you call me."

There were hoots and hollers, and Garcia laughed and accepted the razzing with good humor. Crosby's absence from the team had been hard for everybody, but watching Garcia so obviously trying *not* to miss him had been the hardest part.

The night progressed, and the club got more crowded until around midnight, when it was definitely time to leave. They'd had fun, but Toby's shift as a DJ was over, and Crosby and Garcia had plans to escort him home. Natalia and Emily had children to return to, and Harding and Blodgett had a long drive ahead. And even those without "grown-up" responsibilities still led grown-up lives. Partying until 3:00 a.m. was great until it interfered with a run or a nap or a diet or even doing laundry, because when they hit work on Monday, they had to have their feet underneath them to run.

And Joey, who may have been their only party animal, absolutely needed to come home and finish the night in Gideon's arms.

But they were all seasoned at watching their backs by now. The people who'd driven had parked in the same place, and the people who were flagging down cabs or rideshares would wait together and even crash at each other's places. No single person would be left behind.

Which was why it was such a surprise.

They all hugged Chartreuse goodbye and left her tables empty—and hefty tips on board for the whole staff that had treated them right—and then exited out the back entrance, through an alleyway to an alcove where hailing a cab was as natural as breathing. Gid went first, knowing Harding and the other drivers were bringing up the rear with Toby in their midst, Manny Swan at his elbow since he was still recovering from his ordeal. Gideon stepped out to hail a cab and was unprepared for the black SUV, tinted windows and reinforced grill, to swerve to the side of the road.

The side door popped open, and a beefy set of hands hauled him back into the darkened interior, and then the vehicle pulled away.

The last thing he saw before the door slammed was Joey Carlyle's anguished face.

"Well done," came a voice with a lot of south Boston in it. "I couldn't count on my last bodyguard to do well in such circumstances."

Stevie Carlyle. Well, the least Gideon could do was make it quick.

"Yeah, that's because Joey shoved a knife through his hand," he said before planting his elbow in the bodyguard's throat.

The man gave a strangled grunt and released his arms, and Gideon had his hand on the car door's handle when he felt the muzzle of a *very* large gun against the back of his neck.

"Listen," said Joey's father. "I don't really give a crap who you are or what you are to my son, but I know you're a worse bargaining chip with your brains splattered all over the inside of the car. You calm down and I can at least spare your ugly mug for him. He'd probably prefer it that way."

Gideon was tempted—*so* tempted—to keep fighting, but he'd done his homework. Absolutely unprovable, but still, everybody knew Stevie Carlyle had splattered a lot of brains.

He stilled and allowed himself to slide between Stevie and his bodyguard, who was still struggling for air.

He shouldn't have been shocked when Stevie moved the barrel of the gun from the back of his neck to the side of the guard's head and pulled the trigger.

The noise and the smell and the awfulness that followed blurred, one big gray-and-red-spattered fuzz spot in Gideon's brain, and he tried to breathe through his nausea.

The only reason he didn't throw up on Joey's father was because he knew for certain if he did, he'd be part of the mess too.

"Good," Stevie Carlyle said, taking out a kerchief and wiping the gun and then throwing the kerchief and the gun out the window in front of a school as their SUV whizzed by. He rolled up the window and said, "As long as we understand each other, it was worth losing another bodyguard to make my point."

Gideon felt a black-hearted smile twisting his lips.

"What?" Stevie demanded. "What is that look?"

"You, sir," Gideon said distinctly, "are lucky your son didn't put you down in your sleep like a rabid dog."

Stevie didn't kill him, didn't even go for the other gun Gideon was sure he had in the holster he could spot at the man's side.

"That's funny. I always thought it was the other way around."

Gideon didn't answer him—he didn't want to play the bad-guy banter game. He ignored the mess to his right because he had to, and focused on not being sick.

And remembered that moment in the warehouse office when the needle had slid into his arm, after hearing Joey actually use his father's name to keep them both safe.

He hadn't said anything, but what he'd wanted to say, had been *yearning* to say, was "Don't worry, kid. They're coming for us. They won't leave us in the wind."

Now, in his head, he heard his own voice saying those words, and then Joey's voice, loopy, garbled, saying, "If you hurt him I will burn your families to the ground."

Oh yeah.

All he had to do was survive. Stevie Carlyle didn't have a clue what was coming.

"I'LL GUT him! I'll rip his throat out with my teeth!" Somebody was howling, *gibbering*, and Joey was struggling with all his might. Iron bands wrapped around his shoulders as he stared at the disappearing SUV in a red haze of fury.

"Joey—fuckin' *Carlyle*—stop it!" Crosby boomed in his ear. Were those *his* arms holding him back?

"*Gideon*!" The howl was raw enough to tear his throat, and the echoes were still ringing in his ears when a harsh slap across his face shocked him into stilling his frantic thrashing.

"*Carlyle*!" Clint Harding barked into his face. "Stand down, son, *stand down*!" The military boom, accompanied by the military command, was almost as bracing as the slap, and Joey sagged in Crosby's iron grip.

"He's got him," Joey gasped. "Harding, he's got *Gid*."

Harding nodded. "I hear you. But he could have shot him right here. *Think*, Joey—why wouldn't he do that?"

Joey struggled for breath, for *clarity*. "Same thing he's wanted since I got clear of FLETC," he said. "He wants *me*. He seems to think I'm some sort of weapon. Military, DOJ—like if I joined the organization, he'd be invincible."

Harding nodded slowly. "He's going to need to break you first—make you feel like you've crossed the line. He wants a mini-me. Someone of his own flesh and blood. It's a narcissist's dream."

"He didn't seem to think I was his own flesh and blood when a brown girl squirted me out," Joey spat venomously. His father's words; Joey had heard them a lot growing up.

"Yeah, Joey," Crosby rumbled. "But now he thinks you're a killer. We were in the fucking papers, man, and I'm sure there's folks in the Sons of the Blood who told him about you. How many of them did you put away?"

Joey's shoulders went limp, and Crosby set him down like he was a porcelain doll.

All those lessons with Gideon flooded through him, and he could hear the thing Gideon had never said, probably because Gid hadn't wanted Joey to ever imagine it was true.

"So I'm a killer," he said, dispirited, close to tears.

"No," Harding said, voice firm. "You're a *warrior*. You know the difference between those two things?"

Classes—all that book learning, but it didn't come down to that in the end. His brain said, *Protector—trained, disciplined.* But that's not what penetrated the blinding cold fear of becoming what he hated the most.

What it came down to was a blanket, constructed one stitch at a time, thrown around Joey's shoulders to keep him warm. Every stitch a memory of kindness.

Of love.

Gideon's unfathomable eyes as he buffed makeup into Joey's face.

His approval as Joey had been kind to Crosby, playful with Pearson, tender to Natalia, deferential to Harding.

That dry chuckle he had as he laughed at his own jokes.

His fury when Joey had taken his own life for granted.

That sudden vulnerability every time they were about to kiss.

His resonant baritone as they sang at the top of their lungs, because they were high, and pissed, and very, very glad to be alive.

The way he'd touched Joey softly in the night, when they were hard men meant for hard use.

And contrasted with that?

There was only the lack of expression on Joey's father's face when Joey had threatened him with death at the age of eight years old.

"Yeah, I know," Joey said into the sudden silence.

"The difference between a warrior and a sociopath?" Harding said, his voice firm. "Let's hear it, Joey, or I'm locking you in a padded room while *we* go get our friend."

Joey gave a wolfish smile. "Me. I'm the warrior. Stevie Carlyle's the sociopath. We kill the sociopath to keep our pack safe."

Harding gave a sharp nod. "That'll do." He glanced to his people, all of them dressed for dinner and dancing, all of them with hard faces and squared shoulders, even Natalia's wife, who knew what it was to stand by a warrior when she went into battle.

Even Toby Trotter, their little DJ, who had been rescued by warriors when he'd gotten in the way of the sociopaths.

"Okay, people," Harding said. "What's coming next is off books. Whether you join us or not, you need to keep your eyes peeled—we don't know how much he knows about the whole unit. We meet at the office in two hours to pick up body armor and tactical gear and to map out a plan. Bring your drop pieces and ammo. Anybody *not* up for this needs to let me know—"

"See you in two hours, Boss," said Doba, with Henderson nodding at his side.

"Tal's drop piece is in the lockbox in the car," Emily said. "Let her get that and she can ride with you. Toby, I'll get you home."

"Thanks, honey," Natalia said, giving her the warm gaze of somebody who has seen their every faith rewarded.

"It's Gid, honey. We gotta go get our boy, right?"

Gideon, who had been there from the very beginning, Joey remembered. Gideon who wasn't only Joey's. Gideon who belonged to the unit, and *everybody* wanted in.

"It's a plan," Harding said. "Crosby, Harm and I will take Joey to Gideon's apartment to get his stuff. I'm going to give you two Joey's apartment keys and the location of the cameras his father has been tapping to monitor him. So far we haven't spotted any other tails or cameras, but we need to make sure. Let us know how many people you see waiting for him. I'm pretty sure it's a trap."

Crosby grunted. "Boss, uhm… permission?"

Harding's smile wasn't… pleasant. "With cause," he said temperately, which meant Stevie Carlyle might be out some men that night.

"Course," Crosby said. "Joey, you want us to bring you some, uhm—" He gave Joey an apologetic once-over. "—clothes that won't rip?"

Joey remembered Gideon's comment about seeing when Joey had last waxed and was surprised he could still smile. "Most of my work clothes are at Gid's," he said, not caring. They knew. Everybody had seen that dance, their kiss. Gideon may have dealt with the fallout, but Joey had known what he was doing.

"Then you won't mind what we stash in there if we have to," Crosby said, nodding. "Fair." He was still standing a little behind Joey, and Joey was surprised by the giant, all-encompassing hug he received. "You keep your brains in your head, Carlyle. Remember, we got your back. We got Gid's. Nobody has to be alone, you hear me?"

And Joey remembered that late-night talk with Gid, and how Gid had told him he would be okay, would remain himself, because he had people to remind him who he was.

"I hear you," he said and gave Harding a grim nod. "Can we send somebody with Emily and Toby?" he asked, remembering the night Toby had gotten hurt. "I am not okay with them on their own."

Harding glanced up, obviously reluctant to ask somebody to stand down. His shoulders relaxed when Henderson stepped forward.

"I'm not as good a shot as Doba," he apologized, nodding to Emily. "But I'll be happy to escort you both."

"Harm, do you want to go with them?" Clint asked, and his husband gave him a bored glance.

"No," he said, without elaboration.

Harding let out a soft breath. "Of course not. Okay, people—we all have our assignments. Two hours. First person who gets there needs to unlock the equipment room and start cleaning guns. Let's go."

And they went.

INVASION

TWO AND a half hours later, Joey was dressed in tactical gear—vest, weapons, helmet at the ready, earpiece in—and he and the team were having a spirited game of where are *they* and how do we get *there*?

"Massachusetts," Joey said, no bullshit. "Yeah, I know he does business down here, but the bodies he didn't bury in the basement, he used to dump in the res. He shares property borders with it, and he knew where to leave the remains so the scavengers got there long before the law. He would rather transport a body in the back of his car than dump one somewhere he wasn't comfortable with."

Memories of his father and his habits, long dammed up, were flooding him now. He found they weren't painful anymore, not embarrassing, not infuriating or threatening. Two years of taking classes, of studying perpetrators, of learning how to profile bad guys in order to predict their movements had boiled the information down to its purest form: A weapon to defeat Stevie Carlyle, to remove this painful, dangerous phantom from Joey's life.

To get Gideon back.

"Okay, then," Harding said. "That's a long drive with a prisoner, and we know he's going to be pressed for time. I don't care *who* you are—abducting a federal agent is a quick way to get stopped at a roadblock. I know we're a small branch, but we frequently interact with the bigger boys. Why does he think he can get away with this?"

Joey gaped, suddenly realizing the enormity of what his father had done. *Big pointy brains—dammit, this is why we need Gideon!*

"Because we just alienated a bunch of people," Natalia said, walking in brusquely with her tac bag over her shoulder. "Clint,

I'm not sure if you've been taking temperature readings, but in this climate, putting a bunch of racists in jail does *not* make you any friends."

Clint sucked air in through his teeth in that sound people made when they knew somebody was speaking an unwelcome truth. "I hate people," he said bleakly, which told Joey that all the political bullshit he didn't pay attention to was the shit that put gray hairs on his boss's head. "But," Harding continued on an exhale, "it does explain why I can't get Connie Deavers on the phone." Their FBI liaison should have been open to Harding's call twenty-four seven—unless she'd been told to dodge his number.

"We knew we were on our own anyway," Tal said grimly. "If we send a full invasion force into Stevie Carlyle's compound, complete with news coverage, we will piss off a whole lot of people, only some of them Stevie Carlyle's. No, Clint—the whole team is, uhm…." She gave Joey an apologetic glance, and it took him a minute to realize that he was the only person in the room who could say it.

"Off the reservation," he finished dryly and wished Gideon was there, because he would find the whole thing inappropriately funny.

I'll tell him when we get him back, Joey thought, and it was the first bit of hope he had.

"So it's just us," Harding said. "Fair. Pearson, you and Tal search air traffic for independent flights going to Massachusetts. Joey, I can get us air transpo, but we need to know exactly where we're going. We've got one shot. If we can't stop Stevie from lifting off, we've got to come up with a plan for invading his territory, and that's not going to be easy. You need to walk us through his property—"

"Compound," Joey said, wanting his friends to know what was doing. "There's security everywhere, except…." He smiled a little.

"What?" Garcia asked. Well, Garcia was wily and little, like Joey. He knew how to avoid danger as opposed to clobbering it head-on.

"There's a mountain lion on my father's property," he said. "And a den. And he's got a gamekeeper who hates him and killed the feed for a half-mile around it so nobody thinks it's a cool thing to go blow the mountain lion away from a thousand fucking yards."

"So a blind spot in the security," Harding said, impressed. "Excellent." As usual during a briefing, he had his tablet out and had connected it to the large screens. Front and center was an arial shot of the entire compound, humbled by the perspective of a drone flying three hundred yards above the trees.

"Uhm, Chief?" Manny Swan said hesitantly. "Did you not hear the first part of what he said?"

Harding glanced up. "The gamekeeper who hates Carlyle's father? Why, can we use him?"

Swan was a handsome Black man with a square jaw, tightly shorn hair, and teakwood dark skin. His resting expression was something Gideon had described as "watchfully amused," so to have him cock his head and actually *goggle* at Harding was unexpected.

"What?" Harding asked, yanked out of his game face by Swan's borderline freakout.

"Did anybody else hear him say *mountain lion*?"

"I did," Doba said unexpectedly, raising his hand. "I heard him say that."

Pearson and Natalia turned their heads. "This is a problem?" they asked.

Garcia and Crosby—syncing together like twins—both waggled their hands. "Pretend… like just for a second," Crosby said, sounding unbearably earnest, "that some of us are strictly city cats and are possibly afraid of things with teeth and claws. Not that we *are* afraid, but… you know. In case we were."

Joey stared at them all, a part of him tempted to fly out of the room in a temper, furious at the stupidity of his colleagues.

Unbidden came those early days of him in the unit, when Gideon and Harding, and then Talia and Pearson and even Crosby and Kylie all would spend time with him, showing him things they'd learned in their wide and varied experience and he had not.

He wasn't sure where the smile came from. It must have been a gift from Gideon, given to him in one of those long-ago Saturday classes, a reward for the good question, or the surprise observation. It was his turn to give it back.

"Yes," he said, his quiet chuckle an echo of Gideon's raspy, dry amusement. "Yes, I did say mountain lion. Yes, he can bring down a full-grown deer. No, he's not going to bring down *us* unless we get between his mates and their cubs or get too close to his den. We can go in the back way, but…." He frowned. "Not all of us." He glanced at Harding. "The cameras aren't down the whole way. I did a lot of dancing to sneak in last time, and there's no guarantee Stevie didn't figure out how I got in. We should make sure *we* can still see the mountain lion sometime after Christmas, to make sure Stevie didn't fix the hole in his security, and it should be me and maybe two other people sneaking in the back—"

"While me and the rest of us make a whole lot of noise at the front," Harding said before setting the tablet down and tapping furiously on it. "And that will make it easier to sneak you into town, Joey."

"Why are we sneaking him into town?" Crosby asked. "I mean, isn't the point of snatching Gideon to get Joey to come get him? Wouldn't we want Stevie Carlyle to think he succeeded?"

"To buy him time," Harding muttered, still tapping. "If we show up all bells and whistles in the front, and *make* Stevie ask to see Carlyle, Joey and whoever he brings with him have time to infiltrate the compound and find Gideon. What we *don't* want is for Gideon to have a knife to his throat while we debate whether or not to send Joey to his father in a demented game of Red Rover. That's a great way to get Gideon's throat cut and Joey shot. What we want is for Joey and company to sneak Gideon out so the rest of us can invade like Iwo-fucking-Jima, you think?"

"You don't think we'll catch him before he's out of town?" Garcia asked.

Clint opened his mouth to answer, but Joey beat him to it.

"I think their plane had lift-off before any of us had our weapons," he said. "This was planned. I had to go to my apartment to get my suit—they must have seen me leave with the garment bag. It's…." He wanted to roll his eyes at his own vanity. "It's from a pricey store, not casual clothes. Whether they tracked me to Gid's after that or caught us in a net, they knew—they *knew* we weren't ready for tactical. They *knew* we were down to drop pieces, if that. My dad's a lot of things—asshole, psycho, mobster, blackmailer—but you know what he's not?"

"A fuckin' moron," Pearson supplied. "We did our homework this last month, Joey. We know what we're up against." She gave a tinkling little pixie laugh that was even more terrifying because she was wearing her specially fitted vest and had pulled her hair back into its no-nonsense plait. "In fact, whether we get backup from the FBI or not, I suspect your father just made his first tactical mistake since he took you away from your grandfather."

Joey blinked at her. "How so?"

In the next heartbeat of silence, he could hear the curiosity of most of the unit, and it was Harding who answered.

"Well, taking you away from your maternal grandfather made you his enemy for life," Harding said. "I'm sure he's figured that out by now."

Joey remembered his last visit and narrowed his eyes in what even *he* knew was an unpleasant expression. "I think he knows."

"And kidnapping Gideon—or any member of the unit—made the SCTF not only his enemy, but it gave us an *excuse* to be his enemy. I'm sure he's got dirt or threats or something on somebody at the DOJ, which is why we're getting radio silence from the FBI. But we have authorization to cross state lines and to use lethal force. All those hearings Crosby and I were called in for weren't only to justify our unit's use of force in the Sons of the Blood mishigas. They were to justify our unit to the people who provide our funding and authorize my use of it. Sure, it's just us." And now Clint Harding gave the sort of smile that reminded everybody in the room that the large dark eyes with the unexpected kindness hid the heart of a true soldier, a warrior, and a dyed-in-the-wool motherfucker.

"We gonna say it, Boss?" Pearson asked, that wicked smile lighting up her features.

"Oh yeah," Harding said, and then the whole unit joined him in what had become their battle cry during the Sons of the Blood finale.

"*How many of them can we take out*!"

THEIR BLOOD was up, and their minds focused, which was good, because as the echoes of their battle cry were still lingering in the sound tiles of the office, Harding's tablet pinged.

"Okay, then," he muttered, holding his hand up for silence. "First things first. Joey, I've got three pictures here with dates that the drones picked up since your visit over Christmas. I need you to take a look and tell me what you think they mean."

Joey turned to do that, and Harding held up a finger. "But first—and hear me out completely—an SUV was found on fire near the Teterboro airstrip, with a body inside. The body was identified, and it is *not*, repeat *not*, our agent. Do you hear me, Joey? Not Gideon."

Joey nodded sharply, although his vision was going black.

"Breathe," Natalia murmured in his ear. "C'mon, Carlyle, stay with us."

"Not Gideon," he repeated through numb lips. "I heard ya."

"Good," Harding told him. "Because the male, Caucasian, late forties, was identified as Horst Krentz, a German national who was apparently recruited to America to be mob muscle. His most recent employer? Anyone? Anyone?"

"Stevie fuckin' Carlyle," Crosby supplied.

"Give Crosby something to eat," Harding said. "And Garcia too—you all know the drill. Don't let them go into the field hungry. Anyway, yes. His cause of death was—"

"A gunshot to the back of the head," Joey supplied. "He probably fucked up somehow when they grabbed Gid. Stevie doesn't like his goons to fuck up in front of him." He had a feeling that the guy he stabbed in the hand wasn't breathing too well these days either.

"You're no fun," Harding said. "But the upshot is that yes, your old man is recorded as having boarded a plane with two other passengers bound for Boston—so probably the driver—and yes, that SUV is probably his, and so's the dead guy. So there's our probable cause. Now look at those pictures and tell me if you think your buddy the mountain lion is still alive."

Joey scanned the pictures, frowning. "Oh no," he said sadly, pulling up one from shortly after his visit.

Sure enough, lying bloody in the snow was the body of a friend.

"They didn't need to do that," he said, and in spite of his fear for Gideon, his fury at having his friends put in danger, he could still feel something for the magnificent animal, body destroyed by *many* bullets, lying dead in the snow.

"Oh, Joey," Gail said, her hand—which he'd seen coated in blood on more than one occasion—tender on his shoulder. "I'm so sorry."

"Same," Harding said. "But that's not the last picture in the sequence."

Joey kept studying, and his next intake of breath was less anguished. "The family," he murmured. "The female. She was in another cave, at least the one I've seen, but she and her cubs survived. Check out the cubs—they're mostly grown. I wonder if one…."

He continued to pore over the aerial shots, and what he saw, a picture dated a week or two ago at the most, made him smile. "Look at this one. One of the cubs set up shop in the old man's cave."

He paused. "Clint, this wasn't that long ago. If the female's still alive, and the male set up shop in the old man's cave, that means the cameras are back down again. Either that or Stevie's been distracted and hasn't taken him out yet."

"Well, Joey," Harding said slowly, "what on earth do you think could have been distracting him?"

Joey grunted. "Maybe a pesky little agency that took out some higher-ups that he'd been blackmailing? He told me not to go after them, and we did. Maybe he promised more than he could deliver."

Harding nodded. "So now his clients are pissed, and he needs to get SCTF in line. How better to do that than get his son in line. If he can prove that he's got Joey Carlyle, SCTF agent, under his thumb, then he's back in black, right?"

Crosby grunted. "But Boss, that's crazy talk. That's… he wasn't even fuckin' subtle. He did it in front of all of us. He left a DB in his wake. He's—oh!"

And like that, Joey remembered his first encounter with somebody like Stevie Carlyle who didn't act like Stevie Carlyle.

"He's decompensating," he said softly. "Like Chester Schumer. He's… he can't keep the crazy in check. We brought down the Sons of the Blood, and half his business went down with it. He's *desperate*."

Clint nodded, but it was Natalia who said, "Yeah. Yeah, he is. Which on the one hand may make him sloppy, but on the other…."

"It'll make him dangerous." Joey remembered Chester Schumer, going after Gideon with a stiletto. *I sort of wish it had been a cheese knife, because that would have been* cool*!*

The memory, along with Gideon's dry voice in his head, steadied him. Gideon knew what to do with a decompensating sociopath. He knew how to use somebody's best weapon against them.

It was Joey's job to be that weapon.

"We move out in ten," Clint said. "I got us a helo from the roof, so take your Dramamine or eat your snacks and grab a water—I understand it's stripped down and it's gonna be a bumpy ride."

POINT A AND POINT B

GIDEON SAW the blow coming, but he didn't flinch.

He wanted to say Stevie Carlyle hit like a girl, but the man had lead in his glove, and Tal and Gail could still hurt him worse.

But that didn't mean he wasn't hurting bad.

So this is how it ends. Tied in a chair in Stevie Carlyle's basement, worried about his son.

Stevie backed up, shaking out his hand and blowing hard, and if Gideon's jaw hadn't been aching—probably broken—he would have made a crack about how maybe he shouldn't have blown away his bodyguard before this portion of the program was through.

Something must have shown in his eyes, though, and Stevie must have been more exhausted than he wanted to let on because he paused long enough to ask.

"What? What's so fuckin' funny? What're you laughing about?"

In truth, Gideon had been in this basement, getting the shit beat out of him, for what felt like half his life. He knew what broken ribs felt like, the hairline fractures in each collarbone, knew he'd be pissing blood for a good long time and that Stevie's kicks to his ankles and shins in steel-toed boots had probably bruised his bones at the very least.

If he could laugh, he'd probably spit blood.

"What?" Stevie shouted, lowering his face to Gideon's, spittle flecking his lips.

"Nothing," Gideon rasped. Had he been screaming? Must have been screaming. His throat felt bloody. That was probably the screaming. "Just thinking."

"Thinking what?" Stevie asked, pulling off his gloves—thank fuck—and backing up to sit on a stool next to a bottle of water. "You look like shit. You're probably gonna die here. What's so fuckin' funny?"

"We always ask ourselves," Gideon said, "where do bad guys keep getting their help. Minions-R-Us? Lackeys Incorporated? Is there, like, a dystopian business model for disposable employees?"

The words sounded great in his head, but his lips and tongue were swollen, and he'd spit out at least three of his teeth—some of them he'd just had installed, dammit! For all he knew, he was going to die for telling Stevie Carlyle, "Blargh garble blpt phlorg blargh garble." But then until Joey, nobody had ever really gotten his sense of humor anyway.

To his surprise—and yes, relief—Stevie Carlyle laughed.

"That's funny," he said, surprised. "You're funny. That why you and my son are such good friends? Cause you're funny?"

Also, I have a large penis.

Oops! Better keep that info to himself.

"We like to shed blood," he said, although that wasn't strictly true. "We're good at it." Now *that* was true. "We like keeping people safe." And that was the God's *honest* truth.

"And that amuses you?" Stevie sounded confused.

"And music," Gideon mumbled. In his head he'd had the entire CD of Bruce Springsteen's *The Rising* on loop. He wondered if he'd ever hear it again, but even if he didn't, he figured he'd ironed out all the lyrics in his head. He and Joey could sing it together after they wired his jaw shut for a time.

"Music?" Stevie grunted and took a swig of water. "That's funny. My son didn't like no fuckin' music."

I bet his grandfather sang to him all the fuckin' time, you psychopath. Nobody just picks up music like that kid. It was in his heart, but he couldn't hear it until he met me.

"Evrry conzerd in Mnhattn," he mumbled, his vision going a little dark. Unconsciousness would be great right now. His team was coming for him—he knew they were—and Joey would be leading the charge, but he'd lost track of time a little, and he wasn't sure if he'd still be here when they showed up.

"Sir?"

The voice from the top of the stairs sounded poised and unflappable—Gideon had heard it before, keeping Stevie updated on whether or not they had visitors. A butler, probably—or a flunky—but nobody with the paygrade to watch Stevie beat Gideon to death.

"Yeah? What's up?"

"Your employee watching the road just called. There's two black SUVs approaching from the main entrance—"

"You been watching that back entrance?" Stevie demanded. "Little bastard must be coming in through there."

There was an uncomfortable silence.

"Have you been?"

"Yes, sir, I have been."

"Hasn't that Gray motherfucker been helping you?"

"Sir, he… he seems to have disappeared."

"The gamekeeper disappeared?" The surprise in Stevie's voice might have been comical, but it was *so* complete. Gideon's people were obviously in the SUVs, but the fact that the gamekeeper had disappeared—the one that Gideon knew from Joey's reports had been leaving holes in the cameras from the back of the property—was worth not passing out for.

"Sir, I was watching the feed, and I looked up and he was gone—"

The butler's voice echoed from the top of the steps, but even Gideon could hear the fear. Stevie just waved his hand, though, as if shooing a fly.

"He does that," he muttered. "He does that. He… he said he would tend the game until my end…. I thought…." He shook his head. "Doesn't matter. Doesn't matter. He'll be back. Fucking mountain lions. I…." Stevie shuddered, and Gideon felt stupid. The word snuck into his consciousness, buffeted about by pain and confusion, but once it was there, it stuck.

Decompensating.

Oh yes. Stevie Carlyle had suffered some setbacks, some business problems, and all the things he'd thought he could control were spiraling out of his grasp. And in the middle of it was his son… his intractable, infuriating, perfect killing machine of a son….

And Stevie *wanted* him, wanted him under control, wanted his DNA under Stevie's roof, wanted the skills he had, the connections he must have forged through the SCTF. Wanted him, *needed* him, to comply.

If only, if only Joey Carlyle would come and be Stevie's perfect little soldier, all the other things would be fixed. Stevie knew it.

So he'd seized upon Gideon—and while Stevie's grilling had never indicated he knew about their relationship, he was still madly, insanely jealous.

Gideon, it seemed, had some pull over his son that Stevie didn't understand. Gideon needed to call Joey Carlyle back into the fold. Gideon needed to fuckin' die, but not before Joey watched him.

He thinks it'll break Joey. Thinks the fight'll go out of him if he sees the one person he's connected to die.

Because that'd worked so well with Joey's grandfather.

Without warning Stevie turned his body—powerful, like a boxer's—and yeeted his plastic water bottle to the back of the basement. It clattered there, knocking something over that Gideon couldn't see, and Stevie turned toward him with renewed fury.

Oops, sorry, Joey, know you're coming for me, but I think you just broke his restraints.

"Sir!" cried the butler, sounding like he'd gone somewhere and come running back. "They've *run through the gate*!"

The next sound he heard was the clatter of Stevie's booted feet as he pounded up the old wooden steps that connected the basement to the kitchen. Gideon remembered the kitchen envy, but Stevie's footsteps….

Oh *nice*! SCTF had arrived! Thank you, Clint Harding!

And probably Joey, coming around the back. A conversation they'd had tickled the back of his brain. Something about knowing the compound, knowing *this basement* in particular. Joey was coming for him. Joey was coming. Well, good. So they were coming for him.

Gideon just had to wait—

Can't wait. If Stevie Carlyle comes back down to this fucking basement, he's going to kill me.

Yeah. Yeah. Gideon knew enough about decompensating killers, didn't he. He'd seen it in Chester Schumer. He'd seen it in Morton Donald Johns. If Joey's father made it back down to the basement, Gideon had better be *long* gone.

Fortunately, Gideon knew a little something about restraints too.

Like, zip ties weren't always reliable. There were the *good* ones, the thick nylon ones used by the feds. Those were pretty strong. And then there were the smaller ones, the brittle ones, the zip ties that were originally used for something else—tying bundles, whatever—before somebody thought bigger ones would make easier restraints than rope.

Those could be shattered with enough quick force or some wearing-down at the edges.

As Gideon listened to Stevie clatter up the stairs, he gently tested his bonds—and the extent of his injuries.

Oh! Hey, right wrist was broken. That was *bad.* It was swelling pretty badly too. Yeah, no, that wasn't going to work. But Gideon was ambidextrous, and his left wrist was still rockin'!

And this chair—what the fuck was this chair he was sitting on? Metal folding? No such luck. But it *was* a wooden kitchen chair. Something old that had once been sort of delicate, with lots of decorative lathing.

Oh, this thing would shatter in a *heartbeat.*

With an effort, he widened his swollen eyes, trying to decide what lay on either side of him.

The floor was packed earth—no concrete in sight. Okay, okay—he could work with that. He was currently sitting in a pool of unfiltered light, mob-land style, from a bulb swinging from the ceiling.

As far as he could tell, the floor was untreated, with some underlying moisture but a dry topsoil, so no little electric booby traps. Excellent. Now, which side?

Well, if he landed on his right side, his wrist would break even *more*, and he'd probably pass out.

But Stevie had mostly led with his right when beating Gideon about the head, and the left side of his face was pretty swollen. He probably had a concussion from that. That was the side where his ribs were feeling crunchy and, well, dangerous.

So if he landed on his *left* side, his *head* would break even more, and he'd probably pass out *forever*.

Okay, then.

It was a plan. Probably not a great one, but Gideon could work with it. He couldn't take a deep breath—his ribs were too crunchy. But he could take a *breath*, and he could harden his core, and he could brace himself.

Ass firmly in seat, he began to dance.

And his chair began to wobble.

And then it began to rock.

And Gideon got ready for everything in his body to explode.

BACK DURING the Sons of the Blood thing, Joey and Gideon had taken a precious three days off—with Clint's blessing—and ridden not one but *two* electric motorcycles from Manhattan to Boston.

Gideon could ride like a fucking *champion*, Joey discovered, although they'd both discovered that riding a motorcycle all day wasn't as great for the sex drive as all the advertisements claimed.

Still, they'd enjoyed the ride, had eaten some great chowder as they passed through Boston, and had been a little sorry to see the outskirts of Joey's father's influence come into view in the form of the storage center where Joey kept their stuff.

There was a car rental place about a mile away—Gideon had rented a car to Logan airport there while Joey had driven first one bike then the other to his storage space.

Once again, he had to leave his clothes collection, but this time, since he only had to walk a mile to the car rental place, he managed to smuggle his old leather jacket out.

Only to realize that he didn't really love it like he used to. He loved the one he'd bought in Manhattan more.

They'd given it to a homeless woman in Boston and had been in their apartment in time to take a shower, have a glass of wine, and have some rocking sex to celebrate that they were no longer on the back of motorcycles.

And most importantly, Joey had *two* motorcycles somewhere his father still hadn't thought to look, somewhere that could get him into the reservation unseen and to the back entrance onto the property.

Where the young mountain lion was proudly terrorizing rabbits and deer and probably pissing pheromones to all the female mountain lions in the area.

Good for him.

Joey had picked Crosby and Pearson to go with him—apologizing to Garcia and Swan of course.

"Naw, I get it," Garcia had said generously. "Cowboy there is built like a fuckin' house. You're gonna want some of that with you." That he used "Cowboy" as an endearment *and* a nickname was actually sweet as fuck, but nobody on the team was going to tell Garcia that because it might make him mean.

"And you and Gail could take out an army with knives alone," Manny Swan said generously. "So, you know. Go take out an army, brother."

They'd been on the side of the road in front of the car rental agency, where the two SUVs they'd had waiting for them when they'd arrived at the quiet, federally owned airstrip only five miles away were parked on the side of the road.

After some grim bids of "good hunting" and some quick, hard back-thumping warrior hugs, Crosby, Pearson, and Joey slid away, running quietly in the woods alongside the road until they were out of sight. In ten minutes, the SUVs would pass in front of the storage center, and the motorcycles would draft along for a few miles until Joey took them into the reservation.

With any luck, by the time Stevie knew of the SUVs, the motorcycles would be out of sight in the barren back quarter of the res.

Crosby was deft and powerful on the electric motorcycle, and Pearson was a fearless passenger behind Joey.

They ghosted offroad, through long, dry grasses and powdery dirt for a mile or so before Joey led them behind the little line shack, where they dismounted. Neither of his teammates showed the slightest bit of "bike wobble," as Gideon called it, both of them striding around like they chose that mode of transpo all the time.

Joey had sort of suspected that might be the case.

He was in the middle of pulling a tarp over the motorcycles while Crosby and Pearson re-fitted their flack helmets and adjusted their weaponry when it occurred to him that he might be kissing these two vehicles goodbye.

He'd had such plans, he thought now. Him and Gideon reclaiming them. Taking them to Lake Erie to meet Gideon's stepmother and his father. Of maybe traveling a little, seeing more of the East Coast than places he got sent out to for calls.

And even if they did get Gideon back, there was no guarantee they'd be leaving this way.

He left the keys in the ignition of both bikes, and when Crosby cocked his head, Joey shrugged.

"If we don't get back to them, I don't want them to rot," he confessed, thinking about the leather bomber jacket. It had started to crack after eight years in storage. That was a terrible thing to do to something useful and beautiful.

"We'll get him back," Pearson said, patting him on the back. "Don't worry, Carlyle. It's not just you here. Although—" She gestured to the break in the fence, which hung as rusty and as disused as it had that Christmas. "—you are the one who's got to lead the way."

They'd all brought water and food bars and salt tablets, which was important. Because even though it was only ten in the morning (oh God, had they only gone dancing *last night*? Had it only been that long before Gideon had been yanked inside Stevie Carlyle's vehicle and dragged away?) it was already hot and humid, and they were jogging through some rough terrain.

But Joey and Gideon ran nearly every morning they woke up together, and he had the feeling Pearson and Crosby weren't far off that mark either. They all used the fitness facilities in the office—and they all practiced combat almost daily.

The five or so miles to the mansion was no big deal, as long as they followed in Joey's footsteps as he avoided the pitfalls of what was now barren rock and close trees.

About a mile in, Joey caught the pungent smell of large-cat urine, and he sucked in a breath and stopped.

"Recognize that smell?" he asked.

"It's like cleaning the cat box times a thousand," Crosby muttered. Crosby and Garcia had adopted a giant fluffy white thing named Sampson. The last time Joey had been over there, he and Sampson had spent an hour bonding, leaving Joey coated in long white hairs and cat drool. In a million years, Joey couldn't imagine that massive furry vortex of goodwill exuding this much acid.

"Keep your eyes peeled," Joey said. "My path swings wide of the caves—we should be on the fringe of the big cat's territory but not intruding." He started walking again, but he kept his eyes swinging, left to right, right to left, the hair on his neck standing straight up as they neared the stand of rocks where he knew the cave sat, the mountain lion's lair. There were enough boulders and rough terrain here to make getting this close to the place inescapable—another reason, Joey reflected sourly, that it had taken his father so long to get rid of the grizzled old warrior. Stevie Carlyle didn't like the woods. He liked *owning* them—and he'd definitely enjoyed gloating that he'd taken so much of them from the reservation—but walking through them, not so much.

Maybe it was that thought that distracted him, because he almost startled when his gaze swung toward the rise of rocks again, and he saw the quiet figure, sitting, back straight, observing the three SCTF agents as they jogged toward the house.

Joey stopped short, but when he heard Pearson and Crosby go for their weapons, he shook his head.

The gamekeeper watched them impassively, and Joey gave him a short nod.

"You are going to kill the old man?" the gamekeeper asked.

"Yes," Joey said, not imagining this would end any other way.

"Good. The cameras are out until you get to the house."

"Thank you," Joey said, that tiny part of his back relaxing.

"I did not do it for you," the gamekeeper told him, and he turned his head and watched as the young mountain lion, the one who'd taken the old one's cave, poked his whiskers out. "He is kinder than his father," he said thoughtfully. "But his father was my friend."

"I was sad to hear of his passing," Joey said, and the gamekeeper turned toward him, nodding.

"I know. Your friend is being kept in the basement," he said. "You know the way."

Joey swallowed and suppressed a shudder. Yes. He knew that basement.

"Indebted," is what he said. "Should you need one, there's two motorbikes by the break in the fence, keys in."

The gamekeeper smiled. "Indebted," he said, and then he turned back toward the young mountain lion, whom, Joey knew, wouldn't come out while the three awkward humans dressed in loud armor still lingered.

He nodded toward Crosby and Pearson and took off, going faster now that he didn't have to hop and skip between cameras.

"The basement?" Crosby asked, barely winded.

Joey grunted. "Lot of blood in that basement. Fucking cold. Locked me in there when I pissed him off."

"What a fucker," Crosby replied, parkouring off a rock to stay on Joey's six.

"Yeah, well, you wanna know the good news about that basement?" Joey did the same off another rock and watched from the corner of his eye as Pearson leapt it like a gazelle.

"Tell me," she said, less winded than him *or* Crosby.

"I know the secret way in—and Stevie Carlyle never found it."

"That's a good thing," Crosby said, and then they were quiet as the terrain got *really* rough.

WHEN JOEY told the story of his childhood, he usually said, "Stevie shipped me to military school when I was fourteen," and left it at that.

But there were six long years between the night Joey pissed on his teddy bear to kill the nanny cam and the day he got in the limo for the fuckin' last time to go to military school. Gideon had known. Gideon had asked him about those years one night, after a windfall of catching Bruce Springsteen at the Stone Pony in Jersey once they'd finally brought down the Sons of the Blood. It had been late May, about two weeks before they'd hit the club, and they'd been driving back into the city.

"Why do you ask, Gid?"

Joey remembered the expression on Gideon's lean face, the trouble in his eyes as he'd stared out over the highway, the removable splint still on his wrist from their last adventure.

"Because… because I've memorized every intro Bruce ever recorded, and the ones that connect with his father are heartbreaking. But I think that's because his father, for all his faults and flaws, *meant* well, you know? I just… my dad's doing his best. You know that. Started calling me once a week. Asked for pictures of you. Just… did he even try to connect with you?"

Joey wanted so badly to tell him that yes, yes his father had been a human being, but he opened his mouth to lie and that's not what came out.

"One of the housekeepers used to feed this stray cat," Joey said finally. "I liked it. Fed it too. It was filthy. Stevie got home one night, and I'd just bathed the thing, dried it off. It was eating tuna in the kitchen. Fucker saw me there, feeding the cat, and he grabbed both of us—cat by the neck, me by the ear, and threw us in the basement—cat fell and broke its leg on the way down. Dad told me he'd let me out when the fucking cat was dead. Told me I could kill it quick by breaking its neck."

Gideon's breath had gone all funny in the dark. Uneven and choppy, like he was injured.

"What did you do?" he whispered.

Joey let out a humorless laugh. "Well, first of all, it wasn't the flex the old man thought it was. I'd seen the gamekeeper coming in and out of the basement from a pile of rocks. It used to be a servant's entrance, and then there'd been a cave-in, but the door remained, and if you weren't too big and wide, you could weasel your way through." He paused. "I was too short to reach the light," he said thoughtfully. "One of those ones that hangs by a cord from the ceiling. It took me a long time to pick up the cat, wrap it in my shirt, and make my way outside." He could smell it. The dankness of earth and mold and of rotting blood. He'd realize later that it wasn't just the animal's blood. His father knew every part of this basement—except the hidden door. When people talked about bodies in the basement, Joey knew that some people had *real* bodies in the basement, because that terrible, claustrophobic moment in the dark, he'd tripped over at least two shallow graves.

"What did you do with the cat?" Gideon asked.

"I put it in the housekeeper's car," Joey said. "She quit that night, and I figured she would after she watched him throw us in the basement." He laughed a little. "A few months later, I got a note passed to me in school by a teacher who knew her. It was a picture of the cat, sitting on the porch with her. Leg seemed to be healed okay."

"That's real good," Gideon said, his voice evening out a little. "And you?"

Joey shook his head. "I dunno. Stevie saw me, no shirt, blood all over me, and didn't even ask about the cat. I think he figured I ate it, or maybe didn't think about the body rotting down there or something. But he let me out the next day." Another one of those broken little laughs. "The gamekeeper brought me dinner and a water bottle—to drink from and piss in, he told me." Then, because it was important; Gideon knew this for some reason. "Wasn't my last time in the basement. I figured out where the light was, mapped the whole thing in my head. Figured out that the old man didn't know where the secret door was because it was behind this sort of fake wall, and I kept it a secret. It's funny," he said, although it really was the furthest thing from funny. "There's at least five shallow graves down there, but if the old man had even thought to *look* outside that fucking basement, or improve it, or pay off some schmoes to fix it, he would have figured out he didn't have to live with his own goddamned bodies in the fucking basement."

Gideon had shuddered then, visibly. "So no, then."

"No what?" Joey had forgotten the question.

"No, you didn't connect with your father."

Joey's laughter had the bright red tint of hysteria to it. "No. I did not connect with my father."

"But that's okay," Gideon said, and Joey saw his hand reaching in the darkness while he used the other to drive.

Joey seized it, realized that his own was clammy and he was shaking from telling that terrible story, the thing he'd never spoken of, on this quiet, spooky drive from New Jersey to Manhattan.

"Why's it okay?" he asked, his voice smaller than he remembered.

"'Cause you connected with the gamekeeper," Gideon said.

"And the cat," Joey said, thinking about his fondness for Crosby and Garcia's cat. "I think I like cats."

"Good," Gideon said, squeezing his hand.

"And I like you," Joey said softly.

"Also good."

Joey had used his free hand to call up some more Bruce on his streaming service, and they let the music speak for them all the way back to the city.

RIGHT BEFORE the trail ended and the gravel driveway began, Joey paused before peeling off and took a solid measure of Crosby. Back in March, Crosby *definitely* wouldn't have been able to fit through this passageway—his shoulders were wide and he'd put on muscle like the football player he'd been in college. But that was before the weeks undercover, losing nearly sixty pounds to stress and a peptic ulcer, and finding his way back. He didn't look like death anymore, but he was still a big guy, and Joey wondered if he could make it through.

"Whacha thinkin', Carlyle?" Crosby asked.

"I'm trying to figure out how much weight you lost in the last few months, you big tubby bastard. This passageway isn't for football players, and I don't want you to get stuck, 'cause that would *suck*."

Crosby grunted. "Yeah, it fuckin' would. Where is it in the house?"

They'd studied schematics on the way in, so Joey gave him a quick sketch about the kitchen and the door almost hidden by the walk-in refrigerator that led to the stairs.

"It's not easy," Joey said. "I mean—if Dad's got his goons there, you got a lot of people to shoot through."

Crosby nodded and then said one of those things that made all that effort he put into looking like a meatloaf disappear. "Yeah, but if Gid's hurt, you're gonna need a way out that ain't gonna kill him. And I'm pretty sure all those goons are gonna be focused on the front of the house where Harding's about to throw his little party. You think you'll have comms in the basement?"

Joey grunted. "Naw. Don't think so. Lotta rocks." He glanced at Pearson. "You got a problem with small spaces?"

She shook her head. "Nope. Honestly, you had me at bodies in the basement. I've never seen the set of a horror movie."

God, Joey loved his team.

"All right. Crosby, find your own way in, and don't get shot."

"Yeah, you neither. And don't get stuck either, 'cause seriously…." He shuddered. "That sounds like a fuckin' *lot*."

And then he reached out and gripped Joey's arm and leaned his head in to touch foreheads briefly. Joey returned the gesture, his heart suddenly full. His brother. His team. He remembered what Gideon had said about who would pick Joey up if Gideon didn't come home one day.

And he realized that Gideon had been right. He had family here he'd never reckoned on.

After a quick fist bump with Gail—who told him he'd better not be fucking bleeding when she saw him next—Crosby was gone, and Joey gave Pearson a grim look.

"Ready for the horror movie?" he asked.

"Lead on," she said.

And with that, he took two steps up toward the rock face and disappeared.

Horror Movie 101

GIDEON WAS pretty sure he was still alive, but he was also pretty sure that wasn't a good thing.

His head felt like a splatter on a windshield, and his wrist… oh dear God. Why was his hand still attached? It should not feel like his hand was still attached!

How will I human without you?

Goddammit, Joey. God*dammit*. It would be so easy to just close his eyes and drift into the ether, let his body quietly fail, the lights in his brain flicker out. But Joey fuckin' Carlyle had climbed into *Gideon's* bed of his own goddamned free will, and Gideon wasn't going to die now. Not when he finally *got* that thing about being human that was so great.

He'd had some inklings before. The team had been pretty awesome, he couldn't lie. His father, and his painful, awkward attempts at connection—that had given him some faith. His stepmom had *really* given him something to root for. But Joey? Joey was a whole new level of human. Joey, who had been locked in this very fuckin' basement, had not only emerged with most of his soul intact, he'd saved the goddamned cat.

Gideon hadn't missed that part. That scared, angry little kid had saved the goddamned cat.

By sneaking through a secret passageway.

In this very goddamned basement.

Okay, then.

Gideon closed his eyes and breathed out the pain. Breathed it out. Concentrated on other things. His wrist was an explosion—but it was… oh shit. It was a *free* explosion. The chair had splintered when it had hit the ground, and Gideon's arms, both the real one and the one that felt like a bucket full of nails, were mobile.

With a groan, Gideon repositioned himself, stretching his bruised legs—still zip-tied to the chair—in front of him, and he took stock. His stomach muscles were bruised, and his ribs were broken. But his legs? His legs were bruised but sound.

Rolling to his back, he levered his legs up, the chair still attached, but it was no worse than leg presses in the gym, and he could do those for days.

One, two, three! On three, he lowered his legs and worked to yank them open, trying to break either the chair or the zip ties.

The chair crunched some more, but the zip ties held.

This time.

One, two, three! Ouch! Oh fuck, his ribs. His fucking ribs. Fuck! He breathed carefully, making sure he still could. Yeah, okay. Hadn't punctured his lungs yet, but he had maybe one more of those in him.

Had to make it count.

One, two, three!

By the time he could breathe again and the pain stars had cleared enough for him to see his feet, the chair had disintegrated, save for a jagged splintered piece of wood he clutched in his one good hand.

Okay, then. Time to stand.

First he scooched on the rancid dirt floor to the rough wooden wall. Then, pressing his back against the wall, he walked his way up, ignoring the splinters they'd probably be pulling out of his ass for a month.

Ouch, fuck, ouch, fuck, ouch, fuck—oh my God. Oh holy crapblossom. He was *standing*. And armed. Or, well, one armed.

Okay, then.

Carefully, oh so carefully, following the wall so he could stand at all, he made his way around the edges to the darkness untouched by the swinging lightbulb.

Somewhere there was a door. Somewhere, there was a Joey. He'd just faded into the darkest shadow when he heard two noises. One was from deeper in the basement, in the darkest part, the part Stevie Carlyle probably never explored.

The other noise was from above, from the top of the rickety staircase, to the door above that led to the kitchen.

When that door swung open, Gideon could hear chaos erupting. Gunfire, Harding's voice through a megaphone, grunts of men getting hit, screams of men who were wounded.

Iwo-fucking-Jima in a mansion, Gideon thought with a suppressed cackle.

He wondered if his boy was up there, slitting throats and taking names.

That's my boy, he thought. *Kill a fucker for me.*

As if summoned by Gideon's thoughts alone, Stevie called from the top of the staircase, "Joey! Joey fuckin' Carlyle! You down there? You protecting your fag cop buddy yet? Show your face, boy, or I'll gut him like a fish and tie you up with his guts!"

Oh, nice. Gideon thought his decision to kill himself to escape was probably one of the best he'd ever made. Yay him!

Wait. Wait. What was that other sound again?

'Cause it was getting louder.

"I SWEAR to Christ, Joey, how high were you to think Crosby might have fit down here?"

"Sorry," he grunted, feeling his way to the next boulder. They both had flack helmets with lights, but they were bulky, and you couldn't always point the light to where you needed to wiggle your body.

"Only be sorry if we get stuck."

"Didn't think I'd grown that much—" With a soft gasp he slithered between a fractured brick wall and a pile of rocks. "—since I was fourteen."

"Brag, brag, brag," she muttered. "All I've grown is boob, and I'm still not making it."

He tried not to stumble. "Your boobs aren't that big," he told her. "I think you were born that big."

She let out a breathless little "Ha!" and continued to keep pace after him.

"Didn't know you noticed boobs," she hissed as they took another step, and another.

"Noticed 'em plenty," he told her, wondering if all soul-baring was as awkward as his had been. That trip back from the Stone Pony was probably the most poetic conversation he'd ever had. "Ouch." He tore his knuckles on a ledge of metal embedded in rock. "Careful there."

"You noticed 'em plenty, but you're shacking up with Gideon?" She didn't say "string bean" or "scarecrow" or "scrawny no-assed skeleton," for which he could only be grateful. He knew what she meant. Unless she saw him without his shirt—and why would she?—she wouldn't know he looked good, defined, strong, powerful.

"I don't know," he muttered. "If Gideon's soul had come with boobs, I would've fallen in love with boobs. But Gideon's soul came with that nose and those eyes and that tall scrawny body. Life's a fuckin' mystery. I don't ask questions—I just keep showing up at his apartment."

"Aw, man," she said and then drew up short, as did he.

The terrifyingly narrow path of boulders, hewn granite, and broken walls had stopped abruptly, giving way to a small antechamber barely big enough for Pearson and Joey to stand abreast.

It practically felt like a ballroom after the journey there.

"Aw man, what?" he asked, panting with the exertion of making his body fit where it had no business fitting. The fucking gamekeeper hadn't seemed this small either.

"Aw man, that was really sort of romantic. How do I give you and Crosby shit about being tough guys in love if you do it with grace and charm? It's heinous."

"Yeah, you're just trying not to notice Swan's had a thing for you since the beginning."

She grunted like he'd hit her and then took a breath. "Yeah, well, watching you and Garcia freak out when something happens to your significant other does *not* make me want to dive into the deep end of the pool."

He glanced at her, her piquant face grimy from rock dust and sweat, but as fierce as any man he'd ever met. "Too late," he said softly, and the look she gave him was pained.

"Of course it's too late. Have you *seen* Swan? I mean… dude. He's got *manboobs*, and they're *glorious*."

He glared at her. "How could you?" he asked, only partially kidding. "How could you put that image in my head?"

And then, in case she had something worse to offer, he pulled out one of the daggers from the back of his belt and started working on the lock to the basement door.

One, two, three—*Pop*!

GIDEON HEARD the rasp of the door as it scraped across the ground, and tried to pull in enough breath to yell a warning.

All he got for his efforts was spots in front of his eyes.

The noise at the top of the stairs continued, but there was creaking as Stevie made his way down them. Oh. Huh. He left the door open. Why?

"I know you're in here!" Stevie cried. "All I had to do was follow the bodies!"

Well, Joey couldn't be coming through that scraping deeper in the basement if he was making bodies up top. Who was coming in, then? Bad guy? If he was, Stevie didn't know him.

Stevie never figured it out.

No, that had to be a friendly, but whoever it was, they were coming into a trap. Gideon swallowed—there was a lot of blood in that spit—and tried to think. Big pointy brain, Joey said. It felt pretty mushy now, but there had to be some pointiness left to help his team out.

"Maybe your buddy's dead!" Stevie called, and in the echo of his voice, Gideon heard the rasp of the door.

His heart was thundering in his ears and his breath hurt… hurt… and he couldn't hear…. Where was he?

He forced himself to scan the floor. Stevie was coming down the stairs, which wrapped around one wall and then leveled out to land almost immediately under the yellow light.

That was the center.

The rasp of the door was against the wall in the dark; Gideon didn't know how deep.

The shortest line between them skirted the pool of yellow light. Stevie was going to be in that center in a couple of seconds.

Gideon had to hobble faster.

"Maybe I'll do the both of ya!" Stevie shouted. "Maybe I'll fuck his corpse while you watch. Maybe I'll shoot you in the head while he breathes his last—wanna see? You little pisser, I bet you've been *waiting* to watch me waste him so you can throw me in jail! Cold-blooded little shit—just like the old man!" He wasn't making sense, and he wasn't looking well. His eyes were rolling wildly, and he almost ate it on the stairs twice, his stride was so uneven. The gunfire above was slowing down, and Gideon wondered what was happening up there.

Whatever was going on, it had unhinged Stevie Carlyle to his last fucking gasp.

The voice in the dark scared Gideon so bad he almost fell.

"Is that what you think the problem is?" Joey jeered from the darkness. "That you and me are too much alike? My God, Stevie, get a fuckin' grip."

"Joey, duck," Gideon mouthed, but nothing came out. No air. There was no air in his lungs. Damn, had he misjudged the punctured lung thing? The pressure in his chest, the swimming vision, all of it would seem to indicate that yes, yes he had.

But it didn't matter. Stevie had landed in the center of the light and had aimed his weapon and opened fire, one, two, three times, the roar like an apocalypse in the little room.

Joey.

Gideon didn't give him a chance to set up a fourth shot.

TRAINING—JOEY HAD it. You kept moving, you knew where your partner was, and you didn't open fire if you couldn't see what was beyond your target. He and Gail had come through the door and seen the shattered chair immediately, but no Gideon.

But the minute Stevie opened his mouth about Joey's little buddy, Joey knew Gideon was somewhere in this fucking pit.

So smart, Gid, getting out of his line of sight. Harding's remark about Gideon not having a knife to his throat while Joey tried to negotiate had chilled Joey to the bone, but apparently Gideon's pointy brain had saved them that.

So Joey had gestured Pearson to swing around to under the stairs while he called attention to himself and then sprinted, putting an old freezer between him and the psycho with the gun.

Gideon, where are you?

The three shots rang out, and Joey risked a glance over the obstacle hidden in the shadows. Stevie had been aiming for where Joey's voice *was*, so he hadn't even hit the thing.

And that's when Gideon leapt out of the shadows and onto Stevie Carlyle's back, his left hand rising and falling like a serial killer's while Stevie dropped his gun and screamed.

With a howl, Joey's father stumbled back against the far wall while Joey scrambled toward him, knife drawn. He heard Gideon's thud and groan as he connected to the wooden partition that was backed with brick, and then Joey was on top of Stevie, his own knife slicing the old man's throat before they were both borne to the ground.

With a heave and a kick—and not a backward glance—he yanked his father's body off Gideon's and tried to assess the damage.

Oh God. Oh *God*—he looked like hell.

"Gail!" he cried, and she was right there at his shoulder. "Gail, God, we need a medic! We need… he's coughing blood!"

"Punctured lung," she said, and her voice was shaking but in control. He knew that, he thought, but he couldn't say it. Oh God. "His ribs must be broken. Gid? Gid, can you hear us?"

"Joey…," Gideon gurgled. "Couldn't let him—"

"I'm fine, Gid," Joey said, and his own voice was not in control, *nothing* was in control.

"Carlyle!" The voice at the top of the stairway had Pearson aiming her weapon, but Joey was on his knees, Gideon's head pulled gently into his lap.

"Boss!" she called. "We're here. We need a bus for Gid, Clint. He's in a bad way."

"Can he be moved?" Harding asked.

"No," she said. "No. Punctured lung, broken ribs—"

"We got a bus waiting for the place to be cleared," Harding said. "But I'll have—"

"Move, Clint, I'm coming down."

"Blodgett," Clint muttered, stepping aside. "Who was *supposed to stay outside with the bus*."

"I love you, Clint, fuck off."

Later, Joey would tell Gideon that, he thought. Later, he and Gid would laugh about the big scary Clint Harding's husband telling him "I love you, Clint, fuck off."

But there was no laughing, not now, not when Gideon was struggling for breath. He couldn't. He couldn't. He couldn't—

"Joey," Harman Blodgett murmured, "lay him down again. We need a cervical collar to check for spinal injuries. There's medics coming down. You should go up with Harding so we can tend to him."

"Gideon?" Joey said, and it seemed to be the only word he had as he stroked Gideon's battered face. "Gid?"

"Baby," Harman said softly, "I need you to step aside. We'll stand for him, Joey. You need to trust us with him, okay?"

My mate. My mate. My mate.

You have a pack, Joey. Have some faith.

He still didn't have words, but he allowed himself to be pulled away, led up the stairs by Pearson, until Harding took his hand at the landing and pulled him out of the path of two very determined EMTs, jogging past with a stretcher that might just make it down the stairs.

When he got up to the kitchen, he glanced around, then blinked, then glanced around again.

"Jesus," he graveled. "There's a lotta fuckin' dead people in this kitchen." The white-tiled walls were spattered with blood—it was something out of a horror movie—and no fewer than four guys lay sprawled on the kitchen island, on a counter, on the prep table, on the floor, all of them with holes in their chests or their throats. One guy—a fifth—lay on his front with a knife hilt protruding from directly between his C3 and C4 vertebrae.

"Nice throw," he muttered.

"Yeah," Harding muttered. "It's a beauty. Crosby, you got anything to say about that?"

Joey turned to Crosby in a daze and saw he was being tended to by another EMT for what looked to be a solid knife wound in his shoulder. "All the other guys were in the front yard getting shot by you people," he muttered. "Joey said I needed to clear a path through the kitchen, so I cleared a path through the kitchen. Do you not have a path through the kitchen, Boss?"

"I appreciate not getting unalived by that asshole there," Harding said, with a jerk of his chin to the guy with the knife in his back. "Who got you?"

"That asshole," Crosby muttered, pointing his toe at a very surprised-looking dead man without a throat. "Sorry, Carlyle, I was doing that when Stevie got through." He glanced at Joey and swallowed. "Gideon?"

"Getting worked on," Joey said, feeling dizzy. "He's…." His voice broke. God, he remembered how Pearson and Garcia had fallen apart when Crosby had almost died, and now he knew what that was like. He'd always assumed Crosby would live—but he couldn't assume… couldn't assume….

"He's tougher than you think," Harding said, and before Joey could retort that *of course* Gideon was tougher than *anybody* expected, he added, "but there's something I need you all to see. Tal found it once we'd cleared the hostiles from the house."

"Any arrests?" Pearson asked. What she was really asking was "Any survivors?"

"Not. Yet." Harding's expression was so grim, it took Joey a minute to realize what he might possibly mean. "Follow me."

He led his way up the staircase to the upper floors and the place Joey remembered as his father's study. As he went, he saw Swan and Doba standing guard over a bedroom full of staff—two housekeepers, the young chef Joey had seen over Christmas, and two helpers, one possibly an assistant gardener. Joey called Swan over before they passed.

"Be kind. I know we have to clear them, but if they got shoved up here when shit fell out, it means they have nothing to do with the business. This is a…." He grimaced. "It's a room he let his guys use when they, you know, wanted to *use* someone. Nobody comes in here willingly."

Swan nodded. "I got that vibe," he said, glancing around distastefully. "I'll hand them over to the first flatfoot that comes along and tell him to get their names and addies and let them go. Harding said he had a thing he needed us to see."

"Yeah," Joey said. He was pretty sure he knew what it was.

TEN MINUTES later, the whole unit was there, except for Gideon and Harm. Harm had radioed Harding to tell him that the bus was on its way to the hospital and to tell Joey it was good he'd stayed away. Joey didn't ask what that meant. He understood his assignment.

He had to hold his shit together while Harding explained why having access to Stevie's computer shit was putting that "we're all dead" expression on his face, and then—he had promises from Pearson and Crosby on this—they would sedate him and drag him to the hospital to wait for Gideon.

He was being an adult. Gideon had taught him how to do this. His pack took care of him; he had to take care of his pack.

"Okay," Clint said grimly. "Tal had about five minutes with this shit before she called me. Tal, you want to explain the sitch?"

She turned toward them all. "The sitch is that we have too many goddamned secrets," she said seriously. "You want to blackmail three-quarters of our elected officials? Our DOJ? Homeland Security? The cabinet? Bank presidents? This is the way to do it. Now some of it is dumb shit. We've got a daughter of a congressman who got revenge porned. Somebody's kid brother tried pot in college. Shit that, in a sane political climate, wouldn't mean jack squat, but as you know, those are not the times we live in. And some of this shit is dangerous. Some of it is…." She grimaced. "It's 'secret police force will sneak into your bedrooms and disappear you' dangerous. You all know what I'm talking about. It needs to be released, but if we release it, we're dead, our families are dead, and our unit is dead. So this is big. And whatever we need to do, we need to agree to it. This op, so far, it's not sanctioned by the government. They could just start by putting us in jail for coming over here to murder citizens, and that would shut us all up, and none of this would get addressed."

"But…," Crosby said. "I mean, it *needs* to be addressed. I take it you got a plan to do that?"

Clint nodded. "Oh, I do. I've got a couple of channels I could send this through, and while there's no guarantees it will all be taken care of—"

"It beats us getting disappeared from our beds as we sleep," Natalia said, and Joey had a feeling she knew exactly what channels Clint was talking about.

"So," Gail said slowly, "we wouldn't be going public with this information. Who do we turn it over to?"

Harding and Natalia met eyes, and Harding said, "Joey, this is why we needed you. I know…." His voice went soft. "I *know* you want to be somewhere else right now. But I've got to ask you, was your father the type to, uhm, booby trap his office? Like, with, you know, thermite?"

Joey blinked, and yearned sharply for Gideon to be there next to him to explain what Harding was asking him.

"Like, burn the office up?" he asked dubiously.

"And the entire house down with it," Natalia said, nodding her head. "Garcia, you worked ATF. Could you brew some of that up—I mean *accidentally set some of that off*—in here with some help?"

For a moment they all stared at her, and Garcia started to cackle.

And then Pearson did too.

And then Swan and Doba and Crosby.

And finally Joey got it.

Burn the house down, with the computers, and nobody would be worrying for the information that could get them killed.

And he let out a weak chuckle. Sad and strained, but it was enough.

"Yeah," he lied. "That Stevie, absolutely terrified somebody would break into his study. I never saw the inside of it myself—he was too fuckin' afraid." His father hadn't even been afraid of Joey as Joey was slitting his throat.

Harding nodded. "Okay, then. Folks, we gotta put on something of a show. Talia, you and Pearson download it and store it. Garcia, you figure out how to destroy it. The rest of us, we gotta clear this fuckin' house and all its grounds of anybody with a pulse."

They all nodded.

It was time for operation CYA to commence.

GARCIA ENDED up in the hospital for a third-degree burn across the back of his arm and smoke inhalation—but, he said as the EMTs were pumping him full of morphine and loading him into the ambulance, that's what happened when you set off a booby trap.

What he was really saying, of course, was that while the injury was the result of some hurried attempts at high-powered arson, it was reasonable to assume that somebody would get injured setting off the booby trap that Stevie Carlyle had supposedly set.

It added to the believability.

And in the days and weeks to come, they would all hear Harding lie convincingly over the phone or to dark-suited visitors with flat, sociopathic faces, that the room had erupted into deadly flame before anybody could access the computers. Joey went on record—many times—as saying his father was a decompensating toxic narcissist and a paranoid sociopath who really *would* set a deadly destructive firebomb rather than let anybody else have access to his shit.

And everybody else said that if Joey hadn't been in the basement, looking over the scene where his partner had been tortured, he could have warned the rest of the unit, but he was understandably upset.

But that was in the weeks to come.

Once the house was clear, burning to the ground with the fire services addressing the ashes with all the special flame retardant they had to counter the thermite, Harding and Tal peeled away in the rented SUVs. Both vehicles were now missing grills and damaged beyond repair because they'd both rammed the gates to get into the compound, but neither of them appeared to give a ripe shit.

Gideon had been taken to surgery the minute he'd cleared triage, and as Harman told Harding, sounding breathless and worried, Gideon was in for the fight of his life.

The next six hours were interminable. Joey remembered very little—lots of staring numbly into space, wondering why he was still breathing.

Random snippets of moments from the last two years kept coming back to him.

The occasional shoulder bump from one of his colleagues, making sure he was still breathing.

Somebody—Gail?—helped him out of his tac gear and gathered his weapons to lock away somewhere, probably a local police vehicle, since they were all off duty and not allowed to carry anymore.

A shift to a small prep room, and the sting of antiseptic as Blodgett—probably in an attempt to still his own shaking nerves—tended to the bleeding scrapes on his shoulders, biceps, and knuckles.

They all left him his knives, in their special sheath sewn into the back of his work slacks.

Somebody washed his face and even ran a brush through his hair to remove the gravel. He had no idea who.

When the doctor came out, like they did in the movies, and said the patient had been moved to recovery, and only family was allowed in, Harding stood up and said Gideon's parents were on their way from Philadelphia, but his domestic partner was there and needed to see him.

The doctor didn't even blink when Talia shoved Joey forward.

Joey allowed himself to be led to a recovery room in the ICU, and he almost crumpled at the doorway. Gideon lay there, head and face wrapped in bandages, a tube in his nose to give him oxygen, one arm heavily bandaged and immobilized.

"Oh God," he whispered.

Talia was right at his shoulder. "It looks bad," she said, "but he's still breathing on his own. No intubation. No breathing tube. They reinflated his lungs, cleaned out the pneumothorax, and sedated him—a *lot*—to give the swelling in his brain a chance to go down. His skull was fractured, but that meant they didn't have to drill a hole in it, so that's not always a bad thing."

"None of what you're saying sounds not bad," Joey said numbly.

"How's this," Tal murmured, guiding him to a chair and putting Gideon's uninjured hand in his. "He's alive. And I'm pretty sure he hung on just so he could protect you. If he knows you're here, he's not gonna leave. How's that?"

"Okay," Joey mumbled, laying his head on the bed next to Gideon. Squeezing that callused, ink-stained, battered hand. "That'll keep me from going apeshit for now."

"Good," she whispered. "Good."

HE WAS in the induced coma for a week.

Gideon's parents arrived the next day, and Harding made Joey leave so they could have some time with their son and to get Joey to a hotel to shower and eat.

He wasn't sure where the clothes were coming from—later he found out that Garcia had gone into Boston and bought him everything from jeans to briefs to micro-Ts to pajamas.

He brought pajamas to the hospital so he could sleep in a cot next to Gideon's bed.

He managed to remember words the next time he met Gideon's father. His first thought was that Gideon looked just like him. His second was that the man seemed *really* happy to meet him.

His third was that Gideon's stepmom kept trying to feed him, and Joey ended up letting her because Gideon seemed to think she walked on water and Joey couldn't hurt her feelings.

But all of that passed in a haze.

Most of what he remembered was setting his phone out on one of Gideon's Spotify lists and playing it for hours at a time.

Gerald and Trish seemed to be okay with this.

After a few days of this, Gerald said that Gideon's mother—the one who'd died—had given him his love of music.

Joey had glanced up, his attention caught for the first time in days, and said that he hadn't known that.

Trish said that she used to love it when he played his music so loud it rattled the house. It meant he was a real live teenager, and not some superadult cyborg living in her husband's house.

That had made Joey laugh for some reason, and then he'd started to cry, and he'd stopped making noise altogether so they wouldn't see him. He resumed his position, hiding his face in the starched white sheets next to Gideon, while Bob Dylan sang "Tangled Up in Blue" through Joey's phone.

He was working so hard on controlling his breathing, he almost didn't feel Gideon's hand, awkwardly stroking his hair.

Then he heard Trish gasp, and he glanced up, not caring if Gideon's parents saw his swollen face, his red eyes.

"Gid?" he asked, afraid—so afraid—it wasn't what he thought.

"S'okay, kid," Gideon rasped. "I'm okay."

And then he sobbed while Gideon's stepmother leaned over his back and held him, and Gideon's father went to get the doctor.

His first thought—first real thought—after medical personnel gathered around the bed to do whatever they did to people coming out of comas—was that he needed to let the pack know.

The team. He needed to let the *team* know.

But he remembered that decision they'd made, that lawless, lawful decision, to protect themselves while they went out and tried to do good in the world, and he knew exactly what he'd meant.

"Harding?" he said into his phone. "You there?"

Harding—who had sent the rest of the team home but had remained in Massachusetts to deal with fallout and to make sure Joey wasn't alone—had answered on the first ring.

"Any change?"

They'd all said this a thousand times in the last week.

"Clint, he's awake," Joey said, and he gave it up and let his throat close. "I think he's gonna be okay."

MATES AND LITTERMATES

"YOU UP for this?" Joey asked for the fifty-dozenth time.

"You?" Gideon asked gently.

Joey looked away. "I'm just so glad you're home," he said.

Gideon's extended recovery had been too long for the hospital, and too intense for a place with four flights of stairs. After a month, Gideon had gone to his father's place in New Jersey for six weeks, until he could walk up the stairs without a pounding headache and going to the john didn't send him to bed with spots in front of his eyes.

Joey had visited every weekend, exhausted and sad. His first night at Gerald and Trish's New Jersey suburban palace had been painful—Joey had forgotten how to sleep. He woke up every five minutes, calling Gideon's name, his movement hurting Gideon's battered body.

Gideon had finally woken up after five solid hours to find Joey curled on the floor with a pillow and a blanket from the hallway, and he'd had it.

"Kid, get up here," he'd ordered.

Joey had crawled up on the bed, miserable, in his briefs, looking like a bear on his last fucking berry.

"Okay," Gideon said. "I need you to touch the places I'm talking about, okay? Gently, but touch them. Start with my ribs." Joey's hands, callused and firm, visited Gideon's ribs, and Gideon covered them with his good hand. "They were broken, and, yes, they punctured my lungs. They're not crunchy anymore, but they're sore. My lungs need to heal. Can you feel that?" He breathed evenly, up and down.

Joey nodded.

"How'd that feel?"

"Rough," Joey whispered.

"Yeah. But still way better than in the hospital. Okay, next. Touch my face."

Joey whimpered. The tears from Stevie's rings had scabbed over, but the bruises and broken cheekbones still left swelling.

"Gentle, but touch it."

And Joey had, while Gideon took him through the injuries, one by one.

When he was done, Joey slithered into bed next to him, his head pillowed gingerly next to Gideon's.

"Why'd we do that?" he asked.

"So you could see I'm not dead," Gideon said softly. "I'm sorry, baby. I'm sorry I got hurt, but I'm not dead yet. You gotta see I'm not dead yet, or you'll never trust me to be here again."

The tears came then, quiet and cleansing. Gideon had heard about Joey crying in the hospital and hadn't believed it, but now he believed.

Joey slept quietly after that—but he looked even worse the next weekend, leading Gideon to believe he never slept at home.

He could take short walks by then, and after wandering around his father's property for a while, holding Joey's hand and appreciating the sunshine in the morning, he ordered Joey to eat dinner with Trish and Gerald and retired upstairs, claiming he needed a nap.

He called Harding instead.

"I don't know what to tell you," Harding mumbled, and Gideon wondered if he'd been down for *his* nap too. "We take turns sleeping on your couch, but it doesn't seem to stop the nightmares."

Gideon grunted. "Does he say what the nightmares are *about*?" he asked.

"No," Harding replied, and now he sounded… cagey. "But you gotta know, Gid, that day had plenty of nightmare fuel. You may need to ask Joey about it. He may need to… talk."

Gideon frowned, because that sounded loaded, but you didn't ask Harding questions when he got like this.

"Have them sleep in bed with him," Gideon told him. "Nobody's virtue is at risk—think wolves in a pack when one of them's injured."

Harding grunted. "Gotcha. Good thinking."

"Has he moved out of the old apartment yet?"

"Yeah—he sublet it to Swan and Pearson, who claim to be using the guest room."

Gideon let out a fractured laugh. "Of course they are. Is this healthy? Us with the partners who are partners?"

"No," Harding said bluntly. "But I don't want to break up teams that are working. When they stop working, they stop being partners. I think you've got the right of it, though. We're a wolf pack—hell, even the spouses who *aren't* working with us are our pack. Even Pearson's or Crosby's ex-roommates are in our pack. We don't let pack go it alone."

"Nope," Gideon said, and then he really was ready for a nap.

"Call me later," Harding told him. "And not just to worry about your significant other. I miss your pointy brain."

Gideon smiled. Joey's word for it. "I'm bored," he admitted. And then, in the interest of honesty, "My stamina's still for shit, but when I'm awake, I'm bored."

"Maybe in a few weeks we can have you back to run a desk. Or overwatch." Harding paused. "Definitely overwatch."

Gideon smiled. "Joey still not great at it?"

Harding grunted. "He's not bad, really. The audible he called when we went to get you—"

"Which audible?" Gideon asked.

"He didn't tell you?"

Gideon had to breathe, because his lungs were still weak and he'd taxed them. "Nobody's told me anything. It's like…."

"Like if you know what happened that day, we'll see you in the fucking basement again," Harding said softly.

"Yeah."

Harding took his own breath. "Make Joey tell you some of this. Particularly about how the house burned down. But maybe you need to hear this too. I'm not sure if you know this, Gid, but you were a pretty awesome force of fucking nature."

Gideon grunted. "Yay me," he said, stretching out on the bed and getting ready for story time. "Now hurry up, it's almost time for my nap."

JOEY PAUSED before he entered Gideon's room. He couldn't help it. He'd never dealt with parents, or people in their parents' homes. It didn't matter that Gideon was, in his words, almost forty, which made Joey close to thirty. Or that Gerald and Trish seemed like *genuinely* nice people, who only wanted Gideon to be happy and well.

A lifetime of distrusting parental figures and of not expecting kindness from strangers had made him leery of imposing on their trust.

But Gerald himself had brought Joey's bag up the stairs to put in Gideon's room, and Gideon….

If Joey had ever wondered what love meant, he was starting to think it was the wave of well-being that washed over Gideon's battered features when he saw Joey at the door.

And the feeling that, even though this ordinary (posh!) house in the New Jersey suburbs was alien to him, being this close to Gideon was home.

So it still took him a minute, a breath, before he opened the door, expecting to find Gideon asleep. He'd been planning to sit on the bed and read—his comfort book since he'd been a kid was *Call of the Wild*, and he had a disintegrating paperback in his duffel.

What he found instead was Gideon sitting up, propped by pillows, reading on his phone.

"Whacha doin'?" he asked, trying to be playful. The fact was, his heart clenched, because with the lowering summer shadows, Gideon appeared almost normal.

He yearned for normal.

"Reading the action report from that day near Boston," he said. Nobody talked about "raiding Stevie Carlyle's compound"—that was too close to the truth.

Joey swallowed. "Ya see anything surprising?"

Gideon rolled his eyes. "Well *yeah*. Did you know *I* killed Stevie Carlyle?"

Joey stared at him. "You did not. *I* killed Stevie."

Gideon shook his head. "No, you didn't. According to this, I had actually skewered him in the liver—he was bleeding out from a mortal wound when you cut his throat." He gave Joey a bloodthirsty smile. "Not bad for an old man, you think?"

Joey felt a semihysterical laugh bubble out of his throat. "I'm not sure whether to be relieved or insulted," he said. He shook his head and slid onto the mattress next to Gideon. "I'll settle for impressed. You learn anything else?"

"Yeah. Never to ask Crosby to clear a kitchen."

Joey couldn't help it. He snickered again. "Yeah, that was pretty epic. Clint was like, 'I don't mind that you kept this asshole there from shooting me, but seriously, what the fuck?' and Crosby was like, 'Joey told me to clear a path, and I *did*!'"

Gideon laughed and then sobered. "Calix took one for the team."

Joey sighed. "Yeah. He didn't mean to get hurt, but he told us this made it look real—I mean he said that as they were loading him into an ambulance."

"How's he doing?"

"His arm got infected—it's getting better. We've been stretched fuckin' thin. They keep sending me and Pearson out so Swan can ride with Doba and Crosby with Henderson. It's like trying to balance the new with the crazy, you know?"

"Yeah. Sucks when you can't have your normal partner. But I'm glad that Doba and Henderson are working out. We wouldn't even have a unit without them."

Joey sighed, pleased with the normalcy of talking work.

And then afraid all over again.

"Gid, what'll happen if… if we don't have this. If we don't have… you know. Work?"

He didn't have the heart to explain more than that, but Gideon understood.

"You mean if one of us gets hurt too bad to go back?" he asked gently.

"Yeah."

"I'm not the only one with a pointy brain, Joey," he said. "When we say we have 'skills,' it's not all throwing knives or goring fuckers in the liver. Remember Chester Schumer?"

How could anybody forget Chester Schumer?

Joey snorted. "'Course."

"Think you'd see him on paper now?"

Joey nodded slowly. "Yeah," he said softly. "Yeah."

"Think you could talk to a victim now? And know that somewhere inside you, you knew how that person felt?"

Joey closed his eyes, remembering almost losing Gideon, of being so afraid of his father, thinking he was invincible. "Yeah," he said. "It sucks. Being a victim."

"We got skills, Joey. If one day we can't go back in the field, we've got things we can do. You don't fight this hard, learn this much, for nothing. I mean, not a lot of *money* in it, but that's not what we're here for, right?"

Joey nodded slowly and took what felt like his first deep breath in two months.

"Still," he said, "I can't wait until you're back at work. Even if you're not out there with me, I know you're with me, you know?"

Gideon nodded and kissed his temple. "Always, kid," he murmured. "Always."

And even if they knew there was no "always," they both knew that trying for always counted.

AT THE end of the weekend, when he got back to the apartment, he found Crosby waiting patiently on the steps, reading a book on his phone, an overnight bag at his feet.

Joey stared at him for a moment, and it hit him, fast, like a shuffling deck of cards going from one hand to the other, that he hadn't spent a night alone since Gideon had gone into the hospital.

Emily had brought her kids.

Crosby and Garcia had claimed that the cat needed him to come play.

Blodgett had claimed that Clint was working late at the office.

Clint had claimed Blodgett was working a night shift at the hospital.

Pearson hadn't made any excuses. She'd just been there with pizza.

Swan had said the new apartment was great, but it was too perfect and creeping him out.

Henderson said he'd heard there were no plants there. He'd brought a succulent that he claimed not even Joey could kill. (So far so good.)

Doba had brought a deck of cards and no excuses.

Natalia had said Emily and the kids were out of town at the in-laws and she didn't want to drive all the way out of the city.

Night after night, unless Joey was in New Jersey, somebody had been there, and he'd been too busy holding on to his own shit to notice.

But he noticed now, and it almost undid him.

"Wow," he said, his knees giving out so that he folded on the stairs next to Crosby. Crosby leaned into him, and Joey realized, with a sense of wonder, that this was what a brother did.

"Wow what?"

"You guys. Gideon told me my pack would take care of me. I… it just hit me. You *been* taking care of me. I… how could I not notice? That's fucking *bonkers*."

Crosby chuckled. "You know, when I was under cover, Garcia said you and Gid and Natalia kept trying to feed him."

Joey grunted. "Yeah. He's a skinny fucker. Doesn't eat much."

"Sayin'. Remember when the whole goddamned team put their lives on the line to rescue Toby, because he was my roommate, and he meant somethin' to me?"

Joey nodded and relaxed even further into Crosby. His packmate. His brother.

"I remember. Gideon and his pointy brain. The rest of us just, you know. Assassinated."

Crosby gave an evil laugh. "Yeah, that was good."

"You practically moved into Pearson's apartment when she broke her leg," Joey remembered. "I…," he sighed out. "I never had this before."

"Yeah. Me neither."

"Thanks," Joey said, his voice shaking. "I'll try not to wake you up tonight."

Crosby grunted. "Chadwick told Harding I should crawl into bed with you. Figured I'd warn you now, in case you slept with a knife under your pillow."

Joey laughed a little. He had been. "Sound choice," he said. "I'll put the knife under the mattress. Harder to get to."

"'Preciate it."

Crosby stood and held out his hand. "Didja eat?" he asked.

"Oh my God—Gideon's stepmom has brisket—like half a fuckin' cow. She wrapped it all up and put it in a container and it's in my duffel, probably leaking all over my clothes. But it's good. We got some potatoes. Wanna gain five pounds?"

Crosby chuffed as he helped Joey up. "Who wouldn't?"

That night Joey thought about people in his bed. He'd had plenty of sex before Gideon, but Gideon was the only person he'd ever *slept* with. But as Crosby snored softly on the far side of Gideon's bed, it hit him that sleeping with somebody—only sleeping—was a sign of trust.

He trusted these people. They trusted him.

And he knew that Gideon had been right about having a pack. Having friends, brothers, sisters, family.

He knew why Gideon had wanted so badly for Joey to meet his parents. Knew why it made him so happy that Joey remembered to bring Trish flowers every weekend he came, and always knew the scores of the Knicks game so he could talk sports with Gideon's father.

And he knew why he'd close his eyes and actually get some sleep this night, and the night after that, until he didn't need a body in the bed next to him, and he could sleep just knowing that Gideon was out there and loved him.

He pulled out his phone and texted, *In a thousand years, Gideon, you'll never know how much you've given me. I just wanted you to know that. You're right. We can go out the door any day and not come back. But before I do that, I needed you to know I see you. I can't love anybody else like I love you.*

But I can love our family like our family, and that is a big fucking gift.

There was a long pause then, and Joey started falling asleep, thinking he'd missed Gideon's window. Suddenly his phone flashed.

I didn't give that to you, Joey. You earned it every day. I'll be home soon, kid. I love you.

Love you too. Night.

And then he slept like he hadn't slept when he was a child.

"YOU UP for this?" Joey asked for the fifty-dozenth time.

"You?" Gideon asked gently.

Joey looked away. "I'm just so glad you're home," he said.

A month later, Gideon finally got to return to the SCTF on limited desk duty. He was still walking with a cane to help support his body, and his arm was still in a cast—it hadn't just been broken, it had been shattered.

But his new teeth were in, and his nose had been operated on so it was a little straighter (but still crooked), and he could breathe.

To Joey he was transcendent. The sexiest college professor in the SCTF. His pointy brain practically radiated beauty.

His wicked grin was fully present as he sat down in the conference room and started assimilating the data on their newest case. Clint had handed him the tablet before they'd even gotten to the room.

"Wait," Pearson said. "That's it? He's just gonna sit down and start working?"

"No," Harding said dryly. "We've got confetti bombs and champagne waiting—oh, I'm sorry, I spent that budget on tactical gear."

She blew a raspberry at him, and he smiled with all his teeth.

"You can hug him," Joey said grandly. "He'll hate it, but you know, it's not for him."

Pearson launched herself at him first, and he returned the embrace gingerly, the same with Natalia's and Crosby's. Garcia, Doba, and Henderson shook his hand, and Swan did one of those power handshake things.

Harding gave him a long, hard shoulder squeeze, and then he gave Joey one too.

"We're glad you're back, Gid," he said softly. "Joey, we're glad you're with him." He raised his voice a little. "You all, it has been a *bear* of a year. But we've ended up with the team of my dreams. I'm grateful for all of you. Now come on—we've got people out there who need us. Let's go do our jobs and don't get dead."

"Amen, brother," Gideon said. "Now somebody get me coffee and come back in five minutes. I'll have this ready to go then."

Joey was at his side in a moment with coffee in his mug with the fox wearing full graduation regalia, and then he sat patiently, eyes closed, while Gideon's pointy brain—and apparently fully working digits—went to work on their op for that morning.

"Whatcha thinkin', kid?" Gideon asked as he started pulling up screens over the table.

"No place I'd rather be," he said, and then paused. "Except fishing. Someday you and I are going to have to go fishing."

Gideon grinned at him. "Can my dad come?"

"Yeah. We'll even invite Harding. That guy needs to relax."

"Hey, Clint," Gideon called, "Joey wants us to go fishing."

"You're leaving me out?" Natalia said. "Thank Christ."

"Garcia and I are going *surfing* in September," Crosby told them. "In California."

"Who says?" Pearson asked.

"We already put in for time!" Crosby protested.

"Not if we're going to Disneyworld you're not."

Garcia stared at her. "*That* is news to me."

And so on, the sound of their pack bubbling up around them, tighter than any family, bound by purpose, strength, trust—and blood.

And next to Joey was his mate, the strongest, smartest wolf in the pack.

And also the kindest deer.

"You up for this?" Joey asked for the fifty-dozenth time.

"You?" Gideon asked gently.

Joey looked away. "I'm just so glad you're home," he said. "I'm just so glad we're *home."*

Keep Reading for an Excerpt from
The Grifter
Book 7 in The Long Con Series

Long Way Down

Josh Salinger peered over the edge of the fifteenth-floor balcony and hissed. He was low enough that the high-rise forest of Chicago obscured his view of even the most vestigial sky, and his heart hammered with a combination of fear and claustrophobia.

He didn't feel ready for this jump, and it pissed him off.

In his ear, his comms piece buzzed, and his best friend, Dylan Li—aka Grace—said, "You gonna make this, Recovery Boy, or do we need a Plan B?"

Josh glanced behind him where the darkened "thief-proof" room sat, looking pristine and unmolested as it teased the city beyond its outstretched arms with the treasures contained within.

Thief proof Josh's still-scrawny ass. He and his team had spent *weeks* planning this job. Hacking the temperature control had stumped them for a while, until Stirling had pointed out that instead of trying to pump up the temp to ninety-eight degrees so a human could walk in the room (which would put many of the priceless works inside at risk), all they had to do was account for what the temperature was when disturbed by one human.

And putting the human in a dry suit to contain some of his heat put that difficulty in the bounds of acceptable risk.

Josh had gotten access as an up-and-coming art dealer, his bona fides backed up by Stirling's excellent hacking and his Uncle Danny's references. Uncle Danny's day job was being an art docent for the Chicago Art Institute, so that hadn't been hard, and Josh had grown up around art, both in America and abroad. He knew his shit, so actually *doing* the job of an art dealer wasn't a stretch. Which was good because he had to be doing *something* to keep his cover up. Besides, he and his family liked art. With his family's help, he'd spotted a couple of new talents and gotten them coveted places in nearby shows, even offering to showcase paintings and one sculpture at his parents' home. His father, Felix Salinger, owned a Chicago-based cable network that had gone national. Without his ever asking a broker's fee, a *lot* of art had been sold because somebody had seen it on the wall in the Salinger dining room. His mother had planned the entire room around doing that.

So yeah. The side gig that was supposed to be his real gig had been satisfying, but what it *really* had done was give him unlimited access to the private collection of Celeste Buenaventura, heiress, party girl, jet-setter, and, in his mother's words, "porcutwat." Looked pretty and sexy, had a thousand ways to make any interaction unnecessarily painful.

Sadly, along with her mother's billions, the girl had also inherited her father's ruthlessness and recklessness in business. She ran his enterprises deftly, cheated unions and vendors alike, bought art in quantity and quality to hoard and lord over the masses, and slept with anything that slithered.

She was that rare bird—a person with no moral center but wielding enough imagination to love and appreciate art, even the weird stuff like Otto Dix that made people both queasy and tearful with the horrific nature of mankind at war.

Much of her private collection was stolen; she had a fondness for stuff that had disappeared during WWII after having been confiscated from their victims by the Nazis.

Again, a real porcutwat.

She said it was for "historical significance," but the majority of recovered art that had been stolen by the Third Reich had been restored to the original owners, or more recently their descendants. With the exception of the United States government, most of the world still regarded the ideals of the Nazis with contempt.

No, Celeste Buenaventura liked to keep stolen art because it made her feel powerful over the poor and unlucky, which made her the perfect person to set up for this caper, which was why Josh had spent the last four weeks pretending to be her art dealer—and keeping one step away from her entitled octopus hands.

Ugh. As. If.

But her much-examined history had shown that Josh, of all the men in the crew, was Celeste's type, which was unfortunate, because he was also the guy planning the heist and the guy who needed to be *back* downstairs at the party to give coy, shy smiles and dodge neatly out of the way from Celeste's wandering hands like a champion twat tease.

However, that's what put him on this ledge right now, attaching the paracord to his carabiner and getting ready to leap three stories, catch his weight on the cord, and then rappel three more floors down to the men's room he'd excused himself into fifteen minutes ago.

"Josh? Recovery Boy? You ready to go? That's one hell of a jump."

Josh blinked. The voice was different—no longer the staccato patter of his best friend, the thief who *should* have been doing this if he'd been at all able to people enough to pull a grift. Instead it was the deeper, more gravelly bass of Grace's boyfriend, Hunter.

"How long's it been?" Josh asked hoarsely. His bones felt fragile, his muscles weak. Oh God. He was about to blow this caper because he'd pushed himself too far, too fast, and now he was about to prove everybody who loved him right by wimping out at the last possible moment.

Jesus, boy-o, what in the hell are you trying to prove?

Liam's voice, during their last heated conversation, reverberated through his head.

Josh had scowled and walked away, leaving Liam, curly hair in stunning disarray, freckled face blotched, usually smiling mouth compressed in anger, and, Josh knew in his fragile bones, hurt.

Josh had owed him an explanation, and now, before making a jump that would have been easy fifteen months ago, before the cancer had sucked out his strength and his stamina, he hoped he'd have the chance to give it to him.

God, Liam, I don't want you to see me as wounded. Is that too much to fucking ask?

But he hadn't asked, had he? He'd simply gone about and planned the damned op, politely asking his Uncle Danny—

who'd been the one to bring Interpol Officer Liam Craig into their painfully intimate circle of grifters, thieves, and muscle—to pass along their planning to "anybody who might need to know."

Danny had given him a distinctly disapproving look but had done as Josh asked, probably figuring—as most parental figures did when their children hit adulthood—he would eventually pull his head out of his ass and fix this thing with Liam, who didn't seem to have a petty or bitter bone in his body.

I want to see him again, Josh thought. *I need to tell him I'm sorry. I need to tell him why.*

"Josh?" Hunter asked tentatively.

"Yee-fucking-haw," Josh said grimly… and made the jump.

The first descent was terrifying—and exhilarating—and for a whole heartbeat Josh remembered why he'd done this for fun before. And then a gust of wind came out of fucking nowhere from off the fucking lake, and Josh was slammed sideways and into the building. He let out a grunt of pain, and his left arm went numb.

Oh fuck. He had to be three stories lower and to the left and ready to party in less than three minutes.

"Josh?" Hunter asked, his voice taking on the restrained tension of someone trying not to panic.

"Arm," Josh gasped. "Shoulder. Have Grace ready to pull me in when I hit the balcony."

Hunter muttered something to somebody else, and Josh concentrated on not throwing up. God, he'd hardly ever thrown up as a kid, but since the big C and chemo and recovery and special foods and protein drinks, throwing up was his go-to for any sort of discomfort.

Fiercely, he concentrated on working the rope, the pulley, gloved hands and slippered feet finding purchase on the hundred-year-old stone of the stately apartment building. Oh thank you, Celeste Buenaventura and your great taste in art and living quarters, even if you are a shitty human being!

He'd forgotten how pain could dog even the most fluid movement, could make his breath come short, could… oh God, foot, foot, foot—he was so close. If only he could extend his arm to pull himself closer.

Pain blinded him, and he almost lost his grip on the rope. He fought the urge to throw up and was trying to pull his shit together enough to actually slide onto the balcony when he felt an arm around his waist and a hand at his belt, while a familiar voice, accented with London's East End, conferred with Grace.

"He right bloody bollixed it," Liam hissed. "God. Out of socket, you think?"

"Here," Grace said, sounding flat and unemotional, which meant he was *really* panicked. "Liam, you steady him, I'll hold his arm. Hunter—"

The crack his shoulder made when it slid back into its socket was what pushed him over the edge.

"Gonna puke," he rasped, and before he could even position himself, he felt strong hands on his waist and another under his chin, and somebody—probably Grace—was holding the puke bag.

The stomach spasm was mercifully swift, and Grace—ethereally graceful and beautiful like the stars even with such an awful chore—disappeared with the offending receptacle. Someone—Hunter, Grace's decked, stoic boyfriend—wiped Josh down and thrust a breath mint into his mouth, and Liam…?

Definitely Liam… simply held him upright, whispering into his hair.

"Goddammit, boy-o, you had to do all this without me? Can I come help now? Please?"

Oh God. "Dammit, Liam," Josh rasped, trying to put his weight on his feet. "I missed you so bad. Do you really have to see me like this?"

"I'll take you anyway I can get you, lad. Just don't leave me behind."

And then Grace was back, lint roller in one hand for Josh's all-black suit, bottle of water so Josh could rinse and spit the breath freshener, and a comb for a quick touch-up. Grace—whose real name was Dylan Li—was often described as a firefly in a tornado. Off-the-charts brilliant, a stunning dancer, so much natural beauty most people claimed it was like a slug to the gut. The catch to all this might have been called ADHD on steroids with a nuclear chaser: Grace was lucky he lived through most days, either because his own recklessness and lack of focus would get him killed or because the people around him wanted to kill him before the gods took their share.

But nobody who believed that had seen Grace over this last year, working his ass off to keep Josh alive.

"Thanks, Dylan," Josh said softly, catching Grace's hands as he went for one more swipe of Josh's suit. "I'm fine."

"You are not fine, and I need at least twenty minutes to tell you why you're *fucked* and a fucking asshole, so let me—" He literally spit on his hand, wiped a scuff of dirt from Josh's check, and then flounced off.

"Oh dear," Josh murmured. "Everybody's pissed off, and I've got to go get my ass grabbed."

"Good news is," Hunter said, shining a light in Josh's eyes to make sure he wasn't concussed, "a bigwig entered right when she would have been searching for you. She's been kissing up to him for the last fifteen minutes."

Josh perked up. "Our target?"

"No," Hunter said. "Leon di Rossi, the European shipping tycoon, with his newest belle, Julia Salinger."

Josh groaned. "They didn't—"

"They were on standby, my boy," came a new voice, and Josh hoped the balcony would break off the side of the building so he could die right there.

"Uncle Danny… this was supposed to be—"

"Oh, son," Danny—who was not Josh's real uncle, but Josh had always considered him a second father—said. "This is a big enterprise, but we're a big crew. We've all had a hand in this. You wouldn't want to cut us out now, would you?"

Josh gave him a weak smile. "No," he said softly. "Sorry, Uncle Danny."

Danny gave him a tender kiss on the forehead. "Plenty of people will yell at you—you don't need me. Give your prize to Liam and then go back in there and put on your show. This little caper has had some glitches, but they all do. If you and your mother and Uncle Leon can get out of there without notice, this will all be worth it. Trust me."

Josh felt some strength infusing him. Worth it? Well, then—let the con go on!

At his side, Liam gave a nod to Danny, who nodded back, and with that, Hunter, Danny, and Grace all faded away—probably to scale back down the dark side of the building to the waiting van—and only Liam was left.

"Liam…," Josh said plaintively, hating that his voice was still a little thready with fear and hurt.

"Stop," Liam said harshly. "No. Not from you. You asked me to stay away until you were up to full strength, and here you are. Jumping out of buildings and risking your life. You're up to full strength, and here I am."

Josh grunted. "Not so full strength if I'm fucking up this early in the game, am—"

The self-deprecation died aborning.

Liam Craig had been by his side for so much of his illness. He'd caught Josh when he'd stumbled, carried him to bed when Josh had overdone it, entertained him for hours while Josh's family went out on capers much like this one and Josh had to stay behind.

Secret by painful secret they'd peeled the veils from each other's hearts until Josh felt as naked with Liam as he'd ever felt with another human being, including the few lovers he'd taken in his short span on the planet.

It was a painful sort of intimacy, a frightening sort of need, but Josh had been sick, leukemia ravaging his slender body, threatening to destroy every plan and every hope and every dream he'd ever had.

For all that Liam was to his heart, for all that he'd been devastated when Josh had begged him to stay away these last five months, not once—not ever—had they kissed.

Until now.

Liam's mouth crashed onto Josh's with absolute fury, and Josh's breath caught in his chest as he fought for the strength to keep up.

I Don't Think I'll Make it On My Own

Six months earlier

"Now that's a ship," Liam said, mostly to himself as he approached the yacht in San Juan harbor. Liam had come quite a ways from his mother's East End flat and the five younger siblings he'd worked hard to feed from the time he'd hit fourteen.

Even as a copper, his income hadn't increased that much from what he'd received as a strong back loading freight on the docks. He'd continued to live in the flat until his brothers and sisters got old enough to help their mum, and then while spending his days as a bobby, he'd done a remarkable thing.

A series of small art thefts had occurred in the local museums about his neighborhood. Nothing too large—nothing that would bankrupt the places—but small things, almost whimsical items. A button from a uniform worn by a general rumored to be Oscar Wilde's first lover. The tiara from a cottage maid who'd lived happily with the Archduke of Somebody, giving him many children while he was ostensibly married to his cousin.

Nothing too spendy. Nothing too spectacular.

And nothing to be related to the following month or two, wherein something *fabulous*—a Monet thought to be destroyed when the Nazis invaded Paris, for instance—would suddenly resurface, hung on full display for the world to see where no painting or sculpture had been before.

The events were… sporadic. There was no rhyme or reason to them. No pattern, except that when one small thing disappeared, one large thing took its place. Liam had been… intrigued. In his spare hours, sitting cross-legged on his twin bed in the room he still shared with his younger brother, he'd mapped out the museums that had been hit, the things taken, the things returned.

And had come to an odd conclusion.

Money wasn't involved in either the thefts or the returns. The thefts were *so* small, but they all had to do with, of all things, love affairs ending badly—or held in secret. The returns had to do with righting a terrible wrong.

One day, his day off, he was wandering a small museum—one of the ones that had been hit already—when he came upon a miniature that, Liam could *swear* it, had been painted by Francis Bacon upon the suicide of his lover, George Dyer. He stared at the six-inch painting, heartsickened by the image, trying desperately to remember if the artist ever worked this small. This seemed a sketch, framed, not a fully realized painting, and while Liam wasn't really a fan of the work—Bacon hurt his heart and his senses—he could appreciate the skill and the passion.

"Lovely sketch, that," said a man passing by. He was cute—a good ten years older than Liam but puckish, with curly brown hair and slightly crooked teeth. Slender in build, with a vulpine face, the man shouldn't have been remarkable, but somehow he had Liam's complete attention.

"Tragic," Liam said, giving the man a slight smile. Then, quite seriously, he said, "But this sketch doesn't belong here—these are all nineteenth-century expressionist. I have no idea what a modern-art sketch is doing with this lot."

"You know your art, then?" the man asked, cocking his head. Liam got a faint whiff of expensive scotch and tried not to recoil. It could be as innocent as a businessman having a drink with lunch, but Liam's father had died young of too much drink—and too much driving near country bridges—and Liam had no fond memories of scotch.

"I know my crime," Liam murmured, frowning at the sketch. "Have you seen the art docent nearby? I want to ask him about—"

But the man was gone.

And while there was nothing to suggest it overtly—Liam knew his own freckled features with the slight gap in his front teeth were neither elite nor particularly stunning—he had the feeling it wasn't because the man had found his company unpleasant.

In fact, he was pretty sure it was because he'd spoken to the thief/art restorer himself.

And after a brief, frantic consultation with the docent, who had *never* seen that Francis Bacon sketch before—this, goddammit, *wasn't* that sort of museum!—Liam was quite sure of it.

And after writing a detailed report and sending it to his local Interpol office, he had his guess confirmed and was invited to a one-on-one meeting with Detective Chief Inspector Alec Lawson.

Lawson was about fifteen years Liam's senior, with prematurely silver hair, tired eyes—wandering eyes, as Liam would discover—and a kind, distracted smile.

And two file boxes on a thief he and half of Europe called "Lightfingers."

"You talked to him?" Lawson asked excitedly, like a much younger man asking about a pop star.

"I suspect so," Liam said. "He… he said the sketch was a good one when it clearly didn't belong there."

"What was he like?"

Liam thought carefully over the seconds-long exchange. "Sad," he said after a moment. "That painting. It really… it meant something."

Lawson's face fell. "That's too bad," he said. "In the past he's been… whimsical. Happy paintings, pretty families." He brightened. "He once substituted a child's sculpture of a cartoon character for the sculpture he stole from a private collector who had the original illegally."

"He kept the original?" Liam asked.

Lawson shook his head. "No, no—it found its way back to the French museum where it had been stolen." That soft expression again. "No fatalities," he said. "No big break-ins through glass ceilings. Ninety percent of the time the thefts are to return something where it belongs. I swear to God, he's like king of the goddamned fairies."

Liam—who'd once been given that moniker in school and had to bloody a lot of noses before losing it—grimaced.

Alec caught the expression and misinterpreted it. "I don't know if he's that kind of fairy too, but so what?" That last was said challengingly, and Liam gave a startled chuckle.

"I thought that was my name," he said, and Lawson's sad eyes turned speculative.

"I could have sworn it was mine."

The dalliance lasted only six months, but it was long enough for Liam to get promoted to Detective Inspector and Interpol liaison—and for Lawson to rekindle his romance with the wife he'd never told Liam about.

Disappointed and more than ready to move out of his mother's flat, Liam took an assignment from Interpol that involved a more frightening kind of criminal. Andres Kadjic was a Jack-of-all-trades. Guns, drugs, girls—he trafficked them all, and surprisingly, he spent much of his ill-gotten gains on *art*.

Before Lawson retired into politics, he'd put Liam on a task force trailing Kadjic through North Africa and Eastern Europe.

Liam had been but a tiny cog in a big bureaucratic wheel at the time, but he'd gotten to travel, gotten to see Morocco and Prague, St. Petersburg and Istanbul, and everywhere he went, he'd catch a whisper, a scent, of Lightfingers, the man who sometimes stole for profit (but usually from the filthy rich) and often stole to even the scales. (He was the tinier museums' best friend.)

The hard-core law and order folk at Interpol would loudly decry that a thief was a thief, but the younger generation would file their reports on the crimes—still with that element of whimsy—and say to themselves that they'd be very disappointed if this man was caught.

"Seriously, we've got the likes of Kadjic literally polluting the world with misery, and this guy swaps out the portrait of some noble's wife for a privately commissioned one of his mistress, and we're supposed to go after him, guns blazing? It's a *joke*, for God's sake."

For his part, Liam kept to himself that memory of the puckish, boozy man who had chuckled to himself about the painting being hung in the wrong place. He felt as though he'd been allowed a privileged glimpse of an endangered species in its natural habitat. The gentleman thief was, after all, a rare bird indeed.

And then Liam tracked a pair of forged passports to Moroccco. The carriers of the documents were a father and his son—both artists—but Liam had noted that they seemed to be running from wherever Kadjic was. Which made him think that if he could find *them* before Kadjic did, he could make one of those arrests that young up-and-coming officers only dreamed about—and maybe earn the rank that Alec Lawson had bestowed upon him out of guilt.

He was literally wandering the streets one evening when he heard the chatter of excited children. He walked through that back alley and saw a dozen kids, each with their own set of thick crayons, all of them scribbling on the outside wall of one of the most unpleasant vendors in the square—a man who sold Khubz, and who sold it dearly and would rather feed the crusts to the pigs or chickens than to give even a scrap to the hungry children.

The children were not drawing graffiti, though; they were drawing pictures. Yes, some of them were of the baker, and none too flattering, but some of them were of hawks from the world-famous aerie nearby, and some were of horses, and some were of sparrows.

Liam approached a little girl drawing a dragonfly and offered her a dirham. "Yes?" he asked.

She nodded, her eyes fastened hungrily on the coin.

"Who gave you the crayons?" he asked in passable French.

Her response sounded like "Dwyleje," and it took him a moment to translate.

Doigts Le'gers.

Light fingers.

"Only crayons?" he asked her.

"Khubz," she replied happily, and only then did he notice the paper-wrapped bread in the pocket of every child there.

Lightfingers bringing food and art to street children.

Idly, he wondered which item would be reported stolen next.

In any event, it wasn't his circus—nor his particular monkey—and he had business to attend to in Casino de Monte Carlo, where the current pit boss was trying very hard not to turn on Liam's big fish, who also happened to be the casino's biggest client.

Ayoub Fassi was a muscular man with a stout face and a constantly sour expression. He seemed to have a hatred for everybody—not only Liam, but anybody foreign or who spoke English as opposed to French was on his hit list.

When Liam, wearing a white linen suit and a straw hat in deference to the sun, walked into the man's office and gave his most charming smile, Ayoub had merely wrinkled his nose and launched into a diatribe against anybody with freckles, curly hair and….

Liam had to look up the word the man kept using, and then his eyebrows went up.

"Really, mate," he said in his broadest East End accent. "We're not good enough friends for you to comment on that!"

Fassi gave a hiss, as though knowing damned well he had gone too far. "It is this Kadjic," he spat. "He's one. He and his…." The word that came next was best translated as "concubine," but it had a distinctly male flavor. "He drags the man in, and neither of them are decent. Swilling scotch, laughing—he dresses like a cartoon character. Is insulting."

"Cartoon character?" Liam asked, at a loss.

"Aladdin," Fassi said succinctly. "So insulting."

Well, yes, there was some cultural appropriation involved, but a lot of kids loved that cartoon. Liam wasn't going to dissect the implications *now*.

"So Kadjic and his boyfriend are here?" he asked. "In the city? When did you last see them?"

Fassi shrugged. "An hour ago? 'Aladdin' was trying to get him to forget something… something about a painter. I don't know." He sighed. "If I did not hate that cartoon so much, I might find the young man charming."

Liam blinked. The word was… evocative somehow.

"Do you know where they went?" Liam asked.

"The market district," Fassi said unequivocally. "Kadjic had found somebody there he'd been searching for."

Liam felt his face pale. Fassi might not know this, because apparently Kadjic spent his money prodigiously at this establishment, but "finding somebody" Kadjic had been hunting for did not bode well for anybody.

Without another word, Liam bolted, pulling his comms out and rushing to find a cab that would take him to the market district where he'd just been.

On a burst of breath, he told the other two people he'd managed to drag with him to Morocco chasing the painter lead—oh shit, oh hell, *a painter* that Kadjic had *found*—and told them to search the market district, close to the bazaar where a father and his son might slip in to what was left of the afternoon crowd.

The cab let him out before the streets became pedestrian traffic only, and the absolute stillness of the evening told him something was happening that only the people who lived there would know.

He paused for a moment after the cab roared off, and he listened. He heard a man plead. And a child's scream. And then another man yell… and chaos erupt.

He rounded the corner of the alley, weapon out, badge extended, screaming, "Interpol, put your weapons down!" in time to see a midsize man wearing a very sharp European suit and black leather shoes disappear around the corner. Liam would later hear that he'd allowed his target to escape, but he couldn't regret it.

In front of him was a scene from a nightmare. A man with pale skin and light blue open eyes—poor, with a battered knapsack in his hands and wearing the most threadbare of traditional garments—slumped against the wall, his head tilted to the side, halfway separated from his neck. His mouth was open, blood still oozing from his throat like a dying river.

On the ground next to him was a thug—no other word for it—a thickly muscled man in another sharp black suit (in this heat, for fuck's sake!) He had black hair, white, white skin, and his hands were coated in blood. As was the weapon in his fist. The thug groaned slightly, and a third man on the ground a few feet from him let out a sob.

"Is the…," he gasped. "Is the boy okay?"

At that moment one of Liam's fellow agents rounded the corner, and Liam gestured at the groaning armed man.

"Cuff him," he said imperiously, as though he knew exactly what had happened when all he knew for sure was that the thug with the knife was bad news. When that guy had been secured, he bent next to the bleeding man on the ground, and almost cried to recognize his phantom thief, the giver of crayons and bread.

"Hello, my friend," he said softly, wincing at the mess of blood on the man's midsection. "What happened to you here?"

"Kadjic," gasped the man. "Didn't like it when I jumped on Yuri's back. Said he'd teach me manners. Good thing he forgot how to spell."

"Spell?" Liam glanced up at Carter, his counterpart.

Carter shrugged and spoke into his comms, asking for medical assistance while the boozy, youngish man with the curly hair and the charm—and the blue velveteen harem pants and vest of an expensively dressed Aladdin—tried to talk.

"His name. My flesh. I think he forgot the d."

Liam stared at him in horror, squatting to take his hand regardless of protocol. "Weren't you his boyfriend?" he asked baldly, and that earned him a blood-flecked smile. *Nicked lung*, Liam thought, and prayed the medics would arrive soon.

"Right up until—" The man gasped. "—I stopped Yuri from killing Antoine Couvier's son." He squeezed his eyes closed. "I didn't know he'd kill Antoine. Poor Antoine… seemed like such a gentle man. Fucking booze. I should have known."

Liam smoothed his hand over the man's brow, wanting to give comfort, until it hit him. "His son!" he gasped. "Did he get away?"

Aladdin nodded. "Nicked the paint in his bag. You can see it. Green. Like grass." He let out a little sob. "Like home."

Liam could see the man losing consciousness and thought, *I should arrest him for art theft. He must be Lightfingers—he must be!* But Andre Kadjic had just tried to carve his initials in the man's ribs—after he'd choked out the thug who'd killed Antoine Couvier and gone after his son.

That was a lot of valor in their little thief, Liam thought. Arresting him now would be a poor way to repay him.

At that moment the medics arrived in a small, old white-painted van with a red cross on the front. Liam moved out of the way to let them work, getting the location of the hospital from the driver before he went to talk to Carter.

"What'd he say?" the man asked, stepping aside so a medic could treat the still-groaning mob muscle on the ground.

"Said Kadjic ordered his man to kill Antoine Couvier and then the man's son. L… little guy couldn't stop Couvier's death, but he did manage to choke out the hired help while the kid got away." Liam glanced around at the dark that had fallen dreadfully fast. "Poor kid," he muttered. "Must be scared to death."

Carter, a fortyish veteran with the hide of a Komodo dragon, gave a snort. "Not for long. If Kadjic finds him, he'll be dead!"

Liam's heart started pounding in his ears. He may have moved out of his mother's flat, but that didn't mean he didn't miss the whole stinking lot of them. How old would the boy be? He'd been what? Six? Seven? When his father had first gone on the run after tipping the authorities off to one of Kadjic's operations via a clever flaw in their forged documents. That would make Etienne twelve now. Liam could see his own little brother, Caleb, with spidery arms and legs, thin wrists and ankles, and that sort of perpetually super-excited/super-confused expression that a lot of boys that age seemed to have.

"We need to find him," he said, trying not to let his panic show.

Carter looked around as though there were listening devices on the dirt streets, the clay walls, the colorful canopies set up to temper the brutal daytime sun that only blocked the stars now.

"If we do find him," he said softly, "he needs to *disappear*, you hear me? So he doesn't *disappear*."

Liam blinked. "Any ideas where he should *disappear* to?" he asked, realizing that Carter had just suggested waggling their fingers and making a material witness go away to save the boy's life. It was an unexpectedly human move from the seemingly implacable Carter, but maybe Carter had memories of children he loved too.

"Talk to your Aladdin friend," Carter said. "He seems to feel some obligation to the boy. But first let's find him."

It took them all night.

Writer, knitter, mother, wife, award-winning author AMY LANE shows her love in knitwear, is frequently seen in the company of tiny homicidal dogs, and can't believe all the kids haven't left the house yet. She lives in a crumbling crapmansion in the least romantic area of California, has a long-winded explanation for everything, and writes to silence the voices in her head. There are alot of voices—she's written over 120 books.

Website: www.greenshill.com
Blog: www.writerslane.blogspot.com
Email: amylane@greenshill.com
Facebook: www.facebook.com/amy.lane.167
Twitter: @amymaclane
Patreon: https://www.patreon.com/AmyHEALane

COVERT ★ BOOK 1

UNDER COVER

AMY LANE

Covert: Book One

For Judson Crosby, the transfer to the elite law enforcement branch of the SCTF is a great escape from the death sentence he earned as a whistle-blowing patrol officer. Calix Garcia, the fierce new guy, makes a perfect partner, catching bad guys while minimizing collateral damage. Crosby loves working with him.

Of course, he'd also love to work him over in a totally different way.

Garcia has waited his whole career for a solid, dependable partner like Crosby. But after six months fighting crime together, he's done fighting their attraction.

Their coming together promises to be everything they need… until a threat from Crosby's past comes back to haunt not just him, but their entire team.

When Crosby goes undercover to keep them safe, Garcia is frantic with worry. One false move could get Crosby killed and Garcia exposed. But they have to fight their way clear, because hiding your lover under the cover of darkness is no way to live. Crosby and Garcia will risk everything for the chance to live their lives in the light.

Scan the QR code below to order

A LONG CON ADVENTURE

The Mastermind

AMY LANE

"Delicious fun." – *Booklist*

A Long Con Adventure

Once upon a time in Rome, Felix Salinger got caught picking his first pocket and Danny Mitchell saved his bacon. The two of them were inseparable… until they weren't.

Twenty years after that first meeting, Danny returns to Chicago, the city he shared with Felix and their perfect, secret family, to save him again. Felix's news network—the business that broke them apart—is under fire from an unscrupulous employee pointing the finger at Felix. An official investigation could topple their house of cards. The only way to prove Felix is innocent is to pull off their biggest con yet.

But though Felix still has the gift of grift, his reunion with Danny is bittersweet. Their ten-year separation left holes in their hearts that no amount of stolen property can fill. A green crew of young thieves looks to them for guidance as they negotiate old jewels and new threats to pull off the perfect heist—but the hardest job is proving that love is the only thing of value they've ever had.

Scan the QR code below to order

BOWLING for TURKEYS

AMY LANE

Milo Tanaka was *not* recovering from the mother of all breakups when his best friend barged into his home and gave him a dog. While Julia the dog doesn't like squirrels, cats, turkeys, other dogs, or most humans, at least she gets him out of bed.

When a tiny blond dog rockets out of nowhere to bark ferociously at Garth Potter's enormous Daniff, "the Chad," Garth is annoyed, but Chad simply woofs in Julia's face. But when Garth looks around for her irresponsible owner, he finds a fey panicky disaster desperately trying to keep his dog from getting eaten, and realizes Milo is simply new to dog ownership, not neglectful or cruel.

In fact, Milo is a *truly* decent guy, and he and his best friend have been struggling to find their footing in adulthood and relationships. As Garth befriends Milo and the irascible Julia, he finds himself entangled in Milo's broken heart and fractured life. As much as Garth wants to fix it, he knows that Milo has to fix it himself. With the holidays approaching, Milo realizes that a good relationship won't leave him isolated and afraid, but surrounded with friends, and that the key to thriving isn't just chasing the turkeys out of his life—it's letting a good man in.

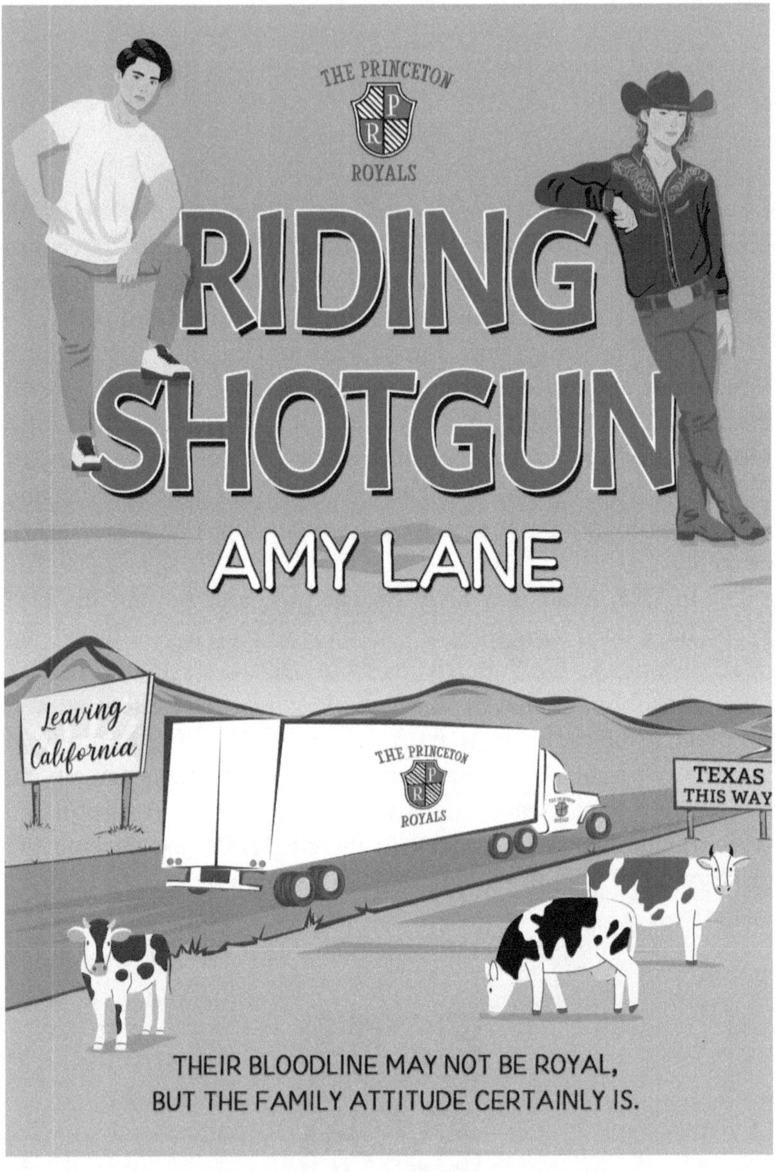
THE PRINCETON
ROYALS
RIDING
SHOTGUN
AMY LANE
Leaving
California
THE PRINCETON
ROYALS
TEXAS
THIS WAY
THEIR BLOODLINE MAY NOT BE ROYAL,
BUT THE FAMILY ATTITUDE CERTAINLY IS.

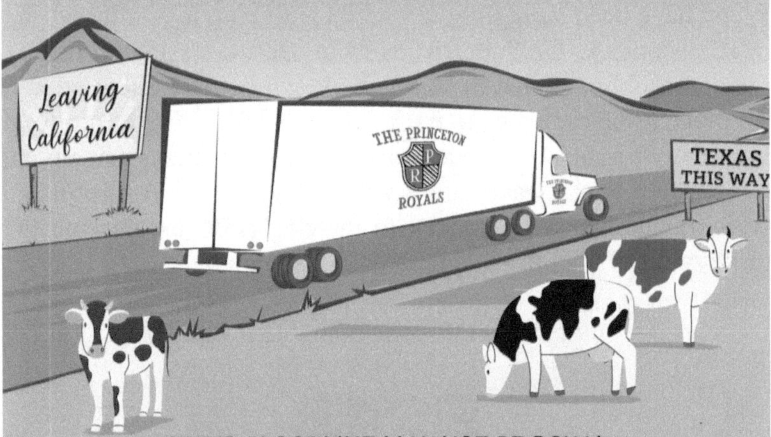

The Princeton Royals: Book One

Val Royal's tight family has always had his back, but they love to interfere in his life. That interference almost sends him over the edge when they arrange for Rory McCauley, security specialist, marksman, and hound-dog smartass, to ride shotgun as security on his latest run.

Hot, bossy, and sharp as a tack, Val ticks all Rory's boxes, but Val's looking for something real, and Rory's allergic to intimacy. Besides, their gig running refrigerated bull semen from Bakersfield to Austin could make or break Val's buddy's ranch, so Val's understandably pretty focused on the job. Rory still wishes Val would let him help Val, uh, *relax*.

As Val and Rory work to keep their payload safe from a couple of determined saboteurs and they get to know each other as smart, competent, fearless professionals, sparks fly, and Val starts to fall for Rory's roguish charm. But can he convince Rory their romance would be worth more than a straight shot to Austin—that it would be a love worth coming home to?

Scan the QR code below to order

AMY
LANE

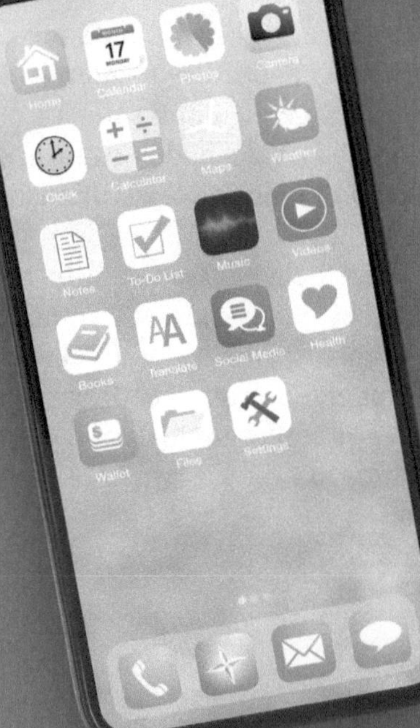

SWIPE
LEFT,
POWER
DOWN,
LOOK
UP

Busy soccer coach Trey Novak doesn't have time for the awkwardness and upheaval dating can cause, but when his cousin stands him up for a lunch date, he meets someone who changes his mind.

Dewey Saunders is dying to get a real job in his field and start the rest of his life, but a guy's got to pay rent, and the coffee shop is where it's at. When the handsome customer in the coach's sweats gets stood up, Dewey is right there to commiserate—and maybe make some time with a cute guy.

Trey's making hopeful plans with Dewey when his professional life explodes. He and Dewey aren't in a serious place yet, and suddenly he's promising to make sports a welcoming place for all people. When Dewey puts himself out to comfort Trey after an awful day, Trey realizes that they might not be in a serious place, but Dewey has serious promise for their future. If someone as loyal and as kind and funny as Dewey is what's offered, Trey would gladly swipe right for love.

www.ingramcontent.com/pod-product-compliance
Lightning Source LLC
LaVergne TN
LVHW041114080826
845145LV00007B/1808

* 9 7 8 1 6 4 1 0 8 9 1 0 4 *